A

City of Drowned Souls

CITY OF DROWNED SOULS

CHRIS LLOYD

First published in the United Kingdom in 2017 by Canelo

This edition published in the United Kingdom in 2019 by

Canelo Digital Publishing Limited
57 Shepherds Lane
Beaconsfield, Bucks HP9 2DU
United Kingdom

A CIP catalogue record for this book is available from the British Library.

Print ISBN 978 1 78863 558 5
Ebook ISBN 978 1 910859 85 8

Look for more great books at www.canelo.co

Printed and bound in Great Britain by Clays Ltd, Elcograf S.p.A.

To the memory of my brother Dave.

It begins and ends with a river.

Always a river.

He could hear it outside, louder and angrier than he'd ever heard it.

He pulled on the iron ring until the metal clasp around his right wrist cut too far into his skin and his blood began to drip onto the cold stone floor. His left hand hadn't been tethered so that he could eat and drink from the bottles of water and bags of food that his captor brought down to him. He tried once more to pick at the metal tie on his right wrist with his left hand, but his nails broke and he only drove the band further into his own skin until it became too painful and he had to give up. He leaned his head back against the rough-hewn stone of the ancient cellar wall and cried.

He thought of his mother.

Always his mother.

And her disappointment.

He could feel cold on the back of his head, different from usual. He leaned forward and twisted around, but it was too dark to see. He ran the fingers of his left hand down the stone. They were damp. He tasted it in case it was his blood, but it was water. Feeling a rising panic that was never far away, he placed the flat of his hand along the wall as far as he could go. There were places where water was running down over the surface. He called out.

Above him, he heard the tugging of the door in its frame. It opened and a weak light filtered into the room. He waited for the ladder, but it didn't appear. In the gloom, he could see the four stone steps that rose from the floor and abruptly ended, the rest of the flight to the door having crumbled away years ago. Still he waited for the ladder to be lowered, but nothing came. Silhouetted against the pale glow, his captor stood and stared down at him.

'There's water coming in,' he shouted up.

Without a word, the figure closed the door and the cellar was plunged into a blacker darkness than before. He screamed once more with fear and frustration and tugged again at the iron ring, but the metal tie cut into his flesh and he cried out in pain. With his left hand, he pulled back and forth at the ring set into the wall but it was solid. He banged again and again on the hard stone with his fist until it too was bleeding. Touching the wall, he had no idea if it was his blood or the water seeping in that he could feel.

He heard another sound. A roaring. The river was growing in anger and coming nearer. Underneath it came a new noise. A sucking. He sat still to listen. His legs were wet. Jumping up to his feet and having to crouch because of his wrist shackled to the wall, he felt the ground beneath him with his fingertips. Water was coming in, bubbling up through the cracks in the stone slabs. Soon, the whole floor was covered. His hand laid flat on the ground was enveloped, the river rising up his wrist. He screamed and the door opened. Again, the figure stood in the gap and stared down.

'Why are you doing this?'

He could hear the panic in his own voice.

'I have no choice.'

Monday

Chapter One

'How does that make you feel?'

Elisenda picked the third imagined piece of lint off her jeans in the last ten minutes and studied the woman seated in the earnest straight-backed chair opposite her. Elisenda herself was half-lying on a modern recliner which made her feel mildly discomforted, the static in the seat fabric clinging to the back of her shirt, tugging it out of her waistband. She felt a sheen of sweat in the small of her back soaking through the thin cotton. She also felt faintly ridiculous. It wasn't solely the fault of the chair.

'Uncomfortable.'

Doctora Puyals leaned forward. 'At being asked how you feel or at being here?'

Elisenda shook her head irritably, her long hair catching painfully behind her shoulders. 'With this bloody chair. It's desperately difficult to sit on. I might consider using it to question suspects.'

'Is that how you feel, Elisenda? Like you're a suspect in some way?'

Elisenda stifled a groan and squirmed on the recliner. There were no arms and she was forced to clasp her hands together on her lap to stop them from sliding down to the floor either side of her. She was conscious of the other woman staring at her fingers clutching tightly to each other, the knuckles white with the strain. She had to fight the temptation to tell her it was entirely because of the chair, not for anything else.

'How do you want it to make me feel?' she finally asked her.

'Curious. You ask me how I want it to make you feel. That's interesting.'

It might be to you, Elisenda thought, glad that one of them at least was enjoying the experience. She sized the woman up without letting it show that she was doing it. The counsellor sat back on her own chair, her head to one side, studying her patient. The unbidden thought came to Elisenda that the good doctor wasn't as good as Elisenda was at reading people's faces without their knowing that that's what she was doing. Behind a professional mask of attentive concern, which Elisenda already had no doubt Puyals genuinely felt, lay deep layers of strength and calculation. It was a powerful face, with inquisitive eyes and a defined jawline that many men would have longed for. Despite herself, Elisenda pulled her own overbite in, aware that it got more pronounced the more anxious she was.

'You feel anxious?' Puyals asked her.

Elisenda could see the attempt to hide the intense scrutiny behind a casual gaze and couldn't help experiencing a surge of irritation. 'I feel it's a waste of our time. Yours and mine. I don't need to talk to anyone. You don't need someone lying here resenting every minute of this.'

Puyals laughed, a gentle sound like water on pebbles. 'You aren't the first person to resent being here, Elisenda. And you aren't the first person who thinks they don't need to talk. You think you're here against your will, I see that. I'm here because I know you're not.'

For the first time, Elisenda looked uncertainly at the counsellor.

'This is a waste of time,' she insisted.

Chapter Two

Thirty-six hours earlier

'This is a waste of time.'

In the moonlit dark, Elisenda could sense Josep behind her bristle at Manel's whispered comment. Before he could reply, the blackness was rent by the scream of a barn owl. Elisenda heard Josep's involuntary gasp at the noise, the needles on the pine trees where they were standing rustling as he jumped slightly.

'City boy,' Manel snorted in a low voice.

'Boys,' Elisenda told them. 'Play nicely.'

Through the darkness, she heard the tortured squeak of a mouse being carried off through the night air along the edge of the dense woods. She also heard Josep mutter something under his breath for Manel's benefit.

'I won't tell you again,' she added quietly. 'Either of you.'

Her eyes had become adjusted to the dark after three hours of waiting, but she sensed rather than saw the two caporals mould into the wooded shadow. The tall and often lugubrious Josep melting into the towering pines, their bark brittle to the touch. The thickset and clumpy Manel fading into rambling gorse, the leaves rustling spikily at the slightest movement. Unlike the woods, their relationship wasn't as symbiotic as Elisenda would have liked.

It was a cloudless sky, a crescent moon washing the narrow track leading up to the converted farmhouse in front of them in a raw lapis lazuli colour, the shadows under the trees either side pools of black where the pale light couldn't penetrate. Ahead of them stood the darkness of the farmhouse. No longer a farm, but a restyled country home for the short commute from Girona, barely twenty kilometres away. Impossible to see in this light, but Elisenda recalled the old stones buffed to an enticing honey glow, the palms in giant pots either side of the massive wooden double door, the mahogany surrounds of the triple-glazed windows set deep into the thick walls. Cooling in summer, warming in winter, bold in its affluent and splendid isolation.

I wouldn't live this far from the noise and warmth of others if you paid me, Elisenda thought for the dozenth time that night.

She froze at a half-caught sound that came from the woods the other side of the track. A rustle of dead pine needles shifting as something glided over them. Unsure at first she'd heard it, she glanced at Josep's shadow and saw him nod in the gloom. Someone was moving through the trees opposite them. She sensed Manel tense. It sounded like just one set of footsteps, which surprised her. She'd expected more, unless this was someone spying out the land first. Checking the pistol in her side holster and silently hefting the heavy armoured jacket to try and find a more comfortable position, she peered through the pines and dense clumps of holm oak leaves.

She was distracted momentarily by the sound of scratching coming from above her and a gentle spattering of pine needles falling to the ground near her feet. She looked up involuntarily and held her breath. A squirrel or a bird, she decided, relieved, exhaling as silently as she could. Returning her gaze to the trees and undergrowth mirroring her own hiding place, she saw a shape in the dark shift. A slight movement on the edge of her vision. She tried looking at it directly but it disappeared. Instead, she had to look to the side of it to catch the slightest of changes in the night. She heard Manel slowly undo the flap on his holster but she could do nothing to shush him without alerting whoever it was coming towards them.

Suddenly, a face appeared in the moonlight alongside a tree by the track.

She felt herself shrink back. Next to her, she heard Josep let his breath out slowly. Her own reaction followed his instantly. To her ears, the sound of it was deafening in the darkness. In the fleeting moment the face was in view, she'd recognised it as Àlex's. The one sergent in her team and her second-in-command, he was positioned in the facing woods. Briefly annoyed with him, she immediately wondered what it was that had made him decide to risk making a move.

She stared closely but could see no more movement. She knew Àlex was on the other side of the track with Montse, the final member of her unit. Hidden in the bushes and rocks beyond and around them and her own small group were other Mossos d'Esquadra. A unit of uniformed patrol cops from the Seguretat Ciutadana and an ARRO team, the support unit that dealt with potentially more dangerous situations like riots, raids and roundups. She'd initially objected to their involvement, but Inspector Puigventós, her boss in the Regional Investigation Command in Girona, had insisted.

'These are violent people we're after,' he'd told her. 'I insist on ARRO support and that's final.'

She was almost grateful now that they were there.

She felt the lightest of taps on her shoulder from Josep. She nodded. She'd heard it too. It explained why Àlex had made his way nearer to the edge of the track. Through the dark, she heard the sound of something sliding very slightly on the small stones of the densely-enclosed drive cutting through the trees. Someone was approaching the house and would soon be coming into their line of vision.

Whoever it was had paused. Elisenda closed her eyes for a brief moment, concerned the person who was coming calling had heard something. A second noise from further away rustled in the night, a second person moving along the path. An aeon of held breath later, the first set of footsteps began to move again, cautiously approaching their position. The newcomer was hanging back, waiting while the leader tested the lie of the land. She felt her whole body tense once more and slowly took out her service pistol, the grip unsteady in the chill sweat of her hand. Josep and Manel strained forward in the shadows. The first of the interlopers stopped again and Elisenda caught her breath as they paused one more time before continuing, finally coming into view.

Sniffing at the breeze, a fallow deer on the path looked directly at Elisenda, its eyes suddenly incandescent white, reflecting the moon. The pale spots on its back shone a tungsten blue, the rest of its coat vanishing into the dark. Elisenda returned the animal's gaze and exhaled. Behind it, the second deer obviously sensed the humans and scampered away. The leader glanced back towards its retreating partner for a moment and looked again at Elisenda, holding eye contact. Staring at her for what seemed an age, it finally wheeled slowly about on its slender legs and gently loped off, away from the house. Elisenda felt her muscles relax and she let out a long breath, leaning her head against the tree next to her.

Violent people, she wryly recalled the inspector's words.

Unusually, Inspector Puigventós himself was on the operation, with the head of the ARRO team, on the other side of the house, covering a footpath that led from a dirt track to the west. Their various vans and cars were pulled up half a kilometre away, off the main road to the east, with more back-up waiting if needed. In all, there were about two dozen Mossos staked out, there on the strength of Elisenda's belief in a tipoff from one of her usual informants.

The only problem was that the violent people they were waiting for hadn't shown up.

'Siset,' Elisenda muttered the name of her grass to herself. 'If you've screwed me over...'

'This is a waste of time,' Manel repeated sotto voce, the fingers on his left hand scratching impatiently at the deeply-scored bark of the holm oak sheltering him, his right hand snapping his holster shut.

Elisenda had to agree with him.

'Quit that noise,' Josep told him irritably, but Manel simply scratched harder with his thumbnail.

'He's right,' Elisenda finally agreed. 'No one's coming.'

She was on the point of breaking the agreed radio silence to speak to Puigventós, when he called through to her.

'*I'm standing the operation down, Elisenda*,' the inspector's voice grated through the handset. He was no longer bothering to whisper.

'With respect, Xavier, shouldn't that be my decision?' she asked, unable to keep the annoyance out of her voice.

'*Not at this stage, Elisenda. We've had a report of an incident near Cassà de la Selva. I'm taking responsibility for standing the operation down*.'

The handset went dead in her hand and after a few moments, Elisenda heard a steady wave of soft noise rolling towards her as the order spread through the police officers in the woods and they slowly began to stamp their feet and move through the pine needles after hours of stiff inactivity. The low murmur of their voices echoed through the trees.

The first of them appeared in the moonlight on the drive, walking away from the house. One or two turned on their torches to see their way more clearly, quickly followed by others. In the dancing light, the riot helmets of the ARRO team banged dully against their owners' heavily-padded right thighs, where they hung on rings when not in use. Two uniformed Seguretat Ciutadana followed, deep in muted conversation, while a third caught them up on the drive. He said something and the other two laughed. Manel grunted something, a bass counterpoint to Josep's stifled sigh.

Leaving her post in the trees, Elisenda emerged onto the drive and shone her own torch at the faint tracks scuffed on the ground by the deer. Josep and Manel followed her and stopped either side. For the first time, she heard the rushing sound of distant water under the crunching footsteps of the retreating Mossos. While Girona and the outlying areas had remained dry throughout the first half of September, the mountains to the north and west had seen heavy rainfall on and off all month, filling the springs and swelling the rivers as they reached the city. She'd noticed the rushing white water of a brook near the house when she'd come to visit the owners earlier in the day, to explain to them that they had to leave their home for a few hours that evening.

'We have reliable reports,' she'd told the couple, architects from Girona, both of them around her own age, 'that the gang that's been targeting houses like yours in recent months is planning a burglary here tonight.'

The couple had been more than willing to pack a hurried bag and go to the wife's parents' house in the wealthy Palau district of Girona. The newspapers had been joyously full all summer of tales of the violence meted out by the gang that had been operating in the area, terrorising any home-owners unlucky enough to be in when they carried out one of their raids.

'Reliable reports,' Elisenda muttered to herself now, caught in the moonlight.

Josep gave a little cough to warn her of something. Looking up, she saw Inspector Puigventós walking along the path towards her, his tall figure in shadow against the negative silhouette of the house. The moon glinted on his glasses, a new addition he still felt self-conscious about, choosing to wear rimless ones to fool himself into thinking they didn't show so much. Subirana, the head of the ARRO unit, strode alongside him, a shorter, stockier, more brooding shadow. Neither of the men spoke.

Sensing a change in the air around her, Elisenda turned to see Àlex emerge from the trees to stand next to her. He was unfastening his armoured jacket, taut anger brooding in his every movement. Montse, a caporala, the same rank as Josep and Manel, had come with him and now stood by Josep, barely a metre away. The calmest in the team, she waited with a controlled athletic grace. Elisenda couldn't see where Manel, the newest member of her team, was.

Puigventós stopped in front of Elisenda and aimed his torch beam at the ground. Elisenda did likewise. The reflected light from below threw dark shadows on their faces, hunting out the ridges and hollows in harsh relief. The barn owl screeched again in the distance, the scene instantly reminding Elisenda of an old Bela Lugosi movie. She had to resist an entirely inappropriate urge to laugh and was momentarily shocked at how close she'd come to really doing it.

Pausing only for a moment, Subirana nodded once to Puigventós and made eye contact with Elisenda, a fleeting smile of support crossing his wide face before he carried on along the path to join the rest of his team. Puigventós waited for him to go before he spoke.

'Would you like your unit to stand some distance away, Elisenda?' His voice was quiet.

She looked straight at him and shook her head. 'They can stay.'

Staring intently into her eyes, he brandished his mobile phone.

'Cassà de la Selva, Elisenda. Three generations of the same family badly beaten. Two parents, a teenage boy and the husband's eighty-year-old father. All four are being taken to hospital now. Their home ransacked, their bank cards taken, their car stolen. While you had your unit, an ARRO unit and Seguretat Ciutadana wasting our time and resources here on the say-so of a petty criminal and drug-pusher.'

Elisenda could feel Àlex next to her tense at Puigventós' words. Silently, she willed her sergent to keep quiet.

'Siset's information has always been good in the past,' Elisenda objected, her voice calm.

'Always, Elisenda? He's a liability, and he's turning you into a liability as well.'

Elisenda couldn't have been more stunned if the inspector had hit her in the face. Before she could reply, Àlex spoke up.

'With respect, Inspector Puigventós, that is uncalled for.'

'I will decide what is called for and what isn't, sergent,' the inspector told him, his anger barely contained. 'And right now, your opinion is anything but welcome.'

Elisenda signalled to Àlex to keep quiet, but was fighting a losing battle with her own temper.

'Liability?' she said, her voice as quiet as Puigventós'. 'In what way am I a liability?'

'Your judgement is impaired, Elisenda. You're letting your personal life mar your professional decisions.'

Elisenda took a step forward, her face centimetres from Puigventós', who recoiled in surprise but stood his ground. Àlex tried to pull her back by the arm, but she waved his hand away.

'My personal life?' In her anger, she saw tiny beads of spittle spatter on the inspector's face as she spoke. 'Not once has my private life affected my work. If others weren't so caught up in their *political* lives, they'd know that. You'd know that.'

'Elisenda,' Àlex pleaded, but she held her hand up behind her back to warn him to keep quiet.

'Political lives, Elisenda?' Puigventós demanded.

'Political lives. Cronies. The right corporate clones helping each other up the ladder, stopping the rest of us from doing our jobs properly. Those are the ones whose judgement is impaired and who serve no one but themselves. Not me. And not my personal life.'

'And you include me in that, do you, Elisenda? A politician?'

The calm in the inspector's voice had an effect on Elisenda, instantly taking the sting out of her anger. Uncertainly, she took a step back.

'Now isn't the time for this,' she told him. 'I need to get my team to Cassà de la Selva.'

Puigventós shook his head and turned to Àlex. 'Sergent Albiol, you will take Caporals Capdevila and Moliné to the real crime scene.' He beckoned Montse forward. 'Caporala Cornellà, you will drive Sotsinspectora Domènech to her home.'

'A senior officer is needed at the scene,' Elisenda objected.

'There is a senior officer there already,' the inspector told her. 'Sotsinspector Micaló. Sergent Albiol, you will report to him. You, Elisenda will go home and you will come to my office tomorrow morning at eight.' He looked again at Àlex, who hadn't yet moved. 'What are you waiting for, Sergent Albiol?'

Shooting a glance at Elisenda, Àlex exhaled slowly to calm himself and led Josep and Manel away. She watched them go. Out of the corner of her eye, she saw Montse staring at the ground, picking at the loose stones with her right foot.

Puigventós made to leave, but paused as he walked past her.

'And bring your ID card and your service pistol with you,' he told her.

Chapter Three

Elisenda walked out of the apartment block on Ronda Sant Antoni Maria Claret and took a deep breath. Narrow and shaded, the street was in the Eixample part of town, the twentieth-century southern extension of the city, the criss-cross of roads like a minuscule take on Barcelona's rambling gridiron pattern. Taking a second and deeper breath after the tension of the session with the counsellor, she was struck at the difference between here and the old town. Just a short distance from the river, the canyons of modern buildings were less humid but the heat of the brick and asphalt felt more stultifying than the ancient and greying stone of Elisenda's side of the Onyar.

'How does that make you feel?' she muttered wryly, repeating the question that the counsellor had asked at least half a dozen times in the last hour.

A woman with a buggy smiled at her, wanting to get past her into the building. Apologising, Elisenda stood aside and watched the thirty-something mother disappear into the chasm of the smart block where the counsellor had her office on the gloomy mezzanine floor. The other apartment on the same floor was home to a *gestor*, one of the very many throughout the land whose well-paid job it was to smooth the path of the country's love of bureaucracy and forms and documentation. The business on the ground floor of the apartment block was a shop selling designer baby clothes. Elisenda glimpsed the price of a pair of cotton mittens and laughed to herself. Her new niece was going to have to make do with more functional gifts from this aunt. Her laugh was short-lived, turning immediately to guilt. Her sister's baby daughter was over five months old now, and Elisenda had seen her barely a handful of times. She glanced at the doorway to the counsellor's building.

'Wonder why that is,' she muttered to herself.

Shaking that thought off, she instinctively reached into her bag for her mobile to check in with Àlex at the Mossos police station at Vista Alegre, but suddenly had to check herself. She still had her work phone on her, but she'd had to surrender her police ID and gun to Inspector Puigventós the previous morning, a semi-deserted and muggy Sunday at the station.

'You need help, Elisenda,' he'd told her in his stuffy office.

She'd simply nodded. Braced for a shouting match, she'd been thrown by his concern for her. She hadn't been aware she warranted it.

'I know you have visions of your daughter,' he'd added.

'How do you know?' she'd asked, briefly angered.

'Your whole unit sees it, Elisenda. It's undermining your authority with them. And it's undermining your judgement.'

'Are you suspending me?'

He'd looked at her ID and pistol lying in surrender on his desk and shook his head. 'No, I'm not, Elisenda, because that would go on your record. I could even have you on a charge for insubordination, but I won't. What I am insisting on is that you take compassionate leave.'

'With these attacks on farmhouses going on?'

'That's covered, Elisenda. They don't concern you for now. Please don't argue. This could quite easily become more of an issue if you don't work with me on it.'

Reluctantly, she'd agreed, but Puigventós had one more demand.

'Counselling?' she'd argued. 'That's the last thing I need.'

'No, it's not, Elisenda, it's the first thing you should have done after you lost your daughter.'

'I lost my daughter six years ago, Xavier.'

Puigventós held his head to one side and examined her. 'And you think matters are improving? When the new law comes in,

Elisenda, all Mossos are going to have to undergo compulsory psychological testing every year.'

'I can wait.'

'You will fail it.' His words had knocked the breath out of her. 'I insist you accept counselling now to avoid greater problems down the line. Every day this week, to be precise.'

She'd jumped up from her chair. 'Every day? You can't. Once a week is more normal.'

He'd motioned her to sit down again. 'Your decision, Elisenda, but I want you to have five sessions before you return to work. Five days or five weeks, the choice is yours.'

On that Monday morning on the pavement outside the counsellor's building, she felt a sudden surge of the same anger she'd felt the previous morning at his words. He'd painted her into a corner. Forced to accept compassionate leave and counselling if she didn't want a greater stain on her record.

Turning right from the doorway and then right again, she walked slowly, unsure of what to do now that her usual routine of solving the world's problems from a police station had been taken from her. She checked her work mobile, which she'd managed to sneak past Puigventós, but she had no messages.

'You'd better not be managing without me,' she muttered out loud as she walked along the narrow pavement, dodging the slender trees in their shallow square beds and the iron posts built to stop cars parking half off the road.

The younger schoolchildren had just started back at school after the end of the summer holidays and they were finishing their morning session now at noon. A small boy holding the hand of an older one as they walked home, both of them in their uniform of a blue and white check knee-length smock over their ordinary clothes, stared at her as she walked past.

'Is that your grandmother?' he asked the older child.

You are so lucky I can't arrest you right now, kid, Elisenda thought. She smiled at him while he waited for an answer.

Considering stopping for a coffee on the open square in front of the swanky hotel that took up two sides of it, she changed her mind and carried on walking, in the opposite direction from the old town and her apartment. She headed instead for the river, crossing it after the road that led the short distance to Vista Alegre so she wouldn't be likely to be seen, and carried on along the east bank away from the centre. Entering the other world contained on the hill that rose steeply to the left of the main road, Elisenda felt the Girona that most people knew fading behind her with the sound of the traffic. She climbed steeply, deep into the poor-quality apartment blocks that had been thrown up in the 1960s to house immigrants from other parts of Spain, encouraged to come to Catalonia by the Franco regime to look for work. Near a primary school, she passed a couple of small children, their smocks not as pristine as the two in the Eixample, the collars patched and sewn. She winked at the smaller of the two and he grinned back at her. A skinny young mother with a drawn face pushing a faded buggy smiled back at her as their paths crossed. The reputation this part of town had wasn't always earned, Elisenda reflected.

'Hey, girlie,' a voice in the shadows to her right called out to her. 'Come and see what I've got for you.'

Stopping, she turned to face the speaker, her gaze directly meeting his. Tanned and muscled, in a tight red T-shirt and even tighter trousers that strained against his crotch, the young man wore his jet black hair swept back in a style that was old enough to be his father's. He blanched when he saw her.

'Sorry, Elisenda,' he said. 'Didn't recognise you.'

Next to him, an obese man, old before his time, was perched on a rickety stool, his belly in a brown nylon shirt overhanging his thighs. He wore old-fashioned lattice summer shoes of a type that Elisenda hadn't seen for years. Gesturing for the younger man to lean down, he waited until he was within reach and quickly slapped him across the head, the sound harsh amid the bleak buildings.

'Show some respect,' the older man told him. 'Now fuck off.'

Cowed, the young guy shot Elisenda a sheepish look and strode quickly away, back into the maze of apartment blocks behind the old man's seat.

'Excuse him,' the older man said. 'He doesn't know any better.'

'Just this once, Tío Juan,' she told him, using the term of deference.

She left him and carried on her way, not a doubt in her mind that he'd sent his younger companion off to spread the word through the neighbourhood that the Mossos had come calling. Instinctively, she quickened her pace until she got to a nondescript block no different from many in this part of the city. The downstairs door was open, so she pushed on in and climbed to the fourth floor.

'He's not in,' the woman told her after Elisenda had been banging on the door for five minutes. She was wearing nothing but a loose and greying vest and baggy gym shorts that seemed to drag her downwards. She looked like she'd only just woken up.

'Mind if I check, Elena?' Elisenda asked.

The woman shrugged and turned away, leaving the door open behind her.

'What's he done this time?' Elena asked, sitting down at a bare wooden table in the living room and reaching for a packet of cigarettes. 'Want a coffee?'

'No, you're all right, thanks,' Elisenda told her. She'd just checked the kitchen and seen the cafetera sitting in a sink filled with week-old water, rainbow colours of grease swirling in and out of the spout.

Siset was nowhere to be found in the tiny flat. Just to make sure, she left Elena alone for a minute to go back out on to the landing and climb to the top floor and the communal roof, but he wasn't there either, hiding among the unused stone sinks and clutter of rubbish strewn everywhere.

'So where is he?' she asked Elena when she'd gone back down the one flight of stairs to the grim apartment.

Elena shrugged. 'Let me know when you find him. I haven't seen him for a week.'

Elisenda studied the young woman. She could see that the thin scabs of needle tracks on her arms were drying out. Leaning forward, she glanced at her right foot, crossed over the left knee and sticking out from the table at an angle. There were no new puncture marks around the ankles or on her toes.

'You seem to be doing all right, Elena,' she told her.

'Just a bit of weed, Elisenda.' She sat and nodded her head for a while, staring out of the open window on to the block of flats opposite, lost in her own thoughts.

'Have you really not seen Siset? He's not in trouble.' Elena snorted at that, and Elisenda had to laugh with her. 'Well, no more than usual. I just want a word with him.'

'Really, I haven't seen him since last week. If you find him, tell the little bastard to come home.'

Elisenda laughed again and got up to go. 'I say the same to you. When he does come back, tell him I want to see him. He's not in trouble.'

He bloody well is in trouble, Elisenda corrected herself on the walk back down the hill, recalling the duff information he'd given her. 'I'll crucify the little sod when I see him,' she cursed under her breath.

'Found Siset, Elisenda?' Tío Juan asked her when she passed his vantage point on her way back out of the neighbourhood.

'Who says that's who I'm looking for?'

'Word travels fast.'

'Have you seen him?'

The man chuckled, revealing two rows of teeth stained brown. 'You know I wouldn't tell you where he was. Even if I knew.'

'He's not your family, Tío Juan.'

'He is where the Mossos are concerned. What do you want him for?'

Elisenda gazed back at the man, and saw in his keen eyes a search for any giveaway sign about why she was really looking for Siset. Despite her annoyance with him right now, she had to protect him as an informant. 'Oh, you know, things go missing,

Siset's usually nearby when they do. I just want to appeal to his better nature and ask him where they are.'

Tío Juan snorted with laughter, the stool creaking ominously under him. Elisenda nodded at him once and turned away, carrying on along the dusty pavement down the hill. Leaving the Font de la Pólvora neighbourhood behind her and walking back into the Eixample, Elisenda couldn't help feeling like a weight had been lifted from her shoulders. It was followed immediately by a sense of guilt. The memory of Elena waiting for Siset in a no-hope apartment in the poorest part of town was the most utterly desolate picture of despair imaginable.

Something else that struck her as she walked without any real purpose through the clean streets of the understated affluence of this part of town were the posters pasted onto the billboards. The forthcoming elections for the Catalan government meant that every last free space – on walls and on TV and in your head – was given over to a succession of scrubbed and earnest faces telling you that they were your best bet for the future. But that wasn't what had struck her. What she only now registered was that she'd seen none of these in Font de la Pólvora. None of the parties or politicians seemed too worried about what the people there had to say about their future. She had no doubt the message would be there somewhere, in public buildings and near the few shops that there were, but there wasn't the overwhelming presence that you found everywhere else in the city. None of the mutual care shown between politics and community that you saw elsewhere. Marginalisation a self-fulfilling prophecy. Then she remembered her own relief at getting back to her Girona and felt a pang of guilt again.

'You need to get back to work,' she told herself, 'or you'll go up the wall.'

She had a sudden vision of Elena alone and aimless again and reached into her bag. She looked one more time at her work mobile, but there were no messages and no missed calls.

'Well, don't think I'm going to be the one to give in,' she mouthed at it, shoving it back in her bag out of sight.

Chapter Four

'Got your feet under the table pretty quick,' Manel commented with a smirk as he, Montse and Josep filed into Elisenda's office.

Seated at Elisenda's desk in her absence, Àlex pointed at the main room outside the glass partition wall. Most of the desks were taken up by officers in the Local Investigation Unit, the bunch that dealt with less serious crimes within the city. Space at Vista Alegre was tight, so Elisenda's Serious Crime Unit, which tackled major investigations throughout the entire Girona police region, was forced to double up with the local team. The only exceptions were Elisenda's office, a goldfish bowl at one end of the room, and another separate office at the other end for the head of the Local Investigation Unit.

'You might have noticed, caporal,' Àlex told Manel, his patience barely contained, 'that the main room is full. We can hardly have a meeting with that lot milling around.'

Montse looked to where Àlex was pointing and nodded her head in agreement. Manel grunted, not convinced.

'Oh, give it a rest,' Josep told Manel.

Manel was about to reply but Àlex held a finger up and looked pointedly at him. 'We're discussing an ongoing investigation. We don't need interruptions from out there. Or from in here.'

The three caporals sat in varying degrees of reluctant silence and waited for Àlex to continue. It was towards the end of the afternoon and this was the first chance they'd had to come together properly since the failed stakeout on Saturday night and Elisenda had been relieved of her duties on Sunday morning. Most of Àlex's Monday had been taken up with reporting to

Puigventós and dealing with Micaló. Now he had to talk to the rest of the team about which way the investigation into the violent robberies at isolated houses was going to be heading.

'Elisenda had been given wrong information,' he told them all now. 'We need to find out why: if it was a genuine mistake by her informant or if he was deliberately misleading her. We need to speak to him, but subtly. Montse, you take care of that, but first we'll need to ask Elisenda if she's all right with you speaking to him. Other than that, we'll be taking witness statements from the family that was attacked on Saturday.'

'Didn't Micaló's unit take statements?' Montse asked him.

Àlex looked frankly back at her. 'We'll be taking our own statements today.'

'Useless tossers,' Manel commented. 'Micaló. The lot of them.'

'Manel,' Àlex told him, 'I think we could all do with a coffee. Go and get us all one, would you?'

Manel stared back at him for a few seconds before picking himself up out of the chair and walking out of the room. He left the door open, so Montse leaned across and pushed it gently shut as he lumbered off.

Àlex watched him go. 'Has either of you spoken to Elisenda?' he asked the remaining two.

'One of us should,' Josep commented. 'She's not going to be taking any of this well. I don't blame her.'

'I'll call her,' Montse offered, but Àlex shook his head.

'It should be me.'

They spoke a little more about the events at the farmhouse on Saturday night, until Àlex suddenly waved his fingers at them to stop talking. Over their shoulders, he could see Manel walking back into the outer room, carrying four cups of coffee on a metal tray. The caporal kicked the door open and walked in, placing the tray down on some folders on the desk.

'Coffee for the team,' he announced.

–

In another office in another part of the city on the same Monday afternoon, another group of people was seated around another desk. Here, too, the man at the head of the table was equally unhappy at being there but making a show of confidence. He didn't own the table or the office or the deep leather chair in which he was currently swivelling from side to side. They were owned by one of the three men seated opposite him.

As, slowly but surely, was he.

Despite his misgivings, the man in the chair felt some degree of his normal state of self-assurance return. 'That's it,' he announced dramatically to the other three men. 'The committee meets in an emergency session tomorrow morning. I've managed to swing it. I've got the quorum we need on board, only two dissenters left and they no longer matter. This time tomorrow, the licence will have been revoked. Wednesday at the latest.'

Two of the other three men turned their heads almost imperceptibly to gauge the third man's reaction. He simply sat and stared in silence, his right hand constantly upending a gold cigarette pocket lighter against the top of the desk and running the smooth metal through his fingers. It clicked softly every time he touched the end on the table to turn it over. It was the only sound in the room.

The man in the borrowed seat was suddenly much less self-assured. 'And,' he finally continued, desperate to break the silence, 'I foresee no problem with the whole matter of the maintenance contracts. I have no doubt the council will award them to your company.'

The third man continued playing with his lighter for a few moments and then clasped it brusquely in his fist. 'Good,' he said. He put the slim lighter down on the table, on his table, next to an incongruous mangled packet of cheap Ducados cigarettes. He had kept them as a temptation to be fought ever since his doctor had finally plucked up the courage to tell him that it really was time to give up smoking or face the consequences. He had since changed his habits, and his doctor. 'Thank you, Marc,' he added. 'I appreciate all your support.'

Opposite him, Marc Comas, a councillor on the housing and planning committee with the city council, felt a teardrop of sweat run down his face.

The man with the gold lighter got up, evidently calling the brief meeting to a close. Uncertainly, Comas stood up too, taking his lead from him. As the councillor was leaving the room, shown out by the larger of the other two men, the man with the gold lighter shook his hand, grasping it tightly in a fist that years in boardrooms had not shorn of the years before them spent working on building sites.

'I trust your predictions about council meetings will be accurate, Marc.'

'Yes, they will.' Comas felt more sweat running down the nape of his neck on to his shirt collar. 'You have my word.'

'I know I do. And the other matter we've discussed.'

Comas looked numbly at him for a moment, his mouth opening and closing. 'I don't know, that's not so easy. It's not for me to decide.'

The other man looked intently into Comas's eyes, his face pushed up more closely than was comfortable into the other man's. 'Who is it for to decide? Your wife? Are you sure you would want me to have to ask her at this stage?'

Pulling his neck back as far as he dared, Comas quickly shook his head.

'Good.' The other man turned to one of his companions. 'See the councillor out.'

Outside the building, a dusty single-storey construction in the middle of an ageing industrial estate, it was all Comas could do not to break into a run to get to his car. Inside, he turned the air conditioning on full blast and drove off, his tyres skidding on the gravel of the forecourt. He drove straight to where the old hypermarket used to stand in Sant Ponç, before the new Carrefour was built, and parked, his BMW slewed across two parking spaces, before going into the self-service restaurant. He was shaking as he sat down at a table by the window overlooking the main road to

France, needing a few moments with his eyes clamped tightly shut to calm himself down. On the table in front of him was a *café americà* – a double dose of black coffee – and a glass of Torres 10, the pungent aroma of the brandy almost making him nauseous.

Taking a hefty draught of both, he glanced around and reached into the left-hand pocket of his lightweight jacket and pulled out his mobile phone. Checking first for any missed messages, he took an earpiece cable out of his other pocket and inserted the jack into the phone. His insurance, he thought. He listened to all that was discussed, turning the sound down as low as he could while still being able to hear everything. His own voice and that of the other man talking about the revocation of the existing licence originally granted to another construction company. The reclassification of the land as industrial in light of the financial crisis, which would be sold to the man with the gold lighter at a cut-down price and then later be changed back to land for housing use once the recession ended. The maintenance contracts for all public buildings, so that unnecessary repairs could be foisted on to the city's finances. What wasn't discussed was the fee that Comas would be getting for all this.

At another table nearby was a fourth man, one that had never attended the meetings with Marc Comas or ever been present at the construction offices. Sipping from a glass of freshly-squeezed orange juice, he sat and glanced casually every now and then at the councillor listening intently to his phone.

Chapter Five

Elisenda finished her late lunch and waited until she was outside in the narrow streets before checking her work mobile again. Shielding the screen from the mottled sunlight filtering down through the layers of ancient buildings, she looked closely for any symbol in the top left corner that she might have missed, but there was nothing. She'd just had a set menu in a down-at-heel place in one of the few remaining less fashionable parts of the old town. It was one of her informant's favourites.

'Seen Siset lately?' she'd asked the owner after he'd recited the short list of the day's first courses, no doubt for the thirtieth time that day.

A stooped and wiry man who could have been any age between forty-five and seventy and who wore the same bleached and faded apron every day, the owner had paused for breath and shaken his head. 'He hasn't been in for a week or so.'

Putting her phone in her bag, Elisenda walked away from the café and back towards the heart of the old town, past the main university campus. The academic year had just started a week or so ago, and students with brand new folders and backpacks were sitting in excited groups on the steps of the arts faculty or among the rows of scooters parked opposite. Further down the hill, even more were milling around Plaça Sant Domènec, the square in front of the main campus. Walking aimlessly across the square towards her, a little hybrid dog trotting perkily at his feet, a slight figure saw Elisenda and smiled, a big, broad beam of a smile.

'Hi, Xiscu,' she greeted the young man. 'How are you doing?'

'Good, I think,' he replied uncertainly.

Elisenda smiled at him. 'You're looking all right.' She knelt down and ruffled his little dog's ears. 'You looking after him, Pujol?' she asked the dog. He was mainly Scottie, but there were other bits and pieces in there somewhere. Xiscu had named him after a diminutive former president of Catalonia because of his short legs. That was the way Xiscu's mind worked. He was the younger brother of someone Elisenda had gone to school with and was one of life's small victims, unable to cope with the world and perpetually out of step with most of what was going on. She felt a special affinity with him today, so she asked him if he wanted a coffee.

'Do I have to pay?' he asked her, a frown of worry across his face.

She laughed and shook her head, steering him across the square. They sat at a table on the terrace of the student bar facing the main entrance and she ordered them both a coffee and a glass of water. She also asked for a cheese sandwich for Xiscu. He often forgot to eat. With their order, the waitress brought out a plastic bowl of water for Pujol, which she placed under the table, fussing over the small dog. Elisenda smiled a thank you at her.

'You studying here, Elisenda?' Xiscu asked her as they waited for their order.

'I'm in the Mossos d'Esquadra, remember. The police.'

Xiscu looked shocked. 'The police? Like the Policia Nacional?'

'They haven't been the police here for a good ten years,' she told him. A very good ten years, she added in her own mind.

'Guardia Civil?' he asked, horror in his voice.

'No, Xiscu. They've pretty much gone too. We've got our own police now, for the whole of Catalonia. The Mossos d'Esquadra, we've taken over from the old Spanish police.'

'Is that good?'

'It's very good. Don't you remember?' she teased him. 'The last time you got charged for possession of drugs, the policeman spoke to you in Catalan instead of in Spanish.'

His face lit up, as did Elisenda's mobile phone screen. 'That's much better,' he decided. 'I much prefer being arrested in my own language.'

Elisenda gave him a broad grin before picking up her phone and looking at the name on the display.

'I'm sorry, Xiscu, I have to take this.'

She told the caller where she was and hung up, surprised.

'So how come you're a woman?' Xiscu asked her. 'In the police, I mean. I thought they didn't allow that.'

Elisenda turned her attention back to him, smiling as he concentrated on which end of his sandwich to start eating. 'They always allowed it, even before, but it wasn't a job most women wanted to do. Certainly not here in Catalonia. And we wouldn't have had much of a chance of getting anywhere even if we'd wanted to. But now things are different. It's our police force now, by us, for us. And they actually encourage women to join. Change, Xiscu, for the good.'

He looked at her, waiting to finish his mouthful of sandwich. 'This cheese is nice,' he eventually managed, evincing a laugh from her.

He was still slowly working his way through the baguette when Elisenda's caller arrived. Rapt, Elisenda had watched Xiscu painstakingly replace the thick slices of cheese each time they slid out of the bread doused in tomato and olive oil every time he took a bite. She was only disturbed from the sight when the metal legs of one of the fake rattan chairs at their table scraped across the cobbled ground.

'Who's this?' Manel demanded when he'd sat down.

'Friend of mine,' Elisenda told him, adopting the tone of patient indulgence she usually did with the newest member of her team. 'Xiscu, meet Manel, another police officer.'

'Making a hash of that sandwich,' Manel commented.

Xiscu looked uncertainly at him and put his unfinished food back on his plate. 'Can I go, please, Elisenda?' he pleaded, not taking his eyes off Manel. 'I don't like him.'

Elisenda laughed. 'We'll talk another time, Xiscu.' She watched him hurry off, Pujol trotting jauntily alongside him, and slowly shook her head.

'He can't quite keep up with life,' Elisenda commented almost to herself. She turned to her new companion. 'So what brings you here, Manel?'

The caporal finished ordering a coffee. She could see he was using the time to consider his answer.

'Came to see how you are. I don't think they should have suspended you. Stupid bloody idea.'

'I messed up, Manel.'

'Bad information, that's all. Not your fault. Would've been worse if you'd done nothing about it and the information had been good. Then it would've been your fault.'

Elisenda studied him and nodded. It was pretty much what she'd been thinking the last thirty-six hours or more, only with worse language. He was big and bluff and reminded her of a brown bear, especially when he wore his chunky dark leather sports jacket in the colder months. At this time of year, he lived in jeans and an open-necked shirt with the sleeves rolled up, his arms, neck and legs thick and powerful. His character was also like a bear, she thought, swatting about with unwieldy paws, upsetting everything around him. The waitress brought him the beer he'd ordered, and he thanked her, his voice suddenly gentle, a shy smile on his face momentarily revealing the gap between the persona he normally showed the world and the self-effacement that lurked beneath the surface. If only he could find a midpoint between the two, Elisenda thought to herself for the umpteenth time since he'd joined her team seven months earlier.

'So what's new?' she asked him. 'Any news on the robberies at the villas?'

He took a sip of his beer and wiped his lips. 'Nothing. We questioned the family who were robbed, but they couldn't tell us anything. The attackers wore masks like they always do, same mix of accents and languages, Catalan and Spanish, same MO as always. We haven't learned anything we didn't already know.'

Elisenda sighed, depressed by his words. Despite the number and nature of the attacks in recent months, the Mossos really had so little to go on. Looking at the caporal, a thought occurred to her, which she decided to keep to herself.

'How's everyone getting on reporting to Sotsinspector Micaló?' she asked instead. 'I can't imagine Àlex is too pleased with that.'

Manel looked at her and shook his head. 'Micaló? He's not in charge. Àlex is. Inspector Puigventós has put Àlex in charge of the investigation.'

Chapter Six

'Right now, Siset, this feels like the only thing of value you've sold me.'

The front door opened after less than five minutes working on the lock and Elisenda stood up straight again, stretching her back. Silently, she put the picks she'd bought ages ago from Siset back in her bag and decided to take one last look around outside before going into the house.

'And I wish I knew where you'd got to,' she added in the lonely silence.

She walked away from the renovated house to where she'd pulled her car up, on the gravel in the middle of the turning circle between the building and the long drive through the trees from the road. Scanning the woods to either side of the path, she could see nothing, the only sound the incessant chirruping of the cicadas in the heat. There was still half an hour of daylight left before night would come in a rush, pushing the old farmhouse into even more isolated solitude. Looking back towards the house, she couldn't help the breath catching in her throat again at the serene beauty of the jumble of mauve and cerise bougainvillea that covered the whole of the right side of the building. Long tendrils of green and purple reached down over the edge of the arched porch sheltering the door she'd just opened. Where the stone of the walls showed, it shone peach in the falling sun. The twin palms in their giant pots rustled to each other in the soft breeze that had sprung up in the last few minutes. Beyond the noise, Elisenda heard the stream behind the house again, its waters still roiling with the flood water from higher up the valley.

'And I still wouldn't live here if you paid me,' she muttered.

After speaking to Manel in Girona, she'd made sure that the architect couple who lived here were still staying with the wife's parents in the Palau part of town.

'Maybe another day or two,' the woman had told her on the phone.

Elisenda had been tempted to ask if she could borrow a key to check up on the house, but had decided against it. News might have got back to Puigventós. And she was supposedly suspended for the week. Instead, she'd driven the twenty minutes or so to the house that the Mossos had staked out the previous Saturday night and broken in using skills taught to her by Siset.

Satisfied that there was no one about in the woods outside the house, Elisenda walked back to the building and in through the door. She'd opened the left-hand side of the splendid double door and stopped to take a look at it. Mahogany, it wasn't original or an antique salvaged from another site, but new and expensive and designed to look grand and ancient. Swinging it back and forth, she found the door was heavy, lined with steel, she imagined, and with round bolts running side-to-side and top-to-bottom inside the wood and into housings in the frame and floor for extra security.

'For all the good that's done you,' she commented.

Inside, she went through all the rooms, turning the lights on in most of them. They made little effect as yet, but they would shine like a beacon in just a short time, once the sun finally disappeared behind the trees to the rear of the house. With that job done, she returned to the living room to see the effect. There was just one main, open-plan room downstairs, which rose unimpeded through both storeys to the ceiling. The centre of the living area was dominated by a quadrant of huge brown leather sofas arranged around a mahogany and wrought-iron table. The owners had had huge skylight funnels put in to channel natural light into what would otherwise have been a dark and dingy space. Between the sofas and the wall farthest from the door, an open hearth, now dark and cold in the summer, divided the room from a small vestibule leading to the kitchen and a bathroom. Stairs rose along most of the length of the wall to the left and emerged onto a gallery that overlooked the living space on all four sides. The upstairs rooms all radiated off this, three big and airy bedrooms, a wet room and a large shared study with framed newspaper articles about their practice and their renovated home.

'Puts my redecorating to shame.'

Finding a remote, Elisenda turned the sound system on, clicking on the button to have the music piped into all the rooms. The song that came through was from some cheesy stage show, and she quickly looked for something else to play, settling on an old Companyia Elèctrica Dharma anthem before turning the volume up. Pouring herself a glass of water from a bottle in the kitchen fridge, she checked the windows and made sure the back door was securely locked. A plastic box on the work surface next to the door held some paper for recycling, junk mail, a religious pamphlet and an empty milk carton. Taking one last look downstairs, she climbed the stairs and went into one of the rooms she'd left dark. Looking out of the window, she could see across the path that led from the rear of the house down towards the brook, but was certain she couldn't be seen. Leaving there, she went into the study at the front of the house and scanned the drive and the woods either side of it. Her car was still alone on the gravel, no other lights coming along the road. The sun had already fallen and she had to strain to see into the growing gloom of the trees.

'So now we wait,' she told the empty house.

Leaning still against the window frame, she dreaded to think what Puigventós would say if he found out what she was doing. Which he would, if things went how she thought they might. The gang they were after didn't burgle empty houses. The pickings weren't rich enough. Instead, they'd developed a fine trade in targeting isolated and restored farmhouses when the owners were at home. Once they got in, they'd terrorise the occupants, threatening one of the members until the others logged into their online bank accounts and transferred money to a temporary account. The beneficiary account was always with an overseas money transfer company and changed each time. After they'd cleared the bank and credit card accounts out, the gang would then turn to any other easily cashable items, usually jewellery and electronic goods. Finally, they'd turn the computer off that had been used to transfer the money and take that too, along with the car keys. Loading the owner's car with their takings, the gang would make their getaway in it, leaving a battered and traumatised family in their wake. The problem had been compounded lately by the gang becoming increasingly more violent in their treatment of their victims. And by the victims' reports being widely disparate in their descriptions of the attackers. Always with their faces and heads covered with black balaclavas, the perpetrators didn't seem to have any fixed description. Sometimes they spoke Spanish, sometimes Catalan, sometimes with a foreign accent and other times speaking a foreign language that none of the families they'd attacked had recognised. Sometimes they were tall and thin, at others they were short and stocky. Sometimes quicker to violence than others, sometimes burning slow and menacing.

Sighing, Elisenda shifted as she grew stiff and went to the rear bedroom to take a look out of there, shaking life back into her limbs as she walked. She'd already decided that the most likely approach to the house would be from the front, as the back was too far from the main road, so she roamed the upstairs a moment before taking up her post again by the front window. She'd left an upstairs window open in the next-door bedroom at the front to allow the sound of the music to tumble out of the house into the darkness, an open invitation to would-be attackers, but she'd left the window in the study closed, worried that a shift in the light would allow her to be seen from outside. The problem was that it meant she couldn't hear any sounds from the road or path through the trees because of the expensive triple-glazing the architect owners had put in.

'At least I can't hear that bloody barn owl,' she mused.

She heard the noise over an hour later, when she went downstairs to fetch another glass of water from the kitchen fridge. Because of the volume of the music emerging from the music system, she hadn't registered a sound until footsteps scraped on the tile floor in the porch, the other side of the front door. Cursing that she hadn't given herself enough time, she ducked back behind the fireplace, standing in the lee of one of the sloping stone sides, which rose to a vent underneath the gallery. Carefully, she put the glass down on the low hearth and frantically looked for something she could use as a weapon.

Expecting to hear either the door battered open immediately or a short wait while whoever it was outside teased the lock open the way she had, she was surprised to hear a key being inserted instead. She couldn't hear the door open above the music, but she heard it slam shut with a decisive crunch of the locks and bars. Footsteps came slowly towards the centre of the room, still about seven or eight metres from where she was hiding, her fingers folding and unfolding in readiness on the hard stone. The sound stopped, only one set of feet as far as she could hear, which surprised her.

Someone spoke. A man's voice.

'Will you turn this hippie fucking racket off?'

Chapter Seven

Letting her breath out in a long feather of relief, Elisenda unpicked herself from the side of the hearth and emerged slowly into the opening between where she'd been hiding and the sofas. On the other side of the leather quadrangle, Àlex had picked up the remote for the sound system and was angrily stabbing his finger at the controls until the music was muted. Throwing the gizmo down onto the nearest sofa, he looked up at her and shook his head in disbelief. The sudden silence throughout the house almost drove her to her knees.

'What the hell do you think you're doing here, Elisenda?'

Elisenda let a brief flicker of anger after the rush of fear subside before replying.

'More to the point, Àlex, what are you doing here?'

'Investigating the case, Elisenda, because I haven't been suspended. I spoke to the owners of this place to ask them when they planned to come back and if they wanted the Mossos to come with them when they did. Only they told me that someone from the police had already called them. You, Elisenda. What do you think you're playing at?'

'I know what I'm doing, Àlex. It was my information that failed, it's my job to put it right.'

'You're unarmed, you're alone. What do you think you could have done had it been this gang instead of me? You're a cop, for Christ's sake, what do you think they would have done to you? You're out of control, Elisenda. You've left Puigventós without any option but to suspend you. And he'd scalp you if he found out you'd come here.'

Elisenda paused and studied him, calming down before answering. The anger at the ills of the world that always seethed under the surface of his angular face and that made him such a good cop now irritated her. His loose shirt and jeans over his powerful frame annoyed her.

'How's he going to find out, Àlex? Unless someone in my team tells him. The way he knew about…'

Àlex watched her falter over her words. 'The way he knew you saw your daughter, you mean?'

'It is not for you to talk about my daughter, Àlex. That is my business, no one else's.'

'I'm sorry, Elisenda, but it is everyone else's. It's not just our team that sees it. And if you really want to know, we're the ones telling other Mossos to shut up about it.'

Elisenda took a step back from him and looked directly at his face. She was shocked to see something in his dark eyes beyond momentary anger. There was genuine concern in his expression. It made her feel more defensive. 'Well, thank you for that. My daughter died six years ago, Àlex, I'm dealing with it. I don't need you or anyone else in the unit to stand up for me or explain my actions to anyone.'

'It's called loyalty, Elisenda. You see visions of Lina, we know you do. We've all tried to help, but you won't let us. So if you won't accept it from us, now you need someone else's help. You're not over her death.'

'Not over my daughter's death.' Her voice was measured, far calmer than she felt. 'Well, terrible me.'

'I'm sorry, Elisenda, I didn't mean it that way. I just mean you need help to deal with it. That's natural, no one's judging you because of it. Just let us help.' He balled his fists against his thighs in frustration.

She looked coldly at him. 'I don't need help.'

His gaze was equally direct. 'You do, Elisenda. Puigventós won't put up with much more. I'm talking to you as a friend, not as a colleague.'

'You aren't a friend, Àlex, you're my subordinate. You haven't earned the right to talk to me like this.'

He looked defeated and simply nodded at her. 'Fine. But you need friends right now, Elisenda. No one else is fighting your corner. Just us.'

'Friends, Àlex? So when were you going to tell me about you taking over the investigation? That Micaló wasn't in charge?'

'Look at your phone, Elisenda.'

'I have been.' She reached into her pocket and pulled out her mobile.

'Your personal phone. And Micaló's not in charge because he's away on a course. We've known that for four weeks. He left for Sabadell at lunchtime today. Puigventós has only put me in charge because there's no one else to do it.'

Elisenda looked at her work mobile with no missed calls showing and back to Àlex. She hung her head, tired. 'I forgot he was going on a course.'

Àlex finally smiled at her, on the edge of a grin. 'He's building up credits. He'll be applying for promotion soon, once he gets enough. Then he'll be our boss instead of Puigventós.'

Elisenda shuddered, her body relaxing after. 'Please don't say that. What course is he doing? How to tell your arse from your elbow?'

'Yeah, but with a grander title.'

Àlex gave one of his full-blown grins. Elisenda watched him and gave a small, wry laugh. He was almost back to the Àlex she'd always known, his voice strong again now, nearly a year since someone had placed a noose around his neck and tried to hang him, his charming rogue character pretty much up to full strength.

'There's water in the fridge,' she invited him. 'Want to hang about, see if the bad guys turn up?'

She got the feeling that he'd acquiesced to humour her, but it was Àlex, less than half an hour later, who suddenly looked up and cocked his head to one side, listening. Then she heard what had disturbed him. The sound of a car driving in a low gear up the drive. She jumped up from the sofas, where they'd been sitting, and ran to the door. She looked through the spyhole but couldn't make out anything moving. Certainly no headlights approaching the house despite the growing sound of tyres crunching slowly over gravel.

Handing her an iron poker he'd picked up from the fireplace, Àlex joined her at the door, his service Walther P99 already in his right hand. The sound from outside stopped and Elisenda whispered to him to check the back door that led from the kitchen into the garden. She watched him hurry across the living room and past the hearth and turned back to listen for movement from outside, but out of the corner of her eye, she saw a change in the shadows by the window at the foot of the staircase leading up to the gallery. With the lights on in the living room, whoever was standing outside was going to get a much clearer view of the people inside than she would of them, but for a fleeting moment, she just made out three orbits through the dark glass, the gaps for the eyes and mouth of a balaclava. The figure was gone in a fraction of a second. She was sure that they would have seen Àlex cross the room and the gun he was holding.

'Àlex, at the front,' she called behind her, pulling the front door open and charging out into the night.

The figure she'd seen at the side window was sprinting towards a car idling on the gravel, past her own and Àlex's cars, parked facing away from the house. Chasing after him, she lunged forward with the poker and caught her prey with a glancing blow to his trailing left arm. A man's voice cried out in pain and the running figure slowed. Trying to catch him up, Elisenda made to swing again, but suddenly felt a searing pain in her left cheek as a second figure emerged from the darkness and landed a punch to her face. She could see his fist being raised again when the sound of a gunshot erupted behind her. She ducked instinctively but realised immediately that it was Àlex firing a warning from outside the front door of the house. Glancing back, she saw that he'd run through the house to emerge onto the porch.

She turned in time to see the two assailants bundle themselves into the car that was waiting for them. The driver gunned the engine and she had to cover her face to protect it from the sharp stones shot up by the wheels spinning on the gravel before they gained traction and the car sped off along the drive. The headlamps came on, reflecting eerily against the curtain of trees either side of the path, and she watched the car pick up speed to take the smooth curve that led to the main road. She felt a rush of noise as Àlex ran past her, following the car. He levelled his pistol at the retreating lights and fired off one shot, but the car kept going. Elisenda heard him swear as he ran after it to the main road, out of sight of where she was crouching, but there were no more shots fired. She ran down the drive and joined him by the side of the road, where she found him talking into his mobile, calling for a patrol car on the road heading northwest from where they were. He hung up and stared hopelessly at the road heading into the mountains, away from Girona.

'I didn't dare fire once they were on the main road,' he told her. As he said it, a small lorry followed by two cars looking for somewhere to overtake it drove past them in the other direction, the lorry driver staring idly at them as he went by.

'Damn,' Elisenda swore. 'We nearly had them.'

Àlex turned to look at her. 'You didn't. You're not here.' He peered at her cheek. 'Better stay out of Puigventós' way for a bit, too, or you'll have some explaining to do about that bruise.'

Gingerly, she put her hand to her cheek and winced, moving her jaw and face to test how it felt.

'Nothing broken,' Àlex assured her. 'There's one thing you should see, though. I noticed it when I was phoning.'

Taking a pencil torch out of his pocket, he shone it at the ground to the left of the entrance to the drive. A small cairn of stones, barely ten centimetres high, appeared in the circle of light, placed there by a human hand. Protruding from the top were three short sticks, wedged in place among the pebbles.

'What is it?' Elisenda asked him.

He shrugged. 'Your guess is as good as mine.'

Chapter Eight

Evening shift on a Monday and the sergent manning the reception desk at Vista Alegre was happy for a quiet night. He and his teenage daughter had cycled one of the new trails running out towards the coast the previous day, an old railway track reclaimed for weekend warriors, and he was paying for it today. Under the desk, he'd surreptitiously put his right leg up to ease the pain in his calf and thigh. He was doing half an hour each leg and hoping the lactic acid would eventually work its way out. In the meantime, he worked on the computer in front of him and prayed that no one would want him to stand up for anything.

He looked up as he heard the glass doors swing open in time to see three people, one woman and two men, walk in from the street. Surprised, he recognised the woman straight away and wondered what would bring her to the Mossos station at this time on a Monday evening. He'd have thought she'd have too many other things to be doing. He knew one of the men to be her husband, but he didn't know who the second man was. Painfully swinging his leg off the stool as quickly as he could, he stood up stiffly and watched them approach the desk.

The man he didn't know spoke to him first.

'We'd like to report a missing person.'

But before he could continue, the woman held up a finger, signalling for him to stop. She turned away from her companions and faced the sergent full on.

'My son has gone missing.'

The sergent blinked a few times before he could think of what to say, his training momentarily flying out of the window.

'Just one moment, please,' he asked them, recovering his composure. 'I'm afraid I have to ask you a few questions first.'

'Please do.'

He quickly went through all the relevant points with them: the boy's name and ID, a detailed description of him and the clothes he was wearing when he went missing.

'I've also brought a photograph of him,' the woman said. 'I know you need one.'

She gestured to the second man, who produced a photo from a canvas satchel and gave it to the sergent.

Going through the checklist, the sergent told them he'd need some information about the circumstances of the disappearance, looking up as soon as he said it. 'I'll find an officer to go through this with you,' he added.

He called through for a sergent from the Seguretat Ciutadana to come out to the foyer and accompany the three people to a quiet room. He also asked a detective with the Local Investigation Unit to join them. Watching them enter the corridor, he quickly opened an enquiry with the Missing Persons Family Care Unit in the central offices in Sabadell, which would be responsible for keeping the family informed of the progress of the investigation. Staring at the name on the screen, he wondered if that would be enough.

Taking a decision, he called up a directory on the computer and checked a number. After a moment's indecision, he made his mind up and dialled the number. It answered on the third ring.

'Inspector Puigventós,' he said into the phone, waiting for a reply before continuing. 'I think you really need to come into the station.'

The sound of the river returned as he climbed down the ladder.

Upstairs, the torrent's growl had been dampened by the thick stone walls of the abandoned farmhouse, its anger briefly entombed below the surface of the compacted earth floors, but down in the cellar, its impatient mutterings seeped once again through the floor and gathered, brooding in the dank corners.

'What is it I'm supposed to be looking for?' he asked the figure at the top of the ladder.

'Over there in the corner.' The figure pointed at the far wall.

At the bottom of the ladder, he turned and looked to where his companion was pointing. Immediately in front of him was a curious plinth. Four solid stone steps reaching up out of the darkness towards the meagre light cast by the open door above. They were all that was left of the original stairs. The rest had crumbled with the damp years ago, the rubble strewn underfoot the telltale signs. That was the reason the other person had lowered the ladder into the underground room.

Getting accustomed to the gloom, he gingerly picked a path through the debris, past the remnants of the cellar stairs. He had no idea what it was his travelling companion wanted to show him in the corner of the cellar. He looked up again.

'Are you coming down too?'

The figure nodded. 'I'll get a torch. I've left it in the car.'

'Well, hurry.'

He turned and approached the far wall, his eyes making out little in the darkness, his own shadow shielding the weak light from above and behind him.

He heard a noise. A scraping.

Turning, he saw the ladder being lifted quickly back up through the doorway. He turned to head towards it, but his only way out of the cellar was gone.

'What are you doing?'

Without a word, the figure at the top of the stairs stared down at him for a moment. Silently, it turned away and closed the door, plunging the room into a greater darkness.

'What are you doing?' he shouted.

The river beneath his feet and beyond the cellar walls rumbled in reply.

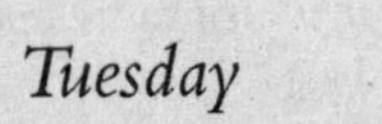

Tuesday

Chapter Nine

'You see your daughter.'

It wasn't a question. It was brutal.

Elisenda flinched on the uncomfortable recliner, or the "rack" as she'd christened it on her punishing run through the quiet streets of the early-morning city. Coming up with the name was the one moment of pleasure she could recall having had all morning. Maybe Àlex was right, she wondered, suppressing a nervous laugh, maybe she was out of control. Snapping suddenly out of her daydream, she could sense Doctora Puyals intensely examining her reaction. So too was Elisenda. It was rare for her to have a problem concentrating.

'No, I don't.'

A knee-jerk reaction. Not entirely untrue.

She thought she saw her daughter. A shadow moving behind a screen. A trail of long hair disappearing out of sight. The shape of a face reflected in a darkened window that vanished when she turned around.

She'd returned home last night to her apartment on Carrer Ballesteries in the old town after leaving Àlex to deal with the aftermath of the failed attack on the architects' country house.

'You go,' he'd insisted. 'You're not supposed to be here. I'll sort it out.'

She'd stopped on the drive back to Girona to check the bruise on her cheek. It was hard to see in the car mirror in the poor light cast by the vanity lamp, but it already looked to be turning a deep shade of purple. She'd also fished her personal mobile out of her bag and checked it for missed calls. Four, all from Àlex, plus one message. So used for so long to focusing her life on her job, she hadn't thought for one minute to look at her non-work phone. Listening to the answering service, to Àlex telling her that he'd been put in charge of the investigation and that he'd keep her posted about developments until she got back, she remembered her words to him about loyalty and hung her head.

Opening the front door to her flat on the top floor of one of the old buildings perched on the edge of the river dividing Girona's compact old quarter from its billowing nineteenth-century expansion, she'd still got a shock at the change she saw in front of her. Not on the grand scale of the house she'd just left, her recent redecoration of her home of less than two years had been to knock down all the walls she could and make what divisions she'd had to with Japanese wood and paper panels. It had been designed solely to exorcise the flat of the dark corners and quiet rooms where Elisenda was haunted by fleeting glimpses of her daughter.

'I hear her singing.'

The words were out before she'd had a chance to check herself, censor how much she would allow the counsellor to hear. She opened her eyes with a start, shocked to find herself still on Puyals' rack. The doctor was relaxed in her straight-backed chair, her head to one side.

'When I'm at home on my own, I hear Lina, my daughter singing. It keeps me awake. It kept me awake last night.'

'You told me you redecorated your flat.'

Elisenda had no recollection of having told the other woman that. 'I don't understand why I see Lina in my flat. She never lived here. I moved back to Girona after she and my ex died.'

'Do you want to tell me about that?'

She was surprised to discover that she did want to tell Puyals about it. 'They were flying to Mallorca for a summer holiday. I was still living in Barcelona at that time, after her father and I separated. Lina lived with me and saw her father at weekends. He had a pilot's licence and a small plane. They just flew there and never came back. A summer storm. They didn't reach the island and nothing was ever found. No wreckage. They were never found. I moved back to Girona because I couldn't face staying in Barcelona where I'd lived with her. And now I'm back here and I still see her.'

'Do you want to stop seeing her?'

'I don't know.' Elisenda stopped speaking for a moment, her eyes screwed tightly shut. 'I think I need to stop seeing her. For my own sake. And I can't help feeling that that's wrong.'

'It's not, Elisenda. What you see and hear isn't your daughter. It's your grief. That's what's haunting you, not Lina. You are.'

'Can I change that?'

'Yes.'

After the session, Elisenda found the first café she could and ordered a black coffee, which was a rarity for her. Drinking the small cup in one gulp, she ordered her usual *café amb llet* and a glass of water straight after. She felt more drained after the hour spent with the counsellor than she had after a sleepless night and a gruelling run. Still shaking, she ordered two sugary donuts and wolfed them down. The woman behind the bar smiled at her. Elisenda wondered what she must have thought the need for so much sugar and caffeine was.

By the time she left the café, the face she showed the world was back in place. Still feeling adrift at the lack of a job to do, she found herself wandering through the regimented patchwork of the Eixample, turning left and right at random. By the time she'd stared in the third shop window, she was happy to feel that the desperate unease she'd felt just a half hour earlier was giving way to irritable boredom with being suspended. Angrily, she checked her work mobile and was surprised to see that someone had left a message for her. Probably Àlex, she thought. Impatiently going through the sequence to retrieve it, she was surprised in the end to hear Puigventós' voice. Telling her to call him or go to Vista Alegre the moment she got the message.

She stopped in the middle of the pavement and pondered for a moment before moving on again. Uncertain of what was waiting for her at the station, her pace was nonetheless more purposeful than it had been at any point in the last twenty-four hours. It was only as she was crossing the footbridge to the east side of the river that she recalled the bruise on her cheek. She touched it once and winced.

Chapter Ten

'I don't do missing children.'

'You do now.'

Elisenda and Puigventós faced each other off across his desk, equally defiant. She'd walked the ten minutes to the police station since getting Puigventós' message preparing herself for best and worst case scenarios. At best, questions about how she got her bruise. At worst, a demand to know what she was doing at the farmhouse the previous night. Àlex was also in the inspector's office, standing behind Elisenda. Unfortunately, his presence in the room seemed to indicate the second scenario was the one she'd find herself having to face.

What she wasn't prepared for was this.

'This is the Serious Crime Unit,' she repeated. 'We don't deal with missing persons. That's a Local Investigation Unit case. They can take it. You can't bring me back from suspension for this, Xavier.'

With a sigh, Puigventós sat down and signalled for Elisenda and Àlex to do likewise. Stubbornly, Elisenda remained standing. The inspector took his new glasses off and polished them before speaking. When he put them back on, Elisenda decided reluctantly that they made his finely honed nose and cheekbones and his keen grey eyes look even more patrician. He looked up at her as he spoke, his voice strained.

'The missing boy is Jaume Comas Miravent. His mother is Susanna Miravent.'

'The politician?' Elisenda finally sat down too, dropping heavily on the stiff chair. 'Again.'

She saw Àlex's look of bewilderment at her last comment.

'Precisely,' Puigventós continued. 'That family again. And that's why we have to treat it as a serious crime. Because of who the mother is and because of the elections. And because of what happened four years ago. This is potentially much more than just a missing person case, Elisenda.'

'I know who Susanna Miravent is,' Àlex interrupted. 'The anti-independence candidate for the elections.'

'The anti-independence, pro-austerity, pro-privilege candidate,' Elisenda added, 'standing for a party that passes itself off as being of the left.'

'The mother of a missing child,' Puigventós corrected them both. He turned to face Àlex. 'What you probably won't know is that they have an older son. Had an older son. He went missing four years ago, when he was twelve, under similar circumstances. He's never been found. This son, Jaume, was ten at the time. The family were on a day out when the older boy just vanished.'

'And no trace of him since?' Àlex asked the question, but glanced at Elisenda, uncomfortable at having to ask it.

'Sightings all over Catalonia, Spain and Europe.' It was Elisenda who answered him. 'But none of them substantiated. And no body was ever found. No ransom demands, nothing.'

'You will have to go back over the case files from that investigation,' Puigventós told them. 'Fortunately, it was after the Mossos took over from the Spanish police, so we'll have the records. Technically, the case is still open, but the family has gone on record as saying that they regard him as being dead and that they'll be applying for a declaration of death after ten years.'

Àlex looked at Elisenda out of the corner of his eye. Her face was impassive.

'And all of that is why I need your unit leading the investigation, Elisenda,' Puigventós added.

She nodded her head slowly. 'So I'm no longer under suspension? Good.'

Puigventós reached into a desk drawer and pulled out her ID card and pistol. 'And nothing has gone on your record.'

Elisenda stood up, with Àlex following suit. 'I certainly won't miss those awful counselling sessions.'

'I said nothing about ending the counselling, Elisenda.' Puigventós pulled up an email on his computer. 'Doctora Puyals seems to think that you need to continue with that.'

'Come on, Xavier. With the house robbery investigations and now this, I'm not going to have time to waste on talking about my childhood.'

'The counsellor thinks otherwise, and I'm inclined to agree with her. That's why Àlex is here. I want your unit to be in charge of both cases, but Àlex will be running the investigation into the house attacks, under your supervision, of course. You'll be running the missing person case and overseeing both investigations. You can use Sotsinspector Armengol's Local Investigation Unit for support if you need it. He's aware of that. And Seguretat Ciutadana for house-to-house and searches evidently.'

'As well as the counselling? Seriously?'

Puigventós nodded. 'Very much so. And the counselling will now include another session on Saturday morning. Doctora Puyals has suggested it and I've already agreed to it. We think you need it.'

Elisenda's head dropped slightly. 'That's the trade-off, I take it.'

Puigventós smiled, the small wrinkles around his eyes magnified behind the glasses. 'How did you get the bruise on your cheek, by the way?'

About to leave the room, Elisenda turned back, avoiding Àlex's gaze. 'Running this morning. I stumbled and caught my face.'

'Where was that?' Àlex asked her, a grin lurking behind his eyes.

She looked directly at him and back at the inspector. 'By the Torre Gironella. The ground's uneven there.'

'Lot of sharp stones too,' Àlex insisted. 'Surprised it's not worse. Anything could have happened.'

Outside Puigventós' room, she spoke to him over her shoulder as they walked along the corridor to their offices. 'You will pay for that, Sergent Albiol.'

-

They drove through the quiet streets and swimming-pooled villas of the Palau district of Girona, south of the city, past the excluding shutters and yawning double garages of the great and the good. The scintillating green of the pines and tended hedges stood guard, shielding the privacy of the houses behind them rising a stark blue-white against the sky, like a morning storm awaiting.

'I've never met her,' Elisenda told Àlex as he wound the car up through the curving roads and gentle inclines towards the Comas Miravent home. 'She's got to be about ten years older than me. Around the time she was coming to prominence, I was living in Barcelona.'

'You mean you don't move in the same circles?' Àlex teased her, waiting for a Mercedes sports car to glide left into an expansive drive.

'Hard to believe, I know.'

Elisenda had decided that they should go and see the parents of the missing boy straight after their meeting with Puigventós, both to reassure them that the Mossos were taking the disappearance seriously and to gauge the situation before deciding on their next step.

'Seguretat Ciutadana are out searching the boy's route home,' she'd voiced her thoughts to Àlex. 'We need to speak to the parents first to see which way we need to take the investigation.'

She glanced at the notes on her mobile. Sunday's election was to decide the ruling party and president of the Catalan government for the next four years. With probably the most far-reaching powers of any non-national government in Europe, the Generalitat in Barcelona was able to raise taxes and pass laws, with exclusive jurisdiction in some areas, such as the environment, trade and transport. Where it shared powers with the Spanish government was in education, currently a sore point in relations between Barcelona and Madrid, and health and justice. Susanna Miravent represented a populist political feeling that had emerged in recent years since the financial crisis that wanted to retain a union with Spain and reduce the powers of the Catalan government. Miravent, Elisenda knew, went as far as to advocate the abolition of the Generalitat. Taking one last look at the screen, Elisenda flicked the mobile off and sighed.

Àlex slowed as they approached a group of two cars and a white TV van waiting outside a house, seemingly one of the biggest in the neighbourhood. So far, a single television camera had been set up on the opposite side of the road, the crew and reporter moving into position as Elisenda and Àlex's car slowed down outside the house. A reporter and a photographer climbed out of each of the cars and moved forward. Elisenda wound her window down to speak to one of the two Mossos standing guard by the front gate.

'Are they giving you any trouble?' she asked the uniformed officer, a caporala with piercing blue eyes and light brown hair pulled up tightly under her cap.

'Not yet. Surprised there aren't more.'

'There will be. Call Vista Alegre if you need extra bodies.'

The other Mosso pushed the bell on the front gate and spoke into the intercom, standing aside as the wide single automatic gate moved slowly backward and inward. As Àlex waited, one of the reporters tried to attract his attention to ask a question, but he shook his head. Revving the engine gently, he squeezed through the gate before it was fully open and drove up the steep drive to a turning circle in front of the house. Elisenda realised that her initial idea of the building being large was inaccurate. It was a typical, nondescript cloned house, a product of the recent construction boom that owed its appearance of opulence to the high hedge and extensive lawn surrounding it rather than to the house itself. As expensive as the architects' place in the country, but with none of the taste. Or isolation, she thought, its one saving grace.

At the top of a raised porch, a blond wood door opened and a Mosso came out to show them in. 'They're in the living room,' he told them, pointing to a door. 'They're expecting you.'

'How are they doing?' Elisenda asked him.

He looked suddenly perplexed, surprising her. 'Best if you see for yourself,' he finally told her.

Elisenda thought that he might have come in with them, but he sat down instead on a straight-backed chair that had been placed in the hall. Going into the room, two things struck her. The first was the sparseness of the decoration, a model of white space and minimalism. She hated to admit that she liked the feel of the room, with its two low sofas, open fireplace and modern art hanging on the walls, and very little else. The other thing that struck her was that there were three people watching them walk up to the sofas. She'd been expecting only two. None of them rose.

'Susanna Miravent,' Elisenda greeted the only woman. 'I'm Sotsinspector Elisenda Domènech, my colleague here is Sergent Àlex Albiol. We're with the Serious Crime Unit in Girona, we'll be leading the investigation into your son's whereabouts.'

'The Serious Crime Unit?' Miravent asked, a faint trace of consternation on her face.

'We deal with major investigations in the Girona area. The Mossos believe that given your profile, your son's disappearance should be treated with the utmost care. It doesn't reflect any concern for his safety that is out of the ordinary for cases such as this. May we sit down?'

Miravent was sitting on the sofa facing the fireplace next to one of the men. She gestured to the other man, who was sitting on the sofa at a right-angle to the first one and facing the window, to vacate his seat. He joined his companions on their sofa, sitting between them. Elisenda took the seat he'd just left, but Àlex stayed standing, his eyes scanning the people in the room and everything else in it.

'Would you care for some coffee?' Miravent asked them. She turned to the man at the far end of the sofa. 'Marc, can you go and arrange that, please?'

Slightly ungraciously, the man she called Marc got up and left the room, returning just a few moments later. Not enough time to put a cafetera on, Elisenda thought. She asked the two men to introduce themselves.

'Marc Comas,' the man who'd supposedly gone out to arrange the coffees said. 'Jaume's father.'

'Are you also a politician?'

'I'm a city councillor. On the planning and construction committee. I'm in charge of green-lighting all new planning projects in the city.' Instinctively, he produced a card from his wallet and handed it to Elisenda.

And not as successful or as high profile as your wife, Elisenda thought, despite your trying to prove otherwise. She looked at the grand title on the business card he'd given to her and wondered how that might affect him. She studied him quickly as she put his card in her notebook. His face was too fleshy for the rest of his body and she could already see he had a habit of pinching his cheek tightly while other people were speaking, as though reminding himself to pay attention.

'And this is Francesc Bofarull,' Miravent said, indicating the other man. 'My campaign manager. He was with us when we discovered that Jaume was missing and when we reported it to the police.'

Elisenda had seen in the notes before leaving Vista Alegre that Bofarull had been with the married couple the previous evening when they'd gone to Vista Alegre. She studied him quickly. He looked like every man she'd ever seen who'd graduated from a business school. A corporate haircut crowning a confident and chiselled face. Slim, good in a jacket and tie, his fingers as manicured as his manner.

'I'm afraid I need to ask you some questions,' she told them, naturally gravitating towards Miravent as she spoke.

Before she could, though, the door opened and a young woman came in carrying a tray full of cups and saucers and a large and spotlessly clean cafetera and milk jug. So that was how come arranging coffee took a matter of seconds. Without a word, the woman left the tray on the table between the sofas and left the room.

'Encarna, our housekeeper,' Miravent explained to Elisenda. 'I'll pour.'

Elisenda watched her as she deftly set out the cups and saucers and served everyone a cup of coffee. For the first time, Elisenda noticed her hands. Despite being Catalan to the core, from a family that traced its roots in the city back centuries, she wore her wedding ring on her right hand, the Spanish way, instead of in the Catalan fashion on the left hand. It instantly irritated Elisenda, who had to fight down the emotion. Everything about the politician was elegant and slender, from her long fingers to the fine cut of her face and figure, the lithe grace of her body at rest and the efficient parsimony of her movements. Elisenda could see why, despite embracing politics most people in Catalonia found unpalatable, she enjoyed the media exposure she did and invited the trust of an increasingly confused and sceptical electorate. Miravent proffered a cup to Àlex, her eyes engaging with his as he leaned forward to take it, and sat back to look frankly at Elisenda, wordlessly inviting her to ask her questions.

Elisenda went through the same process that the team at Vista Alegre had the previous evening. She learned that the boy had left school at the normal time, five-fifteen, and hadn't stayed on for his extra English lessons as he should have done. The classes were extracurricular and optional and term had only just started a week earlier, so the teacher had seen nothing untoward in his not being there. After that, he was supposed to have gone to a friend's house to do their homework together, but he'd told the friend he wasn't going, which was why no one noticed his absence until quite late in the evening. The friend thought he'd gone home, his parents assumed he was at the friend's house. It was only when he didn't show up at the time they expected him that they rang the friend. After that, they'd rung all his other friends and the school head teacher, but none of them had seen him since five-fifteen. The boy whose house he was supposed to be going to reckoned he'd seen Jaume getting on a bus outside the school, which wasn't in itself unusual as that's how he normally went home. Elisenda made a note of the friend's name.

'Do you know if there was anything that was worrying him? Was he being bullied at school?'

Comas grunted. 'Hardly. Jaume wasn't the sort of boy to be bullied by anyone.'

'Might he have gone to see someone of his own accord? Grandparents? Friends from outside school?' As she asked the questions, Elisenda digested Comas's words and how the subtext of what people said was often more revealing than the words they thought they were saying.

'We've called everyone.' Surprisingly, it was Bofarull, the campaign manager, who answered. 'There's no one we can think of that he'd be with.'

'And he would have told us where he was going, anyway,' Miravent added. 'Jaume would never fail to tell us where he was.'

Elisenda knew she had to tread carefully with the next question. 'Do you think it might have something to do with his brother?'

'Jaume was over the death of his brother.' Again, it was Bofarull who replied.

'We'd all talked about Albert's death,' Miravent continued. 'We were all comfortable with it. It isn't something that would have made Jaume go off. And this isn't an anniversary or anything like that.'

'Any jealousy?' Elisenda insisted. She was certain she saw a flicker in Comas's expression. 'Anything else at home that would be upsetting him?'

'Nothing,' Bofarull answered.

Elisenda could sense Àlex behind her drawing in a breath, picking up on the campaign manager's insistence on replying to what should have been questions for the parents to answer. She deliberately aimed her next question at Miravent.

'Given your political beliefs, do you think that someone might have taken Jaume as a protest or to make demands?'

Bofarull was about to answer, but Miravent signalled him to keep quiet. 'My political beliefs, Elisenda? I have beliefs the same as any other person who chooses to enter politics. I don't see why someone should target my family because of my beliefs. They might because I'm a politician, but not because of the views I uphold.'

Nice speech, Elisenda thought. She was willing to place a bet that Bofarull would have come up with almost the same reply.

'Nonetheless,' she told Miravent, 'there is a strong possibility that your son's disappearance is related to the elections and possibly to the stance that your party represents. If that is the case, we would expect to hear from whoever might have taken Jaume with a series of demands. The Mossos would need to see that the moment you received it.'

'You have my word.'

'There are Mossos inside and outside your house to keep you safe and to try and stop the media from harassing you. We will also be sending a member of the Policia Científica here to monitor your landline in case anyone rings with demands. If you receive any suspicious calls on your mobile phones, we will need to hear about it. One other thing: we have a dedicated family support unit based in Sabadell. Their job is to keep you informed of how the investigation is progressing and offer you any comfort you need. They'll be contacting you this morning.'

Miravent put both hands up to stop Elisenda. 'I'm afraid we won't be needing the services of the family support unit, thank you. I would prefer to deal directly with you, Elisenda. You would be far better able to keep us up to speed with matters.'

'That is not how we usually do this, I'm sorry. I'll be too involved with the actual search for Jaume to be able to give you the time you need.'

Miravent smiled indulgently. 'I'm a busy woman, too, Elisenda, especially seeing as we're in the closing stages of an election campaign. I really won't have the time to be dealing with someone on the end of a phone in Sabadell. I would sooner speak directly to you.'

Her tone had the finality of someone used to getting their way. Elisenda had no doubt that once she spoke to Puigventós and the judge, that would prove to be only too true. 'I'll see what I can do,' she promised, willing to cede ground on this to possibly gain a compromise elsewhere. 'You or your representative will also need to be present when we see the judge. We have a time scheduled for first thing tomorrow morning. Can you arrange that?'

'Why do we have to see the judge?'

'You're aware that our investigation will be directed by an examining judge. They'll be the one responsible for deciding on the focus of the investigation and how the Mossos are to run it. In this case, they have to decide on the preliminary procedures to be taken. To do that, they'll look at all the evidence we submit to them and listen to your arguments to establish the nature of the disappearance. Once that's established, the judge will instruct us how to proceed. Don't worry, it doesn't mean that we're not doing everything we can in the meantime to find Jaume, it's simply due procedure.'

'I'll attend as representative,' Bofarull offered.

Elisenda shook her head. 'If it's not a direct family member, it will have to be a lawyer.'

'We'll arrange that by tomorrow morning,' Miravent promised. 'We have our own lawyer.'

'As and when we hear anything, we'll contact you,' Elisenda told her. 'If there's anything you need, please call this number.'

Elisenda gave Miravent her card and made to stand up.

'Just so you know,' Bofarull said, 'we're arranging a media conference for this afternoon. An appeal for information. We need to get this out there as soon as possible to find Jaume.'

Elisenda considered him. 'That's your decision. I would suggest you don't let the media turn it into a circus.'

'We're very experienced at this,' he assured her.

I'm sure you are, she thought.

Chapter Eleven

'Cross the river and take a right,' Elisenda told Àlex as they drove back towards the city centre.

Àlex chose his words carefully before speaking. 'Bit of a cold fish. Miravent.' He paused, but Elisenda made no effort to reply. 'And Comas. They really didn't seem that worried to me.'

'Politicians,' she replied with a shrug. 'Used not to giving anything away.'

'Didn't you find their reaction strange?'

She sighed. 'What should their reaction be?'

'Their kid is missing.' Àlex couldn't keep the anger out of his voice. He glanced nervously at her the moment he spoke. She stared expressionlessly through the windscreen without answering. 'You all right, Elisenda?'

'Why wouldn't I be?'

'With this investigation. A missing child.'

She turned her head to look at him, her face cold, before returning her gaze to the road. 'Tell me what happened last night after I left,' she finally said.

He exhaled silently, knowing not to pursue the matter.

'The bad guys got away,' he told her, his voice unnaturally calm. 'There were no Seguretat Ciutadana cars out and about near enough to get on to them and by the time one got there, they were long gone.'

'Anyone ask what you were doing there?' Her voice was recovering some of its animation.

'Not really. Científica came out to look for any traces, so they were more worried about doing their job, Seguretat Ciutadana didn't ask, and you've seen what's worrying Puigventós this morning.' He turned to face her for a moment. 'So you got away with it.'

'I lead a charmed and fortunate existence.' Even Elisenda laughed wryly at her own words. Àlex grinned, the tension evaporating. 'Did Científica find anything?'

'Nothing important. Unfortunately, you didn't draw blood from that guy you hit, so no possible DNA there. The car was stolen. Uniforms found it burned out on some waste land near the industrial estate in Celrà this morning. They didn't leave anything either at the house or at the car. These people know what they're doing.'

'Celrà? That's a good thirty kilometres away. And in the other direction. So where they went after that is anybody's guess. I can't see the owners moving back any time soon once we tell them about it. Have you had any more thoughts on the stones and twigs we saw?'

Àlex considered for a moment. They'd crossed the Onyar and were heading out of the city, the river to their right behind a thin straggle of trees, to the left scrub-lined hill and sparse, empty buildings. 'I think it's got to mean something. I was going to check up on the other houses that have been targeted recently to see if I can find anything similar there but then this thing with the missing boy came up.'

'Still a good idea. We'll have to sort out how we split these two jobs.' She gestured at a turnoff up ahead. 'You need to take a left here, we're exploring the heady delights of Font de la Pólvora.'

They drove past Tío Juan perched on the same rickety stool as always, clocking everyone coming in or out of his neighbourhood, his hands clasped tightly on the handle of a heavy walking stick, its tip resting on the pavement between his feet. Elisenda knew he'd seen them even though he showed no sign of it, so by the time they got to the end of the road the word that they were around would be spreading through the less salubrious parts of the district. She reckoned he was able to recognise pretty much all of the unmarked Mossos cars in the city. Sure enough, when they tried Siset's apartment, he wasn't there.

'Out,' Elena told them. She was wearing a bra and tracksuit bottoms, her voice slurred, a spliff burning slowly in an old ashtray on the kitchen table, a half-empty bottle of beer next to it. Breakfast.

'Did you tell Siset I wanted to see him, Elena?' Elisenda asked her.

Àlex went into the bedroom and living room to check, but found nothing.

'Yeah, I think so,' Elena told her.

Looking through the kitchen cupboards, Àlex found an old packet of sliced bread. He took a slice out and poured olive oil and sugar on it and gave it to Elena. 'Eat that, it'll do you good.'

She looked at it askance but took a bite out of it anyway. Evidently surprised at the taste, she took another mouthful and munched happily on it. The food seemed to revitalise her.

'He's been back, then?' Elisenda insisted.

'Last night.' Elena took another bite, tiny crumbs spraying as she spoke. 'But I haven't seen him this morning.'

'OK, but tell him I need to see him. It's important.' She signalled to Àlex that they should leave. 'Take care of yourself, Elena.'

'And eat,' Àlex added.

'Olive oil and sugar?' Elisenda asked him on the stairs.

'My grandmother used to give it to me when I was a kid. Instant zing.'

'Ah, the things they teach you in Barcelona.'

Driving the short distance to the next destination on Elisenda's list, they passed a shiny new primary school, the kids sitting in the playground in the sun engrossed in something their teacher was showing them. They split off into chattering groups, excited by whatever task it was they'd been set.

'I look at Elena,' Elisenda commented to Àlex, 'and I think what chance have these kids got? Then you see that school and there's hope.'

Àlex snorted. 'And then we'll see the school that Jaume Comas Miravent goes to and realise that there isn't. That this side of the river and the other side of the river will stay firmly as they are. Especially if politicians like Susanna Miravent have their way.'

'And I was feeling so cheerful.' She pointed to a side road. 'Turn left here and stop where you can. Not too far in, the place we want is fifty metres down the road.'

Parking, they walked quickly to a café, but Elisenda knew the moment they'd got out of the car that if Siset were in there, he'd already have taken flight. Two toughs sitting on stools outside the tatty bar had been giving a running commentary to the shadowy interior ever since they'd pulled up.

'Morning, boys,' Elisenda greeted them.

'Elisenda,' the older of the two acknowledged, the same guy who'd tried to catcall her the previous morning.

Inside the gloomy café, wooden tables lined up along one wall, a dull zinc bar along the other, a motley quartet of dominoes-players sat in begrudging silence at one of the tables, its surface glistening with sticky rings of spilled brandy. Rows of bottles of Ponche Caballero and Licor 43 and other drinks that had gone out of fashion years ago gathered dust on the shelves behind the counter. The owner, a bear of a man with thick black hair on his bare forearms matted with sweat, flicked a grimy tea towel over the glass cases chilling aluminium trays of chorizo and Russian salad and stared at the two Mossos.

Elisenda looked around before speaking. 'Well, I guess that answers that question.' She turned to the owner. 'I take it you haven't seen Siset.'

He shook his head. She asked the four players at the table the same question. None of them spoke. Just one, the oldest at the table, gave the slightest of shakes of his head.

She turned back to the owner. 'So you're saying that Siset hasn't been here and you haven't seen him?'

'Haven't seen him for weeks,' the owner finally said, his voice like gravel soaked in beer.

Elisenda walked over to another table, where an old-fashioned leather satchel was lying on the ground underneath it. She squatted down and fished it out, taking a quick look inside. She recognised it as the one Siset always carried. She stood up holding it and turned in time to see the owner shoot a glance at the oldest of the domino set.

'In which case,' she told them, 'this is most definitely lost property if its owner hasn't been in to claim it for weeks.'

'That's not Siset's,' the owner said weakly.

Elisenda gazed directly at him. 'We both know that's not true. But not to worry, we're the Mossos, he'll be happy to know we're keeping it safe for him. When you do see him, let him know he just has to come to Vista Alegre to claim his property.'

The owner and the oldest man at the table looked at each other, unsure of how to react. One of the younger players puffed his chest out and scraped his chair back, seeming to want to make a move. The harsh sound of the metal on the tile floor echoed around the small bar.

'I take it you have no objections,' Elisenda told them, approaching the counter and looking straight at the owner.

Without a word, Àlex took a step towards the table and effortlessly moved the younger man's leg to one side on his chair. Quickly reaching down, Àlex picked up a domino piece that had been hidden there and placed it gently on the table. He grinned at the player caught cheating and stepped back.

The two Mossos left as the sound of arguing from the players rose in the murk. Retrieving their car, they drove back down through the dusty jumble of apartment blocks, past Tío Juan sitting sentinel to his domain.

Chapter Twelve

'Puigventós,' Elisenda explained, holding her mobile up for Àlex in the car after a message pinged in. They were just entering the built-up part of the city outskirts, nearing the turnoff in the road that led from the river to the police station.

'I'll never get over how the river's suddenly so wide here,' Àlex told her, waiting at the lights.

'Flood defence. The old town used to get badly flooded in the winter when there was heavy rainfall in the mountains, so they widened this bit to ease the flow. Now the flood water is diverted along all the tributaries outside the city. Still gets pretty wild at times, though.' She read the short text. 'And Puigventós is insisting we go and see him the moment we get back to Vista Alegre.'

'You might be needing flood defences of your own. He's probably found out about your extra-curricular activities.'

Elisenda instinctively put her hand to the bruise on her face. It was still tender. 'You will pay for this one day, Àlex, you do know that?'

They were surprised to find a TV van outside the Mossos station. A couple of the terrace tables at the café on the corner opposite the entrance were occupied by what could only be journalists, talking into mobiles or tapping at tablets. Elisenda only recognised one or two of them, the rest were probably from Barcelona.

'How news travels,' she commented.

Inside, Puigventós was a lot calmer than she'd feared.

'It's to be expected. The disappearance of a child is news and Susanna Miravent is a controversial figure. Combine the two and this is what we get.'

'I wonder if the press would bc as interested if a kid from Font de la Pólvora went missing,' Àlex commented.

'They probably wouldn't be, sergent, but it's not our job to worry about what the press think. Right now, I'm more interested in what you both think now that you've spoken to the family. What are we looking at?'

'Àlex and I have discussed this now,' Elisenda told Puigventós. She took a sip of water from the glass that the inspector had poured for them each from a bottle on his desk. 'We see three main options. One is that the boy has absconded of his own accord. We'll learn more about that after we've spoken to his teachers and friends. The family setup is an unusual one, since the mother's in the public eye and most of her time is taken up with the elections. Also, Miravent and her husband don't appear to be the closest of couples, so that might be relevant too. Either way, it might be a case of the boy looking for attention.'

'There's also the possibility that he's injured somewhere,' Àlex added. 'He fell on his way home or on his way to somewhere else. Other kids attacked him. A hit and run driver. We'll be checking up on those possibilities. Seguretat Ciutadana are looking at his possible routes from school and following the route of the bus he took to see if anything turns up.'

'If anything,' Elisenda took up the reins, 'we believe that those are the least likely options, but we need to chase them up to be certain.'

'Why's that?' Puigventós wanted to know.

'More than anything because of the profile of the family. But we'll come back to that. The second option we see is that it's a random abduction; just pure chance that he was the child taken. Again, it's a possibility that we have to investigate, but one that we're not convinced is the right one, especially given his age. We'll be checking on sex offenders, anyone with a history that might indicate they'd take a fourteen-year-old boy.'

'You think it's more closely related to the mother,' Puigventós predicted, the slight nod of his head showing he already agreed with that.

'I think initially that that has to be the main focus,' Elisenda replied. 'Whatever way we interpret it. Miravent's views are unpopular with a lot of people, she will have created a lot of enemies who could conceivably take her son to force her to stand down as a candidate.'

'The family's also wealthy,' Àlex added. 'Or appears to be wealthy. This could be an opportunist kidnapping after someone's seen her on television, meaning it's for financial rather than political reasons.'

'Either way, while we're looking into possible causes and anyone in the mother's or the father's background who could be behind it, we wait for a ransom demand.' She paused before continuing. 'The flip side of the political motive is that it isn't a political enemy who's done it, but a political friend.'

Puigventós rubbed his eyes, already fatigued by the breadth of the possible options. Elisenda could see that it was a possibility that had also occurred to him.

'Another sort of attention-seeking, in other words,' he said. 'Stage a kidnap to gain political ground. Do you really think the mother would go along with that? Or the father?'

'She might not know,' Elisenda replied. 'I want to take a closer look at Bofarull, her campaign manager, he seemed to take over quite a lot. It might be in his canon of acceptable political acts. Susanna Miravent struck me as being very much in control of things, but there's always the chance that there could be areas where Bofarull operates without her knowledge.'

'I think we need to look at the husband too,' Àlex added. 'The dynamic between the three of them at the house this morning didn't seem right. He seemed excluded: maybe he's the one after the attention.'

'His political office too,' Elisenda agreed. 'We'll be taking a look at that. The boy's disappearance might be politically motivated because of the father, not the mother.'

Puigventós took his glasses off and polished them. Like all new glasses wearers, it had become his latest tic, a device to make time while he thought. 'OK, I think we're all agreed that those are the avenues we need to pursue.'

'There's one other possibility that we have to consider,' Elisenda interrupted. 'This is the second time that this has happened to this family.'

Puigventós second-guessed what she was going to say. 'To lose one child is unfortunate. To lose two looks like carelessness.'

'Or worse. Àlex and I have also discussed this. It's something we're going to be looking at closely. Of course, we've also got to speak to the judge to see which way they want us to go. Depending on who we get, they could call for anything.'

The inspector looked at her over the top of his glasses, another new benefit. 'Which you will, of course, observe to the letter, Elisenda. Investigations are led by judges, our job is to do their bidding, in case I need to remind you.'

She looked frankly back at him, the bruise on her cheek throbbing dully. 'You have my word that I shall very closely observe what the judge tells us to do.'

Puigventós grunted sceptically. 'Now, normally, we'd be able to count on Sotsinspector Micaló and his unit for support, but as he's away on this course until next week, we'll have to bring in Sotsinspector Armengol. You can coordinate with him and he can work with his own and Sotsinspector Micaló's teams.'

Elisenda studiously avoided making eye contact with Àlex when the inspector made his remark about support from Micaló. The absence of his self-serving brand of policing and corporate politics was the first ray of sunshine for the investigation and her peace of mind.

'I'm sure we'll manage,' she commented.

'We'll bring Esteve in now so he's up to speed with everything,' Puigventós decided, dialling an internal number on his desk phone.

A few minutes later, Esteve Armengol came in. The new sotsinspector in charge of the Local Investigation Unit, he'd taken on a post just two months earlier that many had seen as a poisoned chalice because of the scandal of his predecessor. Elisenda had to admit that in an irrational way she was struggling to like him because of what had come before, not because he'd given her any reason to dislike him. Just a couple of years older than her, he was slight in build with a head shaved to hide a growing bald patch, and wore stylish thick-rimmed glasses framing piercing, bird-like eyes. Outside work, he always carried a battered brown satchel and was often seen at lunchtime reading a book on a shaded bench in the little Foramuralles park by the city walls. Taken as a whole, it had earned him the nickname of the Professor among some of the Mossos.

'Morning, everyone,' he greeted them affably, taking the seat next to Àlex at the meeting table.

Elisenda also had to admit that she'd hoped to see a woman in his role to even things out in the regular meetings held between Puigventós and the sotsinspectors to coordinate the various investigations, but had similarly had to admit that there were none suitable among the candidates. Inspector Puigventós, who was head of the Regional Investigation Command, which reported to the Criminal Investigation Division in Sabadell rather than to the police station in Girona, coordinated criminal investigations in Girona with three sotsinspectors. Elisenda was one of these and was in charge of the experimental Serious Crime Unit, which took on major cases throughout the Girona region. The second was Roger Micaló, who led the Regional Investigation Unit, which investigated the criminal cases in the region not taken on by Elisenda's unit. They both reported to Puigventós. The third was Esteve Armengol, who was the new head of the Local Investigation Unit, which dealt with lesser criminal investigations within the confines of the city. Unlike Elisenda and Micaló, he coordinated with Puigventós but actually reported to the commander of the Girona station.

Puigventós quickly explained to Armengol the situation regarding the disappearance of the politician's son and handed over to Elisenda, who outlined the main strands that they wanted to investigate.

'Because we're also dealing with the house robberies at the same time,' she finished, 'and because we're still a small unit, I want my team to concentrate on the angle of the disappearance being politically motivated. In that case, we'd be grateful if your unit could tackle the possibility of the boy having been abducted by a possible sex offender, or at least outside the realm of any link to the mother's profile. We'd need you to check on known offenders and look for any other suspicious activity or chatter that could be relevant.'

'You would also be able to count on the support of some of the members of Sotsinspector Micaló's unit should you need it,' Puigventós added. 'All the files you'll need are on the system.'

The newcomer digested what they'd both said, his face impassive. 'The family must be devastated.'

'You'd think so,' Elisenda replied, the words out before she knew why she was saying them.

Armengol stared at her, his eyes unnaturally large through his glasses. He seemed to collect himself. 'Of course. If you need backup in other areas as well, ask me.'

'There is one other problem,' Elisenda continued, turning back to Puigventós. 'Susanna Miravent doesn't want to deal with the missing persons unit in Sabadell but directly with me. Given the nature of this case, I'm all right to speak to her, but we'll need Sabadell to run the website campaign and weed out the nonsense we get back. Josep will monitor it, but he won't have the time to screen everything.'

'Agreed,' the inspector told her. 'Sabadell can also organise the phone hotline and pass on what's relevant. You'll have enough to do without worrying about that.'

'If you need any assistance there,' Armengol added, 'let me know.'

Elisenda thanked him and tried to imagine the same requests being made of Micaló. It would have taken at least another half an hour of wanton negotiation and wasteful concessions. As they all left Puigventós' room, though, she realised that she was still reserving judgement.

-

'I'm back.'

'We know,' Manel told her. 'The whole station's talking about it.'

Elisenda and Àlex had found themselves walking back to their own unit's offices with Armengol, as his team shared a large outer room with the Serious Crime Unit. Fortunately, from Elisenda's point of view, the new sotsinspector spoke most of the time to Àlex as they shared a common bond of being from Barcelona and having studied journalism at the Autonomous University, at the Bellaterra campus outside the city. They even had a few old university friends in common.

'See,' she'd told Àlex when they'd gone into her office, 'Barcelona. Small-town mentality. You're in the big city now. How many times do I have to tell you?'

Àlex spotted Manel at a desk in the outer office, working on a computer. 'And now we have Manel from Lleida bringing civilisation to us all.'

Elisenda looked out through the glass partition wall. Manel was sitting alone at one desk, Montse and Josep were working together at another. 'Give him a chance.'

Àlex raised an eyebrow at her and called the other three in. Josep, the last one in, brought a chair with him. The room was a lot more cramped than Puigventós' office had been. Seeing Siset's satchel where she'd left it propped up against the wall, Elisenda picked it up and balanced it on top of a filing cabinet, tipping a dead plant into the waste-paper basket to make space. She decided she'd check the bag's contents properly after the meeting with the rest of her unit.

'Are you still suspended?' Manel took up the thread again. Swatting with his big paws, Elisenda thought. Josep shook his head in irritation.

'No, I'm not. I still have to go to counselling every morning, but apart from that, I'm back full on.' She considered the two investigations facing her team. 'And is it ever full on?'

She and Àlex explained that as well as the investigation into the violent house robberies, they were also going to be leading the search for the missing teenager.

'The five of us?' Josep asked, aghast.

'We'll have the support of Sotsinspector Armengol's Local Investigation Unit,' Elisenda told him. 'Not ideal, I know, but that's how it is.'

'Why have they given us the missing teenager case?' Montse wanted to know. Seeing the three men in her team filling the room – Àlex with his lean but broad-shouldered build, Manel with his muscular bulk and Josep with his height – Elisenda was struck by how slight Montse looked among them. It was a deception. A serious marathon runner away from work, she was muscle and fibre, a compact powerhouse of stamina resting lightly on her chair, always on the edge of movement.

'Because of his mother and because of the family's history.'

A fellow Girona native like Elisenda, Montse knew of the brother who'd gone missing four years earlier, but Josep and Manel had to be told the full story.

'Only in Girona,' Manel commented, tutting. 'We don't have politicians in Lleida who are anti-independence.'

'Oh, give it a rest,' Josep muttered.

'Yes, you do,' Montse added. 'You've got a member of the same party as Susanna Miravent's in the government.'

'He won't get voted back in, though,' Manel replied, final and gruff.

'You don't know that,' Josep joined in. 'And there's nothing to say Miravent will get back in. Everything's changed since the last election.'

Àlex spoke before Manel had a chance to reply. 'Yes, OK, this isn't the point right now.'

Elisenda paused before carrying on. Àlex's job as her sergent was increasingly becoming one of policing the squabbles of the three caporals, ever since Manel's joining the unit had changed the dynamic. It was becoming her job to try and get that back or find a new dynamic that worked. She looked at them now.

'If you want to discuss politics, go and have a coffee on your own time and do it. Right now, we've got a missing teenager to find and we've got a gang targeting isolated houses who are getting steadily more violent in their attacks.'

Josep and Montse looked suitably chastened. Manel was unmoved, no doubt feeling her comments weren't also directed at him. Elisenda closed her eyes for a fraction of a second, only too aware of the bridges she had to build. One step at a time, she thought.

'OK,' she continued. 'We're all going to have to double up and deal with both investigations more than we'd want to, but some of us are going to concentrate more on one case and some on the other. As you know, Àlex is already running the investigation into the house robberies, so that will continue. He'll be working with Manel on that.'

Àlex looked impassively from Manel to Elisenda. She knew that he normally preferred to work with Montse. 'That's fine,' he told her.

'Good. I think you need to check up on the symbols that we've found at one of the houses and see if there's any trace of them at any of the other houses that have been targeted. We'll keep looking for Siset too, to see why he gave me bad information. I'll be in charge of the investigation into where Jaume Comas Miravent is. Montse and Josep will be working with me on that.'

She caught the last two caporals exchanging a brief glance. There was relief in both looks. Ignoring it, she went through the various strands of the investigation that she and Àlex had discussed with Puigventós.

'The Local Investigation Unit will be looking at the question of whether this is down to the boy being abducted by a sex offender. We'll be looking at whether the boy has absconded. Montse, your first job is to get out to his school and talk to his teachers and classmates, see what that turns up. I want you also to look into the family itself in case there's any cause there for him to run away.'

'Or other causes,' Àlex reminded her.

'Exactly. We also have to consider the fact that this is the second child in this family to have gone missing. Inevitably, that has to raise questions about the parents' part in this, either separately or jointly. Initially, they are to be regarded as victims, but we will also be keeping an open mind as we look into the family setup more closely. Please remember that as you conduct the investigation. That finally leaves the possibility of kidnap, which I think is potentially the most likely and could be for political or financial reasons given who the boy's mother is. I'll be looking into that with help from all of you.'

'Could it be the missing brother who's come back and taken this one?' Manel suddenly asked.

'Be serious,' Josep instantly snapped at him.

Elisenda put her hand up to them both to warn them to keep quiet while she considered Manel's comment. 'I don't know that that's something we should initially be looking at, but we do need to examine the case notes for the brother's disappearance. Josep, that's your first job. I want to know if there was anyone who came under suspicion at the time of the first boy's disappearance who we should be talking to now. Or if there were any other circumstances that we need to take into account with this case. That will overlap partly with Montse looking into the family, as you might come across some pattern common to both disappearances that's to do with the boys' home life. Does everyone know where they're starting?'

She watched them all nod their understanding before making her final remarks.

'Now, I know none of us here agrees with Susanna Miravent's politics.' She ignored Manel's snort, instead composing her own face into an impassive mask. 'But that's not the point here. As far as we're concerned, her politics don't matter. She's a mother. A mother of two missing children, one she'll still be grieving for, another whose disappearance will open up the wounds of the last four years.' She managed to keep her voice from faltering. Out of the corner of her eye, she saw Montse exchange a glance with Àlex. 'That's all we're interested in. Not her politics, but her child. Getting her child back.'

She looked from one to the other of her team, each one evidently forcing themselves to make eye contact with her.

'One other thing,' she added, staring at each of them in turn again, more pointedly this time. 'There will be some crossover in what we find, and we're all going to have to participate in both investigations at some times. That means we have to talk to each other. I hope you're all very clear on that.'

Chapter Thirteen

Escola Mare de Déu del Mont was wholly unlike the school that Montse had gone to and she gave a little silent thank you to her parents for that fact. She'd gone to a state school in Santa Eugènia, the suburb where she'd grown up, not one of the private religious schools like this one that still flourished even today. The one positive she'd give it was its location, which she had to admit was glorious. Almost at the top of Montjuïc, the strange blip of a hill to the north of the city centre, the views of the surrounding countryside as far as the Pyrenees were enough to make her stop and take in nature's display for a moment. A rarity for her. Even as she'd driven her way up the steep twists and turns to the rambling school buildings near the flat peak, she'd had to suppress the urge to park the car and run the rest of the way. Filling her lungs at every step with the less humid air outside the old city while she drained them with the muscle-bursting effort of the relentless climb. It was her idea of bliss.

'I can give you ten minutes,' the head teacher told her. Pulling the folds of his habit together in the light breeze, he introduced himself as Father Besses.

A crocodile of primary-age children stopped its silent progress under the sheltered arcade of the quadrangle to let the two adults wade through them to a door under the cool air of the arches. Montse looked at them, their faces impassive, none of the chattering joy she recalled of that age bubbling through. Unlike the state system, where primary and secondary schools were separate, the private institutions took in children at the start of their education and churned them out through the factory gate at the end, their childhood and beyond forever influenced.

Besses suddenly stopped inside the cold of the building. 'This is terrible, simply terrible.'

It sounded to Montse like a dutiful afterthought.

'Isn't it, Father?'

'I don't teach Jaume Comas Miravent any subjects as such,' he told her. 'I teach the younger children, whereas I deal more with the pastoral aspects of the older boys' education.'

He showed her along a hushed corridor to a spacious office with a large window overlooking the mountains to the north-west. The room was cool, the sun not yet shining in, the air conditioning on low. One wall was dominated by a large wooden crucifix. Montse had to keep reminding herself that this wasn't some ancient institution that had taught generations of Girona wealth, but had gone up in the last thirty years, the whole complex designed to resemble a much older religious building, with breeze-block towers and prefabricated cloisters.

'Has there been anything in Jaume's behaviour or state of mind since the start of the new term that has given you cause for concern, Father?' she asked him, refusing his offer of a coffee.

The head thought for a moment. 'None of his teachers has commented on anything. He has come in for a degree of ribbing from some of the other boys, though. His mother appearing so frequently in the news has contributed to that. But nothing unpleasant or that could be construed as a problem.'

'No bullying?'

'We simply do not countenance bullying at this school. Our boys are taught the merit of humanity and Christian values.'

Montse wondered if the children would have the same to say about that. 'Was he having any problems with his course work?'

In strange contrast to the old-fashioned nature of their surroundings, Father Besses deftly tapped at a computer on his desk and studied the screen intently. 'It's rather early in the school year to say, but there does appear to be some imbalance between his work last year and so far this year. But as I say, it's far too early to read anything into that. Many of our pupils come back after the long summer holidays and find it difficult at first to get back into their school work. It soon rights itself.'

'But it could indicate that something was troubling Jaume?'

In reply, Father Besses shrugged, holding both hands out flat in front of him. 'Conceivably,' he conceded.

'Jaume's brother Albert also studied here, didn't he? Do you think there was anything about his brother's disappearance that might have led to Jaume running away?'

'I wouldn't have thought it likely. Albert's disappearance was four years ago, when Jaume was still quite young. From my conversations with him in the years since that time, I would say that he has come to terms with the loss of his brother. His faith has helped him considerably there. They were quite close but very different. Albert was more academically gifted. Jaume is more athletic. He plays for the school basketball team. Oddly, although Albert was two years the elder, it was Jaume who looked out for his brother, not the other way around as you'd expect. Albert was the quieter of the two, Jaume is more assertive.'

Montse took in his words. 'I'd like to speak to some of Jaume's classmates. His closest friends here.'

Besses peered keenly at her. 'I'm afraid I'm not going to be able to allow that. As you will appreciate, I am *in loco parentis* here. I cannot sanction your speaking to any of the boys without the consent of their parents.'

'In which case, can you give me their names and I'll approach their parents to ask permission?'

He still looked unsure. 'Would you leave that with me, please? I'll speak to the parents of the boys in question and tell you their decision.'

'One of your students went missing, Father Besses, a teenaged boy, while you and the school were *in loco parentis*. You must understand the need to find him.'

The priest shook his head emphatically. 'Jaume was not on the school premises when he went missing. Neither my staff nor the school can be held responsible.'

'Father Besses, we will need to speak to these boys.' Her voice was firm. 'I'll call you this afternoon for their details. I trust you will cooperate if we want to find Jaume safe and sound. And keep your school's good reputation.'

He studied her for a brief moment. 'Yes, of course.'

Montse got up to leave. 'Thank you. I'll be in touch later today.'

–

The house owner spoke to Àlex through a video intercom next to the front door. It looked new. So did the small fenced compound next to the house from behind which an angry German Shepherd was barking furiously at them.

'Mossos d'Esquadra,' Àlex told them, raising his voice above the din. 'Sergent Àlex Albiol and Caporal Manel Moliné from the Serious Crime Unit in Girona.'

There was a short delay between his words and the reply from the man inside the house. He was asking to see their ID. Àlex held up his card to the little camera aperture above the intercom mouthpiece and then moved out of the way while Manel did the same. There was another longer pause in which Àlex wondered if the owner was actually going to do anything. He was about to press the button again when he heard a bolt being pulled back inside the door. It opened a crack and someone peered out over the thick security chain between door and frame. Àlex knew him to be a man in his early fifties, a self-employed website designer who did most of his work from home.

'We met when your house was burgled,' Àlex explained to the sliver of face that was showing. 'I took your statement at the time.'

'What is it?' The man's voice was thin, fear evident in the faltering timbre.

'It's nothing to be alarmed about. We've come to check up on you and your property to make sure you're all right and that the security is in place.'

The eyes stared back at him for a moment and then the door shut. Àlex heard the slink of a chain being unhooked and the door opened again, wider this time. The man peered out anxiously, looking over Àlex's shoulder to the long driveway beyond and the T-junction with the main road at the end of it. There was an intermittent reverberation of metal cutting through air as the occasional car or lorry went past, a low background noise to the constant chirruping of cicadas and the lonely silence of the house itself. The dog had finally stopped barking.

'I refuse to be driven out of my own home,' the man told Àlex and Manel. It was out of tune with the underlying air of fear that he exuded. Àlex wanted to tell him to consider moving back to Girona, but knew it wasn't his place.

'If you'd like,' he said instead, 'my colleague and I will check on the security you've put in place. We appreciate what you went through, so we want to make sure that you're safe in your home. We've also stepped up Mossos patrols in the area.'

The man looked doubtful. 'I haven't seen any.'

'They're there.' Although how many of those would be diverted to hunt for a missing teenaged boy, Àlex didn't know. 'May we come in?'

'If you like, I'll take a tour of the land outside the house,' Manel suddenly offered. 'Check up on all that.'

'OK,' Àlex agreed, surprised. He was used to having to give the new caporal an order before he'd do anything.

Inside the house, the owner gave Àlex a tour of all the extra locks and alarms that he'd had fitted since being attacked in his home over a month earlier.

'It was hard to get someone to fit it all in August,' the man commented, 'because most businesses were on holiday, but I managed to get everything done that I wanted.'

It was impressive, Àlex had to admit, and expensive. Reinforced doors and windows, sensors in all the rooms for an alarm system connected to a central security service, video cameras hooked up to a computer showing various angles of the outside of the house. For a brief, silent moment, they both watched a grainy colour image of Manel walking the perimeter of the land surrounding the property. They went upstairs, where one of the bedrooms and the bathroom seemed smaller than Àlex remembered.

'Panic room,' the man explained. 'With a concealed entrance in our bedroom.'

Àlex nodded, exhaling slowly. He couldn't help feeling the anger he always felt when ordinary people became victims of extraordinary misfortune. The man's house had been attacked on a Monday evening in late July. He'd been home on his own when the gang had forced their way in by battering down the front door. Once inside, they'd tied him to his kitchen table and waterboarded him until he'd agreed to transfer money from his account. They'd also given him a few lumps and bruises for the hell of it. The man thought they were in his house for over two hours.

'I would have paid them anyway,' he'd said when Àlex had interviewed him in hospital straight after his ordeal. 'There was no need to do what they did. I'm just glad my wife wasn't in at the time.'

He'd suffered one of the more violent attacks, others had been marginally less unfortunate. Looking through the rooms of the man's house now, Àlex could well understand his need to install all the security. No matter how much he loved the house, Àlex was certain that had he been the victim, he'd have had no second thoughts about selling the house and moving back to somewhere surrounded by people and light and noise. Manel turned up at the front door as Àlex was taking his leave.

'It's all looking good,' the caporal told the owner, asking him to come to the corner of the house to look at the side of the perimeter. 'Just one recommendation I'd make. That section over there, the fence is weak. If I were you, I'd get that strengthened and put in a sensor light. There's a path the other side that leads to a B-road that's wide enough to get a car along. You should get it sorted.'

The owner looked nervous and grateful. 'Thank you, I will.'

Before they left, Àlex told the owner that they'd be checking the driveway where it joined the road as well. 'So please don't be concerned if you see us taking a look down there.'

What he didn't tell him was that that was the main purpose of their visit.

'Well spotted,' Àlex told Manel as they drove the short way down the drive and stopped. Manel didn't answer for a moment, which Àlex put down to his usual manner. His words, when they came, surprised him.

'I saw him after the attack,' Manel finally answered as they got out of the car. 'The state they left him in.'

Ignoring the whumph of the cars and lorries speeding past by what seemed like bare centimetres, Àlex told Manel what they were looking for. 'A pyramid of stones with twigs stuck into it. Somewhere on the ground.'

Crouched down, they searched under the bushes that grew along the side of the road and around the bare patches of earth up to the edge of the asphalt. A tall cypress stood either side of the drive, marking the entrance. Àlex looked one side while Manel examined the other.

Surprised and feeling a little deflated, Àlex finally stood up, stretching his back. 'Nothing.'

'What's it about?' Manel wanted to know.

'We think we found a symbol at the house on Saturday night. That's why we're checking up on the other houses that have been targeted to see if there are any more and if they mean anything.'

Manel snorted and walked back to the car. 'Sounds a bit fanciful to me.'

Àlex watched him go and closed his eyes, not letting the irritation rise. Taking one last look around him, he gave up and joined the caporal waiting impatiently in the car.

Chapter Fourteen

Elisenda noticed Siset's satchel on top of the filing cabinet in her office and was about to take it down when there was a knock on the door behind her. She turned around to see Josep leaning in through the frame, his head bowed low. It was one of his habits. Conscious of his height, he would often hunch his shoulders while talking to someone shorter or instinctively duck his head when he went through doors. Before coming in, he ran his hand through his shock of mousy brown hair, which started every day unruly as it currently was and ended up like an uncut lawn the more frustrating an investigation became. Elisenda smiled at today's rough patch.

'Josep, come on in. What have you got for me?'

Motioning for him to take a seat opposite her, she sat down behind her desk. He placed some folders on top of it but didn't open them.

'I've been going through the case files for the first boy's disappearance. I haven't turned up anything out of the ordinary just yet, but at least I know the sequence of what happened that time.'

'You'd better run through it with me, then. It's from before I came back to Girona and I don't know all the ins and outs. I wasn't involved with it.'

Josep looked uncomfortable for a moment, dropping his head even further and bringing his shoulders in. 'Sotsinspector Pijaume was in charge.'

Elisenda nodded. Armengol's predecessor. 'Go on.'

'There are some anomalies because Jaume admitted to lying in his first statements because he was afraid of being told off by his parents. It happened on a Saturday in June. The family were rambling in the Gavarres mountains, between Madremanya and Pedrinyà, and had stopped for a picnic a short walk from a river. Before they ate, Marc Comas went swimming with the two boys, Jaume and Albert, and left Susanna Miravent with all the picnic stuff by a tree, reading. After a time, Comas returned to Miravent and left the two boys playing by the river, but told them not to go into the water without him there.

'This is where Jaume lied in his first statement. He initially said that he was running along the bank and that when he returned, his brother had disappeared. What he eventually admitted to was that he'd disobeyed the father and gone for a swim while Albert had stayed on the bank.'

'Meaning he couldn't have seen whatever it was that happened.'

'What he did say was that he saw a car. There's a single-track road a short distance the other side of the river from where the boys were. He didn't see enough to recognise the make or see anyone in it. What's interesting is that both the mother and the father said independently of Jaume and of each other that they heard a car engine. When Jaume got out of the water, Albert wasn't there. He said he didn't think anything of it, presuming his brother had gone back to where their parents were. Jaume was worried that he'd get told off as he didn't have a towel and was wet from the river, so he didn't rejoin them straight away but waited until he'd dried off in the sun. By that time, though, his father had come looking for him, which is when they realised that Albert wasn't there.'

Elisenda digested everything Josep said. 'Good work. As far as I recall, there have never been any substantiated sightings of Albert.'

She noticed him sit taller in his chair, unfolding some of his height. That was one of his tics when he was feeling more confident.

'I've checked the initial phases of the investigation at the time. There were the usual phone calls by people saying they'd seen him, but nothing was ever corroborated.' He checked inside one of the folders. 'In fact, there have been sightings in Catalonia, Spain, France and Germany, but nothing ever came of any of them.'

'They rarely do, unfortunately.'

'My next step is to see what theories the team at the time had about his disappearance. The most common one is that he fell into the river and was swept away.'

'Swept away? They're all small streams in that area.'

'Where they were swimming was calm, but other tributaries were in flood. The investigation felt that once a child's body had been taken, it would be very easy for it to be pulled into the water system and lost. Apparently, he was quite a slight child. They also worked on the possible hypothesis of the boy being abducted. I'm about to start looking into who they had in the frame as suspects if that was the case.'

'OK. Check them against any names that Sotsinspector Armengol comes up with for Jaume's disappearance. If there are any that appear in both investigations, we need to be speaking to them. Armengol's also offered to filter the feedback we get from the missing persons unit in Sabadell. You might as well use it; we're going to have our work cut out as it is.'

Behind Jaume, she spotted Montse coming into the outer office, so she called her in. Josep gave her a brief outline of what he'd told Elisenda, and Montse reported on her meeting with the head teacher at Jaume's school.

'He was reluctant to let me speak to Jaume's classmates without consent from their parents. He seems more worried about the school's good name.'

'Why do you say that?' Elisenda asked her.

Montse looked uncomfortable. She glanced at Josep for support. 'He mentioned Jaume being outside school when he went… when he went missing. Said the school wasn't to be blamed.'

Elisenda looked in her notebook and found the name and address she'd got from Susanna Miravent. 'This is the friend Jaume was supposed to be doing his homework with. You can approach his family directly. I'll be seeing Miravent and Comas later today, so I'll get other names from them.'

Montse took the details and put them in her own notebook. 'I'll still be ringing the school later to arrange to see the boy's tutor. He wasn't available this morning.'

'Tutor,' Elisenda commented, shaking her head. 'Only in a posh school.'

She turned away, missing Montse's controlled exhalation of relief and the wry look that Josep shot the other caporal. Elisenda wasn't the only one struggling with handling the disappearance of a child.

Chapter Fifteen

Susanna Miravent looked more like her real self, Elisenda thought, her real self being the political image she portrayed to the media. That morning, in her own home, she'd seemed strangely outside her proper environment. It was here, at the front of a crowded room of journalists and TV cameras, a speech on a piece of paper in front of her, her appearance designed for public consumption, that Susanna Miravent the product existed. The real Susanna Miravent as the electorate knew her.

Elisenda was in the audience, standing at the back of the exquisite conference room in the city centre hotel. Puigventós was next to her. The family had said that they preferred to be alone on the podium, without the Mossos there. The focus on them and their concern, on their son and his disappearance. The second time that the same tragedy had befallen the same family. Or rather, Bofarull the campaign manager had decided on it, Elisenda imagined. She watched him now, buzzing about on the edge of centre stage, ordering the press and cajoling the cameras into place. The one appendage as far as she could see was Marc Comas, who sat in untidy discomfort next to his wife. Neither of them spoke to the other while they waited for the signal to start the ball rolling to get their son back.

The lights focused on the couple at the front of the room and the noise died down: the signal for Miravent to turn on every gram of her experience at working a crowd. And she did, Elisenda had to admit.

'I normally stand before you as a politician,' she began, her voice steady with just the slightest hesitation. Elisenda glanced quickly at Bofarull. He was living the speech with her. 'But today, I stand before you as a mother. You know me as a woman of integrity, a woman not afraid to stand up and say what she thinks is best for Catalonia, a woman proud to be both Catalan and Spanish, proud to fight for the best and strongest way to overcome the terrible recession caused by a succession of irresponsible governments, proud to uphold good family values. Well, today, it is precisely these values that have suffered a blow. A terrible personal blow...'

Elisenda hung her head to try not to show the annoyance she felt. 'This is pure electioneering,' she muttered to Puigventós. 'It's her son we're trying to find, not votes.'

'And they're lapping it up,' the inspector whispered back.

She looked up and scanned the room. The journalists were rapt, their recorders held high to catch every word, although that wasn't necessary as Bofarull had already promised them transcripts of the speech after Miravent had delivered it. The camera crews and presenters looked on in delight. This was perfect television. Elisenda couldn't help shaking her head in anger.

A face she knew was looking straight at her instead of at the actors on stage. David Costa, the editor of the local newspaper. He and Elisenda had gone to school together, gone to the same bars and excursions as teenagers, kept in touch all through university and her failed marriage, but they'd barely exchanged a word since falling out nearly a year ago. She was about to look away, but something in his expression stopped her. She could see in his eyes the same anger as she felt at the politician's words, but there was something else there too. A collusion, a desire for her not to turn away. To talk to her.

'So what does he want?' Puigventós muttered, surprising her.

She sometimes forgot that the inspector rarely missed a trick. Without meaning to, she raised her hand to the bruise on her cheek. Quickly removing it, she glanced one more time at Costa, who by now had looked away, and turned her attention back to the woman holding the room in her hand.

-

At the end of the appeal, Susanna Miravent picked up her papers and walked swiftly out of the room through a door to the rear of the podium. One or two of the reporters applauded her performance, no doubt supporters of her political views. Taking one last indecisive look at the gathered media, her husband stood up and followed her. He had spoken a few words, unscripted and more directly appealing for his son to be returned safe and sound, but it came across as less powerful than his wife's prepared words. A measure of the strength of her rhetoric and the weakness of his nature.

Elisenda watched as Bofarull hurried into the throng of journalists, making sure each one got a copy of Miravent's appeal. Making her way to the rear of the conference space to follow Miravent and Comas to a small prep room leading from it, she picked up a copy of the handout. Topped by two photos of Jaume, a head and shoulders shot and one of him full-body at a recent sports event, the body of the text began with a description of the boy and what he was wearing at the time of his disappearance, followed by the time he vanished and the route he should have taken home. That was good, Elisenda thought, but the sheet also featured a photo of the mother and a description of her political beliefs as well as the text of the appeal that she'd just given. She could feel her knuckles tense in annoyance, crushing the piece of paper, and she checked herself before anyone saw. Passing by where he was standing, she heard Bofarull stoically assuring a small group of journalists that the boy's disappearance would not be affecting Miravent's election campaign. Elisenda had to bite her tongue. She could sense Puigventós behind her bristling at the attitude.

Passing through the room, she saw David Costa looking towards where she'd just been standing. His gaze roamed the room, no doubt searching for her, but she managed to reach the door behind the podium without him catching sight of her. At the door, two party officials demanded to see their ID before they'd let them into the prep room where Miravent and Comas were. Satisfied, they let her and Puigventós in, when Elisenda's mobile pinged to say she'd had a message. Checking quickly, she saw that it was Catalina, her sister, asking if she wanted to have dinner at her house that evening. Sighing, she put her phone away without answering. Another difficult moment she was going to have to face.

Inside the small room, furnished with just an array of padded upright chairs and a blond wood table topped with bottles of mineral water and pens and notepads in the hotel's livery, Miravent and Comas were sitting next to each other. Both looked drained, the first human moment Elisenda had registered from either of them. It reminded her that despite the mother's evident political use of the situation and the strangely controlled calm of their demeanour, they were also the parents of one teenaged boy who had gone missing and another who was presumed dead after similar circumstances. Before she had a chance to say anything, Bofarull joined them in the room.

'How do you think it went?' Miravent asked him, ignoring the two Mossos.

He made to reply but Elisenda spoke before he had the chance, unable to conceal her anger any longer. 'This is a police investigation, Senyora Miravent. We are asking for information to help us find your son, not to further your party's election chances.'

'I beg your pardon,' Miravent replied, shocked.

'You ask me how the appeal went, not your campaign manager. I understand that it's your right to give a televised appeal, but this is an investigation to find a missing child, not an opportunity for electioneering.'

For a brief moment, Miravent looked like she might lose her temper, but the politician in her immediately came to the fore. 'I'm sorry you feel that way, Elisenda. I felt I was making the most of my position to find my son the best way possible.' Her voice was calm, measured.

'We can't tell you how to conduct these appeals, but it would greatly help us find your son if you would at least consult us on the best way to go about actions like this.'

'Yes, well I'm sure we'll be able to work together on this,' Puigventós interrupted, flashing a warning look at Elisenda. She was struggling to stay cool.

'Thank you, Elisenda,' Miravent added, studied benevolence in her voice. 'I will be sure to listen to what you say.'

'As far as appealing to the public is concerned,' Elisenda carried on regardless, 'right now you are parents, not politicians. The appearance you've just made may be counter-productive. Your family has seen enough grief; my job is to try and make sure you don't experience any more. Your job is to ensure that too.'

'Elisenda,' Puigventós warned her.

'Grief, Elisenda?' Miravent looked at her quizzically. 'We feel no grief.'

Chapter Sixteen

Despite being in one of the more aspirational areas of the Eixample that had been favoured by Girona's professional classes for the best part of half a century, the first-floor flat was surprisingly ordinary. In a forty-year-old block above an old-fashioned *drogueria* selling row upon row of bleach, paint and saucepans, the front door to the apartment led into a gloomy hall with dark wood furniture and no natural light. Opposite the front door was the kitchen, a fluorescent ceiling light casting a pallid glow over the parquet floor in the entrance. Montse was shown to a door on the right, which led into a living room, lined with mahogany bookshelves and framed prints and dominated by two giant brown sofas and a large-screen TV. They certainly went in for the sombre look, she thought, looking out of the window at a narrow balcony with just four metal chairs and a table. Beyond it, she could see the traffic held up in the street below in the reflection given by the window display of a stylish clothes chain shop. No sound of cars rumbling at the traffic lights filtered through the new double-glazing. It was surprisingly old-fashioned for an affluent, modern family.

Both parents were there. The mother was a dentist, her private practice on the mezzanine, one floor below them in the same building. The father was a doctor at the large Hospital Doctor Trueta, on the northern edge of the city. Montse put them both in their mid-forties, both dressed casually but expensively, her with glasses and an inquisitive expression, he with a round face and a gap between his front teeth. Montse couldn't help finding that odd in a dentist's spouse. A grandmother was in the kitchen, getting tea ready for a younger child. The older one was on one of the sofas, sitting between his parents. Montse was on the other sofa.

'I just want to ask you some questions about Jaume Comas,' Montse said, speaking directly to the boy. At just fourteen, he was as tall as her, his limbs still long and ungainly from childhood but his voice firm, no longer a little boy's. He was wearing his school tracksuit, his hair sweaty but freshly combed, just about sticking in place. She could see he'd been crying but was trying to hide it.

He was Carles Pascual, the friend Jaume was supposed to have been doing his homework with the previous evening. His parents had consented without any hesitation to Montse interviewing him about Jaume's disappearance.

'Terrible news,' the mother had said when Montse had phoned her earlier, after getting the details from Elisenda. She had the names of two other boys in her notebook and had arranged to see one of them the following day.

'Terrible news,' the mother repeated now. Her eyes were red and she was holding a crushed paper tissue in her fist. 'It's every parent's worst nightmare.'

Montse nodded in silent agreement and quickly studied the family. Carles was sandwiched on the sofa between his parents, both of them pressed tightly up against him, their closeness a protection for him and a comfort for them. With the hand not clutching the tissue, the mother was squeezing her son's hand. The father had his arm around the boy's shoulder and was holding him tightly. Their reaction looked natural to Montse. A sudden and unbidden image of Elisenda trying to remain objective jumped into her mind and she felt a momentary pang of guilt at her own difficulty in discussing the case with her boss.

'Have you and Jaume been friends for long?' she asked Carles now after putting him at ease with a few general questions about school.

'Only since the summer.' The boy's voice was strained and he looked at one or the other parent before answering each time.

Montse had to coax him a little to get more complete answers from him. 'We're in the same class at school, but we didn't sit together last year.'

'We have a holiday home in La Fosca,' the mother explained. 'Near Palamós. So does Jaume's family.'

Montse turned her attention back to Carles, interrupting the mother. 'So you became friends over the summer holiday?'

The boy nodded. 'We used to go swimming together every day. And just hanging on the beach. We decided we'd sit together when we were back at school.'

'Did you mix much with his parents?' Montse now asked the mother and father.

The couple looked uncomfortably at each other before answering.

'Not really,' the father replied, pulling a slight face. 'The boys got on well, but the parents aren't really our sort. I think we'd have ended up arguing with Susanna about politics.'

'That's not to say we don't feel so sorry for them now,' the mother interjected.

'Of course not,' the father added. 'We can only imagine what they're going through.' Instinctively, both parents held onto their son even more tightly.

'And Marc Comas?' Montse asked.

'He tried a bit. Invited us to a barbecue at their house. Luckily we'd already arranged to go out with some other friends for dinner.' The father instantly looked guilty after his words.

Montse wrote it all down and questioned Carles again. 'So, Jaume coming here to do his homework was a new thing?'

'Yes, we only started last week. He came here last Thursday.'

'Did you go to his house at all?'

'Not yet. He said it was easier for him to come to my house as it's on the way home from school to his house. He said I'd have to get a bus to his house, and then another one back here after we'd finished.'

'So why didn't he come here last night after school?'

Again, Carles looked from one of his parents to the other for reassurance before answering. 'He said he was going out with his parents for dinner. So he couldn't come to my house.'

'Do you know why he might lie about that?'

A small shrug. 'I don't know. He seemed excited. I thought it was because he was going out with his parents. He told me over the summer that they didn't go out together much. He was a bit nervous.'

Montse changed tack. 'Do you know if he was being bullied at all?'

Without looking at his parents, Carles told her that that wasn't likely, his voice assured. 'He was taller than anyone else in our class. He told me he did weights in his bedroom to build up his muscles. No one would bully Jaume.'

'And would Jaume bully other boys?'

Again, the nervous look to both parents before replying. 'He'd stand up for himself if he had to.'

-

Manel drove quickly, with all the self-assuredness that Àlex would have expected of him. He also knew his way around Girona and the surrounding area reasonably well now, even though he took every piece of time off to go back to his beloved Lleida, some two and a half hours' drive west.

'Got a house in the mountains,' he'd once told Àlex in a less guarded moment. 'My grandparents' old house. Beautiful. Nothing like it anywhere else in Catalonia.'

'Or the world,' Àlex had said at the time, poking fun at him to avoid becoming irritated.

'Probably,' Manel had replied, with no hint of sarcasm.

They'd left the owner of the previous house steadfastly putting all the locks and bolts back in place and were now heading for another house. More isolated this time, in the Albera mountains, near the border with France. They'd steadily risen through lush green hills and emerged into a scarred landscape of giant boulders and harsh peaks. Perched on an old stone wall, a huge buzzard watched them drive past, its neck bent, its collar ruffled by the low wind circling. Àlex stared back at it. The perfect predator. Beyond the bird, further up the mountain, he could see an arrangement of granite slabs, a Neolithic burial chamber. This part of the region was scattered with them. Breathing in the ancient moment, he didn't point it out to Manel, not wanting the homesick caporal to spoil it.

'This isn't so bad,' Manel commented at one point as the Mediterranean suddenly came into view in the distance to their right. A deep and unhurried blue soothing the twisted savagery of the mountains.

The house was empty, although there was evidence of its still being occupied, the owners evidently out. It had been targeted the previous month, the height of summer, the attackers arriving one lazy evening when the couple who lived there were watching the sun set over the distant Pyrenees, a bottle of wine on a stone table. Rich Barcelona exiles seeking the good life. Their ordeal hadn't been as violent as others, but equally frightening. Because there was no internet connection up here, the husband had been driven to the nearest town, to an internet café, to empty their bank account and to a cashpoint to do likewise to their credit cards. Two other gang members had stayed at the house with the wife as collateral to make sure the husband did as he was told. The wife wasn't touched by either of the men holding her, but the threat had been there. Àlex felt a muscle in his cheek twitch as he recalled it now. He'd interviewed the husband, Elisenda and Montse the wife. Both more heartbroken that their idyll had been invaded than at any loss of money.

Parking in front of the house, they took a tour around the property, looking in through the windows to make sure that there was no one inside and checking a small stone construction that housed a generator. Seeing nothing of concern, Àlex and Manel walked the short distance from the house to the road. Feeling that its isolation might mean that any mound of stones would be less likely to have been disturbed in the intervening time, Àlex had hoped to find something remaining to bear out their theory of symbols at the crime scenes.

'Not a thing,' Manel announced.

Àlex had to admit that it was hopeless. The ground either side of the track leading to the house was so strewn with small rocks that it was impossible to discern anything out of place. Animal droppings also showed that there was so much movement about the area that anything left there would have been obliterated before long.

'So how would they leave a symbol here?' Àlex asked himself.

'If that's what they do,' Manel replied. 'Doesn't look that likely to me.'

Disheartened, they left, stopping for a quick lunch in a down-to-earth restaurant in the tiny hamlet of Rabós, where the owner didn't have a menu but recited the day's food in a luxurious litany. Àlex had discovered it in his first month in Girona and he still loved the hearty mountain food and no-nonsense atmosphere. In the winter, there was always a fire crackling in the hearth.

'Get bigger portions than this in the mountains back home,' Manel commented at one point between mouthfuls of rabbit.

As revenge, Àlex insisted they get back to work before the desserts. Manel had a sweet tooth and the *crema catalana* here was perfect, the egg custard with cinnamon firm but melting under its coating of burnt sugar.

'See what you get for moaning all the time,' he told the caporal.

They tried one more place, the site of the most recent attack. The house on the fast road past Cassà de la Selva that had been targeted while their unit had been staking out a house to the other side of Girona. The family had moved back there already as they had nowhere else to go, although they were all out when Àlex and Manel arrived. The parents were at work and the son at school. The grandfather was still under observation in hospital, largely until the family decided what they were going to do with him during the day from now on when they were all out.

The track from the road to the house was short and straight, the house in clear view from the fast two-lane highway heading southeast from Girona. Manel pulled off at the side and the two Mossos sat in the car and looked out, increasingly despondent. They got out and began searching, but the side of the road was paved, the house lying on the edge of a small urbanisation of modern houses. Any cairn of rocks would have been toppled over by anyone out walking.

'There's nowhere to leave anything,' Àlex muttered.

A rush of air behind him made him step involuntarily nearer the side of the road. He turned around to see a Sarfa bus go past, on the route between Girona and the coast. It was picking up speed after pulling away from a bus stop further back along the road.

'This is pointless,' Manel complained after the noise had receded.

Àlex sighed, too fed up to lose his temper with the caporal, and climbed back into the car.

Chapter Seventeen

The Seguretat Ciutadana car dropped Elisenda off on Gran Via, by the ornate central post office, and she watched it glide off along the curving avenue that traced the part of the medieval walls that had existed on this side of the river until the 1930s. The city council back then had pulled them down to modernise the city, which had probably seemed like a good idea at the time. Luckily the walls were still intact on the east bank, the old town, where Elisenda lived.

She'd spent an hour with one of the teams searching the vicinity of Jaume's school in Montjuïc. Others were trying to trace the boy's way home, following any permutations of the bus routes spreading out from the mountain, but there were too many to follow quickly. As night was falling, some patrols were out as usual with instructions to be watchful, but the search as such was being scaled down for the night. It would start again at six o'clock the following morning.

On the other side of the road, a trim young guy with a long body and a short beard pulled up on a battered, old moped and got off. A large pannier on the back was filled with rolled-up lengths of paper and a pot. He pulled out a handful and began pasting them to a triangle of wooden panels on the edge of the pavement. They were posters for one of the parties in the elections that were scheduled for the following Sunday. The man was covering up the posters for another party that were already there, adding another layer to the papier mâché politics on the ever-thickening panels. Someone else would have put up another coating of candidates before the night was out, and so on until

Sunday's decision. Even with dealing with Susanna Miravent and seeing her touting for votes, Elisenda had almost lost sight that the new government for Catalonia would be decided by the end of the week. Or not, if the Spanish elections were anything to go by. So far, the seemingly endless dance of hung parliaments and horse-trading that had hamstrung Madrid for years hadn't yet blighted Catalonia, but now it was their turn to vote for a governing party for the Generalitat, the Catalan government, in Barcelona. Despite more and more parties springing up in recent years, the election four years earlier had been relatively clear-cut, albeit not as much as in the past, but there were even more parties and alliances now.

Crossing the lights of the café terraces of Plaça Independència, alone among the few groups of local people and tourists eating out on a Tuesday in September, she caught up with the bill-poster on the other side of the square. This time, he was covering up the patrician face of Susanna Miravent, glue tears running down her cheeks as he swabbed his brush over the old posters, replacing them with the new, even if only for an hour or two.

Miravent would not be getting her vote, Elisenda knew that, even with a changing political landscape ever since the recession that had seemed to alter everyone's desires for Catalonia. For a brief time, independence from Spain had fallen down the wish list of a lot of the electorate, to be replaced by a romance with the new parties offering an end to austerity and the crippling financial burdens placed on ordinary people. They hadn't been responsible for the crash, so they'd been wooed away from the traditional parties by newer alliances taking a stance against the old politics that everyone now blamed for getting them all into this mess. She watched the man slapping on a poster promoting one of the pro-independence parties, aiming to win back the middle ground of lapsed separatists with a promise to get Catalonia out of Spain's mess.

Miravent's party was an anomaly even by current standards. They espoused continued union with Spain and argued that the country had to tighten its belt, austerity for a supposed common good that still hadn't come bounding over the horizon. A party to the right that claimed to be of the left. She'd won her seat in the Catalan government in Barcelona in the last elections, one of only three members of her party to do so, but the landscape had changed again and it was looking increasingly unlikely that she'd repeat the surprise success of four years ago.

Crossing the footbridge connecting the square with the old town, Elisenda looked up to the left at the floodlit cathedral towering above the city. It always gave her a sense of calm, not for any religious reason but because it symbolised her home, a return to her roots. Mundanely, it also made her realise that she was approaching her flat and she couldn't recall having any food in the apartment. Certainly nothing she actually felt like eating. She considered for a moment retracing her steps and eating at one of the terraces on Plaça Independència, but changed her mind and headed instead for Plaça de l'Oli, behind the Rambla. On the steep steps that rose above the tiny square, once the oil market, another terrace sprawled anarchically between the separate flights, the tables at El Bistrot occupying any flat piece of ground to be found.

Sitting down at a table that commanded a view down to the square, she ordered veal and a jug of red wine and took out the text of the appeal that Bofarull had been handing out to the media earlier that evening. Her mobile sounded. Another message from Catalina, her sister. Staring at the screen for a moment, deciding, she sighed and put the phone away. Another time, she thought. She had work to do, she argued, looking at the two photos at the top of the piece of paper.

She couldn't see any great resemblance between Jaume Comas Miravent and either of his parents. In the portrait shot, he was looking frankly at the camera, his expression confident. Brown hair neatly brushed on top of a face growing into being classically good looking. More like the mother than the father in that sense. Eyes firm but the mouth still a child's, tending to weak like the father's, but with the cheeks and jaw well defined. In the other picture, she could see that he was growing out of being a child and into adolescence. At what looked like a sporting event in the bright summer sun, his stance was easy, his arms and chest filling out, a tall grown-up figure taking shape.

Looking at the two photos, she recalled the mother's comment about not feeling grief. Puigventós had hurried Elisenda away before she could ask Miravent what she meant. And before she could lose her temper. He'd reminded her of her counselling, as though she needed reminding, and that she was on thin ice. She didn't need to be reminded of that either. She thought of the words again, the pitying tone. *We feel no grief.* It felt like a rebuke aimed at Elisenda, at how the loss of her own daughter was leading her down a path that was ultimately self-destructive. Quickly, she put the paper away, feeling the anger in her rising.

'Did you know that this has been voted the most romantic restaurant terrace in Spain?' a voice from below said.

She looked up. 'Not for me, it hasn't.'

It was David Costa. They were the first words they'd exchanged in nearly a year. He'd had a crush on her since school and his romantic comment had irritated her already. He looked the same as he'd always looked, rather bookish, with thick-rimmed glasses and a haircut his mother would like.

'Can I join you?'

'I'm quite happy on my own, thanks, David.'

Surprisingly, he didn't put on his hurt puppy look. Instead, he looked frankly back at her. 'I have something on Marc Comas.'

Nodding slowly, she pushed out the other chair at her table. He sat down and asked the waiter for a glass of white wine and the grilled salmon.

'So what have you got?' Elisenda demanded. She still didn't entirely trust him.

'Have you seen the house where they live? Comas and Miravent? He's a city councillor, she's a journalist who was freelance for years before becoming a member of the Catalan government. How can they afford a house like that in Palau? And send their son to one of the most expensive private schools in Girona?'

'Miravent comes from money.'

'No, she doesn't, Elisenda. Her family isn't that wealthy and certainly can't afford to be subsidising them to that tune. I know where their money comes from. Comas is one of the councillors on the housing and planning committee. I have a file of what you might call strange decisions that the committee has taken over the last few years. Land reclassification, tenders that have gone to not the most obvious bidders. I think he's involved with companies that have seen their profits grow over the same period. All this at a time when construction has been in the doldrums ever since the recession began.'

'Do you have evidence of any wrongdoing?'

'Not yet. But I strongly suspect that he's up to his ears in corrupt practices.'

Elisenda sighed heavily. 'I'm not a journalist, David. I need evidence before I start accusing anyone of corruption. They have a big house and he's on committees. That's not enough. Do you actually have anything I can use?'

'No. Not yet, but I'm convinced that something is going on. You in the Mossos would be in a position to find out more.'

'How? If there's nothing I can show to a judge for them to sanction an investigation, I can't get access to Comas's affairs. You know that, David.'

Their food arrived and Elisenda's heart sank, realising she now had to sit through a meal with him in exchange for no tangible information that was of any use to her.

'They're Opus Dei,' he suddenly added when the waiter had gone.

'Oh, for goodness sake. You're not going to give me some conspiracy theory now.'

His face hardened. 'You know perfectly well I'm not. What I mean is how Opus members tend to look out for each other. The classic old-boy network.'

'And you think Comas is helping other Opus members through the committee's decisions? That's a hard one to prove. I'm sorry, David, but you need to give me something more concrete.'

He put his knife and fork down and stared hard at her. 'I will. I know he's corrupt.'

'Change the subject, David.'

He chuckled artificially to lighten the atmosphere. 'Miravent's politics are something to behold, don't you think? At least that's something we can agree on.'

'I couldn't possibly say. Your politics have always been more radical than mine.'

He laughed again, more genuinely this time. 'Come on, Elisenda, I know you. Miravent is just carrying on a long tradition of throwing in your lot with the colonial power.'

'That's a bit strong, David.' Her food wasn't settling well as she was eating too quickly.

'You know what she reminds me of? The Catalan bourgeoisie under Franco who made a point of speaking Spanish and rejecting Catalan, just to be able to ally themselves with power and get on. Miravent's the post-democracy version of that. A desire to sit at the big table, no matter how unpalatable the menu.'

'Maybe change the subject again, David.' What irritated her was that her own beliefs were probably a more tempered version of the stuff David was spouting, but as a Mosso leading an investigation, she had to retain impartiality.

'Come on, you're not going to tell me the Mossos share her politics.'

'It's a broad church, David, with broad beliefs.'

He smirked at that, which annoyed her all the more. What he knew was that the Mossos owed their current existence to autonomy. They were employed by the Catalan government. Inevitably, the motivation of so many like her who'd joined the Mossos but wouldn't have dreamt of entering the old Spanish police was a desire for a break with the past, a desire to be part of Catalonia as a nation. That meant many of her colleagues were at least pro-autonomy, others pro-independence, including an association of officers who campaigned for just that. She looked at her dinner companion and said nothing of what she felt.

At the end of the meal, one of the most hurried meals that Elisenda could recall and that left her feeling bloated, she didn't lean forward for the usual kiss on each cheek and he didn't attempt to do so either. Watching him go, she sat back down again at the same table and asked for a coffee, which she'd reluctantly forgone in her eagerness to get supper over with. The waiter gave her a knowing smile and came back with a *tallat*, a small white coffee, and a *licor de café* in a shot glass.

Opus Dei, she considered, wondering if they really were members. She remembered the reference to family values in Miravent's appeal. But more than anything, the we-feel-no-grief comment now began to make some sense. She'd get Josep to check up on it in the morning, as far as that were possible. If not the secretive and sinister organisation that Hollywood liked to portray, they still liked to be a closed book to non-members.

Climbing the stairs to her apartment, next to the river, she opened the door and switched the light on. A small child was standing in front of her. In her fright, she dropped her keys. Bending down to pick them up, she turned back to look and the child was still there, standing in what used to be the small hall until she knocked all the interior walls through. It was a girl of about six. Motionless, wordless, expressionless. Elisenda looked at her and felt tears sting her eyes.

'You have to go now, Lina,' she told the vision of her daughter. 'Mama needs you to go.'

'What do you want with me?' he shouted at the door above his head.

He could see it now, a rectangle of black in the darkness. A deeper hue of bleakness that danced into the edges of his vision when he looked to one side of it.

He picked up another rock from the rubble strewn around his feet and threw it. It banged against the damp wood with an angry thud and bounced back down to the cellar floor. He could just see it fall in the gloom a metre or so in front of him.

He refused to cry.

Instead, he climbed to the top of the worm plinth of crumbled steps and launched himself into the black one more time. Coiling his legs as tightly as possible, he sprang and reached with his fingertips for the bottom of the door frame, but he still couldn't find a handhold. He had the measure of the space now and was getting nearer each time he jumped, but so far hadn't found anything on which to gain purchase. He landed back on the ground, in the small area he'd cleared of rocks so he wouldn't injure himself when he fell, and swore. A deep, irreligious curse his mother would have scolded him for.

Giving up for the moment, he inched his way back to the spot where he had the best view of the door and waited to get his breath back. He shouted to his captor again.

'I'm cold.'

He looked up expectantly. The sliver of light around the door seemed weaker, the visibility less. He had no idea how long he'd been there. At least a night, he thought, and another day.

'I'm hungry,' he called again. 'I want something to eat.'

He heard movement at the door and it opened. The figure gestured to him to stand up and threw something down. It was a sleeping bag. The slippery nylon felt like the most luxurious thing he'd ever known.

Something else was thrown down. He picked it up to find a long, thin package in silver foil. He opened it to find a sandwich. Tender ham in a long baguette, the inside of the bread dowsed in tomato, oil and salt. He breathed in the aroma and felt almost sick with hunger.

'Catch this,' the figure above said.

He looked up in time to see a plastic bottle of water arcing down at him from above. Dropping the sandwich onto the sleeping bag at his feet, he caught it in time before it could crack open on the hard floor.

'What do you want with me?' he demanded again.

The figure stared at him in silence for a moment and retreated, shutting the door, plunging the cellar in shadows again.

He sat down with his treasure and resisted the urge to cry.

Outside the walls, he heard the river whisper in the dark.

Wednesday

Chapter Eighteen

'She's six.'

'And how old was Lina when you last saw her?'

Elisenda sighed impatiently. Unlike the previous morning, when she didn't have the inclination to go through with counselling, now she felt she didn't have the time either.

'I've got two investigations to keep on top of,' she'd argued with Puigventós on the phone that morning, trying to get out of going.

'You're on a knife edge, Elisenda,' he reminded her. 'In more ways than one.'

She found herself breaking out into a nervous sweat now, lying on Doctora Puyals' uncomfortable recliner. After another sleepless night, she'd punished herself on her morning run, leaving herself retching with pain at the end of her sixth ascent of the cathedral steps. She realised she was still overheating because of her exertions, despite a cool shower at home before walking as calmly as she could to the Eixample and the counsellor's office. Her gentle walk through the morning streets had turned into a frenetic quickstep somewhere along the way in an irrational impatience to get it over and done with so she could start the day properly.

'How old was your daughter when you last saw her?' the counsellor repeated.

'When she died?' Elisenda replied brutally. 'She was six.'

Puyals straightened her jacket lapel. 'And that was six years ago. So she'd be twelve now. I can't help you until you see that this isn't your daughter you're seeing. This is a projection of her. Your projection of her. Of your guilt.'

'My guilt? I wasn't the one who flew her into a storm.' Elisenda opened her eyes. She was wary of making any more admissions like yesterday's. 'Anyway, I thought this was supposed to make me feel better. Shouldn't this be non-confrontational and non-threatening?'

'Normally it would be, Elisenda. But you thrive on confrontation and threat. If not to yourself, then to the people you try to help. So maybe that's the only way you're going to feel you're making any progress.'

'The only way I'm going to make any progress is by finding a missing teenager and stopping more people being terrorised in their own homes. That's what I should be doing.'

'I agree.'

'You do?' Elisenda made to get up but Puyals signalled her to stay where she was.

'Yes, I do. If all you had to worry about was your job. But it's not. You have a ghost to exorcise, Elisenda, and it's not your daughter.'

'I'll call a priest,' Elisenda said, instantly regretting her flippancy. It was born of anger.

'No need. The visions will end when you're ready for them to end.'

-

The man standing under a young plane tree outside the court buildings was familiar in a younger, friendlier and more attractive sort of a way. Seeing him turn as she approached, Elisenda did a double-take, her nerves on edge after the session with Doctora Puyals. She wondered if she was going to need yet more counselling to cope with this bout of counselling and decided it was best not to say that even in jest to Puigventós. Shaking off the thought, she looked up at the spanking new court complex, tacked on to the Institut de Medicina Legal and covering the block between the post office and the old overhead railway line from France, and was struck as always by the current obsession with horizontal slit windows on public buildings. She felt they had to say something about our view of the world outside our own. Her daydreaming was disturbed by the clanking of a local train trundling along the track opposite, slowing down as it headed for the station a few streets away.

She greeted the man and introduced herself.

'Joan Bellsolà,' he replied, handing her a card. It had a Barcelona address on it.

She looked at it and him. 'So what relation to Gerard Bellsolà are you?'

'He's my uncle. I didn't want to go into the family firm here, so I moved to Barcelona.' He gave a wry smile. 'You can have too much family.'

She was surprised to find herself liking a member of the Bellsolà legal dynasty, at least three generations of which had smarmed their way through Girona's courts. Joan's uncle Gerard was Elisenda's current nemesis, seeming to defend every one of the city's worst white-collar criminals.

'Shall we go in?' she suggested.

Their appointment with the judge who'd be instructing the investigation, insofar as the search for the missing boy was deemed to be a criminal investigation, was at nine thirty. They were a few minutes early. Reporting to the front desk, they were given a room number and a name. Elisenda stifled a sigh. The misery of the morning run and the counselling that followed were like hot ice cream muffins at Rocambolesc compared with the stultifying nausea of working with Jutgessa Roca.

'I've never had dealings with her,' Joan said innocently.

'A pleasure all to come.'

Despite only being a couple of years older than Elisenda, Jutgessa Roca more closely resembled a throwback to the unresponsive authoritarianism of the courts in Franco's day than the sort of judge that democracy was supposed to provide. A stickler for form and procedure at the expense of common sense, she was able to veto even the most reasonable request of the Mossos if it wasn't fully covered by jurisprudence. A pity, then, as far as Elisenda was concerned, that the Catalan and Spanish legal systems required an examining judge to dictate how a police investigation was to be conducted.

As it turned out, the judge proved to be more amenable than usual. At least at first.

'This is a simple case of abduction,' she decided five minutes later after Elisenda had put forward the facts as they knew them.

Elisenda questioned the use of the word simple but let it ride. 'It is most probably a case of abduction,' she said in a measured voice, 'but there are avenues within that supposition that we need to explore.'

Roca considered that for a moment and turned to Joan. 'What is the family's view of this?'

He smoothed his already perfect hair before replying and turned on a tentative smile. Still a Bellsolà, Elisenda reminded herself.

'We agree with the Mossos d'Esquadra that there is probably a political motive behind this. Or at least some sort of attack on the Comas Miravent family because of Susanna Miravent's political profile. Because of that, we would welcome the focus of the investigation centring on that.'

'Sotsinspectora Domènech?' the judge asked Elisenda.

'While we agree that that is the probable main focus, as I said, we need to consider other possible motives. We would want to look at an abduction not only for political motives but also for financial ones. There haven't been any ransom demands as yet, but we can't rule that out. Neither can we rule out the possibility of the boy's identity being random and that these are the actions of a sexual predator. I'd request the investigation to be open enough to allow us to explore those avenues.'

The judge looked down at the notes in front of her and agreed to their requests. Dumbfounded by a minor victory, Elisenda asked for a further moment alone with her.

'There are other matters we need to consider,' she explained to both Roca and Joan.

Waiting for the lawyer to leave, the judge turned to Elisenda, her voice a few degrees cooler now that Joan had left the room. 'Well, Sotsinspectora Domènech?'

Elisenda chose her words carefully, trying not to antagonise. 'We also want to look at the possibility of the family's involvement in this matter. This is the second child of this couple that has gone missing. We have to consider that their actions might not be as innocent as might appear. I want to request the right to look into the family's affairs, if only to rule them out as being above suspicion.'

Which is when the Jutgessa Roca that Elisenda knew reappeared. 'No. This is a family that has suffered more than any family should. They are pillars of the community. I refuse to allow you to put them through further tribulations.'

Elisenda stared back at her and thought quickly. She could probably investigate what she needed to assess the parents' possible implication through the channels open to her from the other strands that the judge had sanctioned, without worrying too much about the niceties of her ruling. As Puigventós had warned her, she would observe the judge's decision. From afar. And get on with finding the missing child without the help or hindrance of the court's blessing.

'Of course,' was all she replied.

Joan was waiting for her in the foyer.

'Not such a dragon,' he commented, a smile on his face. Elisenda thought it strange how the same smile on his uncle's face looked vulpine. On his, it was charming.

'A real charmer.'

He left her outside the court and went off in search of his car to go and see Miravent and Comas at their house. She watched him go and turned back to look at the court towering over her, blotting out the morning sun.

'New police, new courts,' she murmured, setting off briskly back into the centre towards Vista Alegre, 'same old useless Jutgessa bloody Roca.'

Chapter Nineteen

Marc Comas took a huge bite out of his Serrano sandwich and chewed steadfastly through the gristle and fat, savouring the tomato and olive oil with which the inside of the long, crunchy baguette was liberally coated. His second breakfast. A big, milky *café amb llet*, awash with three sachets of sugar, and a glass of Torres 10 brandy stood on the bar counter in front of him. His first breakfast had been the same since his childhood, a glass of cold milk sweetened with sugar and three dry Maria biscuits, taken standing in the kitchen. Unfortunately, Susanna's retrograde political stance didn't stretch to what they should eat for breakfast. She insisted on muesli and fruit. Wholesome, healthy fare as befitting a champion of family values. It tasted to him like something you scraped off a dusty farmyard.

'Stuff that,' he muttered out loud between mouthfuls.

And stuff that idiot Bofarull too, he thought. His wife's campaign manager had turned up for breakfast empty-handed and helped himself to his coffee and his cereal, he recalled, forgetting for one righteous moment that he hated the foul stuff. Susanna and Bofarull had discussed his missing son like he was another election to be won. A campaign based on personality and percentage shares, public profile and popularity. Ignoring any thoughts or feelings that Comas might have had on the matter. The overwhelming worry and dread at the idea of their son missing subsumed by a cold strategy of political logic.

And none of it had removed any of the everyday worries that were left up to him to manage, he mused now at the bar, not his wife and her genius campaign manager. He was the one to sort out their finances. The school fees, keeping up appearances, mixing with the right people, the summer home, holidaying in the right winter resorts. He and his wife came from old families. Sadly, that didn't equate to old money. And what money they did have was gobbled up by his wife and son, although he'd never dare say that to Susanna. What he forgot for the moment were his own hugely expensive hunting trips to Soria twice a year, his own expansive generosity to all the right people in Girona's finest restaurants, the accumulated cost of breakfasts and lunches and snacks such as this and his insistence on buying a new and increasingly more impressive car every year.

Alone in a small bar off Carrer Sant Josep, enjoying a brief respite from home and the search for his son that he felt he deserved, he figured their money worries were behind them. But it hadn't come without an entirely new sense of unease, tainting the taste of the brandy burning his throat and gullet down to his stomach, where he was convinced he had ulcers. Like everything in his political career, this semblance of financial stability had come at a cost, he realised, checking yet again that his phone, with its recording of his recent dealings with the owner of one of the province's largest construction and property management companies, was still in his jacket pocket. His light summer coat was slung over a hook on the underside of the bar and hanging securely between his tightly-clamped knees.

He'd only recently taken to using this bar for his breakfast, previously preferring one of the ones on Plaça del Vi, the square in front of the Town Hall, where he had his office. But ever since his first meeting with his new and rather informal business partner, he'd taken to parking on Plaça de Sant Josep, through the warren of streets behind the Town Hall, to stop putting in a daily bill for parking in his usual and expensive underground car park, wrongly believing that it would prevent any suspicion arising about his expenses and stop any further investigation of his finances. It was a change of pattern that had also led to a change of route from his car to his office, where he'd discovered this unassuming old bar, which served up a much more traditional breakfast that reminded him of happier times.

'*Hala*,' the bar owner suddenly exhaled in surprise. An unshaven, grizzled old guy, he could have been anywhere between fifty and eighty and normally limited himself to serving up food and drink and criticising the modern world. Comas jumped too. Not so much because of the car alarm that had just begun blaring out somewhere in the streets outside but because of the bar owner's instant and unusual reaction to the intrusion of the real world.

Like many people, Comas had never heard his own car alarm and had no idea what sound it made.

The bar owner's constant grumbling about the keening alarm spoiled what was left of Comas's breakfast and he wolfed his sandwich down quicker than he should have, exacerbating his inevitable indigestion with a hasty gulp to polish off the brandy. He paid and left the small bar, his head spinning slightly. Outside, he let out a long, low belch and noticed for the first time that the sound of the alarm seemed to be coming from where he'd parked his car. When he'd been inside the bar, the distortion from the echoing little streets had made him think the sound was coming from another direction entirely, but out here, the noise was funnelled along the narrow dogleg lane from the tiny Plaça de Sant Josep.

Rounding the corner to investigate, he saw his car in the distance, its indicators flashing and what looked like a broken rear side window. An elderly man was staring in curiosity at the car. Two old ladies dragging wheeled shopping baskets walked by, oblivious in their discussion. For the first time, Comas heard the sound of his car alarm.

'*Merda*,' he muttered, reaching for his phone to call the police.

What he didn't hear were the footsteps behind him. Or the whistle of the extendable metal baton before it hit him between the shoulder blades, knocking him to the ground. He did see the expensive black leather shoes in front of his face, and the cobbles lying harshly against his cheek that fanned out before him. He also saw the hand reach down towards his right hand, the one in which he was clutching his mobile. Instinctively, he held on, but another crack of the baton broke the bones in two of his fingers and he released his grip. The phone was taken from him, along with all the damning evidence it contained. He watched the fine footwear recede quietly back down the lane, tears brimming in his eyes as he slowly began to get to his knees.

He had no doubt who was responsible.

Chapter Twenty

'Nothing?'

'Nothing,' Àlex confirmed. 'We tried four houses in all, over the whole of the region in four different counties, and we found nothing. No symbols, no stone circles, no markings on the ground, nothing at all.'

Elisenda muttered a curse. 'It looked promising.'

Àlex raised his arms in frustration. 'We're always going to be chasing this gang. If the symbols thing had been real, we might have been able to anticipate them, without having to rely on dodgy information from people like Siset.'

Elisenda looked guiltily at the satchel on top of the filing cabinet and pulled it down, placing it on her desk so she wouldn't forget to check its contents. Probably his usual smutty DVDs, she imagined.

'Six counties,' Àlex reminded her. 'These people are covering a wide area. Even if we had found that the symbols meant anything, no matter how much we tell the various stations to keep an eye open, that's just too large an area to control.'

'Look for patterns. If the symbols aren't what we thought they might be, look for patterns in their past attacks. See if there's anything there that would help us anticipate their next move.'

Àlex sighed. 'We've looked, Elisenda. You know we have. We're back to square one.'

'We have more to go on now. Every time they target a house, they give a bit more away. A pattern might emerge that we haven't seen.' She looked out at the big office and saw Josep and Manel at separate computers. Montse had already gone out. 'I'll ask Josep to look for anything, but he's pretty much tied up with the missing boy. Do what you can.'

As always, Elisenda felt hamstrung by the lack of funding for her unit while it was still regarded as experimental. They were seriously understaffed. She worried it was a self-fulfilling prophecy: don't throw money at it until it fully proves its worth, but until it has the resources it needs, it's unlikely ever to be able to do that.

'To cheer you up,' she carried on, 'I saw the wonderful Jutgessa Roca this morning. She's been assigned to instruct us in the missing child investigation.'

Àlex groaned. Elisenda told him about the meeting with the judge and the Comas Miravent family lawyer.

'The one thing she wouldn't consider was that the parents might be implicated in the boy's disappearance. Which of course we should, so we're ignoring her on that. I've also got Josep checking up on anyone connected with the parents who we need to look at. It could turn up something. One other thing is that David Costa came to see me last night.'

Àlex whistled. 'I'll look for a truthful report of it in today's paper.'

'Don't hold your breath. He told me he suspects Marc Comas of corruption. He didn't seem to have any concrete proof and I'm not sure how far I want to trust him, but it's still something we should be considering when we look into the parents.'

'Against the judge's orders.'

The grin was back, Elisenda was pleased to see. Less than a year ago, Àlex had nearly been killed in the line of duty and it had left him for the best part of the intervening period racked with self-doubt. Someone had tried to hang him, and his voice had lost its strength for several months, a reflection of his lost confidence. But now his vocal cords were fully recovered and he seemed stronger than ever, the frustration he felt at his symbols theory not panning out simply further evidence that the old Àlex who took policing as seriously as any Mosso she'd ever met had returned. She filed those thoughts away.

'He also said that they were Opus Dei,' she continued.

'Only in Girona,' Àlex muttered.

'A bit less of your Barcelona cockiness, if you don't mind. Were you never wooed at school?'

He laughed. 'Wooed? You evidently moved in different circles, Elisenda. Opus never troubled me.'

'I was. A girl in my school who'd never bothered talking to me before suddenly wanted to become my best friend once her family found out my mum was a teacher and my dad a lawyer. She kept inviting me to picnics by the river and days out with right-minded, God-fearing people. She even asked me once to the family's beach house.'

'I thought Opus Dei was all shadowy figures wielding power behind the scenes and secret handshakes.'

'Everyone does now, thanks to books and films. But it's much more mundane than that, I'm afraid. Certainly here. For some it's spiritual, but for a lot, it's just the local big fish wanting to join a club with some of the other local big fish. Help for the boys. Just another ladder for social climbers to jump on. A sort of Catholic country club. I told her to sod off.'

Àlex got up to leave. 'So you were already like this as a kid, then.'

She watched him go with a stern look on her face and turned her attention to Siset's battered leather satchel.

'Gross insubordination,' she muttered, pleased that at least one of her team was in a good mood these days. As a reflex, she glanced up to see Josep and Manel continuing to ignore each other and wondered for a moment what she was going to have to do to pull the various strings together.

The top layer of Siset's bag was a couple of scruffy T-shirts, stiff with dried sweat and with logos that had long since faded. They were there to cover from a casual observer what lay underneath, she imagined. Sure enough, she pulled out several piles of bootleg DVDs held together with elastic bands, some with black and white photocopied covers of blockbuster movies, others with lurid lettering and pictures of large swathes of flesh that were anything but Hollywood classics.

'You really are a piece of work, Siset,' she commented. In an age when everyone got their entertainment of this sort from the internet, her grass still clung to a dying technology.

Underneath was an assortment of old dross, possibly stolen, possibly not, but that would have been no good to anyone. It was little wonder he needed to supplement his income by selling her information; he was never going to become Mister Big from passing on this rubbish. Looking through, she felt relieved not to find any drugs. That would have been harder for her to overlook. At the bottom, she found a small fabric drawstring bag. Opening it, she tipped the contents out on to her desk.

'Oh, Siset,' she muttered.

It was a matching necklace and bracelet. Silver and stylish with inset turquoise stones, it chimed with her. Logging into the computer system, she searched through the records until she found what she was after. There on screen was a photograph of the same matching set of jewellery, the picture taken by the owners as an insurance record. They'd been stolen from a house in the Albera mountains, one of the ones Àlex had told her that he and Manel had visited the previous day looking for stone symbols. It linked Siset to the raids on isolated houses. She called Àlex in to take a look.

'It probably explains why he gave me false information,' she told him. 'The little bastard's playing both sides against the middle.'

'Dangerous game to be playing with these people,' Àlex replied.

'I really need to find him now.'

Elisenda reached for her bag at the sound of her mobile ringing. Answering it, she was shocked to hear the news relayed to her by a sergent in Seguretat Ciutadana.

'Thanks for letting me know.' She hung up and looked at Àlex. 'Marc Comas. He's been mugged, his phone stolen.'

Àlex looked as shocked as she felt. 'Want me to go and interview him?'

'No. I'd better go. You go and look for Siset, you know where he normally hangs out.' She glanced at the two caporals in the outer office. 'You'd better go on your own. If you take Manel into Font de la Pólvora, he'll start a riot.'

Chapter Twenty-One

The mountains in the distance were shrouded in dark cloud. From the movement of the light between the sky and the land, Montse could see that it must be raining heavily up in the mountains. The rivers that fed into the Ter, which brushed the northern edge of the city and eventually gobbled up the Onyar past the Devesa park, would be filling, getting wilder. South and east of the city, so many streams fed into the Onyar, she wondered when they'd see a difference in its flow through the city. Despite the storm protection in the river course as it entered Girona, the water could still run wild under the bridges connecting the old town with the new. She turned away from the view and entered the school. Here in Girona, there was no rain, but there was a humidity curling into the air down in the city centre that had been enervating. Up on Montjuïc, she was making the most of the cooler, dryer air that blew gently on the back of her neck.

Father Besses didn't come to meet her today. Instead, a secretary in a tartan kilt and thin sweater that looked ideal for the air conditioned environment of the school offices but would have been a millstone in the outside world showed her to a small interview room. A table and four chairs and posters on the walls showing children happily learning religion and sports told Montse that this was one of the rooms where tutors would meet parents to discuss their child's progress. After a short while, a man in his thirties came into the room and sat down. He was carrying a cup of coffee in each hand.

'Milk, no sugar,' he announced. 'Hope that's how you like it. I'll get sugar if you want it.'

'That'll be fine,' she told him.

He put the cups down and took a seat on the side of the table at a right-angle to her.

'Joaquim Benach,' he introduced himself, shaking her hand and pushing one of the cups across the table in front of her. 'I teach French and I'm also Jaume's tutor. Neither monk nor priest.'

Montse smiled, deciding she liked the man. Seeing him closer up, she revised his age upwards to early forties, but well preserved, with laughter wrinkles around dark eyes and flecks of grey through neatly cut black hair. His movements were easy and he looked like a runner, although she would most probably have known him from the circuit if he had been.

'You know I'm here about Jaume Comas Miravent,' she began, turning the handle of the coffee cup to face her but not taking a sip. 'Really, I want to ask you if you've noticed anything in his behaviour that might explain his disappearance.'

Benach idly stirred his coffee even though Montse suspected there was no sugar in it. He was evidently giving himself time to gather his thoughts.

'I was Jaume's tutor last year too,' he told her, 'which is helpful from your point of view as I can see a progression from one year to the next. If this had been my first year as his tutor, it would have been much too soon in the term to be able to tell you anything of any use.'

He stopped stirring and gently touched the bowl of the spoon against the inside lip of the cup, watching as the capillary action drained the liquid from the spoon. Despite his outward friendliness, he seemed suddenly reticent.

'Did you go to a religious school, Caporal Cornellà?' he asked her.

'Please, call me Montse.' She realised she had to put him at his ease. 'No, I went to a state school in Santa Eugènia.'

'So did I. Not in Santa Eugènia, I mean, but here in Girona.' He looked up from his cup. 'They're different beasts, these schools. The parents are the clients, the children the product, the priests and the directors the gatekeepers. And as teachers, you can often feel caught in the middle. I owe a loyalty to the children in my care, but my employment to the clients and the gatekeepers.'

'I appreciate that you have to be considered in what you tell me, but I do need to know everything possible to be able to find out what's happened to Jaume. As far as I can promise it, I will be discreet about any information you can give me.'

He smiled and took a sip of coffee. 'Nice to meet another state school kid.' He paused before continuing. 'There are a couple of issues that I see. There has been some change in Jaume from the summer term. Very much for the good, I might add, which makes his disappearance all the more distressing, if that's possible. All last year, Jaume hung out with two boys in his class, but after the summer holiday, it was evident that they'd fallen out.'

'Could I meet these two boys?'

'You'd really have to go through Father Besses for that. And I know that he'll insist on getting consent from the parents first. I can give you their names, but I'm afraid it'll be up to you to work out how you speak to them.'

He told her a couple of names, the same ones that Elisenda had given her. 'Thank you. I know that he's now friends with Carles Pascual.'

'That's right. Apparently they became friends over the holiday. You see, the two boys that Jaume used to hang around with like to think of themselves as being a cut above the rest. So did Jaume. All three are from similarly affluent families, from the same part of town. I have to say I was delighted at the start of term to see that Jaume had switched allegiances. Carles is a really nice kid, more grounded, and he brought out a much nicer side to Jaume. Had he not disappeared, I would have said that Jaume changing his friends was a good thing, but of course now this has happened.'

'Do you think these other two boys could have something to do with Jaume's disappearance? Revenge for changing friends, perhaps? Do you think they were bullying him?'

'I think you should speak to them to form your own conclusions.' His stare was more candid than his words. 'As for bullying,

Jaume's big for his age and quite well developed. He plays basketball for the school and for a local team. I would say that he'd be too much of a match for the other two.'

'Could he have been bullying them?'

Benach put his head to tone side. 'In the past, I would have said that it was a possibility, but he's been a lot calmer since the summer. That's thanks to Carles. I wouldn't have thought so based on his attitude this term.'

'You said there were a couple of issues.'

'I wasn't teaching here when Jaume's brother went missing, but I have met the parents on several occasions, and other members of staff remember Albert. After his brother went missing, or died, Jaume's parents doted on him. The father, especially, has always been very protective. That, unfortunately, has had a detrimental effect on him. He could be very self-centred, which has led in the past to his being rather confrontational with other children and some of the staff. But then, with the elections coming up and his mother's involvement with that, he was no longer the centre of his parents' world and I got the impression it put his nose out of joint. He can be a rather jealous boy. I think that may also have contributed to his falling out with his friends. This is why I was delighted that he'd become friendly with a kid like Carles Pascual. Jaume's had his problems, but he's a good kid at heart. Carles brought that out in him.'

Montse remembered something that Father Besses had said. 'His work hasn't been as good this year. Is that right?'

'Not quite. The first week, he was better if anything, but then this last week something seems to have happened that sent his work plummeting. Normally, at this stage, I wouldn't have thought that a problem unless it didn't settle down. Teething problems at the start of the year. But now, given his disappearance, it might be relevant.'

'Do you know what caused it?'

'No, but by the drop in the standard, I would say it was either because of the fallout with his friends, or there was potentially something seriously troubling him.'

Chapter Twenty-Two

Marc Comas had already been discharged from A&E and was back home by the time Elisenda caught up with him. He was sitting enveloped in one of the deep sofas at the house in Palau with a glass of whisky on a small table next to him. The small and ring fingers on his right hand were heavily swathed in a cast that extended back as far as his wrist, the whole of his hand wrapped in a blue sheath, and he was holding his hand up against his chest. He leaned sideways to take a drink and winced in pain, arching his back where the first blow had struck him.

The first Mosso on the scene had recognised him immediately and had accompanied him to the hospital, ensuring that he was hurried through the system and not troubled by any journalists.

'There were already a few journalists there by the time we left,' the uniformed Mosso had told Elisenda when she got to the house. He handed her a copy of the statement that he'd taken from Comas and she read it quickly.

'Thanks, Francesc,' she said. 'News travels quickly.'

'It does in Girona.'

He left to go back to the station. Two other Mossos were already at the house, standing guard against the growing throng of journalists outside. She watched Francesc Paredes go. He was still at the rank of mosso, one below caporal, but he was bright and eager and she'd earmarked him as a potential member of her unit. If the higher echelons ever decided to increase her budget, that is.

She sat on the sofa opposite Marc Comas, leaning forward on her haunches. The hospital had given him some heavy-duty painkillers and his voice was low, his words slurred. Elisenda could see his eyes coming in and out of focus. Susanna was sitting next to him, her right hand resting lightly on his lower arm against his chest, her wedding ring dull against the blue of his shirt sleeve. It was the first show of affection Elisenda had seen between the two. For once, Bofarull wasn't in the room, dominating the answers. Elisenda had seen him at the kitchen table with Joan Bellsolà: the campaign manager and the family lawyer going over some papers. It was a different world from Elisenda's. Encarna, the housekeeper, brought in a tray of coffee and set it down on the table, leaving again without saying a word. Elisenda tried to make eye contact to thank her, but the young woman kept her head down all the time she was in the room.

Recalling the statement that Mosso Paredes had taken, Elisenda asked Comas to confirm that he hadn't seen his attacker.

In reply, the councillor gestured to his back, wincing again with the movement. 'He came from behind me. I didn't see a thing.'

'And when you were lying on the ground, did you see what your attacker was wearing?'

'Jeans. Dirty jeans. And trainers. With stripes on them. That's all I saw.'

'And the attacker took your phone and your wallet? Nothing else?'

'That's enough, wouldn't you say?' Miravent entered the conversation. She spoke to her husband. 'I've cancelled all your credit cards, by the way, darling. You don't have to worry about that.'

He smiled weakly back at her and closed his eyes, either from the pain or the pills he'd been given to numb it.

I'm sorry, Marc,' Elisenda told him, 'but I do have to ask these questions. We have to ascertain whether this is just a random mugging or if it's related to Jaume's disappearance.'

Comas opened his eyes, anger in them. 'It's a mugging. They took my wallet. What else would it be?'

'Why would kidnappers attack my husband if they've taken my son,' Miravent asked, 'and steal his wallet? Surely they'd want to make sure we had access to money to be able to pay a ransom.'

'That is presuming their demands are going to be financial.' Despite her words, Elisenda was surprised that no contact had been made by any kidnappers yet. It had been nearly forty-eight hours since the boy had gone missing. Were there going to be any demands, financial or political, she would have expected them by now. Every hour that passed opened up other possibilities to explain Jaume's disappearance.

'And you really haven't had any contact from anyone in relation to Jaume?' Elisenda insisted. 'I know that the family of kidnap victims are often told not to contact the police, but it really wouldn't be in anyone's interest if you dealt with anyone without our knowledge.'

'I can assure you, we've heard nothing,' Miravent told her.

'We've been considering this mainly from the angle of your political profile,' Elisenda told Miravent before turning her attention to Comas. 'But I need to know if there's anything in your professional life, Marc, that might lead to someone doing this to target you. Your role as a councillor, perhaps. Is there anyone you can think of who might want to hurt you in this way?'

Comas opened his eyes one more time. 'No one.'

'I also have to ask this. You're members of Opus Dei, I gather.'

Miravent raised her eyebrows. 'Members? We prefer to use the word "faithful". If that's what you're referring to, yes we are.'

'But you don't send Jaume to the Opus Dei school in Girona. Or Albert.'

'You don't have to go to church to pray, Elisenda. Or join a party to have political beliefs. We choose to send our sons to a different school for other reasons.'

'The cost,' Comas suddenly piped up, his eyes shut, his words increasingly less intelligible. 'The more exorbitant the better.' He laughed once. It had a bitter sound to it. Elisenda said nothing but filed the moment away.

'Could your son's kidnapping have anything to do with your faith? Anyone who is opposed to Opus Dei? Or anyone who might feel that they've been discriminated against by not being members?'

'This is too ridiculous. If you really want to know,' Miravent told her, any politician's pretence at empathy gone, 'it is precisely our faith that keeps us going in all this. That has kept us going through all these years and that has made us stronger.'

'You said you felt no grief.' Elisenda could feel the words catch slightly in her throat. She knew she was being dragged away from the point but couldn't help herself.

Miravent pulled herself up straight on the sofa. 'Grief? Why would we feel grief?'

'Because your child died,' Elisenda all but shouted, her own anger and sorrow rising in equal measure. 'And your other child is missing.'

'Our child was chosen. Albert was chosen to sit by God's side. And he was chosen at an early age. That is not a cause for grief, that is a cause of pride. God chose our son. He chose us.'

'And Jaume? What if anything happens to Jaume?'

'Then so be it. That is also good. It is also good because it's God's will. Our family has been chosen, favoured.'

'What sort of parents are you?' Elisenda whispered.

'Parents with faith. It's something I cannot imagine you will ever understand.'

Elisenda looked at the other woman across the chasm that lay between them. 'No. No, you're right. It is something I hope I will never understand.'

-

Comas waited until his wife had shown Elisenda out of the room and opened his eyes, looking around him. Getting up quickly, he hurried into the small home office next to the living room and used his left hand to pull his wallet out from where he'd hidden it in his underpants. Looking at them as he took them out, he passed his credit cards one by one into the shredder and removed any other piece of paper that could connect the wallet to him. When he'd finished, he hid the wallet in one of the desk drawers. He'd throw it out with the non-recyclables when the coast was clear.

Feeling his headache getting worse, he rummaged through the drawers for the sleeping pills he always kept there, prescribed by his doctor but unknown to Susanna. He was needing them more and more lately. He couldn't find them and panicked, worrying that she'd found them. He cursed when it was obvious they'd gone and he thought of his wife.

'Faithful,' he mimicked in a low voice, tears welling in his eyes as he thought of his two sons. 'Bullshit.'

Chapter Twenty-Three

'I need to get out.'

Josep looked taken aback at her words. 'I've been looking through Pijaume's investigation,' he told her.

Elisenda sighed and sat down heavily at her desk. 'I suppose you'd better tell me, but then we're getting out of here.'

She told him a little of her conversation with Susanna Miravent. 'Gruesome,' she concluded, not wanting to talk any more about it just yet. She waved Josep to sit down. He was looming over her.

'Sotsinspector Pijaume's investigation into Albert's disappearance,' Josep said. 'It drew a blank but it was very thorough. Pages and pages of interviews, suppositions, conclusions. All good. I don't see how it could have been conducted any differently.'

She looked at him. He looked as defeated as she felt.

'He was a good detective,' she concluded. 'Unfortunately.'

They sat in silence for a moment, lost in thought.

It was Josep who spoke first. 'The original investigation's conclusion was that the boy had drowned in the river and the body been swept into the river system and either lost somewhere in there or taken out to sea. An accident. No human hand involved.'

She turned to look at the map of the Girona region on the wall to her right. There was a network of small blue lines in the mountains leading almost at right-angles into progressively bigger and bigger lines, flowing eventually to the sea.

She exhaled slowly. 'I forget how extensive the river system is. Maybe he was right.'

'But you still want to check,' Josep guessed. 'Because it's Pijaume.'

'So do you.'

He nodded. 'They had suspects. No one in particular. They questioned known sex offenders, but those were the only leads they really had. Nothing came of any of them.'

'What about the car that Jaume says he saw?'

'The parents heard it too, but nothing. No one ever came forward to say they'd been in the area. The cars of the suspects they did have were seen in Girona on that day, so they couldn't have been involved. Added to that, there'd been another incident on the same day about an hour earlier. It was seven kilometres away, a fatal hit-and-run, and Seguretat Ciutadana had set up road controls, which meant that cars going in and out of the area were controlled. Anyone snatching Albert would have had to go through the controls, which makes it unlikely that he was abducted. It also means they were very aware of sightings of cars in the area, and that still turned up nothing. From the notes, I get the impression that Pijaume's team began to doubt the boy's and the parents' seeing or hearing a car.'

'What about the hit-and-run driver? Could they have been involved?'

'Never caught. They never found who did it.'

'See if Seguretat Ciutadana still have records of the cars that went through the control. It's long shot, but there might be something that makes more sense now.'

Josep made a note of that. 'I haven't spoken to Sotsinspector Armengol yet. He was going to be looking at sex offenders.'

Looking through the glass partition, Elisenda saw that Armengol was in the outer office, talking to a member of his unit about something. He caught her eye and signalled that he wanted a word, so she beckoned him in. He leaned in through the door, his left hand holding on to the frame, his body only half in the room.

'Your sex offenders,' he told Elisenda. 'We've taken it down to five that we want to have a word with. They're the only ones whose profiles that we can see might lead to them taking a fourteen-year-old boy.'

'We have two who were questioned at the time of the older brother's disappearance,' Josep told him.

'Have you got the names?' Armengol swung into the room and leaned over the caporal.

Josep asked Elisenda if he could bring up the files on her computer screen and twisted it around to show Armengol. The sotsinspector pushed his glasses up his nose to see it more clearly.

'Yup,' he told them. 'Both on our list.'

Elisenda turned the screen back to face her and looked at the names. She didn't recognise either. 'Can you give these two priority, Sotsinspector Armengol?'

'Esteve, please,' he asked her, not for the first time. 'Yes, we'll look at those two first and I'll let you know if they look like they're worth pursuing further. What conclusions did the previous investigation reach regarding them?'

'Ruled out,' Josep replied. 'I think they were questioned as a matter of course. It was only as no other avenues appeared to be opening up that the investigation came back to them.'

'Belt and braces,' Armengol commented. He turned to go. 'I'll get on to it.'

After he'd gone, Josep turned back to face Elisenda. 'With respect, Elisenda, you're still not sure about him, are you?'

She watched Armengol in the outer office, talking to a couple of officers in his unit. 'I've just got to get used to him.'

'He seems all right.' Josep's voice was tentative. 'Maybe we need to give him more of a chance.'

'Maybe.' Elisenda looked at her caporal. 'And maybe we all need to give Manel a bit more of a chance.'

Josep puffed his cheeks out. With his unruly hair and slumped posture, he looked like a recalcitrant teenager. 'Maybe Manel should try not to make that so hard.'

'Make what so hard.' The voice was Àlex's. He walked into the room and flopped down on a chair. 'Christ, it's humid outside today. We need a good thunderstorm to clear the air.'

'Ah, but that doesn't always help,' Elisenda told him. 'Any joy.'

Àlex shook his head. 'Siset's nowhere to be found. I've tried all his usual places and he wasn't in any of them.'

'And no one's seen him, I take it.'

'He's invisible.' Àlex laughed. 'I spoke to Elena again. I told her that you were looking after his bag for him and that there was a reward waiting for him for information about the house robberies. He may be just dumb enough and greedy enough to fall for it.'

Elisenda considered her informant. His canny sense of self-preservation battling it out with his low-grade hustling. 'Worth a try. What's your next move?'

'Manel and I are going to be going through the attacks to see if we can find a pattern we've missed. We can't just let them carry on what they're doing until we get lucky.'

'Sounds good.' Elisenda picked up her bag and stood up. 'Let me know if anything comes up. Josep and I are getting out of here.'

As she walked past, Josep turned to Àlex and mouthed 'We are?', jumping up to follow her. Àlex grinned back at him and shrugged his shoulders.

Quarter of an hour later, Josep found himself driving a pool car along the Pedret road. They were heading north, out of the city. To their left, the Ter flowed heavy, already full from the rainfall higher up its course and now enriched with the waters of the Onyar.

'We're going to the mountains,' Elisenda told him.

'Right.'

He waited for her to elaborate, but she put her sunglasses on and stared out of her window, deep in thought. They drove through Celrà, stopping and starting at the traffic lights and skating round the roundabouts, past the low skyline of old stone houses and new industrial buildings. They drove in silence for ten minutes before Josep tried engaging with her again.

'How are the family taking it?' He glanced across at her, but she didn't react. 'Their press conference has had a mixed reception,' he persevered. 'The public are always sympathetic in these cases, but Sotsinspector Armengol told me this morning that the flow of calls had reduced, whereas the media seem to be taking more interest.'

'We'll be turning right up here soon,' Elisenda suddenly told him as though she hadn't heard what he'd been saying. She pushed her sunglasses up onto the top of her head. 'I want to see where Albert went missing.'

'Right.'

'We need to get a feel for it. It might help give us some idea of what's going on now.'

Josep turned right where she indicated and followed the smaller road past stone farmhouses and wheat fields, the landscape either side raw from where the crops had been harvested. 'Seguretat Ciutadana and the local stations are still here,' he told her. 'They've been checking this area closely in case Jaume returned for some reason.'

'No ransom note,' Elisenda muttered. 'Forty-eight hours and we've got no one claiming they've got Jaume or demanding something for his return.'

'Letting the family suffer to up the ante?' Josep suggested.

'Or he's left under his own steam.'

'And he's gone back to somewhere safe to him. Or meaningful. Like this place.'

'Or this is something else entirely. Either way, it means we can't gauge exactly how much of a risk the clock ticking is.' Watching the scenery change as they slowly climbed, Elisenda brushed her top teeth back and forth over her bottom lip. 'They've found nothing,' she muttered, 'but it's still worth looking. Them and us.'

The road narrowed and began to wind more, through a dappled shade of holm oaks and pines. Josep turned left off onto a smaller road, a raised wall of greenery one side, the mountains a short distance across more wheat fields to the other. He'd scrutinised enough maps and files over the past twenty-four hours to know the route to take. A short distance from the stretch of the stream they were heading for, they came to a Seguretat Ciutadana patrol car. Stopping, Josep showed his ID to the mosso standing by the car.

'Serious Crime Unit,' he told the younger guy, who was almost as lanky as Josep was. He stood with the same stoop. 'We're on the missing boy case, checking the area where the older brother went missing.'

The mosso signalled them through. 'We've got teams searching through the woods up ahead,' he informed them, his strong accent almost a caricature of Barcelona's flat vowels.

Sure enough, they passed Seguretat Ciutadana and support officers drafted in especially, scouring the forest in a straggling line on both sides of the narrow road. For a brief moment as they drove by, Elisenda watched the rows of officers in blue fatigues patiently scanning the ground ahead of them, and then they were gone, taken from sight at a bend in the road. Reaching their destination, Elisenda and Josep got out of the car and breathed in the quiet air. Elisenda filled her lungs and wondered at its crisp cleanness. It had none of the humidity of Girona of the past few days.

'We don't get air like this in Girona,' she commented.

'We really don't in Hospitalet,' Josep replied, mentioning his home town, the sprawling industrial city sprouting to Barcelona's south. He laughed. 'Or this quiet.'

It seemed unnaturally still, even the sound of cicadas hushed for the moment, scant wind blowing through the trees. They both watched as a hoopoe flew across the path in front of them in its curious dipping flight, its black and copper comb fanned out on top of its head, its dark brown and white striped wings vivid under its auburn mantle.

Josep broke the silence. 'It's this way.'

As they walked across a field into the shade of a gnarled cork wood, a sound began to grow in the hush. Running water. Louder than Elisenda would have expected it normally.

'The rain they've been getting higher up,' she commented. 'The rivers are fuller.'

'The files say it was the same when the older brother went missing,' Josep told her.

They passed a spot in a clearing the other side of the wood where an ancient holm oak tree stood. Josep told her it was where the family had been picnicking on that day four years earlier. Beyond it, the noise steadily grew and they emerged by a river bank.

'Well, I didn't expect that,' Elisenda muttered.

Below them, the water was calm, a clear blue mere with roots and branches tumbling down gentle, dusty banks to the edge of the stream. It was about the width of a swimming pool. The noise was further away, to their left. As they stared, a sudden eddy appeared near the bank where they stood and vanished just as rapidly. Josep picked up a leafy branch lying nearby and threw it into the water. It floated gently for a moment, scarcely moving from where it had entered, until another eddy emerged and pushed it to the middle. There, it was quickly snatched, borne away downstream by an invisible current, swirling as it was dragged towards the source of the noise, the smaller offshoots shaking their leaves against the main branch until they were sucked under the surface. Within a moment, it was gone, tumbling out of sight beyond a turn in the river.

'And then it was gone,' Elisenda said.

'Undercurrents,' Josep agreed. 'It could easily carry a small kid away. Albert was supposed to be pretty slight.'

'But Jaume isn't. He'd probably be strong enough.'

They quickly followed the route of the stream and came out where it met a larger river. The water bucked and foamed as the two sources merged and whirled away towards a bigger and faster flow of water further down the valley.

'Easy to see how a swimmer could get into trouble,' Josep said. 'I wouldn't attempt it when it's like this.'

Elisenda shook her head in agreement. 'And it's deceptive, too.'

Over the other side, she saw a track, wide enough for a car to negotiate. Looking either way, she couldn't see anywhere to cross. She asked Josep if there were any bridges nearby. He looked at the map of the region that he'd been carrying but shook his head.

'Nowhere. Fords higher upstream, but they're probably impassable when it's in flood.'

'So, if Jaume was telling the truth and he did see a car over there, he couldn't have got over to it and the driver couldn't have crossed over to here.'

'But the driver might have been able to get to Albert if he was in the water.'

'In which case, why did no one come forward to say they'd seen the boy or tried to save him? It also hasn't told us anything about whether Jaume's come back here.'

Retracing their steps, they searched the area where Jaume had gone swimming at the time Albert disappeared and all along the bank upstream but found nothing. There was no evidence of Jaume or of anyone having been there recently.

'Seguretat Ciutadana have already searched here,' Josep told her, 'and they came up with nothing.'

'Any houses?'

'Just the one we passed on the road here, and the owners have been questioned. Apart from that, there's an abandoned house the other side of the river, heading north. We'd have to get back to the road and drive three sides of a square to get there.'

Elisenda looked at the treacherously calm river and at the trees and fields opposite.

'We'll try it.'

Chapter Twenty-Four

It was a regular noise. Like ticking slowed down through a mist.

The abandoned house stood derelict at the end of an overgrown and potted track that had gouged and kicked at the underside of the car as they'd laboriously bounced towards it. The stream where Albert had disappeared had vanished behind them as quickly as it had re-emerged after their cross-country trek to get to the other side. As they stopped the car, Elisenda heard another river beyond the old building, stronger and more forceful. Through the windscreen, she saw that most of the roof was still intact, apart from a few pantiles that had slithered to the ground on the right-hand side, where they lay in a broken pile. The exposed roof timbers were dank and rotting. The first metre of stone walls above the foundations were green with damp, moss growing in the cracks and rough hollows, more extensive on the right than the left.

'You can see why they abandoned it,' she muttered.

'It was already derelict at the time Albert went missing,' Josep told her. 'It was searched at the time, and it's been checked again now.'

They got out of the car. What the Basques called a *txirimiri* was falling, a spectral drizzle that felt like a soft mist caressing your face but that would soak you to the core in ten minutes. Josep fetched two waterproof coats from the boot and gave one to Elisenda.

'Still a surprise no one's bought it,' she commented, putting it on. She looked around at the tranquil setting. Even in the mizzle, the scenery was enchanting, with distant mountains a rolling backdrop to the green scented pines and holm oaks surrounding the house. 'It's just the sort of place people are buying to do up these days. And getting attacked in.'

Josep grunted a laugh. 'Too damp.'

She looked at the green walls as they walked towards the house. 'Bet you it's got an earth floor. That's easy to cure, you just put in a proper one.'

She forced the rickety wooden door inwards and saw that she was right. The house was very old, no doubt long abandoned by a smallholder, their children unwilling to live the harsh life all the way out here. The ground inside was compacted earth, the building blessed with none of the fineries of life of even sixty years ago. It was exactly the type of property that people from Girona and Barcelona had been picking up for a song before the recession and restoring to an unprecedented state of luxury. The smell of damp and mud pervaded the house. She rubbed at a piece of the door between her thumb and finger and the wood crumbled away.

Scraping the rotting door further over the earth to get in, she heard a sound from above and saw a sudden movement out of the corner of her eye. Ducking and reaching instinctively for her holster, she quickly looked up. A dove was fluttering its wings in panic, their underside a storm white against the dark of the roof beams as it darted back and forth looking for a way out. After a few attempts, it finally found a small window at the front of the house, the glass long gone, and darted out into the wet air. Elisenda let out a deep breath and pulled her hand away from her holster, slowly going further into the old house with Josep at her heels.

Together, they searched the ground floor, what there was of it, but there were no signs of anyone having camped there. Not recently, anyway. The remnants of an open fire in the middle of the main downstairs room bore witness to someone having taken shelter there once, but it looked to have been some time ago. To the rear of the house, the sound of the river stormed wildly over the rocks in its course. The upstairs floor was easier to search. They simply looked up where the ceiling had gone. The sky was visible in the front corner where the tiles had fallen, the *txirimiri* gently enveloping the two Mossos.

Josep stopped and cocked his head to one side, pulling the hood of his waterproof down. He signalled to Elisenda to listen. She heard it too. A knocking. It seemed to be coming from the rear of the house, but neither of them could make out its exact source.

In what had been the kitchen, Elisenda found a door near the back that she'd assumed led into the main room, closing a circle with a twin door near the front of the building, but she now realised by the layout that there had to be a gap between the two rooms. Pulling it open, having to force it against the rusted hinges, she saw it gave directly on to a narrow flight of stone steps leading down into the damp darkness. The ticking was louder now she'd opened the door, and more insistent. It was coming from beneath their feet.

'I'm so glad we found that,' she whispered to Josep, taking a deep breath.

She shone her torch down the steps and began the steep descent, but as she progressed, she was puzzled to see that there was a source of light somewhere below. Josep followed her down, also sweeping ahead with the beam of his torch. The stones to her right ran with water, the outside wall she guessed, and she avoided brushing up against it. Listening all the while, she realised that the regular sound, which had speeded up when they'd opened the door, had calmed down now to its previous rhythm. Reaching quietly for her holster again, she took out her pistol and hefted the grip in her right hand, holding it against the torch so both barrel and light followed the same course. She heard Josep behind her do the same.

The source of light was coming from what would be the left-hand side of the house. With it came a steady stream of air, the moisture from the drizzle borne on it. Reaching the foot of the steps and turning, she saw a window cut into the back wall of the house. She hadn't realised from the front of the house that the rear of the building was a storey lower, the house built on a slope. Looking out of the window while Josep went deeper into the basement room, she saw how the land fell away to the river, now visible behind the old house. Another door set into the back wall opened onto a stone stoop overlooking the riverbank, with the mountains beyond. She had the unbidden thought that the house and setting were just ripe for someone with money to turn into a creation for the new age. And for someone else to come along and take it from them.

'Elisenda,' Josep called from behind her.

She turned and went back in. The knocking sound was still going, she realised. She'd become lulled by its insistence. He beckoned her over to a rusted iron frame leaning against the wall. It looked like an old bedstead. He pointed at it.

Part of a small skeleton hung down from the top of it, the tiny skull tapping at the hollow frame in the breeze blown in through the broken window. Other bones, darkened by mud and time, lay scattered on the earth floor. Elisenda looked up at the window just a metre or so away and then back at the skull. It was caught on one of the curling shapes of the bedstead, lodged upside-down, the base of it still tapping against the cold metal, the sound chiming through the room.

'It's a deer,' she told Josep. 'It must have got trapped on the bedstead.'

–

Her phone rang as they bumped their way back along the track towards the narrow lane that would lead to the main road. It was Armengol, calling from Vista Alegre to tell her that of the two sex offenders he was checking up on, one of them couldn't have been involved with Jaume's disappearance.

'*He's in hospital after an operation on his knee. There are complications so he's been there for nearly two weeks. We're still looking for the other suspect. I'll keep you posted.*'

Elisenda thanked him and hung up, telling Josep what Armengol had said.

'I don't think they're where we should be looking,' he told her.

'Neither do I. That's why we've got Armengol looking into it instead of us. But we still have to be sure.'

'I was going through more of the notes on Albert's disappearance when you came in this morning. I found that Francesc Bofarull was questioned at the time.'

'How significant is that?'

He shook his head. 'Not very. He was already Susanna Miravent's campaign manager back then. All the family's friends and colleagues were questioned eventually, after the investigation started going nowhere.'

'I thought as much.' Her voice was glum, but she suddenly signalled him to stop before the track joined the small lane. 'Just to satisfy my curiosity, I want to see if there are any symbols marking out the house.'

'The ones Àlex is looking for? I thought he wasn't having any luck with that.'

'No harm in checking. If they are staking out their targets, I also want to see if they're leaving symbols for houses that aren't worth bothering with.'

Josep pulled over and they both got out to look. The *txirimiri* was turning into full-blown drizzle, a steady fall spattering the hoods over their heads. They found nothing.

'Which,' Elisenda commented with a sigh as they climbed back into the car, 'means nothing. The pile of rocks and twigs at the architects' house was too deliberate for us to disregard it, so I think Àlex is right. They must have a meaning.'

They set off along the lane, eventually heading for Girona, when Elisenda asked again about Miravent's campaign manager.

'Do you remember anything the first investigation said about Bofarull?'

'Nothing out of the ordinary. He'd got his MBA in Barcelona the year earlier and had moved back to the Girona area when he got the job with Miravent in time for the last elections. He was interviewed twice, but I think the second time was when the investigation was getting desperate.'

'Is he Opus Dei?'

Josep looked surprised. 'I haven't found anything. I'll check.'

'He possibly is if he's working with Miravent's political campaign. I can't imagine her employing the wrong type of person.' She looked out of the window as they approached the main road. 'There's something about him that I can't put my finger on.'

'He lives not far from here.'

Elisenda sat up. 'He doesn't live in Girona?'

'No, his family's from the Baix Empordà and he's got a house there. Just past La Bisbal, in Vulpellac.'

Not far from Elisenda's own parents in Monells, this side of La Bisbal, she thought. She didn't know the Bofarull family, but then she'd grown up in Girona, the Monells house being her grandparents' home when they were alive.

'Turn right at the main road,' she told Josep. 'Let's go and check it out.'

Chapter Twenty-Five

'I grew up on the other side of the village. Over there.'

Francesc Bofarull pointed out of the window towards the north side of Vulpellac. The mountains beyond were vanishing in the steady fall of rain. It was much heavier now, with dark, thunderous clouds unfurling in the sky, seemingly barely metres above their heads. Elisenda always found the village to be a charming anachronism. Half a dozen restored medieval streets book-ended by new houses made to look ancient, it stood in quiet and timeless splendour to the left of the roundabout by the industrial estate after you left La Bisbal.

'I didn't expect to find you in,' she'd told Bofarull truthfully when he'd answered the door.

He'd quickly invited her and Josep in out of the rain and offered them coffee, leading them up to a room on the third floor, which boasted what would have been wonderful views over the village if the skies hadn't just opened. The house was seventeenth-century, he'd told them, and had belonged to his mother's family. His parents still lived in his father's family home. It was a fairly similar story to Elisenda's own, although unlike Bofarull, she'd grown up in Girona. Her parents now lived in her grandparents' old house after years in the city, these days commuting to their jobs there, all to keep the home in the family. And like her parents, Bofarull had modernised his home while still keeping the heart of the old house intact. She had to confess to liking the traditional but new La Bisbal ceramic floor and stair tiles and the light wood throughout. The room they were in now was Bofarull's home office, a political starship with a bank of top-end electronics on hewn stone shelves and a laptop open on an antique walnut table. A framed newspaper article on the wall featured Bofarull at his desk surrounded by his high-tech domain.

'I work from home a lot,' he explained. 'Not so much right now with the elections going on, so you're lucky to find me in.'

'You were questioned at the time Albert went missing,' Elisenda stated, watching his reaction. 'Do you know why?'

He was taken aback. 'Everyone who knew the family was, I thought.'

'And do you have any theories about Jaume's disappearance now?' She deliberately kept her voice cold.

The campaign manager sat down at his desk to gather his thoughts. He quickly jumped up to his feet again. 'Sorry, did you want coffee?'

'Your thoughts on Jaume's disappearance,' Elisenda insisted.

'I could really do with a coffee.'

He led the way to the door out on to the landing and waited there, ushering Elisenda through.

'I'll be down now,' Josep told him, lingering by the window.

'I'm afraid I can't allow that,' Bofarull told him.

'And why's that?' Elisenda wanted to know.

The campaign manager waved his arm around the room. 'We're four days from an election and I run the campaign for one of the leading figures in it. You must understand that I have a lot of sensitive information in this room. I can't allow you to stay here without me being present. Unless you have a warrant.'

'A warrant?' Elisenda asked. 'Why would we want a warrant?'

'You wouldn't. But if you want to search my house, you'll need one.'

Elisenda stood in front of him and studied his face. He was as cool and collected as ever, not a hair out of place or any undue colour to his cheeks. 'There was no question of searching your house. We're simply here to ask you a few questions about Jaume.'

'Which we can do over coffee. So that's good, then.'

He gestured them both out of the door and followed them down the three flights to the ground floor. The same traditional but modern ceramic and wood theme ran through the kitchen, the same state-of-the-art appliances resting in carefully restored niches. Bofarull busied himself pouring water into a stylish, new machine that took the coffee from bean to cup and set out ceramic cups and saucers, a modern design made in traditional La Bisbal green and yellow. Elisenda couldn't help feeling irritated by the all-singing, all-dancing gadget for making a hot drink.

Outside, a wide patio with aluminium tables, potted palms and an olive tree was getting a soaking from the downpour as the rain took a firm hold of the village. At a right-angle to the glass door leading out from the kitchen, a wooden door reminded Elisenda of the door in the abandoned house they'd just left. The design of these houses had changed little in centuries.

Josep tried the door but found it locked. 'Is this the toilet?' he asked Bofarull innocently.

'It leads down to the cellar.' He pointed to a door just outside the kitchen in the hall. 'That's the toilet if you need it.'

'It can wait.'

Josep wasn't stooping for once. He always stood more upright, less self-conscious about his height, when he was feeling confident or in control. Elisenda had to stifle a smile.

'What do you keep down there?' she asked Bofarull.

He glanced at the door. 'Down there? Wine. It's my vice. It keeps perfectly in the cellar, just at the right temperature.' He poured out three cups of coffee and set them down on the kitchen table. 'You asked me what my thoughts about Jaume's disappearance were. To me, it's quite clear. As far as I'm concerned, it's a politically-motivated act to throw Susanna's campaign off course.'

Elisenda let the contents of the cellar off for the time being. 'And who do you suspect of being responsible for it? One of her political competitors?'

He shook his head emphatically. 'No. Someone in the political arena simply wouldn't do anything like this, it would be too high-risk a ploy. It would backfire too easily. No, this is someone outside politics but who is opposed to Susanna's high set of values regarding the right way our country should be moving forward.'

Elisenda took a sip from the coffee on the table, hating to admit that it tasted very good. 'There will be a lot of people who disagree with her stance. The majority, in fact, I should imagine. Can you narrow it down to any particular group? Or person?'

'The more radical anti-austerity or pro-independence groups.'

Elisenda shook her head. 'Unfortunately, that's still the majority.'

Bofarull bristled at her reply. 'I wouldn't be so sure of that. Come Sunday, we'll see where the wishes of the majority lie.'

'No doubt. The problem is we can't wait until Sunday to make sure that Jaume is safe. We need something more specific to go on now if we're going to find him soon.'

Bofarull held both hands up. 'That's how I see it. I couldn't say who specifically would do it, but I do believe it's to do with the elections. An attempt to subvert democracy.'

Trying to tease answers out of him, and wanting but not wanting to engage in political debate, Elisenda glanced again at the cellar door. It was possibly irrational, but after the scene at the abandoned house in the Gavarres, she needed to know for sure what lay downstairs.

'Would you permit us to take a look at your cellars?' she asked him.

He shook his head. 'It's wine, I told you. And I'm sorry, but I really am very busy. We go to the polls in four days' time and Jaume disappearing like this is causing us any amount of headaches. I have a lot of work I need to be doing.'

'Headaches?' Josep barked. 'A child is missing.'

Elisenda hushed him and he turned away in disgust. 'Headaches?' she echoed. 'An odd way to describe it.'

'You know what I mean. It's an extra cross for us to bear at this time.'

'The extra scrutiny in the press,' Elisenda agreed. She watched his face closely as she made her next comment. 'And all the extra air time your party's getting.'

His look stayed calm. 'You imagine a woman with the deep faith that Susanna has would use a situation like this for political gain?'

'I'm sure Susanna's faith would mean she wouldn't contemplate using her own son like this. Are you also a member of Opus Dei?'

As Bofarull searched for the words to say, Elisenda heard her phone ring in her bag. She ignored it, waiting for the self-assured man opposite her to answer. The moment her phone stopped ringing, Josep's started. He answered it. She tried to ignore his conversation, but the interruption had given Bofarull the breathing space not to say anything rash. It was Josep who spoke instead.

'Elisenda,' he said after hanging up. 'That was Àlex. There's been another house robbery.'

Chapter Twenty-Six

'I want a warrant to search Bofarull's house,' Elisenda told Josep. 'There's something about him.'

Josep nodded. It was the third time she'd said it since they'd left his house in Vulpellac.

'Do you think the boy's in his cellar?' he asked her now.

'No. If he was holding him, I don't think he'd be that stupid. But I'd like to know what is down there. Who keeps a locked door in their own house?'

She was distracted by a reflection of flashing blue and red lights skating across the windscreen. The strands of colour were caught in the raindrops lashing down on the glass, the wipers struggling to push one lot away before the next onslaught hid the outside world from view. Josep was forced to drive slowly through the torrential downpour, peering through the rain at the jumble of cars ahead of him. A uniformed Mosso, miserable and drenched in his waterproofs, flagged them down, but signalled them through when he saw Elisenda in the passenger seat. It was still daytime, but the dark clouds and sheets of water had turned the scene before them into a crepuscular chaos. None of it was helped by the rain churning up the dirt track leading up to a house they couldn't yet see, sending their car skittering across the mud.

'This is useless,' Elisenda told him. 'We'll have to walk from here.'

Luckily, the ground was less treacherous when walking than in the car, and they hurried towards the flashing lights outside the house, the sound of the rain on their waterproof hoods making any further conversation until they were under cover impossible. Àlex was waiting for them on the porch.

'It's a bad one, Elisenda.' He pointed to an ambulance behind them. 'One of the members of the family has a head injury. The paramedics are looking at him now, but it's not looking good.'

As he spoke, the ambulance siren was turned on and it began to pick its way carefully down the track towards the main road. They watched it emerge onto the asphalt and pick up speed immediately. A Seguretat Ciutadana patrol car followed behind.

'Where are they taking him? Girona?' Elisenda asked.

Àlex nodded. They were at an isolated house just off the winding road from La Bisbal to Cassà de la Selva, at the other end of the Gavarres mountains, not that far from one of the houses that Àlex and Manel had checked out the day before.

'These attacks are getting more frequent,' Àlex told her, leading her and Josep into the house, past a team of Científica scouring the floor. They'd marked out a path for them to follow. 'Counting the failed attempt on Monday, this is the third one in less than a week.'

Elisenda scanned the rooms in the house as Àlex explained what had happened. The story, like the house, was the same one they'd been getting used to since before the summer. A restored house out in the sticks, the family at home, terrorised until they'd transferred money and handed over anything else of value in the house, including the car.

'Where are the other family members now?' she asked him.

'Gone to the hospital. It's just a husband and wife living here. The wife has gone with Montse to the hospital in a Seguretat Ciutadana car. She wasn't hurt, but she's obviously concerned about her husband's injuries. Montse was taking a statement in the car while they were waiting for the ambulance to go. The wife didn't want to stay in the house.'

'OK. Montse will call if there's anything we need to know straight away. Anything turn up to shed light on who's doing it?'

Àlex shook his head. 'Nothing. And with this weather, Científica can't do very much outside.'

They watched as two forensic officers in white coveralls dusted a table where a television set had once stood. One looked at the other and shook her head. Elisenda didn't expect them to find much that would be of any use.

Àlex's phone rang and he answered it. 'You can't be serious,' he muttered into it. 'OK, I'll be there now.'

'Problem?'

'Manel. He wants me to go outside and look at something. In this rain.'

Elisenda and Josep followed him outside, walking gingerly past the parked cars and through the mud towards the end of the drive. The ground underfoot was getting steadily more slippery, and they struggled to keep their feet.

'Better be worth it,' Josep shouted above the deafening noise.

At the end of the track, where they'd watched the ambulance join the main road, they saw a torchlight sweeping the area, the light from it reflecting against the thick rain back onto Manel, swatting about in the downpour.

'Never rains like this in Lleida,' he yelled at them as they arrived.

'You got me out here to tell me that?' Àlex called back.

Manel shook his head, his face swivelling comically from side to side inside the hood while the waterproof material stayed in the same position. Elisenda could see a laugh reach the corners of Josep's mouth. Manel shone the torch at a point over her right shoulder and, with his free hand, gestured to them to follow him back along the track. Grumbling over the roar of the rain, they turned and gingerly retraced their steps a short distance. He suddenly stopped and turned back to face them, shouting something, but his words were snatched away. Pointing again, this time behind them, he directed his torch at something.

'This had better be good,' Àlex shouted.

Elisenda already knew it would be.

Carved into the gnarled bark of a pine tree by the side of the main road next to the track leading to the house was a small triangle. It looked freshly made and was meant to be visible only if you knew what you were looking for. Projecting from the apex, two further cuts had been made, two lines sticking out of the top. It resembled the cairn of stones that Àlex had found on the ground near the house on Saturday night. Another cut had been made in the bark. A horizontal line scything through the middle of the triangle.

Manel shouted again, his voice barely audible.

'There's your symbol,' was all Elisenda heard.

He reached for the sleeping bag to pull it up and an intense, raw pain surged the length of his arm. Tears sprang instantly to his eyes and he gasped for breath. He tried moving his right arm again, more gingerly this time, and something cut into his wrist. More by touch than by sight, he discovered there was a thin metal ring clasped tightly around it.

He pulled it again, but it was attached to another ring. He felt it. A thick iron hoop set into the wall he recalled seeing when he'd first descended the ladder into the cellar. He had no idea how long ago that was now. Two days? Three? Without letting the thin metal ring move on his wrist, he tugged at the hoop. Gently at first, then more frantically, pushing it hopelessly first one way then the other. It was as solid as the wall holding it.

It was only as he leaned his head against the wall in despair that he registered the dull ache behind his eyes. When he closed them, the darkness behind the lids rushed in and out, making him feel he wanted to be sick. He quickly opened them again and the dizziness abated.

The water, he remembered.

He found the bottle with his right foot and lashed out at it, sending it skittering across the stone floor. He recalled feeling drowsy just a few minutes after gulping down great mouthfuls. He remembered it had tasted odd, but he'd thought that must have been because of the plastic. He knew now that his captor had drugged the water. In the darkness, he could make out the pedestal of crumbled steps and immediately knew why. He'd been getting closer and closer with his leaps to the bottom of the door. It must have worried his captor, who'd drugged him so that he could come down into the cellar and manacle him to the wall.

In his anger, he tugged with his whole arm at the ring, the thin metal cutting into the raw flesh of his wrist. Wincing with the pain, he leaned his head down to lick away the blood he could feel welling up around the metal. It tasted sharp but comforting. It soothed the wound.

'What is it you want with me?' he shouted in anger, but this time, no one came to look at him through the door.

He leant his face against the wall. He could feel a trickle of water running down it. The river beyond began its murmuring.

He closed his eyes again, ignoring the nausea, and cried.

Thursday

Chapter Twenty-Seven

'And how does that make you feel?'

Elisenda had no idea how any of it made her feel. What she did know was that if she stayed on the couch a moment longer, she'd be asleep, in spite of the studied discomfort of Doctora Puyals' torture furniture. Unwillingly, she closed her eyes for a moment and opened them immediately. She'd seen Lina again in that brief instant.

'You saw your daughter last night?' Puyals asked her. 'Your visions of her are becoming more distinct.'

Elisenda looked at the wall opposite her, at the jumble of the doctor's framed certificates dancing in front of her. She was dazed and replied without thinking.

'And this morning.'

'You saw her in your apartment this morning?'

Elisenda shook her head.

'Out. By the city walls when I was running. I stumbled on the rocks by the Torre Gironella and she was standing by the wall. She was just looking at me.'

'Did you hear her say anything?'

'She never says anything. I only hear her when I can't see her. When she sings.'

'How well did you sleep last night?'

Elisenda cast her mind back to the hours of darkness in her still unfamiliar redecorated flat. She'd spent the night on the sofa, wrapped in a sheet, watching out for the shadows flitting behind the paper screens. Looking one way when the sound of a lullaby suddenly floated at her from another. Softly crying in a way she never would in public.

'I didn't.'

'Do you think that might be why you had a vision of her when you were out? Because of your exhaustion?'

I don't know, Elisenda thought. Probably. She was already beginning to compose herself for work. If nothing else, the counselling sessions were acting as a decompression chamber between the dread of the night and the controlled mask of the day. Her eyes focused on the wall in front of her.

'Why so many certificates?' she asked, gesturing vaguely with one hand.

'Because I can help in so many different ways,' Puyals said after a pause. Elisenda imagined she heard the wry smile underpinning the counsellor's comment.

Needing to get off the lounger, she swivelled her legs to one side and stood up, the pins and needles instantly stinging her feet and calves like a column of red ants. Puyals made no move behind her and she walked forward to look more closely at the certificates on the wall. She turned and looked at Puyals, confident in her chair.

'They're bits of paper. And this is just talk. It's not doing any good.'

'Just talk? Have you talked to anyone else about your daughter before now, Elisenda?'

'No. What good does it do? I'm seeing Lina more than ever. That's why I've always kept it to myself. Telling someone about it just makes it worse for me.'

Puyals wrote something down on her pad and tore the page off. 'I'm setting you some homework that I want you to do.'

'Homework? Are you serious?'

The counsellor gave her the piece of paper. 'Yes. Are you?'

–

In the street outside, Elisenda remembered for the first time that the dentist she'd gone to as a child used to have his practice in the building over the road from the counsellor's. Another painful memory.

'At least he never used to ask you to talk,' she muttered angrily. She caught a man and a woman in summer office clothes looking at her talking to herself and pointed at her ear. 'Bluetooth.'

She hurried away from the Eixample and along Carrer Santa Clara, heading for the court buildings. Crossing Plaça Independència, she had to sidestep all the boxes and crates being delivered on unwieldy trolleys to the various bars and restaurants in their early-morning ritual of restocking for the day ahead. The clattering industry of the delivery lorries and of all the bleary people hurrying to work amid the enticing aromas emanating from the various doorways made her slow down momentarily. She looked longingly at a couple drinking huge cups of breakfast coffee on a café terrace and checked her watch. Not enough time. She had the pleasure of a morning appointment with Jutgessa Roca awaiting her. She expected the usual answer.

'No, Sotsinspectora Domènech, I cannot agree to this.'

Elisenda attempted not to roll her eyes in the judge's modern office and tried again.

'I think Francesc Bofarull could be of interest,' she insisted.

'Because he has a locked cellar in his house?'

Elisenda tapped on the form lying on the judge's desk requesting a warrant to search Bofarull's house. 'And because of everything we've set out here.'

'No, Sotsinspectora Domènech, and that's final.'

Defeated, Elisenda went back outside and breathed in the air. It hadn't rained so much in Girona the previous day, but the storm in the mountains outside had helped freshen the atmosphere in the city. It did little for her mood.

'So much for talking and doing your homework,' she muttered, crumpling the request for a warrant and stuffing it into her bag next to the piece of paper the counsellor had given her.

Past the traffic on the busy roundabout between where she was standing and the Devesa park, she saw a lot of coming and going under the slender, towering plane trees. It was odd, she thought, as Thursday wasn't market day, until she remembered the date. The coming weekend marked the commemoration of the sieges of Girona by the French in 1808 and 1809. First celebrated to mark the bicentenary, in recent years it had grown into a festival, with re-enactors doing battle through the streets of the old town and period tinkers and traders setting up shop in the park. It would all be kicking off tomorrow. Normally, she enjoyed it.

Her phone rang and she was surprised to see it was her mother.

'*Elisenda, call your sister. She's upset that you haven't answered her calls.*'

'I will, mama. It's just been a busy time.'

'*It's as though you don't want to see your new baby niece.*'

Elisenda promised she'd call and hung up, letting her breath out in a long sigh. A new pang hit her. Despite her resolve and all her arguments to the contrary, mostly to herself, she found seeing Catalina with her baby freshly harrowing every time, another reminder of her own loss. And the more she fought it, the more it hit her, a new splinter flaking off her brittle mask. She closed her eyes and quickly reopened them, filing the guilt away. Looking once more at all the activity under the trees, she turned away and hurried back towards the centre, past the jumble of posters freshly pasted the previous night clamouring for the city's vote on Sunday. Susanna Miravent looked blindly out at her, seeking her trust.

'We're all under siege,' Elisenda exhaled.

Chapter Twenty-Eight

The sky was a deep summer blue unblemished by a single cloud after the violent downpour of the previous day. Àlex opened the side window a few centimetres and took a deep breath of the sharp, crisp air that blasted in. He glanced across at Manel, silent for once, driving fast along the road to Cassà de la Selva, and closed his eyes, enjoying the almost overpowering force of the fresh wind blowing into his nostrils and filling his lungs. He slowed his own breathing down accordingly, relaxed. Something in the investigation felt like it had turned a corner and was finally heading in the right direction.

'Bollocks,' muttered Manel. 'Traffic lights.'

The caporal's voice and the rapid change down through gears brought Àlex out of his reverie. He opened his eyes and looked around. They were already in the small town on the main road from Girona to the southern end of its coast. Just a few minutes later, they reached their destination, the house that had been targeted on the Saturday night and that the two of them had checked out two days earlier. They parked by the side of the road where the drive led up to the house and began searching. Only this time, they were holding their gaze up, not scouring the ground.

'Not a single tree,' Manel said, frustration in his voice.

Àlex knew how he felt. There was no tree anywhere near enough for a symbol to have been carved into it. After last night's discovery of the markings on the pine by the house in the mountains not far from where they now were, it seemed like the whole theory was going to be blown out of the water at the first attempt to verify it.

'Try down that way a bit,' Àlex told Manel.

He watched him walk away, looking for anything a symbol could have been left on. Giving up, Manel waited for a lull in the traffic and ran across the road in case there was anything to be found on the other side of the road. Àlex's phone rang. It was Elisenda asking him how the search was going.

'Nothing.' He couldn't keep the disappointment out of his voice.

Hanging up, he noted a change in the air, a small vortex. He looked up to see a bus pulling away at speed from the nearby stop. Àlex stared at it. With its own short piece of slip-road, the shelter stood some fifteen metres from the entrance to the drive leading up to the house.

'Too far away?' Àlex asked himself, but it was the only construction, natural or artificial, near the house, and the house was the nearest to it of any of the other buildings nearby.

Walking quickly along the pavement towards it, he spotted Manel on the other side of the road waiting impatiently for a break in the traffic.

Standing on a low concrete plinth, the bus stop was a three-sided glass shelter with four round aluminium pillars at each corner and a flat aluminium roof, with a metal bench on the back wall. Advertising posters obscured both ends and a panel with routes and timetables was fastened to the glass at the rear. A low wall circumvented the back, an embankment holding back a landscape of fields and distant trees and power lines. A grey plastic litter bin stood on a post outside the shelter.

He quickly searched the construction, inside and out, looking for a symbol sprayed on or drawn in felt pen, but found nothing. Frustrated, he turned to see Manel finally crossing the road towards him.

'Nothing,' he told the caporal in annoyance before registering his expression.

'Gotcha.'

Manel was pointing at the strip of metal at the top of the stand, visible when you approached it in traffic if you knew what you were looking for. On the side nearest the road, someone had painted in black marker a triangle with two pins sticking out of the top and a horizontal line through the body of the figure.

Àlex looked at Manel and grinned.

'Gotcha.'

–

Àlex called Elisenda back to tell her about their find just as she was entering Vista Alegre. She hung up, happy at any small breakthrough with the house attacks, and hurried along the corridors to Puigventós' office. Sotsinspector Armengol was already there when she arrived. For a brief moment, she was relieved that she wasn't the last to show up, but then she remembered that Micaló wasn't going to be at the morning meeting for the heads of the various investigation units. He was still off learning all manner of new things on his course. Not all bad, then, she thought.

'I've got a warrant from Jutgessa Roca,' Armengol told her and Puigventós.

Scratch that, she amended.

'She just gave you a warrant?' she demanded.

Armengol looked surprised. Both he and Elisenda had given progress reports on their various investigations and he had told her about the second sex offender questioned at the time of the first boy's disappearance.

'He's since left Girona and is living in Celrà. I've got a warrant to question him and search his house.'

'And Roca went along with it?'

Armengol nodded, evidently mystified by Elisenda's irritation. 'I'll let you know what we find,' he told her uncertainly.

She murmured a vague thank you.

'Any other business?' Puigventós interrupted them.

'I'm concerned there's been no demand made,' Elisenda told him. 'It worries me we're not looking in the right place. We need more uniforms out; I want them to retrace the search around the school for anything they might have missed. Check up on Jaume's favourite places, in case he's the one that's absconded.'

Puigventós sighed. 'Anything else, Elisenda?'

'Yes, I want uniforms talking to people in the street, here and outside Girona. Someone must have seen something or thought something was unusual. We just need to trigger that memory.'

'I'll do what I can,' the inspector promised her.

'I'll keep on top of Sabadell,' Armengol added. 'They're getting people sending them sightings. I've got my unit and Sotsinspector Micaló's team looking into them, but there's been nothing substantial yet.'

'One other thing,' Elisenda said. 'Marc Comas's mugging.'

'You think it's significant?' Puigventós asked.

'I think we have to regard it as significant. It's quite a coincidence that he should be attacked just after his son has gone missing. I've spoken to him about the attack and I get the feeling that there is something he's not saying. Again, I could do with help from the Local Investigation Unit with any known muggers, if only to rule them out.'

'Only too happy,' Armengol told her. 'I'll let you know what we turn up.'

Elisenda thanked him again and Puigventós called the meeting to an end. He asked her to stay when the other sotsinspector left the room.

'How's the counselling going?' the inspector asked her.

'Well.'

'You're sure of that?'

'I'd sooner be getting on with my job, if that's what you mean. Has Doctora Puyals said anything?'

Puigventós smiled. 'She said you were challenging. I think we can interpret that any way we want.'

Elisenda left his office. 'Challenging,' she muttered. 'Good.'

Back in her own unit's offices, she called Josep and Montse into her room and told them of Àlex's phone call.

'So he and Manel are checking up on other houses to make sure these symbols are real and to look for a pattern.' She turned to Montse. 'Did the victims' statements throw up anything we don't know?'

Montse shook her head. 'The husband's injuries were so severe, he's in an induced coma. The doctors couldn't tell me how long for. I took a statement from the wife. She said the attackers had their faces covered at all times, two of them spoke Spanish in a South American accent, one in what she called a foreign accent and another one in a Spanish accent.'

'So nothing we haven't already heard. Where is she now?'

'Still at the hospital. She refuses to leave until she knows her husband's going to be all right.'

Elisenda turned talk to the missing boy. She told them about her interview with Marc Comas after he was mugged and about Armengol's unit looking at convicted muggers.

'There's something not right about it, so we're going to be looking at the mugging from the point of view of his son's disappearance. Josep, I want you to check up on anything in his professional life that would indicate that someone might abduct his son. This might not be to do with Susanna Miravent's political career but with her husband's work. David Costa from the newspaper told me something about his involvement in corruption. He didn't seem to have much, but I'll be talking to him again to find out more.'

Josep nodded, but it was Montse that spoke. 'I've got to go out to interview Narcís Pujol. He's the second of Jaume's friends that he fell out with. I spoke to the first one yesterday, but I didn't get much from him. He was with his parents and didn't say much. I'm seeing Pujol with his tutor at the school, so I'm hoping he might open up more.'

Elisenda picked up her bag, noticing again Siset's on the filing cabinet. 'I'll come with you. I want to see for myself how far the school or someone there might be involved.'

'I'll check up on Comas to see if there really is any suspicion of corruption,' Josep told her.

Elisenda sighed. 'And then there's still Miravent and the elections and Bofarull and his locked cellar. There are just so many strands to this and we don't know which is the right one to pull.' She looked at the two caporals. 'So we might as well just pull the lot, see what falls out of the tree.'

'Until we find another one we hadn't seen,' Josep muttered as he left the room, his head bowed.

Chapter Twenty-Nine

'Of course, we still haven't got a clue what they mean. Or where they're going to happen next. Or when. Or how we're going to catch the bastards who're doing it.'

Manel didn't take his eyes off the road as he spoke. Àlex looked across at him, a half-smile of wonderment on his lips.

'Do you know, Manel, I'm beginning to like you. You make Josep look like an optimist.'

Manel shrugged, lifting his right thumb off the wheel while still looking straight in front. 'That's good.'

Àlex turned back to face the road ahead and tried not to laugh. They were crossing the lowlands by Sant Pere Pescador. To their right, the Mediterranean lay hidden beyond a wetland reserve, saved from the depredations of an earlier construction boom. To their left, they were being shadowed by row upon row of apple orchards, stretching along the coast and inland for kilometres. After the house by Cassà de la Selva, they'd checked a second house, the one where the owner had installed cameras, fences and a panic room. The new guard dog had barked once when they'd pulled up.

'He's filled the gap in the fence,' Manel had commented, standing at the entrance, looking at the perimeter through binoculars at the perimeter.

They hadn't gone up to the house out of a desire not to spook the man even more. Instead, they'd stayed at the start of the drive, where they'd found the symbol almost immediately. It was on a cypress tree on the left-hand side of the drive. Carved into the bark at waist height was another triangle, this time with three pins sticking out of the top.

'What's the significance of the two or three sticks at the point of the pyramid?' Àlex asked again as the orchards slipped by on both sides now. 'Or triangle, or whatever it's supposed to be.'

'We don't know that, either.'

Àlex did let out a laugh this time. 'Another thing we don't know is why go to the bother of the symbols in the first place.'

'They're checking out places for future reference? Come back and rob them later?'

'So why not just write down the address?'

Manel shrugged. 'They'll have a reason.'

Alex turned away. Out of his side window, he saw teams of workers picking the apples. Different groups in different fields working up and down the rows of trees. At the end, near the road, lorries waited to take away the tall stacks of wooden crates piled up at the start of alternate columns. It was a quietly industrious scene.

'At least I'm getting to know the area,' Manel suddenly said, gesturing with one hand at the orchards around them. Ahead of them, in the distance, the Pyrenees stood out bold against the blue sky. Àlex waited for the usual but-it's-still-not-as-good-as-Lleida comment but none came. 'Where are we?'

'Just past Sant Pere Pescador, in the Alt Empordà county,' Àlex told him. 'The first house was in La Selva county, the second was in the Baix Empordà county, and we're now in the Alt Empordà, where the last house we're checking out is.'

'The nice one way up in the mountains? The proper mountains?'

'That's the one. They're the three counties that follow the coast.'

Manel grunted at that, his interest in his new home over for the day. Past the lowlands, they climbed once again into the Albera mountains. A buzzard was perched on the same section of stone wall as two days earlier. Àlex was convinced it was the same bird. This time, knowing what to look for, he noticed more Neolithic burial chambers on the steep slopes rising above him. The last time they came, the slabs had blended in with the natural stones and he hadn't spotted them. The same was true of the symbol by the house, he realised. With no trees nearby to check and without the distraction of focusing on looking for an artificial cairn of small stones, they looked instead at the rocks and boulders either side of the track leading to the house.

'Got it,' Àlex said.

It was painted in black on the side of a large mottled grey boulder, more visible from the other direction than from the way they came, but easy to find once they knew what they were looking for.

'Just one stick this time,' Manel said.

Sure enough, there was just one line protruding from the top of the triangle. As he had with the previous symbols, Àlex took photos of it on his mobile and they left.

'Just satisfy my curiosity,' he said to Manel when they were getting nearer Girona.

Taking a detour, they took a look at the house that they'd originally staked out on the Saturday. It seemed ages ago. By the look of it, the architect couple who owned it had still not moved back. They stopped and examined the ground. The cairn they'd found that night had gone.

'They've removed it?' Manel asked.

'Or last night's rain did. It's impossible to tell.'

The downpour had opened up small channels in the earth on the track leading to the house where the rainwater had drained into the ditch by the main road. A trail of pebbles had been deposited on the asphalt, carried there by the localised flood. A couple of new potholes had been gouged into the ground too.

Àlex looked up and down the road. 'No trees, no bus stops, no posts. That's why they marked the symbol with a cairn. There's nowhere else to leave it. It's not how they normally do it.'

Manel followed his gaze and sniffed. 'We still haven't got a clue what they mean, though,' he muttered. 'Or what we're going to do with it.'

'They need to turn the air conditioning down,' Elisenda complained. 'It's glacial in here.'

'That's not the air conditioning,' Montse replied.

They were in the same interview room in Jaume's school as Montse had been shown to the previous day. The same secretary had ushered them in with the words that Joaquim Benach, Jaume's tutor, would be with them shortly. The head teacher, Father Besses, had greeted them aloofly when Montse had introduced him to Elisenda in the mock-ancient cloisters when they'd arrived. He seemed unhappy at their presence in his school, containing his emotions as a subdued line of children in overlarge start-of-year uniforms shuffled past them. They'd watched him march off at the head of the little column.

'Glad I went to a state school,' Montse had muttered.

'If only because of the clothes,' Elisenda had agreed. Unlike most private schools, state secondary schools didn't require students to wear a uniform.

The door to the rather ascetic interview room opened and Benach came in, carrying a tray with four cups and saucers on it. Steam coiled up from each cup, carrying a waft of coffee on the air.

'I know, I know,' he announced to them. 'I spoil you.'

He was preceded into the room by a teenaged boy in the school uniform of powder blue polo shirt bearing the school's crest and dark grey trousers, in his case long trousers, unlike the knee-length shorts the younger boys in the cloisters had been wearing. He walked in and sat down at one of the chairs, not waiting for Benach to take his place. He had fine dark brown hair over a savvy face, and black-rimmed glasses threatening to fall off a button nose that gave a child-like air to an otherwise confident expression. His naturally golden complexion was toasted after the long summer holiday, his parents evidently not of a new generation worried about the effects of the sun on young skin.

Benach busied himself handing out the cups of coffee and sat down. 'This is Narcís Pujol,' he introduced the boy. 'His parents have consented to my being present while you ask him about Jaume.'

'Thank you,' Elisenda said, introducing herself to the tutor. She turned to the boy and thanked him too.

'There's very little I can tell you,' Pujol told her. His voice was surprisingly deep, only adding to the aura of self-confidence he exuded. 'I've had very little to do with Comas since the summer.'

'Can I ask why you fell out with each other?'

The boy took a sip of his coffee. In that moment, Elisenda could see the adult he'd turn into, the unhurried entitlement in his attitude.

'He changed friends. That's all. He chose to sit with that little weed Pascual instead of with us.'

'There must have been a reason,' Montse insisted.

'You'd have to ask him that. Or Pascual. We didn't have an argument. He just came back after the summer holiday and started hanging out with Pascual instead of with his usual friends.'

'Maybe he outgrew you,' Elisenda said, pushing him a little bit.

He laughed. 'Outgrew me? Hardly. If anything, it was the opposite. But he'll come back with his tail between his legs as soon as he sees that no one likes Pascual.'

'You seem more upset than you try to make out,' Montse commented.

He turned his glance lazily towards her. 'Not really. As I said, he'll soon get sick of his new best friend.'

'So why are you so worried he went off with another friend?' Elisenda pushed him. 'Were you bullying him because of it?'

Elisenda could sense Benach growing uncomfortable with the way her questions were going, but she ignored him.

Pujol's eyes flickered briefly. 'Bullying Comas? Have you ever met him? He's the tallest boy in our year. No one bullied Jaume.'

'Were you bullying Carles Pascual, then?' Montse asked. 'And Jaume didn't like it?'

Elisenda knew the answer to that one. Not while Carles was Jaume's friend, he wouldn't dare. 'Have we got this the wrong way around?' she asked him. 'Was he bullying you? Is that why you felt you had to bring him down a peg or two?'

The boy looked surprised. 'What do you mean?'

Elisenda leaned across the table. 'What do you know about his disappearance, Narcís? Was his changing friends part of bullying you? Were you forced to do something to defend yourself?'

'I must say I'm not comfortable with this line of questioning,' Benach suddenly spoke up. 'Should Narcís's parents be present?'

Elisenda studied the boy's shocked expression and turned to smile at the tutor. 'That's really not necessary.'

'I am able to answer questions,' Pujol snapped at the teacher without looking at him.

Benach exchanged a look with Montse and rolled his eyes slightly.

'What do you know about Jaume's disappearance, Narcís?' Elisenda asked again, her tone softer.

The boy looked back at her, his confidence only partially restored. 'Nothing. I've barely spoken to him since the new year started.'

'But you argued.'

'Who told you that? It wasn't an argument. We just had a bit of a go at each other playing basketball. It wasn't anything serious. We were always arguing, but we always stayed friends. He just hangs out with Pascual because Pascual's impressed by him. Jaume likes to be the centre of attention, so he sits with someone like Pascual because he'll hang onto his every word.'

'Has he always been like that?'

Opening up now, Pujol rolled his eyes. 'Always. Especially since his brother died. His parents give him everything he wants so everyone wants to be his friend. And his mother's on TV all the time.'

'Where do you think Jaume is, Narcís?' Elisenda asked him. 'You've been a friend of his for a long time. Is there somewhere he'd go if he needed to?'

Pujol shook his head, thinking. 'I can't think of anywhere. They always go to La Fosca in the summer. They've got a house on the beach.'

Elisenda nodded. The house and the one owned by Carles Pascual's family and the surrounding area had already been searched thoroughly. 'Is your family in Opus Dei, Narcís?'

Benach took a deep intake of air at that but Elisenda waved a hand at him to calm him.

'And Carles Pascual? Is his family Opus Dei? Is that why Jaume no longer sits with you.'

'No, that's not why,' Pujol said.

Before he could say any more, Benach put both hands flat on the table. 'I'm sorry, Sotsinspectora Domènech, but I think I'm going to have to terminate the interview here. This is irrelevant and beyond what I understood you were going to be asking.'

'Are you?' Elisenda asked again, looking at Pujol.

He nodded. 'But Pascual isn't.'

Benach stood up. 'I must ask you to leave. If you wish to pursue this line of question, I think Narcís's parents should be present to give their consent.'

Elisenda gathered her bag and stood up. 'Thank you, Senyor Benach. And might I ask if you're a member of Opus Dei?'

'This is irrelevant.'

Elisenda stood in front of him as he tried to usher them out of the room. 'I will decide what is relevant.'

She and Montse walked back in the warm sunshine to the pool car parked outside the school gates.

'Do you think it is?' Montse asked. 'Relevant, I mean? The whole Opus Dei thing?'

Elisenda gazed out across the plain to the distant mountains. 'I don't know. Maybe not directly. But every now and then you have to shake a few branches to see what falls out of the tree. What I don't see is that this is anything to do with a couple of schoolkids falling out with each other. There's more to it than that.'

They were almost by the car when Elisenda's phone rang. She looked at the screen and mouthed 'Josep' at Montse before answering. She listened to him speak for a few moments and then hung up.

'You know we were complaining about so many strands to this investigation?' she told Montse. 'Well Josep's just found another. Someone else we apparently need to talk to seems to have gone missing.'

Chapter Thirty

'Pere Vergés Gumbau.'

Elisenda shook her head at the name Josep gave her. 'Don't know him.'

'Convicted of fraud. Arrested just under four years ago, came to trial three years ago and came out of prison last Friday.'

They were standing in their unit's outer office. Elisenda and Montse had gone straight to Vista Alegre from Jaume's school once they'd got the phone call from Josep. The inside of the station felt cold and gloomy after the bright after-storm sunlight of the day outside.

'Less than four years for fraud?' Montse questioned.

'Out on appeal,' Josep told them. 'He was retried last week and the conviction thrown out. Released on the Friday.'

'So why's he of interest to us?' Elisenda asked.

Josep sat down at a desk and called up a screen on the computer to show them. 'I've been checking anyone reported missing in the last week and his name came up, so I took a look at him. He worked for the IT department at the city council.'

'The city council? Where Marc Comas works.'

'A different department, but still a link of some sort,' Josep agreed. 'An external audit about four years ago turned up a fraud. Money was being paid to a series of providers that supposedly worked with the council, but the audit showed that although the providers existed, they'd never had any dealings with the council. There were invoices for services that had got through internal audits, but they turned out to be fake. And the amounts invoiced were only ever for small sums that individually wouldn't have been questioned. It was only when they were taken as a whole by the external auditor that a pattern of fraud was noticed. They looked further and found that the accounts the money was paid into had nothing to do with the providers; instead they were temporary accounts each time in different banks and the money was then transferred onwards each time the account was closed. The second transfer was always offshore.'

'And it was all traced back to this Pere Vergés?'

'It was at the time. The fraud did seem to come from the IT department, and specifically from computers he had access to. But he always denied it. The thing is they've never been able to trace the trail of accounts beyond the second transfer and the missing money has never been recovered. Vergés has certainly never had any unexplained income traced to him. I've looked at the original trial and it really wasn't a safe conviction. The evidence was so flimsy and circumstantial, I really don't see how he was found guilty in the first place.'

'Was it investigated by the Mossos?'

Josep pulled up another screen. 'The Regional Investigation Unit investigated it.'

'Micaló's lot? Oh please let it be my lucky day.'

Josep smiled wryly and shook his head. He was sitting confident and tall in his chair, his head at the same height as Elisenda's and Montse's even though they were standing. 'Sorry. This was under Sotsinspector Micaló's predecessor, a couple of years before he took over.'

Elisenda sighed. 'I knew that really, but a girl can dream.'

'But as I said, Pere Vergés always denied any involvement in the fraud,' Josep continued, 'and he won a retrial last year, which has just been held. And that found no real evidence to link him to any of it, so his conviction was quashed.'

'And you think he's now out of prison, wanting to know who put him there,' Elisenda surmised. 'After waiting a year for the original hearing and the best part of a year for the retrial. It might fit.'

The time a defendant could wait until their case came to trial had improved a lot in recent years, but it was still a slow and laborious process. She recalled as a child a case that her father was involved in, when a man spent two years in prison awaiting a hearing for an offence that carried a one-year sentence. He was found guilty, sentenced and released all on the same day with no compensation for the extra year's imprisonment.

'What's happening with the investigation into the missing money?' Montse asked.

'When Vergés was convicted, the Mossos continued to look but haven't turned up anything, so it eventually became a cold case and slipped down the list of priorities. But you can be sure that with his release, it'll come back to the fore again.'

Elisenda sighed. 'I hope they give it to Micaló, not us.'

'You said he'd gone missing,' Montse prompted.

'Apparently he saw his lawyer on Monday morning about an application for compensation. He was supposed to return the following day but didn't. He was also supposed to see the judge with his lawyer yesterday about his release, but he didn't show up to that either.' Josep nodded at the computer screen. 'That's why he's come up on the system. The court flagged up that he failed to show. Otherwise we wouldn't have got to hear of it.'

'Who's his lawyer?' Elisenda asked. 'They may be worth talking to.'

Josep failed to hide a smile as he turned to face Elisenda. 'Gerard Bellsolà.'

She hung her head. 'Two Bellsolàs in one week. That's just living the dream.'

'I take it no one's seen him at home?' Montse asked.

'That hasn't been checked yet. The court hasn't asked the Mossos to follow it up, so officially he's not missing, and his name's only just come up in our investigation. No one's been to his house yet. I'll get Seguretat Ciutadana to pay a call.'

Elisenda took a note of Vergés's address. 'Don't. We'll go. This might be nothing, but it's at least worth ruling him in or out of the investigation. We could also go and see Marc Comas again. If he and Vergés did know each other, it'll be interesting to hear what Comas has to say about it. Anyway, I want to ask him again about the attack on him. This guy Vergés might not turn out to be at all significant, but we need to check it out. Are Àlex and Manel back, by the way?'

'Still out, checking up on the houses that have been attacked.'

'Let me know when they get back.'

'There's one other thing about Vergés,' Josep added. 'Before his conviction, he lived with his mother. She died when he was in prison. Earlier this year. He wasn't released for her funeral.'

Elisenda looked shocked. 'Why wasn't he released? Especially if his application for a retrial had been accepted.'

'That's one more reason for him to want to settle a score,' Montse commented.

Elisenda considered everything they'd been looking at. 'OK, let's not get ahead of ourselves with this. But if he really is out to settle a score, it would be interesting to see who he blames.'

–

'Driving in Girona,' Elisenda muttered, a helpless mantra everyone in the city knew.

'This part of town's the worst,' Montse agreed, pointing the car's cold airflow at her face to stay cool.

They'd driven round the same block in the Eixample three times, looking for somewhere to park, before a spanking new white Mercedes left them a space outside a boutique bakery in the ever-expanding squares of the one-way system. Getting out, Elisenda sucked in a deep breath of the aromas of fresh, warm bread trying to entice her into the baker's. She closed her eyes and pictured her apartment in winter, the new wood-burning fireplace she'd had installed and not yet used crackling as she crunched into a toasted slice of *pa de pagès* country bread.

'Elisenda,' Montse called, shaking her out of her daydream.

'The smell from that baker's,' she murmured.

Montse looked at the window display and shrugged. 'Bread. Never touch it.'

'And that's one more reason why running's just so wrong,' Elisenda told her.

They walked in silence the short distance to the apartment block in the narrow and affluent canyon of Carrer Migdia. Oddly, Elisenda felt her reaction to the smells coming from the shop was a small victory. A return to an older, more sensuous and sybaritic version of herself that had been in abeyance for so many years. She wondered for a moment if the sessions with Doctora Puyals maybe were doing her some good. That was something she'd never admit.

Inside the block they wanted, they climbed a dingy stairwell to the fourth floor, the timer on the landing lights ticking down loudly. Unfortunately, there was no porter in the block, so no one to have a key to open the door for them should they need it. It was nearly lunchtime, and cooking smells pervaded each landing, some enticing, some not. On the third floor, they heard the rhythmic beating of a metal spoon on a ceramic bowl coming from inside one of the apartments.

'Someone's having omelette for lunch,' Montse commented.

'Go nicely with that bread,' Elisenda teased her.

No one answered the door to Pere Vergés's apartment. Elisenda rang for the fourth time, but she couldn't hear a bell inside, so she also banged on the ornate wooden door, realising it was pointless. Crossing the landing, she knocked on the door opposite and waited until footsteps shuffled up to the door and someone evidently examined her through the spyhole.

'Mossos d'Esquadra,' she said in a loud voice. 'We'd like to ask you about your neighbour, Pere Vergés.'

The door chain rattled and it was opened by an elderly woman wearing canvas sandals and a blue cotton housecoat. She held herself up with the aid of a stick.

'He's not here,' she told them. She looked down the stairwell to her left and lowered her voice to a stage whisper. 'He's been in prison, you know.'

'Yes, we did know that. Might we come in?'

Elisenda and Montse showed the woman their ID and she led them into a flat that had last been decorated in the late 1970s. Chunky wooden furniture on light brown terrazzo tiles flecked with dark brown and grey. She went to the kitchen to make coffee while they sat themselves down in a living room cluttered with framed photographs and fading memories. The woman's husband was sitting in an armchair, the sofas and chairs perhaps the only pieces of furniture in the room that were younger than Montse. He greeted them and apologised for not getting up.

'Not very gallant,' he told them, 'but I'm old and buggered and I don't move so easily anymore.'

'Not a worry,' Elisenda reassured him, a laugh in her voice.

The wife came in and set a tray down with steaming cups of coffee. 'Language,' she warned her husband. He pulled a face at Elisenda but smiled a toothless devotion at his wife and squeezed her hand when she sat down next to him.

'It's Pere Vergés you're after?' the husband asked them.

'He was at home all weekend,' the wife added. 'He came back on Friday after he came out of prison.' Again, she whispered the last word.

'But we heard him go out on Monday and he hasn't been back since.' The husband's turn to speak.

As witnesses, Elisenda realised, they were gold.

'What time was that?'

'First time was in the morning,' the wife told her. 'About ten o'clock. He was wearing a suit. I saw him through the spyhole when he left.'

That was most likely when he was going to see his lawyer, Elisenda realised.

'He came back at noon,' the husband continued. 'She saw that, too. Through her spyhole.'

The wife slapped his thigh in rebuke.

'And the second time?' Elisenda asked.

'Twenty to five,' the husband told them, no shadow of doubt in his voice.

'*La Riera* was just finishing,' the wife explained, a home-grown soap on television that had all the daytime crowd talking.

'Load of bollocks, but she loves it.'

'Language,' the wife told him, but without any conviction. If anything, Elisenda saw an indulgent smile on her face.

'You wouldn't know where he was going?' she asked them. 'Or what he was wearing?'

The wife shook her head. 'We only heard him that time. I did, anyway, this one's deaf as a doornail.'

'Did anyone come to see him in the meantime?' Montse asked this time.

'Nothing,' the husband told her, gesturing with his thumb to his wife. 'This one would have heard.

'And you haven't seen him since?'

They both shook their heads, the pair of them reaching at the same time for their coffee cups and taking a sip. His was a long and noisy gulp, hers a repeated pecking at the rim like an inquisitive bird.

'How did he seem to you over the weekend?'

'Oh, we didn't talk to him,' the wife told Elisenda. 'We never really had much to do with him when he lived here.'

'Bit full of himself,' the husband explained. 'We weren't good enough.'

'Although I saw him coming through the downstairs door on Sunday morning,' the wife said. 'He was just coming in as I was leaving. I went out to get bread and cakes for breakfast and the newspaper. He said hello nicely enough. Didn't seem as sure of himself as he used to.'

'Prison will have done that to him,' the husband said.

'Language.'

'I understand his mother died earlier this year,' Elisenda changed tack. 'Did she speak much about her son?'

'His mother?' the wife said surprisingly vehemently. 'Oh no, she never spoke to us.'

'Stuck-up cow,' the husband added.

'Language. They both thought they were a cut above the rest of us on the staircase, you see. Neither of them ever used to come to the residents' association meetings. They did everything by letter. Inside the building, can you imagine?'

'Their sort are like that,' the husband muttered.

'Their sort?' Elisenda asked.

He took another gulp of his coffee, his movements painfully slow. 'You know. Their sort. Think they're so much better than the rest of us.'

'All the good it did them,' the wife offered. 'None of their lot wanted to know them after the son was sent to you-know-where.'

'I'm afraid I don't know what you mean,' Elisenda said, mystified.

'Opus,' the husband said simply. 'They were Opus Dei.'

Chapter Thirty-One

'Is Bellsolà Opus Dei?' Montse asked her as they climbed on foot up the cobblestones of the narrow and embracing Carrer de la Força. They'd decided to pay Pere Vergés's lawyer a visit after all once they'd heard he was Opus like Miravent and Comas.

Elisenda laughed. 'No. Our Gerard's much too worldly and pragmatic for that, although that's not always a barrier to membership. You have to be careful, or you end up seeing Opus in everyone and everything.'

Montse mumbled an agreement. 'I've heard more about Opus Dei in the last two days than I have in my life before now. Except in the movies.'

'You see. Girona. We did it first.'

'You sound just like Manel with his beloved Lleida,' Montse accused her.

They laughed and sidestepped a string of elderly American tourists emerging from the Jewish history museum, checking their purchases from the gift shop. Gerard Bellsolà had his legal practice a few metres further up the incline and on the left. An unremarkable doorway in a fourteenth-century building led into a tiny and tranquil courtyard. Just one single oblong of light shone down from the open square of sky above and illuminated a potted palm, its fronds still in the quiet air, dust motes floating in suspension around it. A powerful red BMW motorbike stood incongruous on the ancient flagstones, a sleeping modern beast in its medieval lair. To the right of the patio, a flight of ornate stone steps behind a banister of carved curlicues and mythical animals led along the side wall and continued up the rear to the first floor.

They climbed as far as a heavy wooden door into an office and announced themselves to a snooty receptionist with a lacquered helmet of dark blond hair seated behind the protection of a high-fronted desk.

'Senyor Bellsolà will see you,' she told them after a few moments in which she didn't appear to have told anyone of their presence.

'I know he will,' Elisenda replied with a smile. 'We know the way.'

The lawyer was sitting behind a huge and old-fashioned mahogany partners' desk, even though he occupied the splendid oak-panelled room on his own. Probably from his grandfather's day, Elisenda thought, the first in the dynasty of lawyers to blight the city. Despite the grandeur of the office, she always found it uncomfortable, one of those rooms where no matter how many lights and lamps you put in, it was still dingy. She forever had to fight the urge to look around for more switches to press.

'Pere Vergés,' Elisenda announced, taking a seat. 'You were representing him.'

Bellsolà didn't make eye contact with the two women, checking something on his computer instead. 'What of it?'

'I understand it was in relation to compensation.'

'You know perfectly well that client confidentiality means I don't have to answer that question, Sotsinspectora.'

'Your client has been missing since Monday,' Elisenda told him patiently. 'He missed an appointment with you and he missed an appointment with the judge. Does that not concern you?'

Finally, Bellsolà looked at her to reply. 'My client has spent nearly four years in prison for a crime he didn't commit. I understand that he may need some time before continuing with his application for compensation.'

'Have you spoken to him since Monday?'

'Client confidentiality, Sotsinspectora.'

Elisenda sighed, determined to remain calm. 'He has gone missing, Gerard. His neighbours haven't seen him since Monday.

It may be a cause for concern. Did he say anything to you that might make you think there was something worrying him?'

'I repeat, he had just spent four years in prison and he was innocent. Isn't that cause enough for worry?'

'Gerard, I am just trying to do my job, protecting your client. Without compromising client confidentiality, you can tell me something that would help me ensure his safety. I need to find him. I need to know his state of mind. You know as well as I do that I could get a judge to order you to release the details of your meetings with him.'

Bellsolà laughed, a coarse, confident bark. 'You believe a judge would do that.' He paused and took a deep breath. 'Listen, he did ring me on Monday afternoon. He said he wasn't sure he wanted to go ahead with the application for the time being. Now if you don't mind, I have other clients, and that's all I'll tell you.'

'What about his manner? Did he seem agitated?'

The lawyer looked for the right words. 'He seemed distracted. That's all I can say.'

Elisenda tried a further few questions, but the lawyer had clammed up. She realised they were going to get nothing more out of him.

Outside, once the meeting was over, Elisenda and Montse walked back down the narrow cobbled street.

'I always feel I want to scream out loud after talking to Bellsolà,' Elisenda commented.

'I need to go for a long run,' Montse agreed.

'Screaming out loud's better.'

They crossed the footbridge leading to Plaça Independència. The river below them was flowing faster and deeper than usual, the water swollen by the rainfall in the mountains. Elisenda could just make out a couple of large carp in the muddy, swirling water, their mouths gaping open to catch the flies and insects washed towards them in the low flood. The sun was high in a crystalline sky over the exposed bridge and there was no breeze to soften the high temperature. She took her jacket off and slung it over her shoulder.

'Do you think Vergés could be our guy?' Montse asked her as they neared the square on the other side.

'I don't know yet. I think we need to find out a bit more about him, and where he is, before we start seeing him as a suspect.'

They waited until a group of four businesspeople walked past them, all of them wearing clothes that were too warm for the sunny outside world but that were perfect for the air-conditioned offices where they worked. One of them caught Elisenda's eye and took off her jacket as she walked, smiling in over-heated sympathy.

'The thing that I find odd,' Elisenda carried on once they'd passed, 'is why Vergés decided not to go ahead with seeking compensation. If you've just spent four years in prison and you really are innocent, surely the one thing you'd make sure you did was get some recompense for it.'

'Or revenge?' Montse asked. 'Maybe that became more important to him.'

'If that's so, what made him change his mind? He came out of prison and started the ball rolling to get compensation, but then something happened to make him want revenge instead. What would that be?'

'And why not just carry on with the compensation claim, anyway?'

'Could be he thinks he needs to keep a low profile because he's planning on doing something. We need to talk to him.'

'So what do we do now?' Montse asked.

'Now? Now we go and talk to Marc Comas and Susanna Miravent to see if they can tell us anything about Pere Vergés.'

-

The house in Palau was guarded by two bored-looking Mossos and besieged by a hard core of journalists and TV crews growing impatient with the relative lack of movement.

'Can you tell us if it's paedophile-related, inspectora?' one of the press shouted from the other side of the road.

Elisenda grimaced at the mosso who had called through to the house for the gate to be opened and got out of the car for a brief moment. She knew she had to say something to quell any easy backlash.

'We feel that that line of enquiry is unlikely,' she told the gathered reporters, who had all stood up and were craning forward on the opposite pavement, 'and the Mossos are grateful to you all for your professionalism at this time.'

Ignoring a barrage of questions lobbed over the road at her, she got back in the car and Montse sped into the drive.

'But how long that will last is anybody's guess,' Elisenda muttered to her caporal.

They found Miravent in the living room in discussion with Bofarull. They were talking about the election and a live televised debate she was scheduled to take part in that evening.

'Do you think that's wise?' Elisenda asked her.

'We live in a democracy,' the politician replied when they were shown into the room by the maid. 'I would be failing in my duty if I allowed this matter to prevent democracy being served.'

'This matter?'

'Do you have any news for us, Sotsinspectora?' Miravent asked them. Without waiting for a reply, she spoke to the maid without looking at her. 'Coffee for everyone, please, Encarna.'

Elisenda introduced her to Montse, as it was the first time the caporal had met the politician. 'We have some,' she told Miravent. 'Might we ask where your husband is?'

'He's in his study.' She turned to Bofarull. 'Would you go and get him, please, Francesc?'

'And if you'd care to return also,' Elisenda added as he left.

The three women sat down on the sofas, the silence uneasy between Elisenda and Miravent since their last conversation.

'I presume no one has contacted you about Jaume,' Montse said, more to break the impasse while they waited than out of any real enquiry.

'Nothing.'

Besides the two Mossos at the gate and a third one inside the house, there were two Científica set up in a spare bedroom with recording equipment, monitoring incoming calls and there to alert Elisenda the moment anyone did make contact to say they were holding Jaume. She knew they'd heard nothing. What the Mossos didn't have was any access to Miravent or Comas's mobile phones, her request to monitor them turned down by both the couple and Jutgessa Roca. She had to take it on faith, Miravent's magic word, that they would tell her of any phone call to their mobiles that they received about their missing son. There were days she grew tired of the people supposedly there to help her proving to be the greatest hindrance.

Comas came into the room, followed by Bofarull, and sat down on the same sofa as his wife but at the opposite end. The campaign manager remained standing, with the window behind him. Comas was more composed than he had been the previous day and much of his self-confidence was back.

'How are your fingers?' Elisenda asked him, gesturing to his splinted and heavily-bandaged hand.

He looked at it before answering. 'Sore. And itching like hell.'

Miravent bristled at his last word. Not for the first time, Elisenda got the impression that where the wife's faith was more genuine, if rather intense and distasteful to Elisenda's view of life, the husband's appeared to be a lot more pragmatic.

'Have you had any more thoughts about the attack on you?' Montse asked him.

He shrugged. His self-deprecating smile was almost boyish, one that he evidently knew from experience usually won people over. 'A mugging. I was in the wrong place at the wrong time.'

'I see you've replaced your phone,' Elisenda commented. In reply, Comas waved a new mobile at her. 'I presume it's the same number.' He nodded and she continued. 'Really we're here about what we see as a development in Jaume's disappearance. A man called Pere Vergés has come to our attention.'

As she spoke, Elisenda watched Comas closely for his reaction. She knew that Montse would be studying Miravent. It was the husband who spoke first.

'Vergés? Why would he have anything to do with this?'

'You know him, then?' Elisenda asked.

'Of course. It was quite a scandal. He worked in computers at the city council. I never really had much to do with him at work because I'm in a different department, but he seemed all right. It came as a bit of a shock when he was found stealing.'

'His conviction has been overturned,' Elisenda told him. 'He was released from prison on Friday.'

'Oh yes, I know. But still, no smoke without fire, as they say.'

'Have you heard from him since his release? Has he been to the city council offices? Or called you?'

Comas shook his head. 'No, I haven't seen him since he was imprisoned.'

'Senyora Miravent?' Montse asked. 'Do you also know Pere Vergés?'

The politician seemed to be weighing up her answer, fishing for what the Mossos knew before committing herself. 'Yes, I did. But I imagine you already knew that, otherwise you wouldn't be asking about him.'

Elisenda saw Comas's head begin to turn sharply towards his wife, but he caught himself in time. She found the reactions of both husband and wife surprising: Comas's attempts to keep up suspicion on Vergés and his response to his wife's words, and Miravent's evident testing of the water to see what she and Montse knew about the couple's relationship with Pere Vergés.

'Have you seen him since his release?' Montse asked Miravent.

She shook her head. 'I have had no contact with Pere since he was found guilty of fraud.'

'May I ask what your relationship with him was?' Elisenda asked her.

Miravent turned her gaze to Elisenda and gave a cold sigh. 'You evidently know that Pere was also a good Christian; a member, as you call it, of Opus Dei. Perhaps my husband was not as forthright as he should have been about his relationship with Pere, but we both knew him socially, through our faith.'

'I haven't not been forthright with you,' Comas complained, his words over-complicated. 'I said I had little professional contact with him despite both of us working for the city council. Yes, I knew him socially. We used to meet at church and on social outings organised by our organisation. There's nothing wrong with that.'

'Well, evidently there's nothing wrong with that,' his wife snapped at him.

'Is there any reason that Pere Vergés might have to hold a grudge against you?' Elisenda asked them. 'Either professionally or personally?'

'You think he could be responsible for Jaume's disappearance?' Miravent asked her, stunned.

'Can you think of any reason why he would?' Elisenda insisted.

'None. I mean we knew him as a member of our church. Perhaps he brought shame on his family and on our community, but we certainly did nothing for him to punish us in this way.'

'And you, Senyor Comas? Would he have any reason to hold a grudge against you professionally?'

Comas shook his head vigorously. 'None whatsoever. I told you, I had very little to do with him at work. I only really saw him through church. I haven't done anything that he could remotely blame me for.'

Elisenda pointed to his fingers. 'Was it Pere Vergés who attacked you in the street?'

A look of panic ran across his face. 'No. I told you, I don't know who did it. It was just a mugging.'

'Do you genuinely believe that the attack you suffered had nothing to do with Jaume's disappearance?'

'Nothing. I told you.'

Elisenda nodded. There was some movement in his eyes that was out of place, a hurried rubbing of the good fingers on his right hand, a response that was a fraction too quick. She was convinced he either knew more than he was saying. Or feared more.

'As Jaume's mother,' Miravent suddenly said, 'I really don't feel that this is a profitable line to be pursuing. Pere was a very mild-mannered man, he lived with his mother. Even if he did for some incomprehensible reason believe us to be responsible in some way for his fall from grace, his was not the sort of character to exact revenge in this way. He had his faith; that would preclude any such behaviour.'

'He's spent four years in prison without cause,' Elisenda replied. 'That precludes no behaviour. Does he know Jaume?'

Startled by the change in tack, Miravent replied immediately. 'Of course. They would have met at one of the community's outings. We go to Montserrat or sometimes to the country.'

'And has he been to your house?' Montse asked.

'Yes, I think he has. We occasionally used to throw parties for the community. I'm sure he came to one or two with his mother.'

'Did you know his mother well?' Elisenda took up the reins. 'Apparently, Pere Vergés wasn't released from prison to attend his mother's funeral.'

Comas looked at his wife for guidance, but it was she who answered anyway. 'We were there. Sadly, after Pere's trial, when it was thought that he was indeed guilty of fraud, his mother felt deep, deep shame, and I'm afraid that that led to her disowning her son.'

'Did she visit him in prison?'

'Not that I'm aware. You might not understand, Elisenda, but our community is based on faith and on high moral values. To his mother, Pere failed in that duty. She couldn't forgive him. We have to accept that.'

Struggling not to rise to the bait, Elisenda asked her, 'What about faith in your child?'

Miravent smiled indulgently. 'I see you don't understand. That isn't faith, that's semantics.'

'You're a politician, you deal in semantics. Why would your faith prevent a mother from wanting to comfort or protect her child?'

Without waiting for a reply, Elisenda stood up. She'd asked them all the relevant questions she'd wanted to ask, and she was worried that staying any longer would only make her lose her temper. Montse stood up, too, but the politician and her husband remained seated. The only other person in the room to move to see them out was Bofarull. He stepped forward, away from the window, and Elisenda was able to see his face without the glare of the sunlight behind him.

'Did you know Pere Vergés?' she asked him.

He shook his head, the spin doctor in him embarrassed by the turn the conversation had taken with Miravent. 'I don't, I'm afraid.'

Back in the city centre, Elisenda asked Montse to drop her off. 'After Bellsolà and those two, I need to walk to clear my head,' she commented. 'Tell Josep to find out as much as he can about Pere Vergés and to look into his relationship with both Miravent and Comas. There's maybe more to him than we thought.'

Her caporal left her near the covered market and she walked briskly down Ronda Sant Antoni Maria Claret, past her old dentist's and past Doctora Puyals' building, and on as far as Plaça Poeta Marquina. She was instantly deafened by the noise of the starlings bickering with each other for space in the trees above the Café Núria, a city landmark. The sound of them calmed her. Taking out her phone, she dialled a number she hadn't dialled in nearly a year and waited for a reply.

'Meet me for a coffee,' she told the person at the other end.

Chapter Thirty-Two

'Tell me what you know about Marc Comas and corruption.'

David Costa stared across the table at Elisenda. They were sitting under one of the square parasols in the shade of the plane trees behind Café Núria. The shelter was there more as protection against the birds' over-active digestive systems than from the heat of the sun. It had taken him under ten minutes to walk there from his newspaper's office after her phone call.

He stirred sugar into his coffee. 'It's all still vague. I was hoping you'd have something when I came to see you on Tuesday night. I know there's something going on, but I don't know what. And it keeps going on. There's a piece of land heading south out of the city that was earmarked for construction for houses before the recession. A builder had the licence, but a meeting of the housing and planning committee on Tuesday that Comas chaired revoked the licence. It was confirmed yesterday and I can't print anything in the paper other than the bare facts of the meeting's ruling. The builder is perfectly solvent and has never defaulted on any payment or social security or anything, so it just seems an odd decision. The problem is, as always, there's nothing tangible I can put my finger on to say "there's your corruption", but I know it's there and I'm certain that Comas is involved.'

Despite all that had happened and his unrequited crush on her since their school days, she had to admit that she found this dogged and impassioned David eager for evidence attractive. More attractive than the puppy-eyed David she'd known for years, at any rate.

'Do you know who else might be involved with him?'

He shook his head, his expression one of frustration. 'There's got to be someone, but whoever it is, they're covering their tracks pretty well. I've got names of people I think are involved. Robert Vega, Salvador Canet, Antoni Planas, any one of them.'

Elisenda filed the names away, all ones she knew. 'We've had Salvador Canet and Robert Vega in our sights for some time, but we've never found anything.'

'That's why I was hoping you'd take a look.'

It was Elisenda's turn to shake her head in frustration. 'Comas's son is missing. There's no way on earth the judge is going to grant me the right to start investigating him.'

'Roca? I sympathise with you.'

She grimaced. 'And right now I don't have the resources to start a Mossos investigation into him so that I can put together my own recommendation that I could take to Roca. Without that, my hands are tied. I wouldn't be able to proceed.'

David laughed and mimicked her. 'New police, same old legal system.'

'Watch it.' She wagged a finger at him. 'Do you think Comas had anything to do with what happened to Pere Vergés?'

He looked surprised. 'Pere Vergés? Why are you interested in him?'

'Just keeping an open mind. Do you think Comas could have been involved?'

'Why? Do you?'

'Stop being a journalist and answer a question for once.'

'Well, it's not something I'd thought of, I have to confess. I always thought there was something dodgy about Vergés's conviction. He looked like he'd been set up. I know he was in the IT department, but anyone with a knowledge of computers could have done the scam. It didn't mean Vergés had to be involved. But I don't see that it necessarily has to mean that Comas is involved either. I think he's got much bigger fish to fry.'

'It was four years ago. He could have started out that way. Worked his way up to greater things.' She took a sip of her coffee.

Her glass of water stood untouched on the table. 'You know that Vergés is Opus?'

David snorted. 'Who'd have thought we'd be talking about Opus in this day and age? But the way Madrid's going, they'll be taking us back to those times before we know it.'

'Do you remember the two girls who died when we were kids? A car crash. Two school friends were killed.'

'What about it?'

'Their families were Opus. I remember the reaction. My mum saw one of the mothers in the street just afterwards and tried to tell her how sorry she was for their loss. This woman looked at my mum like she pitied her and told her how happy they were that their daughter had been chosen by God. They never spoke to us again.'

'Your point?'

Elisenda sighed. 'My point is it's hard to gauge the reaction of Miravent and Comas. Just because they're not showing the normal grief or concern we'd expect, doesn't mean we have to read too much into that. But that in its turn is confusing the issue. For all we know, they are involved in their son's disappearance in some way and their beliefs are shielding that. I'm finding it impossible to read them, especially Miravent. To me, they seem an odd set-up, like three individuals in search of a family.' She looked directly at David. 'And when I was married and had a child too young, I sometimes felt like a family in search of being an individual again.'

Her own confession shocked her, because that was where so much of her guilt came from. And because it was a thought she'd never voiced before. David looked like he was searching for the right words to say, but she carried on speaking before he had to, her voice restored to a professional calm.

'And now we know that Vergés is Opus, I don't fully know where he fits in.'

David paused before answering, struggling to pull back from her revelation. 'If it helps, he's always been part of the in crowd. Or he was. They all shunned him after he got arrested.'

'I know his mother did. He didn't go to her funeral. I thought it was that he hadn't been given leave, but I get the impression now that he chose not to go because she'd disowned him.'

'She wasn't the only one. None of them would have anything to do with him. Normally, when one of their number is in trouble, they move heaven and earth to help, with lawyers and what have you. But in his case, they just left him out in the cold. No one lifted a finger. I think they felt he'd brought shame on Opus Dei at a time when it had come under greater scrutiny since making the big time in the movies.'

'Did that include Miravent and Comas?'

'Most definitely. Miravent was already in government by then, she could have done something, raised questions, but she didn't. She used to organise family days out for Opus, which were big on their social calendar. I remember I was reporting on it at the time. Between the judge opening the investigation into Vergés and him being arrested, they held one of their jamborees out in the country somewhere and he was told that it would be best if he didn't go.'

'How did he take it?'

David laughed wryly. 'I think he had other things to worry about at the time.'

Elisenda finally took a sip of her water. She put the glass down thoughtfully. 'And now he's had four years to worry about little else.'

–

Back at Vista Alegre, Elisenda was surprised to see Àlex and Armengol leaving the building.

'Going for a coffee,' Àlex told her. 'Sotsinspector Armengol wanted to brief us on his part of the investigation. And I need a coffee.'

'Come with us,' Armengol invited her. 'I was waiting to see you but no one was sure what time you'd be back, so I thought I'd pass what I had on to Àlex.'

Elisenda studied them both for a moment and shook her head. 'Got to get on. Àlex will keep me posted. Thanks.'

She watched them go and went on into the building. Josep had more news for her when she got to her office. He sounded a little embarrassed at having to tell her.

'Out with it, Josep.'

'Pere Vergés had counselling in prison.'

Her head snapped up. 'All the best people do. Do you have a name for the counsellor?'

He checked his notes. 'Doctora Puyals. She's got an office on Ronda Sant Antoni Maria Claret. I've tried calling her, but there's no reply.'

'Right.' Elisenda stared at him. Her unit knew she'd been forced to undergo counselling, but none of them knew who her counsellor was. 'Don't worry, I'll try and get hold of her.'

'There's one other thing. Vergés had a car that was later registered in his mother's name when he went into prison. A blue Renault. I've put out a notice for Seguretat Ciutadana to look for it.'

'Have you checked if he has a parking space?'

'Not yet, but I will.'

Before she could speculate further on Josep's news, Montse came into the room and pointed to the filling cabinet.

'The sergent at the front desk has just rung through. Someone's come in to claim Siset's bag.'

Elisenda smiled for probably the first time all morning. It felt as good as the freshly-baked bread had smelled.

'Oh, Siset, you're so predictable. Montse, can you ring through and get them to show him to an interview room and keep him there so he doesn't chicken out and do a runner?'

The caporal went into the outer room to make the call. Manel was at another desk studying a computer screen, but he didn't appear to be typing anything or scrolling down any screens. He didn't react at all when Montse began speaking into the phone opposite him. Without waiting for Montse to finish talking to the sergent at the front desk, Elisenda jumped up, leaving Siset's bag safely where it was.

'Come with me, Josep.'

The two of them hurried along the corridor and down the flight of stairs to the foyer.

'Room two,' the sergent mouthed at them.

Elisenda pushed open the door into the interview room back along the corridor and saw a woman sitting at the table under the gloomy light. She stopped and Josep almost piled into the back of her. Deflated, they both entered the room slowly and closed the door. She could tell by his look that Josep didn't recognise the woman.

'Elena,' Elisenda greeted her. 'What are you doing here?'

Elena looked up, her movements faltering, her eyes torpid. Elisenda could see she was only there thanks to some artificial encouragement.

'Siset sent me. His bag. It was stolen. He's only just discovered it.' She paused and seemed to be casting around for the rest of the script. With a jolt of her head and a faint triumphant smile, she remembered it. 'Anyone could have planted anything in it without him knowing. Can he have it back, please?'

Elisenda sat down opposite her and wasn't sure whether to laugh or cry. 'Oh, Elena, why do you let him make you do his dirty work?'

'Because I love him.' She laughed and sneezed a fine spray.

Elisenda wafted the air away in front of her. 'Well, I'm going to be on a high for a week now. Josep, could you go and ask someone to bring Elena a cup of coffee? And a bottle of water. I think she could do with it.'

The caporal left the room and Elena slumped forward, resting her head on her arms on top of the table.

'I'm sorry, Elena, but I can't give you Siset's bag. I need to give it to him.'

Through her tangle of hair and arms, Elena said something that Elisenda couldn't understand. Struggling, the young woman raised her head up and focused on Elisenda to try again. 'He said he trusts you, Elisenda, and that it's all right to give me the bag.'

'He told you to say that?'

'Yes.' Her head slumped forward again as the door opened and Josep came back in with a bottle of water and a plastic cup.

'They're bringing the coffee now,' he told Elisenda.

They waited until a mosso came in with a hot drink and asked him to stay with Elena, while they went back to their unit's offices.

'Now what?' Josep asked.

'We give her the bag.' She turned and saw his look of surprise. 'Siset knows you, doesn't he? We'll have to ask Manel.'

Back in their outer room, she gathered Montse and Manel into her office and explained to them and a mystified Josep that Siset had sent Elena to collect the bag. 'The thing is, our Siset won't trust Elena to look after it for too long, so he'll be waiting somewhere nearby for her to take it to him.'

Josep suddenly saw what she was driving it. 'Manel. Siset doesn't know Manel, so he follows her until she gives the bag to Siset.'

'Exactly.'

'I am in the room, you know,' Manel complained.

Elisenda turned to him. 'When Elena leaves with the bag, you follow her until she meets someone. You'll be looking for a scrawny little affair with unwashed hair and a broken nose. He'll be wearing jeans and a filthy T-shirt for a band that split up at least fifteen years ago.'

'You can't fail to spot Siset,' Josep confirmed.

'When she does,' Elisenda carried on, 'you arrest the little sod and bring him back here. Try not to lose your temper with him.'

Elisenda pulled Siset's bag down from the filing cabinet. The piece of jewellery that had been in there had already been removed and bagged and placed in the evidence room.

'I'll give this to Elena,' she told Manel. 'You wait on the corner outside until she comes out. You'd better bring her back in with you as well. She needs to sleep it off.'

After giving Elena the satchel and sending her on her unsteady way, Elisenda had been back in her office for less than ten minutes before Manel rang her on her mobile. She could hear the faint exertion in his voice and the sound of whining in the background.

'You've got him,' she guessed.

'*He was waiting down by the river. Less than a hundred metres away.*'

'Well done. See you here in a moment.'

She could hear an interruption. Some scuffling and a plaintive howl. Manel growled something away from the phone before talking into it again.

'*Do I really have to keep my temper?*'

Chapter Thirty-Three

'Your boss doesn't like me much, does she?'

Àlex stirred his coffee, even though there was no sugar in it, and tried to find the words to say. He called to the waiter and asked for an orange juice.

Armengol laughed. 'Buying time while you think how to answer that one. Good, I like it. Loyalty.' He waited in silence, not filling the gap.

'She has to get used to change,' Àlex finally answered. 'Your post has connotations, not you.'

He looked up to see Armengol nodding slowly. The sotsinspector looked down and concentrated on slowly moving the slice of lemon around in a cup of chamomile tea. They were in La Llosa, the café next door to the Mossos station.

'We've drawn a blank,' Armengol finally told him. 'With the sex offenders. The second guy we wanted to see has got nothing to do with it.'

'How do you know?'

'For one thing, he's got a watertight alibi. He was at a convention from Friday to Tuesday. Also, his profile's wrong.' Armengol sounded uncomfortable as he said it. 'He was convicted for having sex with a fifteen-year-old boy twelve years ago. He was nineteen at the time. They're now married. There are sex offenders and there are sex offenders.' He looked up. 'But I think your boss has felt all along that Jaume's disappearance is nothing to do with these offenders. Otherwise, she wouldn't have farmed it out to us.'

Àlex could only agree. 'We have to cover all possibilities.'

'Oh, I'm not criticising. I would have done exactly the same.'

–

'It's my property.'

'No, it's not, Siset, you stole it.'

Siset looked at Elisenda, aggrieved. Manel was sitting next to her in the interview room, an irritable presence that was cowing Elisenda's informant.

'The bag's mine.'

She showed him the stolen jewellery. 'But this isn't.'

Siset sniffed. 'Never seen it before, Elisenda.'

'Do you know, you're right. It's all our mistake. Tell you what, we'll drive you back to Font de la Pólvora and drop you off right by where Tío Juan sits. We'll all get out of the car in front of him and Manel here will shake your hand and I'll apologise to you for all the inconvenience we've caused you and tell you that I hope we can carry on working together so profitably in the future. It'll be like a little race. See if you can get to your apartment before all the people in the neighbourhood who hear about it can get there. What do you say?'

'You wouldn't.' He looked at her cold stare and hung his head. 'You would.'

She picked up the jewellery again. 'But I can make this go away. All you have to do is tell me about the people you got it from.'

She could see the calculations behind his eyes. Slow in so much else, he was quick in surviving the street and could work out his options in fractions of a second. Not that he had many that she could see.

'They'll kill me,' he suddenly whined. 'They'll literally kill me.'

'And if you don't tell me, I'll kill you. I'll figuratively kill you.'

'Figuratively?' He blanched.

'And after that, we'll be through. You'll be no use to me, so I'll have to remove your protection as a trusted member of society. The next time you're caught with something like this, Siset, and believe me, you will be, you'll be looking at years. In prison, with all the others you've helped send there.'

'They don't know about that.'

'Not yet, no.' Elisenda put on a thoughtful face. 'But if I have to remove your protection, who knows what might get out.'

'You wouldn't.'

She could see the thoughts race across his face again, like a rat trapped in an experimental maze, treat or punishment waiting at one end or the other. He appeared to reach a decision.

'I'm not saying anything. I can't.'

Elisenda studied his face. She knew he needed a bit more softening up. 'OK. I'll ask you again in the morning.'

'Can I go now?' He started to stand up, but Manel reached across and pushed him back into his seat.

'You're not going anywhere, Siset,' Elisenda told him. 'One other thing. What do you know about Marc Comas?'

He looked genuinely mystified. 'Nothing. I've never heard of him.'

'He was mugged on Plaça de Sant Josep on Tuesday. His attacker took a mobile phone and a wallet with credit cards. Has anyone tried to sell any of those items to you?'

'No, I don't know a thing about that.'

'Have you heard anyone saying they'd done it? Or talking about someone else doing it?'

His reply was the same. She'd worked with him enough over the last couple of years to know the telltale signs when he genuinely didn't know something. One of them was scratching idly at his left armpit with his right hand while he thought. He was doing it now. It was no surprise. She'd had a feeling all along that Comas's assault was anything but a normal street mugging.

'Thanks, Siset,' she told him. 'You've finally said something helpful.'

'I have? Can I go now?'

She packed up the jewellery and stood up. 'You're staying here. Manel will show you to a nice room for the night. Talk to you again in the morning.'

She left Siset to stare at Manel's expressionless face.

Chapter Thirty-Four

Elisenda took one last look at the photo of Pere Vergés and put it away. It was the most recent one they had on record, taken on the day he was formally charged with fraud. She'd visited his elderly neighbours quickly that afternoon to ask them to take a look at it and tell her if his appearance had changed much.

'Bit thinner, that's all,' the wife had said.

'Weedy little bugger, ain't he?' the husband had added. 'Not a looker like me.'

'Language,' Elisenda had chorused with the wife.

She watched the audience now file into the television studio and start filling up the seats. The stage, crowded with eight lecterns arranged in a crescent, was empty for the moment. The stars of the show would be turning up once everyone was in their place. She looked around. The other four members of her team were standing at various points near the stage or by the audience. Half a dozen more Mossos in plain clothes were at the rear and sides of the studio, scanning the room. Puigventós was standing next to her. He'd agreed with her that Pere Vergés now had to be considered a suspect in Jaume's disappearance, and consequently a potential danger to the boy's mother.

In front of her, a floor manager was explaining to the audience how the debate would work and reminding them that it was going to be broadcast live. Elisenda had also reminded her team not to get annoyed with the politics they'd be hearing from the stage.

'Particularly from the woman we're here to protect,' she'd added with a stern warning. She checked now that they were all tuned in, speaking quietly into the mouthpiece attached to her ear. Each one replied in turn.

The lights in the room dimmed and the spots were directed at the stage as the moderator, a news presenter from Barcelona, introduced the candidates one by one on to the stage. The programme was being made by the Catalan television channel for broadcast throughout Catalonia. The four main cities were getting the same treatment. Lleida and Tarragona had been done the previous two evenings, tonight was Girona's turn and tomorrow night was Barcelona, completing the series before Saturday's day of reflection, the day when voters considered their vote and parties weren't allowed to engage in any electioneering.

'I don't need protection,' Miravent had insisted just an hour earlier, when Elisenda and Puigventós had visited her to tell her of events.

'You do,' Elisenda had replied, accepting no argument. 'There is a potential threat.'

'I have a job to do,' the politician had objected.

'So do I,' Elisenda had countered, and that was that.

The first to speak for three minutes was one of the candidates seeking independence from Spain. Five of the eight on the stage were seeking the same, but all from differing perspectives, ranging from the far left to the moderate right. One of the remaining three also sought an independence referendum but was standing for the Catalan branch of a Spain-wide party whose official line was anti-independence so as not to alienate voters elsewhere. Since the recession, politics in Catalonia had got a whole lot more complicated and the middle ground of voters more perplexed.

Next up was Miravent. Like all the others speaking, she was the head of her party's list for Girona. A percentage of seats in the Catalan parliament was awarded to each party, proportional to the number of votes they won. If that meant that a party won four seats in Girona out of a possible seventeen, then the first four candidates on the list were elected to those seats. At the last elections, Miravent's party had won one seat, which she'd taken as head of the list.

'Catalonia is Spain,' she began, 'and Spain is Catalonia.'

'Fuck off,' Manel muttered in her ear. She heard three other sharp intakes of breath at the politician's words, each one masking her own. Telling herself that she had to concentrate on the job in hand of protecting Miravent and searching for Vergés in the audience, she tuned in and out of the woman's words.

'Independence is a myth. Our country was never independent. On the eleventh of September 1714, when we all celebrate the loss of our freedom, we were as much a part of Spain as we are now.'

Around her, Elisenda could hear large parts of the audience getting restless. The studio manager struggled to stop a few boos.

'You've got to admit,' Puigventós whispered, leaning in to her, 'she does make good television.'

Elisenda looked at him and rolled her eyes. His eyes sparkled in a hidden grin.

'We are voting now for our regional government,' Miravent persevered.

'We are not a region,' someone in the audience shouted. 'We are a nation.'

There was a widespread cheer, which the studio manager tried to flap down with his tablet. Some in the audience shushed the hecklers, not necessarily because they agreed with her.

'You should be out looking for your son,' someone called.

The room suddenly hushed and Miravent looked intently at the heckler. 'I am looking for my son, but I am also a democrat. Our democracy, our right to remain a part of a nation, cannot be endangered by those who would undermine that. I best serve my son by serving the people, by ensuring we are not led astray by lies built on a myth that seek to destroy our family.'

'Nice,' Elisenda whispered to Puigventós, anger clear in her voice. 'Imply her opponents are behind it without actually saying it.'

'Bullshit,' a heckler in the audience yelled.

'Don't interrupt her,' another shouted. 'Let her speak, then vote against her.'

That not only got a cheer, it also seemed to placate the crowd, which settled down to let her have her say, interrupted only by the occasional shocked gasp or the sight of almost an entire studio shaking their heads.

'A regional government,' she continued. 'We are dependent on Madrid and that makes us greater. We will always be dependent on Madrid and I welcome that. With or without the pipe dream of independence, we will always be bound to Spain by language, by culture, by history and by common bonds that will never be broken.'

Elisenda turned and scanned the audience. Marc Comas was sitting at the front, to the left, his face impassive. Elisenda wondered not only how well his wife's politics went down at his place of work, but also just how far he agreed with it. Little, if his stony look was anything to go by. It was a marriage with little mutual support for each other, particularly now that their second son had gone missing.

Miravent summed up her argument before the remaining speakers and the free-for-all of the open debate were due to start.

'Unity,' she said, pausing for effect. Elisenda saw Bofarull again living the speech with her. 'In unity, there is strength, a common purpose, a common language. The widespread teaching of Catalan at the expense of Spanish in our schools holds our children back. The widespread use of Catalan in our businesses holds our economy back. The widespread use of Catalan in our institutions holds our culture back. I am not advocating a relegation of the Catalan language and culture, I am advocating a call for its equality with the Spanish language and culture. I am advocating equality through unity.'

In the relative quiet at the end of her words, when the ensuing commotion had died down, Manel's voice came loud through her earpiece. 'Are we sure the kid didn't just make a break for it to get away from this bollocks?'

'Manel,' Elisenda heard Montse's voice, 'there are times when I could love you.'

Next to her, she saw the smile on Puigventós' face and realised that it was mirroring her own. At least there was one form of unity that Miravent was contributing to.

–

After the broadcast, Elisenda and her team ferried Miravent and Comas back to their home as a precaution, even though there'd been no other incidents than the vitriol sprayed liberally around the television studio. There had been no sign of Vergés or of anyone trying to approach the politician or her husband. In Palau, the Mossos' presence in and around their house had been doubled. Elisenda asked the Científica holding fort in the spare bedroom if there'd been any activity, but they said there'd been nothing. She could see they were getting bored at the seeming lack of any purpose in their being there.

'If this is Vergés holding Jaume,' she told Puigventós, 'why hasn't he contacted the parents with any demands?'

'Maybe he has no demands. Maybe this is simply revenge.'

'Or maybe we're barking up the wrong tree.'

Puigventós took his glasses off to rub his eyes. 'Are you going home now?'

She shook her head. 'I want to head off to the Devesa. We've had Seguretat Ciutadana there this evening showing Jaume's picture to the sideshows and stands that have set up in the park ready for the weekend. I want to see if that's had any joy.'

Montse dropped her off by the park and then headed back to leave the pool car at Vista Alegre. Elisenda watched the tail lights lose themselves in the fine drizzle that had just started to fall in the city and turned to walk into the shelter under the towering plane trees. Planted close together centuries earlier, their only way to grow was up, so they were tall and slender with sparse foliage lower down, the leaves seeking sunlight towards the tops of the trees. It meant they provided a cathedral-like canopy of shade in the sun and refuge in the winter. But the park had other connotations for Elisenda, the scars healing but still livid, and she shuddered involuntarily.

It was less than a year ago that one of her team had been murdered in the Devesa. The stripped bark of the plane trees disappearing into the night and the thick bushes at their foot in parts of the park she now walked through brought back the memories. She struggled to push them away, but the pattering of the drizzle on the dry leaves seemed to whisper a hidden threat at every path leading off the dusty central avenue. In the gloom, she looked down to see the ground swirl into a deep crimson veneer under the fine mist that made it through the trees.

She stopped and stood still, telling herself to hold it together. He had died at the other end of the park, where the undergrowth was more unfettered, the bushes more overgrown, the shadows more menacing. That was far from where she was now, there was no threat. Only her. Up ahead, she saw a figure approaching. He raised an arm in recognition and carried on walking towards her, his face in darkness under the night trees, his movements spectral in the floating haze. Slowing her breath down to stay calm, she stared intently at the man. The glow of lamps behind him and the meagre moonlight that filtered down from above blurred his outline, his silhouette slowly dancing as he came near. His face was in shadow. It was only as he emerged into a less dense patch of the park that she finally saw that he was in uniform.

'Sotsinspectora,' the man said when he stopped in front of her.

'Francesc,' she replied, her voice hoarse. She exhaled quietly, not to draw attention to her panic.

Mosso Paredes brandished a small pile of papers in a plastic folder. Photos of Jaume Comas Miravent.

'We've been handing these out,' he told her. 'Asking questions, but there aren't many people here yet.'

'Any luck?'

He shook his head. His eyes were in darkness, concealed in the shadow cast beneath the peak of his cap. 'We'll be back again tomorrow when more of them have turned up.'

Another Seguretat Ciutadana joined them. A mossa that Elisenda recognised. She too was holding a plastic wallet of photos. She also shook her head when Paredes asked her if she'd spoken to anyone who had any news.

'Do you want us to join you, Sotsinspectora?' the mossa said, peering at her in the gloom and the drizzle.

'It's OK, thanks. I'll just take a look for myself. You get on home if you've finished.'

Paredes shrugged. 'Back to Vista Alegre. Two more hours till we go off shift.'

Elisenda watched them head towards a patrol car parked where the path emerged on to the road by the traffic lights and saw them drive off. Turning, she walked on into the darkness, aiming for the lights and noise that were coming from an anarchic jumble of tents. As she approached, she saw that they were modern but made to look old. The re-enactors who'd be staging mock fights through the park and the city, telling the story of the 1808 and 1809 sieges of Girona, a strategic point on Napoleon's supply route into Spain, would be arriving the next day, but some of the sideshows and curiosities had come early, setting up camp under the trees for the weekend.

She entered a passage of low, flickering lights and cooking smells, the seemingly haphazard camp opening into a narrow avenue of tinkers and traders. Over the days of the siege celebrations, they'd be vying good-naturedly with each other for the attentions of the people of the city passing by. Touting for their favour, just as the politicians in the studio had been clamouring for the souls of the voters, drowning them in promises and clever words.

She walked deeper into the heart of the camp. At the end, where the light faded into the surrounding black of the trees, another figure rose, standing up from a seat on a piece of wood. He was part of a small group of men and women sitting in a loose circle by three tents on the edge of the encampment, all of them in period costume. In the light cast up from the lamps on the ground, Elisenda saw he was dressed as a dandy, but a dandy who'd fallen on hard times. His red and gold frock coat with silver epaulettes was slightly too small, as though it had once belonged to someone else. He wore a greying white shirt with ruffles running exuberantly down the front and flowing out of the sleeves of his coat. His green breeches were held up with what looked like a curtain sash and fastened over bright red silk hose and scuffed brown heeled shoes with large silver buckles. Unsteadily, he placed a tricorne hat over the long and curly black wig on his head, adjusting the flamboyant red and green feathers flowing back over his shoulders from the brim. The lantern cast shadows up his face, accentuating a full mouth and pencil moustache, like an old-fashioned movie idol. His eyes glinted like sparks from an untamed fire.

He saw her. Smiling, he took his hat off with a flourish and bowed low, never once taking his eyes off her. In the same flowing movement, he stood up and replaced his hat, the feather catching on an epaulette and curling over his shoulder. He nodded his head in salute and smiled at her, a laugh at the corners of his mouth.

'You seem a troubled soul,' he told her, his voice as velvet as the night.

She showed him her Mossos ID. 'I'm looking for a missing child.'

She took out the photo of Jaume and held it up for him to see in the light from the lamps.

'Ah, another missing child,' he replied, studying the picture.

'Another missing child?'

'Another Comas Miravent child gone missing. Very unfortunate. I'm afraid I haven't seen him.'

'How long have you been in Girona?'

'We arrived today.' He gestured to the others around him. 'Our merry band.'

'Re-enactors?'

'Of a sort. We are storytellers. A *cercavila.* We will be roaming the fine and ancient streets of Girona the next few days, stopping here and there to bring you timeless tales and wanton entertainment. You should really try and catch us. You might be interested.'

Elisenda's phone rang, shattering the past in one shrill sound.

The man laughed and she turned away to answer.

It was her mother. Telling her again to go and see her sister and her new niece. She told her something else.

Elisenda began to walk away from the man, her pace quickening.

'She's what?'

Hanging up quickly, she ran back to the city.

Chapter Thirty-Five

For a brief moment waiting at the traffic lights in La Bisbal, Elisenda wished she'd brought a Mossos pool car instead of her own. Hers didn't have lights and sirens and the ability to make slow drivers get out of the way. Not that there were many this late in the evening.

At the end of the dual carriageway to the coast, she had to slow down for the annoyingly poor road surface when she got to La Fosca, the jumble of holiday villas and apartments near Palamós. Her rear wheel clipped a verge as she wound too quickly through the snaking development and she had to struggle to keep the car straight. She was dismayed to see that the house she was looking for was a beacon of light by the sea, one of only very few she'd passed in the whole of the development and the only one that looked lived-in at the end of a lonely road. Parking on the landward side to the rear of the house, in front of the garage that occupied the ground floor, she looked up to the kitchen window on the first floor. The lights were on but she couldn't see any movement.

Sprinting round the side of the house and up the stone steps, she climbed to the path that led along a low cliff to the front of the house, one of a row of four. None of the other houses looked occupied. She ran to the front door and rang the bell, banging her fist on the wood when there was no reply. She pulled her mobile out of her bag and checked it for a signal. Nothing. She'd tried to ring before leaving Girona, but the signal here was always so erratic and she hadn't been able to get through. Impatiently, she rang again and banged harder on the door.

When there was still no answer, she searched through her bag for the lock picks she always carried in a leather pouch. It felt like it took her an age to fumble through them and find the right ones to open the door. The security bolt wasn't in place and it finally swung inwards. She wasn't sure that was a good sign.

The first thing she registered inside was a baby crying.

She took out her service pistol and went in. The lights were on. Quickly and silently, she descended the three steps from the hall into the spacious, white living room. It was empty but for the overpowering statues and giant antique oil jars and trio of large cream leather sofas.

The crying was coming from upstairs.

She glanced into the kitchen and saw no one there. Taking the stairs, she followed the sound of the baby, first looking in through the open doors of two smaller bedrooms until she came to her sister's room.

Beneath the sound of crying, another noise bubbled underneath. It sounded like running water. Elisenda recalled the robbers' victim who'd been waterboarded until he'd told them his bank codes and she quickened her pace, running into the room on the balls of her feet. Her niece was in the room, lying on her back in a Moses basket, her crying more insistent. There was no one else.

She heard her sister in the en-suite bathroom, a low moaning noise framed by the running water. She glanced at the baby to make sure there was nothing wrong and hurried to the doorway. Steam billowed out into the bedroom, and she had to wave a clear path through it to see better. Glancing rapidly either side, she went in.

Her sister screamed.

'Jesus Christ, Elisenda, you scared the shit out of me.'

Catalina had the sliding door open and was standing in the shower, the water now off, and reaching for a dressing gown.

'I've been battering your fucking door down, Catalina.'

'I'm in the shower.'

'You were moaning. You sounded in pain.'

'Cheek. I was singing.'

Elisenda turned away and put her gun down, shaking her head in fury.

'Haven't you seen what's been going on, Catalina? These house robberies? What on earth are you doing out here on your own?'

Catalina looked surprised. 'It's La Fosca. It's all right here.' She got out of the shower and followed Elisenda into the bedroom. Seeing her daughter crying, she picked her out of the basket and soothed her.

'It's empty, Catalina. The summer's over, no one's here but you. You're the perfect target.'

'Well, you're here now.'

'We're not staying,' Elisenda told her. 'Any of us.'

'Oh, stop fussing, Eli, we're perfectly safe here.'

Shaking her head in annoyance, Elisenda looked out at the path running along the front of the row of houses. It was deserted, the only sign of life the lights of a ship out to sea. As she turned back, something on the bed next to her sister's overnight bag caught her eye. She picked it up. It was a pamphlet by some religious group calling itself New World Missionaries. She stared at it. It was familiar. She'd seen one like it recently, but couldn't place where. Then she got it. There'd been one like it at the architects' house that had been targeted by the robbers.

'For Christ's sake, Catalina. How did you get this?'

Catalina glanced at it. 'Someone came to the door. I said I was busy so they left the pamphlet.'

'When was this?'

'This evening. Just as I got here.'

Elisenda stared in disbelief at her sister. 'We've got to go, Catalina. This is serious.'

'Honestly, Eli, it's just a pamphlet.'

Elisenda checked her mobile again for a signal. Not one bar was showing.

'Please, Catalina, you have to listen to me. You're not safe here. This gang is targeting houses like yours and I don't like the sound of these people who came to the door. Look around you, the place is empty, everyone but you is at home. Why would these people bother coming here in September when hardly anyone's around?'

Catalina sighed heavily. 'All right, I'll go home. Hold your niece while I get dressed.'

She thrust the baby into Elisenda's hands. Elisenda stared at Enriqueta, who stared back at her. The baby gurgled and bobbed up and down in her outstretched arms and laughed, a short bubbling noise from deep in her throat.

'Hello, kid,' Elisenda told her, studying her.

Enriqueta reached forward and held on to Elisenda's nose in her tiny fingers. Elisenda carried her downstairs to check the house while Catalina got her things together.

'Who calls their kid Enriqueta these days anyway?' she demanded. She knew that the name was her brother-in-law's maternal grandmother's.

Going into the kitchen, she turned the light off and went to the window to look back along the road leading to the house. Enriqueta began to moan, upset by the dark, so Elisenda rocked her up and down to soothe her. Gazing out into the black night, she saw nothing, but her sense of unease grew by the minute.

Catalina turned the kitchen light on, startling her. 'I remember that song,' she said.

'What song?'

'The one you were singing to Enriqueta. Our mum used to sing it to us.'

Elisenda looked at her sister, nonplussed, and handed the baby back to her. 'I was singing?'

They went down the stairs to the garage and Elisenda helped her sister put the baby and the bag in the car. Elisenda's was parked outside.

'Just drive straight home, please, Catalina. I'll take one last look and then I'll be on my way.'

She watched her sister reverse her car out of the garage. Enriqueta in the back seat gurgled and flexed her fingers in a goodbye wave as they drove off. After they'd gone, Elisenda pulled her torch out and quickly checked the lamppost and trees near the house, one eye on the road behind her all the time. Àlex had told her what to look for, so she searched in the less immediately visible places but couldn't find any symbols marked anywhere. She finally got in her car and drove through the development, her thoughts on the religious pamphlet and its significance. She tried to reconcile it with the lack of any symbols to mark the house out as a target. Detouring to see if there were any other houses with the lights on and suspicious cars roaming the streets, she found none and turned to drive back to Girona.

Parking in her underground space on the new side of the river, she crossed the footbridge and saw the lights on in La Terra. Her favourite seat in the window overlooking the Onyar flowing past was empty, the soft luminosity beckoning her. The drizzle that had fallen in the city earlier in the evening had given over, but there was the smell of a storm in the air.

Succumbing to temptation, she went into the cushioned haven of La Terra and hungrily inhaled the aroma of coffee and whisky and late-night conversation. Sitting alone on the brightly-coloured tile settle, she sipped a *licor de café* and gazed past the shadows reflected in the window and out into the night. The lights in the restaurants and homes on the other side of the river were mirrored in broken shards on the unusually fast-flowing water. She heard the river sing. Looking around, she realised that no one else had heard it. Two women opposite looked at her and smiled. Opening the window a little, she smelt the scent of the impending rain and listened to another sound. Somewhere under the gentle flood of tears from the mountains, a lullaby was being quietly sung, and she was the only one to hear it.

He awoke with a start.

It wasn't the sound of the river, constantly menacing below the surface. It was a change in the quality of light. He opened his eyes to see his captor a little over an arm's length away from him, his face distorted by the beam of a torch lying on the floor. He scrambled back in panic, the sudden movement forcing the metal band to cut into his wrist, drawing fresh blood.

'What do you want?'

He waited for the pain travelling the length of his arm to subside and repeated the question. The other figure stared at him for a moment and glanced at the fastening around the prisoner's wrist, ensuring it was still tight.

'I've brought you food.'

He slid over an old piece of wood, part of a plank that had rotted with the damp and split in two. Another tin foil package was on it, with a bottle of water.

'I'm not drinking the water.'

'It's not drugged. I just had to do that because you were trying to escape.'

The captive instinctively looked at the ancient iron ring set into the wall and the metal clasp binding him to it. For the first time, he could see it was a thin metal tie, the sort you'd buy in a DIY store.

'Why are you doing this?'

'I've also brought you a bucket.'

The captor placed a plastic pail on the ground and pushed it forward with a stick so that it was within the captive's reach.

'What's that for?'

'What do you think?'

The captive looked at it aghast and back at his captor, the hatred finally burning in his eyes. 'No, I won't. I'm not an animal.'

The captor shrugged and backed away, heading for the ladder, which had been lowered from the doorway above.

'What are you going to do?'

The captor stopped before climbing up out of the cellar and looked at the figure shrunken against the damp stone wall.

'I don't know.'

Friday

Chapter Thirty-Six

Puyals was late.

Normally, Elisenda wouldn't have minded, the minutes joyfully eating into the time she had to spend raking over the coals of her persistent grief. She would have held her face up to the sun searching down through the leaves of the trees planted at intervals on the pavements and savoured the fresh crispness of the air after the previous night's storm. Looked up at the line of perfect blue sky framing the buildings enveloping her in warmth.

Normally, she would have waited a judicious ten minutes, counting the seconds down and hoping the counsellor wouldn't show up so she could hurry off to Vista Alegre to get on with her work. She had a ready-made excuse to Puigventós for skipping counselling in that she'd waited and the counsellor hadn't turned up.

But Doctora Puyals had treated Pere Vergés when he was in prison and so Elisenda looked instead at her watch with a different anxiousness.

She waited outside the street door amidst parents taking children to school and cars queuing at the lights and she rang the intercom buzzer again. No one had left or entered the building since she'd been waiting, so she hadn't been able to squeeze in through the door on their coat tails. She also realised she didn't have a mobile number for her counsellor. Deciding on one last try before ringing Vista Alegre to get uniforms to check up on the counsellor, she did the postman's trick of pressing all the buttons on the panel and hoping someone would buzz her in without asking what she wanted. It worked. As she went in, a voice behind her called, asking her to hold the door. She turned around to see a flustered Doctora Puyals hurrying along the pavement.

'Sorry to make you wait, Elisenda,' Puyals said, catching her breath. 'We had a power cut in my building in the night and my alarm didn't reset. One of those dawn alarm clocks. Very calming way of waking up to the day.'

'Except when the power goes off.'

Elisenda held the door open and they took the one flight of stairs together up to the counsellor's office. Once in her office, Puyals was instantly professional without the need for a large coffee. Elisenda had to admit to being impressed. She was already longing for her second of the morning. The two women settled into their respective positions, Puyals resting lightly on her more functional chair, Elisenda easing herself gingerly into the torture recliner.

'Did you do the homework I gave you?' the counsellor asked.

Homework? Elisenda remembered the piece of paper that Puyals had given to her the previous morning. It was still in her bag, unread. She'd forgotten all about it.

'Yes, I did.'

'No, you didn't.'

'How do you know?'

Puyals half-smiled at her. 'Believe me, I'll know when you've done it.'

Elisenda nodded that she would, uncertain herself how honest she was being. Puyals carried on speaking, the gentle tone of her voice belying the harsh truth of her words.

'Believe something else, Elisenda. Only you can help yourself. If you don't try to solve your problems, no one can solve them for you.'

Chastened, Elisenda listened to the counsellor's words for a few minutes. She was talking again of grief. In her tiredness after yet another sleepless night of disembodied lullabies and fleeting shadows, she felt herself drifting off, soothed by the timbre if not the sentiments. The storm that had threatened had finally broken in the small hours. She'd finally dropped off wrapped in a sheet on her sofa only to be awoken by the rain beating at her window. She'd gone out onto the balcony and looked down at the river. The level had risen dramatically and was careening under the bridges. Someone somewhere was getting a soaking, she thought. She raised her head and let the wind and the rain drench her to the core, the force of it taking her breath away. The memory of it now in Puyals' chair threatened to lull her to the sleep she couldn't get in her own bedroom. She had to stay awake. Without opening her eyes, she suddenly spoke, surprising even herself.

'You treated Pere Vergés in prison.'

The counsellor was taken aback. 'Yes, I did.'

'Can I ask what his state of mind was?'

Puyals stared frankly back at her. 'Of course. Only yesterday, I was telling another client what you and I had been talking about.'

Elisenda's eyes snapped open and she turned to look at Puyals.

'Precisely, Elisenda,' the counsellor continued. 'Just as I wouldn't divulge anything you tell me to another client, neither would I tell you about my treatment of Pere Vergés.'

Elisenda turned on the recliner and sat up, stretching her back at the discomfort caused by even a few minutes in it. She felt instant relief. 'He's a suspect in an investigation. I'm a police officer.'

'Not here for this hour you aren't. Here, you're my client. If you had a warrant and this were part of your investigation, then I'd have to disclose that information. But not like this.'

'I could get a warrant.'

'Indeed you could.'

Elisenda considered in turn how much she wanted to tell Puyals. 'Just answer me one thing. You've spoken to Vergés, I presume he's trusted you, you know what his state of mind might be. Do you need protection?'

Puyals looked shocked. 'Protection?'

'We think he might be involved in something serious. I imagine he feels he has grievances against some people. In your appraisal of him, how far do you think he might act on those grievances?'

'I don't need protection.' Puyals shook her head. 'Not at all. Pere was quite calm all the time I spoke to him. His grievances were real to him but in the time I spent with him, he showed nothing that would make me think he was a threat to anyone. To himself possibly, but not to others.'

'Could he have hidden that from you?'

Again, the half-smile. 'Can you?'

Chapter Thirty-Seven

'New World Missionaries,' Elisenda announced.

On getting to Vista Alegre, she'd photocopied the religious-looking pamphlet she'd found at her sister's beach house the previous night and handed one out to each of her team. The three caporals were sitting opposite her. Àlex was in his usual position, standing close to the wall to the left of her desk, between Elisenda and the others. He was flexing the fingers on both hands, folded across his chest, as he always did, always impatient to be getting on with things, but also always listening intently.

'I know we're not all equally involved in the investigation into the house attacks,' Elisenda went on, 'but we might be called on at any time to help out with one or the other case, so everyone needs to know what's happening across the board. Àlex, you and Manel will be dealing with this, but the rest of us need to be aware of how things stand, just as you do with Jaume Comas Miravent.'

Àlex peered at the flimsy copy of the pamphlet. 'What makes you think this is relevant?'

Elisenda told them about the two people who'd visited her sister's house and given her the leaflet. 'I remember seeing one exactly the same at the architects' house. If it is relevant, there'll be more at the other houses that have been attacked. I need you and Manel to check up on all the past victims to ask if they remember anyone coming to the door with one of these.'

'We'll also check up to see if this lot really exists,' Àlex replied, waving the piece of paper.

'My feeling is they don't. If that's the case, we can take it as fairly certain that this has something to do with the robberies.

They could be recceing the houses to see which ones are worth going for, which would then tie in with the symbols we're finding to mark them out. First of all, though, we need to talk to Siset to see what he knows. If he's selling on some of their stuff, he might have some idea how they work.'

Manel snorted. 'He's too scared to talk.'

'A night here might have softened him up a bit,' Elisenda replied. 'Although I wouldn't count on it. The cells here are more salubrious than his place.'

'Where's the original pamphlet now?' Àlex asked.

'I've taken it to Científica for them to take a look at it. They'll get it back to us when they're through.'

Àlex stared at the copy. 'They won't find anything. These burglars are too street-wise to leave anything. Did Catalina remember if they were wearing gloves when they gave it to her?'

'Good question. I don't know. I'll ask her. Right,' she continued, changing topic. 'Jaume Comas Miravent. I think we have to begin to rule out by this stage that his kidnapping, if he has been kidnapped, is for gain. If it were for either financial or political profit, someone would have made demands by now.'

'Are we sure they haven't?' Montse asked. 'We don't have access to either Miravent's or Comas's mobiles.'

'Or Bofarull's,' Josep added. 'Anyone could be going through him and we wouldn't know unless he told us.'

'Jutgessa Roca.' Elisenda exhaled the judge's name. 'I'm seeing her again this morning to apply for a warrant to search Pere Vergés's home. Even she's got to grant us one for that if she won't give us one to search Bofarull's house.'

Àlex looked doubtful of her chances. 'You said it's not for gain. Do you think this is revenge?'

'I think it's a possible motive. And if that is the case, then I think Vergés has to be the most likely candidate. He was ostracised by his old Opus Dei circle. He might regard Susanna Miravent as representing that.'

'Or Comas might have been involved,' Montse added. 'They worked in the same place where Vergés was wrongly sentenced for fraud.'

'Either way,' Elisenda concluded, 'until we can confirm otherwise, I think we have to consider that he could be a threat to Miravent. Another option is that Vergés, or someone, is putting pressure on either Miravent or Comas, not necessarily for political or financial gain, but for something we don't yet know about. We still need to check up on this mugging. I don't think Comas is telling us a fraction of what he knows about it or if it's relevant to his son's disappearance.'

'Is Vergés a victim?' Manel suddenly asked. 'What if him disappearing is nothing to do with the kid going missing? He's hanging from a tree somewhere and we just haven't found him?'

'So where's Jaume Comas Miravent then?' Josep challenged.

Manel shrugged his wide shoulders. 'I'm just saying they might not be related.'

The room fell silent. Elisenda was the first to speak. 'That is something we might have to consider. For the time being, though, we still have to work on the assumption that he could be involved, which makes him especially dangerous and unpredictable. If this is revenge or a punishment, he could be capable of doing anything to Jaume, which makes finding him even more imperative. It could also mean that Miravent or Comas are in danger, as he's using the boy to get to them. Now, today's the last day of canvassing before the election the day after tomorrow, and Miravent is going to be out and about looking for last-minute votes. That makes her vulnerable. I've asked for Seguretat Ciutadana to shadow her all day, but I want one of our team with her as well.'

Montse laughed. 'That's got to be Manel.'

'No way,' he objected.

'As tempting as that is,' Elisenda replied, a smile on her lips, 'I think it needs to be Montse. We need somebody discreet. Montse, you and I'll go and see her now. Ideally, I'd put you and Josep on this, but with two investigations going on, we can't tie up two of you with Miravent. Àlex, you and Manel check up on the homeowners about these pamphlets. We'll speak to Siset when I get back.'

'Shall I keep looking into Bofarull?' Josep asked.

Elisenda checked her watch and gave him a smile. 'How do you fancy going to see Jutgessa Roca instead of me to apply for a warrant to search Vergés's house?'

Josep groaned. 'Sure I can't just stay here and check out Bofarull?'

'The judge will probably be more amenable to you than to me,' she argued. 'Do that first, then check up on Bofarull when you get back.'

Àlex stepped forward, ready to get on with work, but he couldn't help grinning at Josep. 'Jutgessa Roca. You get all the dream jobs.'

Josep glared back at him and waited behind for Elisenda to hand over the documents he'd need to see the judge.

'Smile, Josep,' she told him. 'You're living the dream.'

-

'I'm sorry, Sotsinspectora, but I have work to do. I can't have the Mossos hindering me in that, not today of all days.'

Miravent was dressed for election battle and ready to go out, hunting down drifting voters on the last day of canvassing. Her campaign manager, Bofarull, was with her, reading out a list of places they were going to be targeting.

'We will be discreet,' Elisenda insisted. 'Only Caporal Cornellà here will be with you. Other Mossos will be patrolling at a distance, no different from any other occasion when we expect crowds of people.'

'I can promise you,' Montse added, 'I will be in the background at all times. No one will know I'm a police officer, no one will be aware you are being protected.'

'And what about the other Mossos?' Miravent argued. 'In a marked patrol car? Potential voters will be only too aware of a police presence. I insist I don't need it.'

From his place by the window, away from the three women standing in the middle of the living room, Bofarull suddenly looked up. 'Susanna, would you mind for a moment?'

He beckoned her over. A brief flash of irritation lit her face, but she quashed it and went over to where he was standing. Elisenda watched as he spoke quietly to her for a moment, her face quickly registering his words.

Elisenda turned to face away and hurriedly whispered to Montse. 'I'll bet you anything he's just told her that a police presence will raise her profile with voters, make her more appealing.'

Miravent returned to her and Montse. 'Agreed. I'll accept one of your officers with me, but that is all. And the patrol cars at a discreet distance.'

'I'll make sure they go unnoticed,' Elisenda replied, directing a smile at her campaign manager, who didn't look entirely happy with that. 'I'll take it you'll be canvassing too, Senyor Bofarull?'

'Yes, I will.'

'He manages my diary,' Miravent interrupted. 'I'd be lost without him.'

'And we'll be organising another media appeal for Jaume tomorrow,' Bofarull added. 'To keep his disappearance fresh in people's minds.'

Elisenda looked at him. 'To keep Jaume fresh in people's minds,' she echoed.

Before she could add any further comment, Marc Comas came into the room. 'What's this about Jaume? Do you have any news?'

'None yet, I'm afraid,' Elisenda told him. She saw a brief flicker of emotion in his face, something he normally kept hidden in his wife's presence. 'Will you be out canvassing with your wife?'

It was Miravent who answered, her voice brusque. 'I think my husband will be better employed staying at home in case there is any news.'

'Quite,' he agreed with her.

Elisenda looked from the politician to the husband to the campaign manager.

'Quite,' she echoed.

Chapter Thirty-Eight

Elisenda left Montse in Palau with Miravent and drove back to Vista Alegre to find Àlex and Manel at facing desks. Àlex was on the phone when she walked into the unit's office. He signalled that he'd be off in a moment. Manel was tapping industriously at a computer keyboard. She watched the caporal for a short while before he became aware of her presence. His normally clumsy bear paws flitted delicately across the keys as he rapidly took in what was displayed on screen. That's Manel, Elisenda thought, ninety per cent of the time battering carelessly at everyone's irritability threshold, the remaining ten per cent oddly gentle and perceptive. You just had to allow the ten per cent to outweigh the ninety. Sensing her presence, he turned and faced her but before he could say anything, Àlex finished his call and hung up. She could tell from the annoyance in her sergent's eyes and the slightest flutter of a muscle in the taut skin on his cheeks that he wasn't getting anywhere.

'I've only managed to get hold of two of the homeowners who were attacked,' he explained, 'and neither of them recalls anyone coming to the door with a pamphlet.'

'Keep trying. It's not the sort of thing most people would remember, especially if they've then suffered the trauma of an attack.'

Àlex looked at the list of calls he had to make on the screen in front of him. 'I know. It wouldn't have seemed important at the time, but someone's got to remember. If not, we might have to get back out to check up in person, but that could be a hiding to nothing. I can't see many people hanging on to it. Or it's a false lead.'

'I'm having better luck with the pamphlet itself,' Manel offered. 'I've checked all the registers of charities and associations, and New World Missionaries doesn't come up on any of them. The church has no record of them, and there's no tax code registered for them.'

'So they simply don't exist,' Elisenda concluded.

'Look at the pamphlet too.' Manel pointed to the original, lying on the desk on top of the evidence bag. 'Científica just sent it back to us. Only two sets of prints they can identify, one of them yours.'

'And the other one is probably my sister's.' Científica wouldn't have been allowed to check Catalina's as she didn't have a police record and they weren't permitted to check fingerprints kept on national identity card records if she wasn't suspected of having committed a crime.

'That's what Científica said.' He showed her the pamphlet. 'Apart from that, charities have to put their details on any advertising. There's nothing on this, not even a website. And it's been printed on a domestic printer, not professionally done. It's not even a good job.'

'It doesn't have to be,' Àlex commented. 'It's only meant as a pretext for checking houses out, not part of any scam. They know no one's going to take a proper look at it, so they don't bother too much with it.'

'They've still got a printer good enough to do this,' Manel argued.

Àlex grinned. 'Of course they have. They've nicked enough good quality kit, they're bound to have a printer and a computer that'll do the job.'

'So,' Elisenda summed up, 'it's obviously fake, and most likely part of the setup. We just need to find an owner or two who remembers seeing one to confirm it.'

'And then decide how it's going to help us,' Àlex added. 'We could ask every station in the region to check up on houses that have received these, but that would be a huge job.'

Elisenda sighed. 'We know they've been out in the La Fosca area, because my sister had one at her house. There might be a way to whittle it down to that.'

'We'll keep looking,' Àlex promised.

'I take it Josep isn't back from seeing Jutgessa Roca?' Elisenda asked. 'If that's the case, we'll have a word with Siset now, see what he's got to say. Manel, you come with us too to observe.'

-

'I want a lawyer.'

'You watch too many American films,' Elisenda told Siset. 'You know the score. We haven't charged you. Until we do, you don't get to see a lawyer.'

'So I can go?' He made to stand up, but she waved him back down.

'Is this your first time, Siset? How exciting. Now sit down. You know we've got seventy-two hours, then you can go. Unless I can think of something to arrest you for and forget about you.'

'You need me,' he whined back at her.

In reply, she just looked wryly at him. He'd been brought up from the cells to an interview room. Elisenda and Àlex were sitting across the bare table from him. Manel was sitting behind them, by the wall. Always hangdog, Siset looked even more hopeless than usual. His unwashed hair was sticking out at odd angles and his T-shirt could have done with freshening up. Elisenda doubted they'd be able to take the ripe atmosphere in the enclosed room for too long.

'Tell him to stop staring at me,' Siset moaned again, nodding at the caporal.

'Answer a few questions and he will. And you'll be able to go home.'

Although his eyes were tired, the informant's street cunning was never far away. 'Been thinking, Elisenda,' he told her. 'I won't complain about you planting that jewellery in my bag if you let me go. Deal?'

Elisenda simply stared at him, not saying a word.

'OK, OK, how about this?' he said. 'Maybe I do know something about the jewellery, so what I'll do is return it to you so you can give it back to the owner and we're all quits.'

Elisenda leaned forward and whispered. 'Siset, you know Àlex here, don't you? You know he's a pretty scary guy, no nonsense, you don't mess with him.'

Siset glanced at Àlex and back again, nodding his head nervously.

'Well,' she gestured over her shoulder, lowering her voice even more, 'the guy behind me, that's Manel. He's from Lleida. Ever been there, Siset? No? Well, don't. It's a terrible place. So terrible, the people from there grow up bitter. Bitter and twisted and scary. They make Àlex here look good-natured. Now, I really need you to help me with what's going on with these robberies, but I've got to go soon, so I'll have to leave you alone with Àlex. And Manel.'

Siset glanced over her shoulder and looked directly at her. 'That's bullshit, Elisenda.'

She stared back at him. 'I know it is, but if you don't tell me what I need to know, you and I are at an end. I'll throw you back out on the street and make sure everyone knows you've been passing me information for the last couple of years. You know I don't need an Àlex or a Manel to put the fear of god into you, Siset, I've got me for that.'

She held his gaze for what seemed like an age until he finally looked down at the table.

'I don't know who they are, Elisenda,' he said in a low voice. 'Really, I don't. I just know they're evil bastards. They pass on some stuff for me to sell, jewellery and watches and stuff, and I have to give them sixty per cent of what I get.'

'Do you have any names?'

'I don't even know what they look like. They always wear those black masks, where you just see the eyes and the mouth.' He shuddered. 'They come to me and tell me what they want me to sell. That's all I know.'

'So how come you knew about the house they were targeting?'

'One of them said something one time they came to see me. I went for a piss and they were talking. I heard them. They said the name of the place I told you about. I swear, Elisenda, I thought they said they were going to be raiding it last Saturday. I wouldn't stitch you up.'

'What else did they say?'

'Something about someone finding the place for them to rob. Someone else who goes around looking for these places and then telling them about it.'

Glancing sideways at Àlex, Elisenda opened a folder on front of her and took out a couple of photos of the symbols they'd found at two of the houses. 'Do you know what these are?'

Siset looked at them and shook his head. 'I don't know. I've never seen them.'

She put them back in the folder. She could tell from his expression that they meant nothing to him.

'They talk odd,' he added. 'Accents. Don't know what they are. Some of them do, anyway. I think they're foreign.'

'Do you know anything else, Siset?'

He shook his head vigorously. 'Nothing, Elisenda, I swear.'

She picked up the folder and stood up. He looked up at her hopefully.

'Can I go now?'

'Not yet, Siset. I think there might be more that you're not telling me.'

He looked crestfallen, but quickly perked up. 'Well, can I have the jewellery back then? It's good stuff. I could treat Elena to something tasty.'

Elisenda had been sorry for him for a moment, but now she almost felt like laughing.

'Nice try, Siset.'

The three Mossos left and Manel arranged for a uniform to take Siset back to the cells.

'Do you reckon he does know more than he's saying?' Àlex asked her on the way back to their unit's offices.

'You can never tell with Siset. You just have to make him sweat and see what he's prepared to give up. Half the time he doesn't know the importance of what he knows.'

Josep was waiting for her in the outer office. He was holding a piece of paper.

'Warrant,' he announced. 'To search Pere Vergés's apartment. Jutgessa Roca had no problem with it. I've also discovered that he has a parking space in the same block. The warrant covers that too.'

Elisenda looked at it.

'That is really bloody annoying.'

Chapter Thirty-Nine

The elderly neighbours came to the door when they heard Elisenda and Josep trying to get into Pere Vergés's apartment. A couple of Seguretat Ciutadana officers were on hand with a ram if needed, but Elisenda's lock-picking skills were more than a match for the ageing lock set in the ornate door. She sent the two uniforms back downstairs to check the underground parking space to see if Vergés's car was there just as the woman from across the landing opened her door.

'Would you like a cup of coffee, Elisenda?' the old lady asked. 'And your nice young man?'

Elisenda laughed gently, more at Josep's rising blush and falling shoulders than at the invitation. 'Thank you but no. I'm afraid we have to get on.'

The husband appeared, slowly hobbling on his walking stick. 'He hasn't been back,' he told them. 'We've been keeping an eye out. Well, she has.'

Elisenda thanked them and accompanied them back into their own flat and sat them down comfortably while Josep waited outside. She had to admit that she'd developed a soft spot for the couple, they were so similar to her grandparents, now both gone.

'Just let me know if you do see him,' she reminded them as she left.

Her phone rang as she crossed the landing. It was one of the two uniformed Mossos calling to tell her that there was no car parked in the space downstairs. She thanked him and hung up.

'So you're using your car, wherever you are,' she muttered to herself.

Josep was waiting for her inside the hall to Pere Vergés's flat. It smelled musty, but that was all.

'No bodies waiting for us,' Elisenda commented.

Off the hall, the shutters in the living room were pulled down all the way to keep the sunlight out, not even the strings of small oblongs between the slats letting in any respite to the gloom. Elisenda switched the light on but nothing happened. She went back to the hall and clicked the light switch there a few times.

'No electricity,' she muttered.

In the living room, Josep pulled the cord by the side of the window and the shutters concertinaed open with a loud scraping, disappearing into the housing above.

'They haven't been used much for months,' he decided.

Elisenda joined him in the room. With the shutters up, what little light from the enclosed courtyard outside filtered in and was diffused by the oppressive choice of decor. It was a dingy and old-fashioned room. A fussy chandelier hung from the ceiling, heavy furniture in dark wood made the side walls seem like they were closing in and a red leatherette sofa of a sort she hadn't seen in years clung to the wall opposite an old square TV.

There was an old Bakelite phone on a narrow console table. She picked it up, but there was no dial tone. On the stained wood and tile coffee table in front of the sofa, a pile of letters stood in two piles, the envelopes on the right opened, the ones on the left not. Elisenda looked at them. Sitting down on the sofa, she stared at the lifeless television screen on the opposite wall and at the letters standing in a clearing in the dust on the table where an arm had evidently just swept months' worth of emptiness to one side. She tried to imagine him there on the Friday night he came home, alone amid the darkness and the must. And then on the Saturday morning, using the light from outside the window to go through the mail until he couldn't face it any more.

'So you've come out of prison for a crime you didn't commit,' she murmured, 'come home to a flat you shared with your mother, who disowned you, your electricity and phone have been cut off because the place has been empty since she died, your old friends don't want to know you, you don't have a job or an income.' Her gaze scanned the room. 'You might be our perp, Pere Vergés, I don't know yet, but you're definitely a victim.'

Getting up, she went into the kitchen and tried the tap. The water had been cut off too. Checking the cupboards, she found the remains of a baguette and some tomatoes and olive oil sitting alone on a shelf, together with a half-finished supermarket pack of cured ham.

'The question is,' she continued to ask herself out loud, 'why you had cold feet about going ahead with your claim for compensation. If anyone deserves it, you do. And why you didn't turn up to see the judge.'

Josep came to find her, his tall frame filling the doorway and blotting out the meagre light that found its way through. 'He's been using one of the bedrooms. There are sheets on the bed and some clothes in a wardrobe. The bed's made, but it's impossible to say when he last slept there. There's also an old desktop computer in the bedroom, but without electricity, it's useless.'

Elisenda followed him through the rest of the rooms in the apartment. They gave nothing more away than the conclusions they'd both already shared.

'We'd better get Científica in to go through all this,' Elisenda decided, 'but I don't think they're going to find anything. They can take the computer away, too, and see what's on it.'

Josep rang to make the request while Elisenda roamed once more through the apartment. When Vergés had first been discovered to have gone missing, Josep had checked the hospitals and Mossos stations in Girona and the towns in the region as a matter of course, but nothing had turned up. He hung up as she returned to the living room.

'Check all the hotels,' she told him. 'And see if you can find out where he used to go in the summer holidays, places that meant something to him. This place is so depressing, for all we know, he's just checked into a hotel to get away from it.'

Josep made a note. 'Do you really think that's possible?'
Elisenda took one last look around.
'No, not for one minute.'

Chapter Forty

Elisenda left Josep at Pere Vergés's flat waiting for the Científica team to arrive. She had another interview, one she'd arranged the previous evening. Taking a pool car, she drove past the Devesa. More sideshows were setting up for the weekend, brightly-coloured canvas flapping amid the green and silver trees and the harsh sound of mallets hitting metal pegs. A coach was parked near the traffic lights and was letting off a group of men of all ages chattering like schoolchildren out to play, their bags an assortment of curious shapes and sizes. They were re-enactors, Elisenda knew, ready to do battle to defend the city from Napoleon until Sunday evening came around and they'd go home to watch the football on television.

She drove out of the city, skirting the western end of the park and crossing the Ter. Glancing left and right quickly, she saw that the river running below the new bridge was higher than normal, tumbling over itself in full flow, a roiling muddy brown capped with foaming white crests. It looked incongruous under such a benevolent sky. Turning left to find the shiny motorway exit that had only been opened recently as the city grew, she passed through the horizontal beehive of toll booths and put her foot down, heading for Figueres, three quarters of an hour north. She wished she were in her own car and could listen to music as she drove. She found she was better able to think laterally to the changing rhythms of a familiar soundtrack than to the monotonous beat of the asphalt under the wheels.

With Figueres to her right, the second largest city in the Girona region, she came to the exit she wanted shortly after and turned off into a barren stretch of semi-occupied industrial land sporadically scattered with the odd prefabricated factory building. An island in the middle of the brown scrubland was home to another new construction, a sprawling complex of low-rise buildings that had never failed to depress Elisenda ever since it had been built. Parking in the visitors' area, she nonetheless had to admit that it was still infinitely better than its predecessor, a hundred-year-old misery in one of Figueres's suburbs that had finally been pulled down a few years previously.

Breathing in the cool air coming down from the Pyrenees, she gazed at the new prison for the region and had to admit that her dislike stemmed from her own prejudices. Just as the replacement of the old police forces by the Mossos d'Esquadra had revolutionised policing in Catalonia, so the takeover by the Catalan government of the prison system thirty years ago had slowly dragged the service into the modern era. Like the police, the prison service had seen a change from the old ways of punishment and retribution to a new climate of reform and reintegration. In the past, prisoners of all ages and levels of offence had been shoved in together and left to their luck, now the wisdom was one of a second opportunity. The bag she was carrying had been designed and made by prisoners as part of the rehabilitation process and were sold throughout the country. It was just that she couldn't help seeing prison as the sad and unfortunate result of the whole process of which she was a part. She knew that not many of her fellow officers would have shared her worries should she ever dare mention them. Looking once more at the multi-coloured wall strips, like a giant Neapolitan ice cream, she took in one more deep breath and entered the building.

Inside, she told the man behind the front desk that she had an appointment and he asked her to take a seat. In the end, she'd barely sat down before the director came down to fetch her in person. About ten years older than Elisenda, the director walked with a quiet assurance and smiled when she saw her.

'Anna,' Elisenda greeted her. 'Thanks for seeing me.'

'Not a problem, Elisenda. We'll just go to my office.'

Elisenda had met Anna Casellas a few times since their first meeting, when the prison authorities had given senior Mossos a tour shortly after Elisenda had set up the Serious Crime Unit. Softly-spoken but confident, the director had an earnest face, tanned at the end of the summer and framed by mid-length dark blond hair. Her dark eyes were inquisitive, with tiny lines at the corners, and she had a habit of holding her head to one side when she was listening.

'You wanted to ask me about Pere Vergés,' Casellas said once they'd sat down in her office, a modern but fairly sparse room cooled just a bit too much by the air conditioning. Elisenda saw why the director continued to wear a jacket over her matching bright red skirt, despite the warmth of the day outside. Elisenda started to feel the cold in her short sleeves and thin cotton trousers.

'He's been missing since Monday afternoon and we think he might have some involvement in an ongoing case.'

'Yes, I'd heard he failed to show up at court. Can I ask what the case is?'

Elisenda had no reservations about telling her about the missing boy and Vergés's involvement with the family and with Opus Dei.

'My honest opinion, Elisenda?' Casellas continued when Elisenda had finished. 'I really can't see him as having any involvement. Pere was adamant that he was innocent, but there was a fatalism about him rather than any sense of grievance against anyone.'

'But he must have felt some sense of injustice at what had happened to him. Wouldn't that have led him to want to blame someone?'

'And punish them?' Casellas shook her head. 'Pere was a model prisoner. He just wanted to stay out of trouble until his case came to retrial or he'd served his time. He even helped teach computing to some of the other inmates on the courses we give here. I had recommended that he be transferred to the open prison in Girona, but then his retrial finally came through and he was found innocent.'

Elisenda digested her words. Girona's prison, in the Pedret part of town to the north, had once been as chaotic as pretty much every other prison in the country, but since the opening of the one in Figueres, the Catalan government had designated Girona's an open prison. That meant it was reserved for low-risk inmates and those nearing the end of their sentence, who only went there to sleep.

'So if you were recommending him for Girona,' she asked, 'would that mean there was nothing in his attitude that would make you think he'd be capable of revenge on the people he thought had put him in prison?'

'I really can't see it. He was determined to clear his name, but I would say that was the extent of it. In my conversations with him, I would say that he saw his situation as more of a fault of the investigation rather than anyone actively trying to set him up.'

Elisenda found that odd. From what she'd seen of the original case, she felt that anyone would have felt they'd been set up. She couldn't help doubting Vergés's motives for being the model prisoner. Or, looking at things very differently, for something in him snapping the moment he got out and tried to return to an old life that was rejecting him.

'And what about his old Opus Dei crowd?' she continued. 'Didn't he feel any antipathy towards them for not supporting him?'

Casellas gazed out of the window for a moment before replying. 'I think it went deeper than that. Pere lost his faith in Opus Dei and the people he'd once known. He was given leave to go to his mother's funeral, but he chose not to. He'd given up on people, on his past life. He had moments of severe depression, enough for me to refer him to the psychiatric services. It was a loss of faith in general, not an antipathy towards individual people, but despair with everything he'd thought. He didn't only lose his faith in Opus, he lost his faith, full stop. His faith in Christianity, all his beliefs, had been taken away from him.'

Elisenda gazed back at her. 'Wouldn't that be enough for a devout person to do something out of character?'

After her meeting, Elisenda left the building and walked across the car park. She couldn't help stopping for a brief moment to suck in lungfuls of fresh air. Checking her phone before getting into the car, she saw she'd missed a call from Josep. She rang and asked him what it was about.

'*Marc Comas. He went out for lunch, and the unmarked car following him lost him.*'

'He went out for lunch? Does he know his son's missing?' She cursed silently before continuing. 'Did it look like he tried to lose them?'

'*No, it was the traffic system. The tailing car got snarled up in the one-way and Comas kept getting further away as other cars nosed in. He wasn't speeding or doing anything unusual.*'

'Doesn't the tail car have lights and sirens?'

'*They didn't want to draw attention.*'

'Seriously? Where is he now? Have you tried his mobile?'

'*We don't know. I've called his mobile, but it's switched off.*'

'OK, get Seguretat Ciutadana to try and find him.'

She hung up and swore again. Getting into the car, she thought of Marc Comas and Pere Vergés.

'So what is really going on with you two,' she muttered to herself as she left behind the prison and headed for the motorway back to Girona.

Chapter Forty-One

'There's a telephone call for you, Senyor Comas.'

Comas was surprised. No one was supposed to know he was here. He looked at his half-finished plate of *botifarra amb mongetes*, a good old traditional Catalan meal of thick pork sausage with haricot beans fried in garlic and parsley, and closed his eyes. Just one moment, he wanted, just one moment away from his wife and the elections and his missing son and the Mossos d'Esquadra.

'For me?' he asked the waiter. 'On your phone?'

The waiter, a young man, the third generation in his family to serve table at Comas's favourite restaurant on the northern fringe of Girona, nodded.

'Apparently the gentleman didn't give his name.'

Irritated, Comas turned his mobile on quickly but he had no missed calls. He turned it off again just as quickly. 'You're sure it's for me?'

The waiter nodded again. Sighing heavily, Comas got up and followed the young man. This was his favourite restaurant precisely because no one knew it was and he could be left alone here to enjoy the sort of meal in the sort of place his wife claimed her status no longer allowed. At least that would soon be changing, Comas thought with grim glee.

The waiter showed him to an office where he could take the call. He waited until the waiter had closed the door behind him and picked up the receiver.

'Hello,' he said, trepidation suddenly entering his voice, but all he could hear was tinny music playing that year's summer hit. 'Who is this? Is this about my son? Who are you? Where's my son?'

His voice steadily grew with his frustration, but no reply came, just the endless vapid summer sound. After a few more minutes, he slammed the phone down in helpless anger. Outside, he told the waiter that no one was on the phone. 'And you don't have number recognition?' he asked him, but the waiter told him they didn't.

He returned to his table, but his appetite had gone, and with it, the brief moment of respite and his peace of mind. Giving up on his meal, he paid up and went out into the warm sunlight. In the car park behind the restaurant, he was even more annoyed to see that someone had blocked him in. A top of the range grey BMW was skewed across where his own car was parked facing outward. He checked the BMW but no one was in it and they hadn't left a note to say where they could be found.

'For God's sake,' he muttered.

He opened his own car door and was about to hold the horn down until the BMW driver came to reclaim it, when he heard another car door closing nearby, quickly followed by a second one.

'Good afternoon, Marc,' a cold voice said before he had a chance to press the central pad on the steering wheel.

Comas jumped. He recognised the voice immediately.

'Please don't sound your horn,' the voice said.

Comas snatched his hand away as though it had been stung. At the same time, a strong hand pulled at his arm to make sure he didn't sound the horn out of reflex.

'Thank you,' the voice said.

Comas turned to face the speaker. He couldn't see the man's eyes behind the heavy sunglasses, but the mouth was set in a firm line. It was Salvador Canet, the man he'd met on Monday, his rather informal business partner who was paying him to turn council decisions in his favour.

'Rather hot today, don't you find, Marc?' Canet said. 'Would you care to sit in the rear seat of your car, out of this sun?'

He signalled to the thickset man holding Comas's arm, one of the two at the meeting the other morning, to release him. The third man was seated at the wheel of a white Mercedes parked nearby. Canet ushered Comas into the rear seat of Comas's own car and pulled the door closed behind them.

'We really shouldn't be seen together in public,' Comas said, recovering a little of his composure.

Canet took his sunglasses off and stared at him. 'Oh, I think we've gone past that now, Marc.'

He pulled a mobile phone out of his pocket. Comas closed his eyes. It was his, the one that had been stolen on Wednesday.

'I see you recognise it,' Canet said. 'Good, that will save us so much time.' He turned to face Comas more fully. 'Forgive me if I'm wrong, but I had assumed we had a relationship based on trust. On a matter of mutual interest.'

'We do. I...'

'Shut. Up,' Canet whispered. Comas flinched more than had the man shouted. 'Yet I find you've been recording our meetings. Not just the one on Monday, but all the times we've spoken.'

'Just for my own records.'

Canet held his hand up to quiet him. 'The thing is, Marc, what you failed to see is that they work equally well for my records. Details of all the payments you've taken, all the council decisions you've helped sway, all the discussions we've had regarding our mutual business concerns. And all spoken in your own voice. And what's more unfortunate from your point of view is that now I have this, I really don't need to pay you for your services anymore. I have all the promises I need to aid me in my business ventures on this one phone. And on the backup copies I've made and deposited with my layer.'

'It incriminates you as much as it does me.'

'Not the version as I've left it.' He played part of Monday's discussion. Canet's voice didn't appear at any point. 'You will, of course, continue to work for me.'

'I'm broke,' Comas said, fighting back tears of frustration.

'Don't worry, Marc. It's not in my interest for you to go under. That's what we do, we help each other. Which brings us to that other matter you appear reluctant to discuss.'

Comas gulped. 'I can't. You're not a believer. They'd never let you in.'

'I'm sure your wife could swing things my way, Marc. Opus Dei, Marc, we help each other. I'd be able to make sure your fate was always tied to mine. You'd never go under with my support as a fellow member.'

Comas struggled to keep his voice straight. 'Why do you want to be in Opus Dei?'

'The same reason you do, Marc. The same reason you do. To open all the right doors. Now talk to your wife and sort it. I won't ask you again.'

Comas looked at the other man and searched for the courage to ask his next question. 'Have you got my son?'

Canet laughed. 'Oh, Marc, I wouldn't go through your children, you know that. I'd deal directly with you. But don't worry, I see you're concerned about your son, so I won't take your question as an insult.' He held his hand out. 'Let's shake on it.'

Without waiting for a reply, Canet took hold of Comas's right hand and squeezed hard. The fingers held together with splints and bandages cracked and Comas screamed in pain. Canet got out of the car and leaned his head back in to look at Comas.

'I won't ask again.'

Shaking with fear and pain, Comas got out of his car and called to Canet. 'Aren't you going to let me out,' he said, gesturing to the BMW.

Canet looked at the grey car and shrugged. 'Not our car. You'll just have to ask someone to move it. I'll be in touch.'

Canet and his companion got in the car and the driver slowly pulled away from the parking space and out into the main road. Comas watched them go and let the tears come.

Chapter Forty-Two

Elisenda had one more visit to pay on her way back from the prison in Figueres. Walking through the double doors of the newspaper building, she recalled the words of her first sergent.

'The media have no place in a police investigation.'

It was a saying he'd liked to repeat, and it was one that Elisenda had always found short-sighted, a throwback to the distant past when Franco's police preferred to be unaccountable and secretive. Oddly, despite the Mossos being more amenable to the press, there were still some who were wary of involving them. She wasn't among their number.

'Thanks for running the piece,' she told David Costa now when he'd come down to reception. She'd asked him to print an article calling more explicitly for the public's support in finding Jaume Comas Miravent.

'I hope it works,' he told her. 'We seem to be getting a good response so far.'

'That's good to hear. We need to keep the profile up. In these cases, there's always the risk of people's interest waning and moving on to the next story if there isn't much news to give them.'

He agreed with her. 'It's a strange situation, this. Everyone wants to help when a child is missing, but our readers are generally unsympathetic to Susanna Miravent's views.'

'They're not helping,' Elisenda had to admit. 'That's why I'm grateful for your help.'

David looked at the photo of Miravent on the cover of that morning's edition. For once, she was portrayed as the mother of a missing child, not an unpopular politician.

'How you can ask people to vote for you to enter an institution that you profess to want to bring down is beyond me,' he commented. 'The hypocrisy of it.'

Elisenda turned to leave. 'You just have to put that thought on hold for the time being.'

-

It all hinged on an apple.

Àlex and Manel had spent the day ringing the houses of people who'd been attacked by the gang. Manel put his phone down and ticked another name on the list.

'They also got a call from the God squad,' he told Àlex. 'That's all of them so far.'

'Same here. I don't think we need to ring any more, there's an obvious correlation.'

Since the first few negative responses, virtually every owner they'd called and been able to speak to had come back with the same reply. Shortly before the attack on their home, they'd all received a visit from some religious group trying to drum up trade for some sect or other. None of them had thought any more of it.

'They're the ones looking for the right houses,' Àlex continued, 'and marking out the ones for the gang to attack.'

On the table between them, they had a series of pieces of paper spread out on the desk, each one with one of the symbols that they'd found at the houses. A triangle with one, two or three lines coming out of the top, all but one with a horizontal line through the centre of the triangle.

'Even if we do work it out,' Manel said for the countless time, 'I still don't see what we're going to do with it.'

Àlex had to agree. He'd sent messages to all the Mossos stations in the Girona police region telling them to be watchful for the symbols, but it was like looking for a needle in a haystack.

'I'm famished,' he said, fishing in a bag near his chair. 'Want an apple?'

He took one out for himself and tossed a second one over to Manel, who made no attempt to catch it. Instead, he simply watched it bounce off his chest and roll across the desk in front of him, knocking over a container with pens in.

'Like the reflexes,' Àlex mocked him.

Manel didn't reply. He just stared at the apple, a frown across his forehead.

'Apples,' he finally said. 'The orchards we passed. Where was that?'

'Sant Pere Pescador.'

Manel called up a file on the computer screen and stared at it. 'Apples. The orchards. There's so much work, they use teams to pick the apples at harvest time. All working under a gang leader, working in shifts. Some of the teams work better than the others, so they get more apples picked.'

Àlex leaned forward and tilted Manel's screen so they could both see it. 'There are different gangs robbing the houses. No, one gang, but different teams, each one working a different way.'

'Three teams,' Manel said. 'The three sticks at the top of the triangle. They're nothing to do with the house itself. They just say which team is to do the job.'

The two of them studied the list of attacks in chronological order on the screen and matched the brutality of the attacks with the number of sticks. They only had the symbols for a small number of the homes, the ones they'd visited, but there was a link. The more violent attacks were where two or three sticks had appeared.

'That explains the different levels of coercion used in the attacks,' Àlex commented. 'Teams two and three are more vicious, so they were probably used for the potentially more profitable homes or the ones where there was possibly more of a chance of the owners being able to defend themselves.' He looked at Manel. 'You bloody beauty.'

To hide his embarrassment, Manel fixed his gaze on the pieces of paper with the symbol on. 'I don't get the line through the middle.'

Àlex looked at his own sheet of names and numbers and the ones he'd ticked off and saw the pattern. 'We didn't find that on the architects' house, and that was the only one that hadn't happened when we saw the sign. They're just marking the triangle to show the job's been done.'

Manel grunted. 'Bureaucratic burglars. Only in Girona.' He suddenly looked crestfallen. 'I still don't see how knowing this helps us stop them.'

Silently, they both turned back to the computer screen and studied it for a few moments.

'Can you see the pattern?' Àlex asked.

'Yup.'

'Me too. It's obvious when you know.'

A voice behind them made the pair of them jump.

'What's obvious?' Elisenda wanted to know.

'The robberies,' Àlex told her, beckoning her over to the desk. 'The sequence. We've worked it out. They're leapfrogging the attacks, doing one in one county, then two in another, then on to a third county and two attacks back in the first county. It's two steps forward, one step back. It looks random, but there is a pattern.'

Elisenda sat down and studied the screen while Àlex and Manel explained to her their theory about the symbols and that there were three different teams carrying out the attacks based on the judgement of the fake religious callers.

'So the next attack would be…' Elisenda said, studying the list of past attacks. 'Two in the Baix Empordà.'

'And then back to the Gironès for a third one there,' Manel added.

'That makes sense,' Elisenda said. 'My sister's beach house is in the Baix Empordà, and the gang is obviously looking for places to attack as she's had a visit from this fake religious lot.'

'Were there any symbols around?' Àlex asked her.

'Not on her house. I didn't have time to check the neighbouring houses or anyone else in La Fosca.'

'So we get the local Mossos stations there to check up on houses,' Manel suggested.

Elisenda and Àlex just looked at him. Elisenda leaned forward and opened another screen in a tab. 'Baix Empordà,' she recited. 'Seven hundred square kilometres, a hundred and thirty-odd thousand people, thirty-six towns. And we've got two stations and four sub-stations there. It would take us months to get round all that.'

'And the next attack could be any day now,' Àlex added.

'Even so,' Manel argued, 'we know they're looking near where your sister lives. We could get the local stations to check up on that.'

Elisenda considered that. 'It really is a long shot, but it's worth a try.'

'I've already mailed the stations throughout the region telling them to keep an eye out for symbols,' Àlex told her.

'Update them all to tell them to watch for religious callers as well,' Elisenda told him. 'But it would be worth you going to talk to La Bisbal and Palamós to get them to check up on the La Fosca area. It's the only real lead we've got to go on, even if it is vague.'

'One thing I don't see,' Àlex commented, 'is why the religious caller lot don't just give the gangs the address of the houses they select. They've got to tell them the area where the house is for them to find the symbol. Why not just give the address?'

Manel smirked. 'City boy. Most of them are isolated houses, they don't have proper addresses, maybe just a house name or a kilometre marking. Or the road itself doesn't even have a name, just a number. There's no address they can give.'

'Probably just a satnav coordinate and a rough description,' Elisenda agreed. 'That and the symbol would be enough.'

Àlex looked at the two of them and tutted. 'Typical Girona.'

He nodded at Manel and the two of them stood up. Elisenda watched them go, Àlex patting Manel on the shoulder as they walked out of the door. She allowed herself a half-smile.

Her smile vanished when the phone in her office rang. Shaking off her weariness, she got up and went into her room to answer it. It was Puigventós, asking her to go and see him.

'There have been a lot of complaints, Elisenda,' he told her when she got there. 'With this siege re-enactment going on this weekend, there's a *cercavila* parading around the city and they're upsetting people.'

'A *cercavila*?'

'I don't mean the main procession through the streets,' Puigventós explained. 'Storytellers. There's one of the usual groups wandering about the city stopping every now and then to act out a story.'

'Why should that concern me?'

'They're telling stories about a child that's gone missing.'

Chapter Forty-Three

Two gunshots rang out loud on Plaça de l'Oli, the echo washing back and forth, trapped among the ancient buildings. The noise was deafening and left Elisenda's ears muted with an underwater numbness. She looked around her, gauging the people's faces.

A third shot rang out, moments later, and the crowd laughed. The hapless shooter shrugged in exaggerated embarrassment to his two companions and the audience laughed some more. All three were dressed in tattered clothing, scruffy uniforms caricaturing the city's defenders of two hundred years previously, their cheeks rouged, their noses prosthetically elongated. Their weapons were blunderbusses and they were reloading them now with gunpowder and blanks, the third one as always lagging behind and suffering the expansively wagging fingers of the other two.

Taking her eyes off the leader of the *cercavila* troupe for one moment, Elisenda glanced around at the audience packing the small dog-legged square. The children stood with their eyes and mouths wide open, some of them tucked into their parents' legs for protection. The adults were expectant, some of them awaiting an amusing story, others aware of the minor scandal of the leader's words and hoping to be shocked.

One of the other members of the troupe banged on a drum, while the remaining two blew into bombards, the shrill reeds keening around the little square as deafening as the sound of the blunderbusses. The music suddenly stopped and Elisenda looked back at the leader. He spotted her for the first time and bowed down low, doffing his hat with a flourish and replacing it, pulling himself up once again to his full height.

He was the man she'd spoken to in the Devesa the previous night. The matinee idol with a flowing black wig and comically extravagant nineteenth-century finery.

Taking one last look at her, he turned back to the crowd and cleared his voice, his forefinger on his lip, his little finger cocked, the faded lace of his cuffs cascading down around his hand. The audience hushed.

Out of a wheeled trunk next to him, he pulled out the lifelike figure of a small boy and held it up to the crowd.

'Nice, Rich Boy,' he pronounced, his voice already resonating rich and hypnotic in just those few words. 'He always cleans his teeth and says goodnight to his parents and goes to bed when they tell him and his room is always tidy.'

The leader looked around at the crowd. 'And he's rich.' He bellowed the last word, drawing out the syllable until it was all you could hear in the square.

'Rich and from a good family and we all have to care about him.'

He set the figure down and pulled a second one out of the trunk. Another small boy, but this time dirty and unkempt, the hair a spiky wig, the clothes grey rags.

'Horrid, Poor Boy.'

The troupe behind him moved forward and whipped the audience up into a loud booing and baying.

'He eats dung for his supper and sleeps in the pigs' trough.'

The crowd laughed and booed some more as the other players went among them.

'He picks his nose and farts into his sister's pillowcase. He licks the sweat off stray dogs and pops their fleas.'

The drummer banged her drum once loudly and the crowd gasped in shock and then burst into embarrassed laughter.

As he held a figure in each hand, two troupe members ran up to him, one on either side, and stuffed the two dolls into a sack each and ran off with them.

'And then they were gone. Missing. Where they went, no one knows. Poor Nice, Rich Boy. And the Mossos went searching for him and they hunted high and low and they turned the city upside down.'

Other troupe members had put comedy police caps on and ran along the front of the crowd pretending to lay into the people with toy batons, gesticulating at them and demanding to know what they'd done with Nice, Rich Boy. The drummer had put her drum down and now walked forward, placing a small podium on the ground and miming a speech, reminiscent of a politician. Every now and then, she sobbed her eyes out for a few seconds and then her expression stiffened and she went straight back to her mimed speech.

'And his parents did all they could to keep reminding everyone of how important Nice, Rich Boy is and how we have to do everything to find him.'

The leader turned his face and spoke in an aside. 'And by the way, vote for me.'

Another of the troupe had thrown a striped shirt on over his head like a silent-movie prison uniform and wandered past the leader.

'So there you are,' the leader said. 'We all thought you'd gone missing. Not that anyone cares.' He tapped the side of his nose. 'You are the right sort, after all.'

Elisenda couldn't help gasping at the obvious reference to Pere Vergés.

The drummer went back to her drum and the first two members came back with the two sacks. The leader emptied the first one and Nice, Rich Boy fell out. He held the figure aloft and the musicians started a screeching celebration while the other three danced wildly in joy around the square.

The music stopped as suddenly as it had started and the leader held his hands up for silence. Lifting the second sack, he shook it, but it was empty. He tried some more, but there was nothing, so he threw the bag over his shoulder, to be caught by one of the players behind him.

'And horrid, poor boy?' he asked.

The fake cops stood still and looked bored, filing their nails and whistling to themselves.

The leader stayed silent for an age, the crowd leaning forwards, waiting for his next words. Slowly he raised his arms to the sky, and with one final flourish, he shrugged.

'Fuck him.'

To a stunned silence followed by a loud gasp, the troupe quickly turned and melted through the thinner crowd behind them and up into the tiny streets rising from the square.

Elisenda struggled her way through the audience, but it was dense and excitable and by the time she'd made it to the foot of the steps leading up into the heart of the old town, the troupe had gone, just the echo of shock lingering behind them. She stood at the bottom and looked up, the steps bifurcating halfway up, the alleyways beyond twisting and multiplying. She would never find them.

'And what would you say to them if you did?' she asked herself.

Chapter Forty-Four

Montse knew that her face rarely gave away any emotions, but she was finding it hard to keep up an impassive expression, especially when Bofarull caught her eye and smiled at her in some sort of imagined triumphant collusion, evidently delighted with the reception he felt they were getting. Glad not to have to respond with the valid reason that she was working, Montse turned away to scan the large factory floor once more.

To her right, Susanna Miravent was standing on a pile of three pallets with her back to a tall scaffolding of storage shelves stacked with large cardboard boxes. In front of the politician, a smattering of workers in the plastic moulding works, an old family business on the edge of Salt near the motorway, were listening, to a greater or lesser extent, to her words. Six reporters and a television crew were recording the event, a last-ditch attempt to win votes in one of the more marginal and marginalised districts. Montse reckoned that was five more reporters and one more television crew than she would have got had it not been for the disappearance of her son.

Despite the campaign manager's optimism, the day had not gone well. Bofarull and Miravent had obviously targeted Salt as it had a high percentage of immigrants, both from other areas of Spain and from outside the country. Evidently, they felt that offered easy votes for Miravent's brand of centralism. The responses they were getting were proving them wrong.

'We pay much more in taxes in Catalonia,' a young woman in the heart of the small throng now called to the politician, 'than the central government spends on Catalonia. It's the highest tax deficit in Europe, higher than what Germany gets back from the EU compared with what it pays.'

Other workers turned around to look at her, some of them nodding.

'We make the money, Madrid spends it,' someone else added. 'And it's never on us.'

Miravent raised both her hands to placate them. 'I hear what you're saying. But at the moment, you pay to support two governments, one in Barcelona and one in Madrid. It's inefficient. You'd all be better off if you only had to pay for the one in Madrid, which would then be able to fund Catalonia properly, as it deserves.'

The young woman laughed bitterly. 'Yeah, like that's ever going to happen.' It drew similar laughs from the people around her.

'Why should we vote for you in Barcelona if you don't believe in the Catalan government?' another voice shouted. 'If you don't think it should exist, you shouldn't be standing for election to it.'

Miravent hushed them again with her hands. 'Because all the people who disagree with the Catalan government as an institution deserve a voice in it, to overturn the excesses of those who would split this great country up and lead us out of a union that has served Catalonia well for three centuries.'

Montse had to give Miravent credit for remaining calm in the face of such little acceptance of her views at best, a mocking of them at worst. Hers was a blind and all-encompassing faith, the caporal decided.

At the end of the one-sided rally, as the workers drifted away back to their workplaces, ignoring Bofarull and his pile of glossy leaflets, Montse kept a firm eye on Miravent, but no one approached her, either to threaten her or to engage in discussion. Studying her, Montse realised that the politician had little concern for whether they did or not, her faith in her beliefs outweighing any sort of empathy.

The room emptied and Bofarull rejoined them. His phone rang as he was about to say something to Miravent. Answering it, he suddenly looked concerned and hung up.

'I have to go,' he told Miravent. 'I'll only be an hour or so.'

'What is it?' Montse asked him.

'My home might be flooded. There's been a burst pipe in the village. The water company's just called to say they need to get into my house in case it's been affected.'

'Can't one of your neighbours see to it?' Miravent asked him. 'Or your parents?'

'My neighbours don't have keys and my parents are elderly. They'd panic.'

'Go on then,' she told him. 'I'll manage on my own.'

Montse studied the concern on his face. 'Do you want a Mossos car to take you?'

'No, really, it's not a problem. I'll take my car. If you could drive Susanna home, I'd be grateful. This was the last place on today's itinerary, so it hasn't messed up the schedule.'

'You might need our help,' Montse insisted.

'No, really, please. It's not important.'

'I'll see you back at the house later,' Miravent interrupted, looking to Montse for her lift home.

Montse watched Bofarull hurry off.

'One moment,' she told Miravent.

Moving a discreet distance away, she rang Josep at Vista Alegre to tell him to send a Seguretat Ciutadana car to Bofarull's house to check up.

'Shall we go?' she asked the politician once she'd hung up.

–

'What a cold fish,' Montse complained to Josep.

She'd left Miravent in Palau with Seguretat Ciutadana watching the house and had gone back to Vista Alegre. Comas had been sitting with a whisky in the living room, looking pale and sorry for himself. The couple had barely greeted each other.

Before leaving, Montse had checked with the two techies in the spare bedroom, but they'd told her there'd been nothing of interest.

'If my kid was missing,' she carried on telling Josep, 'I'd be kicking up a shitstorm to find him. I'd make a complete pain of myself. All she does is look martyred and hide behind her religion.'

Josep looked up from the computer he was working on. 'Had a good day?'

'It's her own son, for Christ's sake.' Montse wasn't to be deterred. 'What sort of a mother just accepts they've gone missing and they'll be back if it's God's will? And the husband's worse. He just goes along with it.'

She was about to say more, but Josep was in time to signal to her with a glance to keep quiet. Looking quizzically at him, she heard the outer door open and turned to see Elisenda come into the room. She turned quickly back to Josep and mouthed a thank you.

'Please tell me something of interest,' Elisenda asked them.

She pulled out a chair and sat down heavily in the outer room with them. Before either of them could reply, she told them quickly about the *cercavila*.

'They haven't done anything illegal,' she concluded, 'and it would be heavy-handed of us to stop them, but I'd like a word with them to find out what they're about. Especially the bit about the prisoner going missing.'

'Pere Vergés?' Josep asked. 'Just got this in the last ten five minutes. I was about to call you.'

He turned his screen to face Elisenda and Montse. It was a group photo of about a dozen people that looked to be taken from an academic yearbook. He pointed to a man on the left of the picture.

'That's Francesc Bofarull. This is his class at business school in Barcelona.' He pointed to a second man nearer the centre of the group. 'And that...'

Elisenda peered closely at the figure.

'That is Pere Vergés,' she said. 'Bofarull said he didn't know Vergés.'

'I haven't got much more,' Josep told her. 'Just the names of the class and where they were working at the time. Vergés was with an IT company in Barcelona, and Bofarull was with an agency that took care of all of its marketing.'

'So conceivably they knew each other from the course and through work. So why did Bofarull lie about knowing Vergés?'

Montse spoke up. 'Bofarull got a call about an hour ago, saying he had to go home. His house was flooded.'

'I asked the La Bisbal station to check it out,' Josep added. 'They said they were busy, but that they'd get on to it when they could.'

Elisenda stood up, the weariness gone. 'Àlex and Manel are in the area. Get hold of them and tell them to get out there. And ring La Bisbal again, get them to send a car.'

'You think it's significant?' Josep asked.

'I think Bofarull has had more questions to answer all along. He could just be sheltering Vergés, or he could be holding him against his will if there's something more sinister about their relationship.'

'You think he framed Vergés for the IT fraud?' Montse asked.

'He lied about knowing him,' Elisenda explained. 'Judging by the equipment in his house, he'd know enough about computing to do the fraud. It's more than possible.'

'It could be the other way around,' Montse argued. 'Vergés is a threat to Bofarull. If he thinks Bofarull framed him, he'd be out for revenge.'

'Then why take the boy? Either way, we need to get into Bofarull's place. Josep, get a warrant to search his house and join us there. Montse and I will go on ahead. I want to see what really is in that cellar he keeps locked.'

Chapter Forty-Five

Elisenda hung up her mobile with her left hand and clung to the strap above the car door with her right.

'Water company,' she told Montse. 'There've been no burst pipes in Vulpellac today.'

'Damn,' Montse muttered and put her foot down perceptibly harder on the accelerator.

The car bucked forward, bouncing on the endless ups and downs of the road. Elisenda clung more tightly to the strap and decided that the colour of hell was blue. Through the side window, the car's flashing light reflected against the night-time fields and streets zipping by in a blur, the icy flare crowding the trees and buildings towards her in frightening relief. At least by looking to the front, the sensation of rushing dread was lessened, replaced by a more considered onrush of nerve-jangling awareness of what lay ahead. She also reckoned that the fast road had sprouted a few more roundabouts in the last twenty-four hours.

'You've done nothing wrong,' Elisenda told her, closing her eyes for a second as they passed a lorry. 'Although, get us killed and I'll be a bit pissed off.'

Montse managed a small laugh, but didn't slow down.

With one hand, Elisenda tried ringing both Àlex and Josep again, but was sent to voicemail both times. To take her mind off the drive, she voiced the questions that came to her now it had been confirmed that the water company hadn't been whoever it was that had called Bofarull.

'Either Bofarull lied to you and Miravent,' she said. 'Or the person that called lied to him. Either way, could it have been

Vergés?' She glanced over at Montse, concentrating firmly on the road. She had to slow down to go through the centre of La Bisbal, putting the siren on to ignore the traffic lights. Even the noise echoing harshly back at them in the narrow main street was a relief after the white-knuckle terror of the open road. 'And did Bofarull really go home, or is this just a wild goose chase and he's somewhere else entirely?'

She saw Montse grimace under the glare of the street lights as they crossed the river. Quickly glancing the other way, she saw the river flowing heavily under the seventeenth-century bridge, built to replace an earlier one washed away by flood. She shook her head in wonder. Usually, there was just the merest trickle of water over a riverbed rich in grass, but the rain in the mountains was driving torrents through the towns even though little rain was actually falling in them.

Vulpellac was just a few more minutes past La Bisbal, and Montse slowed to turn into the little hamlet. A Seguretat Ciutadana car was just stopping outside Bofarull's house when she and Elisenda got there. A uniformed caporala got out and rang the doorbell, turning with a questioning look at Elisenda and Montse as they approached her. Elisenda introduced herself and showed the caporala her ID.

'Is this the first time a patrol's been out here?' Elisenda asked.

The caporala nodded and rang the doorbell again. 'We've had an incident on the Palamós road that's taken up a lot of our resources. A lorry hit a car. We're the first to be able to get here.'

'There's no one answering,' Elisenda said, so the caporala banged on the door with her fist, but it made little noise on the heavy wood. Her cap wobbled on her hair with the effort, dark and long and tightly-packed in a bun underneath it.

'Reinforced,' Elisenda commented, looking closely at it by the weak light of a street lamp. The lock was a heavy-duty one, the frame made of steel coated to look like wood. Bofarull really didn't want anyone to get in. Or out.

'I'll check the neighbours,' the caporala said.

She was joined by her companion, a caporal with a shaved head under his cap and a stylish little moustache and goatee. Elisenda couldn't help thinking they'd been teamed up because they were a tonsorial match for each other. Each one took the house either side, and each one came away without getting an answer. They tried another couple of doors opposite, but got no luck there either, so they returned to Bofarull's house. Elisenda took one more look at the lock and realised that not even Siset's training in door-cracking was going to open it.

'Best get at it with a ram,' she told the two uniforms. 'It's not going to open itself.'

They looked at each other uncertainly. 'We don't have cause to break in,' the caporal said.

'It's all right. We have a warrant. It's on its way.'

Elisenda turned to Montse and pulled a face to say she hoped one was on its way. Just in case, she rang Josep again while the two Seguretat Ciutadana went to the boot of their patrol car. He called back ten minutes later, when Montse was taking a turn at battering at the stubborn door.

'*Got the warrant*,' he told her.

'Good. You'd better get here.'

A neighbour from the end of the street came out to see what the racket was, clutching a cotton housecoat around her shoulders. Elisenda asked her if she'd seen anything suspicious or any movement at the house.

'Only you lot,' the woman told her huffily and went back indoors.

It was only after Josep had arrived and all five of them had taken turns with the ram that the door finally gave in and slowly swung backwards, heavy on its hinges. The lights inside were off. Elisenda went first and flipped the switch. It came on, revealing the small anteroom typical of a house this age. It would once have been for the animals, but was now a windowless space too big for a hall and too dark for a sitting room. She had the unbidden thought that no one ever knew what to do with them. Bofarull was evidently no different as there was just a table and two upright chairs and nothing else. She sent Josep and the caporal up the stairs to the right, while she and the other two crossed into the downstairs rooms at the rear.

The first thing she noticed in the living room was that the large LED television she'd noticed the other day had gone. Looking around, she saw too that a sound system of speakers and dock that had been on a shelf by the TV was also missing. She couldn't remember enough from her last visit to know if that was all. Montse overtook her to go into the kitchen, through a door to the rear of the room they were in. Taking one last look around, Elisenda followed her and the caporal. She could see nothing that appeared to be missing, but a glass lay broken on the floor. Elisenda crouched down by the glass. It lay in a small puddle of water, but nothing else on the tiles gave any hint as to what might have happened. Montse tried the handle on the door out into the back garden, but it was locked.

The uniformed caporal suddenly made a shushing noise and held his finger up, looking into space as he listened. Elisenda heard it too. A dripping noise. It was very faint. There were long gaps between each sound and she found herself holding her breath until the next drop fell. Her two companions scanned the kitchen looking for the source, but Elisenda was drawn inexorably to the cellar door. It was open, a crack showing between the door and the frame.

Crossing the kitchen, she slowly pulled it open fully and waited. The first sound of a drip had grown in volume. It was coming from below, down the narrow flight of stone steps. The light was already on and she signalled to the other two to follow her. As she descended, she listened out for any other noise that would indicate what she might find in the cellar. She had expected the air to be musty, but it was surprisingly fresh, the temperature a few degrees cooler than in the upstairs rooms. As she descended further, a smell began to pervade her nose, getting stronger the deeper she went. She began to feel light-headed with it. The strong scent of red wine. Filling her nostrils, intoxicating her.

At the bottom of the stairs, to the left, there was a cage, its bars heavy. A door to it gaped open. Shocked, she stopped a brief moment to gather herself before pulling her gun out of its holster, where she'd placed it on her waist. Exhaling slowly and trying to shake the growing headiness that was engulfing her, she pressed on, walking quietly across the cement floor, the dust making light scratching noises under her shoes. The dripping continued, amplified in the enclosed space.

Reaching the gate, she looked left, where the cellar seemed to open out. The walls were lined with shelves, each one stacked with bottles. The necks of the bottles were face-out, pointing to the centre of the room.

Pointing to the ancient and stained wooden table and two upright chairs in the middle of the open space.

Pointing to the body that lay on its back on the table.

Another smell reached Elisenda's nose.

Chapter Forty-Six

'Waterboarded,' Albert Riera, the pathologist told Elisenda. 'With his own wine.'

From the edge of the cage, Elisenda watched Riera at work. The smell of the wine that had been poured over the dead man lying face-up on the table was overpowering. It was still making her feel light-headed over an hour since finding the body. She and the Científica forensic team scanning the cellar had had to keep taking turns outside in the fresh air. At least two dozen empty wine bottles were on the floor, some intact, many shattered where the attacker had simply thrown them to the ground. The wine had been poured onto the man's face, over a tea-towel that had been placed over his head. What liquid hadn't been forced into his mouth and nose had cascaded down and collected in a pool on the modern stone floor tiles, spreading across the large room in a gridiron along the joins.

'His own wine?' Elisenda questioned absently, although she knew whose face to expect under the thin material. When she'd discovered the body, she hadn't removed the towel before Científica and Riera had had a chance to get what they could from the scene, but Montse had recognised the clothes he was wearing.

'Someone's wine,' Riera replied irritably. From her distance, Elisenda could see his eyes streaming from the fumes. His mouth and nose were covered in a sterile mask, concealing the salt-and-pepper goatee and moustache that made him look like an old-fashioned grandee.

Carefully, he folded back the drenched tea-towel and handed it to his assistant to bag it. Elisenda moved forward gingerly over the pads set down by Científica and craned over to see the man's face.

'Francesc Bofarull,' she confirmed.

The source of the other smell she'd noticed became apparent, as the campaign manager's mouth and nose were encrusted in vomit from where he'd struggled to breathe as he was drowning in wine.

'Would that be the cause of death?' she asked Riera.

He looked up at her and she saw the annoyance in his eyes. It was nothing new. At least he was reining in his usual foul language.

'You know it's far too early to say. I'll let you know. Now fuck off back to where you were and let me get on with my work.'

Elisenda smiled at him and leaned forward. 'You know that doesn't work with me, Albert, so don't push it.'

He stared back at her for a few seconds, before mumbling what was probably an apology. His assistant looked surprised and flashed a quick conspiratorial roll of the eyes at Elisenda. Contrition famously didn't come easily to the pathologist.

Elisenda retraced her steps to the door of the cage, wondering once again at the structure. Her initial reaction had been that it had some sinister motive, but she quickly realised that it was simply extra security for the wine. The metal construction took up most of the room and was filled with row upon row of bottles. Bofarull had been telling the truth when he'd told her that he kept wine in the cellar.

'How many people would it have taken to do this?' she called to Riera. 'Could one person have done it?'

Riera stood up and stretched his back to consider. Bofarull's legs had been strapped to the table with a length of rope. More rope was stacked with some tools in another part of the cellar, outside the cage, so the attacker had most probably used it opportunely.

'He would have been immobile from the waist down,' Riera said. 'But they'd have had to have held his upper body down. Possibly by sitting on him. Maybe with one hand if they were strong enough or the angle was right. I'll be able to tell you more about that when he's back at the forensic institute, if there's any bruising on the chest. I should say it's possible, but it would be easier with more than one person doing it.'

Elisenda took in his words. She had to consider Pere Vergés as the prime suspect for the murder, but she was trying to reconcile the descriptions she'd heard of the man with the scene before her. It bore too many of the hallmarks of the gang attacking houses, even though Bofarull's home wasn't as isolated as their usual targets. The atmosphere in the cellar was becoming unbearable. The Científica team had already taken a break while she'd been talking to Riera.

'I'm going upstairs,' she told the pathologist.

Riera looked up, his face red. 'I think we'll join you.'

As they carefully moved away from the table and out of the cage, the Científica team came back down the narrow steps.

'Stay away from the body,' Riera warned them.

The leader watched him go and mouthed "prick" at Elisenda. She shrugged and asked him to check the dimensions of the cellar compared with the upstairs.

'Any discrepancy in size,' she explained. 'Any hidden partition or door in the wall or floor. We need to check in case there's somewhere we're not seeing where something or someone could be kept.'

The leader nodded and pulled his mask up. He had sleepy eyes that were accentuated when they were the only feature showing, but he was one of the sharpest members of the forensic team. Elisenda was glad he was on duty.

Out of the cloying atmosphere of the cellar, another Científica told her that the other two members of her team were in the victim's office on the top floor. She climbed the stairs and found Montse and Josep with two forensic cops going through the room. All the state-of-the-art computer equipment she'd seen the other day had been taken. The framed article she'd noticed was still on the wall. Josep stood next to her as she looked at it.

'Did that prove to be his downfall?' he asked.

'Sometimes it doesn't pay to advertise,' she commented. 'If this is just a burglary gone wrong, that is.'

'I've got hold of Àlex,' Montse told her. 'They were out in La Fosca with no signal and then they were delayed by some road accident. They're on their way here.'

Elisenda thanked her and waved her hand around the room. 'So what's our take on this? A robbery gone too far or a revenge killing? Is it a genuine burglary or faked to look like one?'

Montse sucked in her breath. 'If the reason were the murder downstairs, would the killer really go to the bother of taking everything? They might take something to make it look like a robbery, but I don't see that they'd take everything. That would take a lot of cool-headedness. Especially after killing someone like that.' She pointed down at the ground, indicating the cellar.

Elisenda sighed. 'My thoughts precisely. This looks too similar to the house robberies to be anything else, but Vergés has to be a suspect too.' She recalled the victim lying bound to the table. 'But does it tie in with what we know about him?'

'He was innocent and he spent four years in prison,' Josep commented. 'That's more than enough time to make someone change.'

'And his loss of faith,' Montse conceded. 'That and a sense of injustice.'

'But would it lead to him doing this?' Elisenda asked. 'And to taking Jaume?'

'I think it could,' Josep said. 'Although I agree he'd have to be pretty calculating to do all of this to cover it up.'

Elisenda turned to go back downstairs. 'We can't rule it out,' she had to agree. 'But I would like to know more about his relationship with Miravent and Comas. If he did do this and he has taken the boy, they have to know more than they're saying.' She turned back to the two caporals. 'Check up on their house, make sure they're both there, make sure the protection is in place. If this is Vergés, they're at greater risk.'

Once more in the cellar, she saw that Riera and his assistant were already back at work. The Científica she'd spoken to before leaving told her that they'd found nothing unusual about the room so far.

'Fucking Philistines,' she heard Riera mutter.

She turned to see him holding one of the empty bottles.

'Why's that?' she asked, curious.

He gestured at the walls around him. 'I don't know what these people think they stole with the computers, but this is where the money is.'

He moved back from Bofarull's body and beckoned her to one of the shelves. Taking his glove off, he pulled a bottle off the wall.

'Vega Sicilia Único 1964. About six hundred euros a bottle. Two whole shelves of them.' He moved along to another shelf and took another bottle. His movements were almost reverent. 'And this is also a Vega Sicilia Único. But from 1936. That's about a thousand euros a bottle.'

Elisenda looked along the wall. She counted at least five dozen of the dust-caked bottles, just from what she could see.

'There's a fortune here,' she whispered.

Riera gazed around. 'Hence the cage. There's got to be millions' worth here.'

She looked at him thoughtfully. 'And where would the money for that come from?'

She heard her name being called from the direction of the staircase. It was Àlex, peering down into the cellar.

'Nightmare on the roads,' he told her when she went to join him. 'We've been checking out La Fosca with the local station. All the occupied houses had leaflets, but we couldn't find any symbols anywhere. They don't seem to have singled anywhere out for an attack.'

'We're going to have to find a way to anticipate their next step,' Elisenda told him. She rubbed her forehead, tired from the overpowering wine fumes and the enormity of the two investigations facing them.

'There's something else you need to see,' he told her, gesturing for her to follow him.

He took her outside to the front of the house, where Manel was waiting, and pointed to the metal shutter over the niche set into the wall where the meters were kept. In the bottom corner, barely visible in the light from the street lamp, was a symbol. A triangle with three lines jutting out of the top.

'Which makes it a robbery,' she murmured.

'Only one thing,' Àlex commented. 'There's no line through the triangle. If this were the gang, they'd have marked it as job done.'

Chapter Forty-Seven

It was late by the time Elisenda got back to Girona.

Bofarull's body had finally been taken to the city's Institut de Medicina Legal. At that time of night, no judge or court secretary had come out to the scene to authorise the removal of the body as the law required. Instead, as so often happened in practice, they'd delegated that task to Riera as pathologist. He and Elisenda had been among the last to leave. She'd sent her own team off earlier in two cars, while she'd taken the third so that she could drive back to the city alone with her thoughts.

But before that, she'd had one more task to do. Crossing the small hamlet where Bofarull had lived, she went to see his parents. This was never easy, but telling an elderly couple that their one child had died before them, murdered just a few streets away, was one of the hardest experiences she'd ever known. She'd been able to do little but watch the two people hold on to each other and try to understand. At their neighbour's suggestion, she'd called their nephew, who also lived in Vulpellac, and she waited with them until he came. Completely different from his cousin, the man had hugged the couple warmly and told Elisenda it was all right for her to leave.

Entering Girona, she couldn't help being drawn by the lights under the trees of the Devesa, growing weaker in intensity as they reached for reflection in the tall branches towering high above them. On impulse, she parked nearby and walked into the park again. She immediately felt the chill of recollection of a member of her team dying so grotesquely in the shadows, his body staged as cruelly as Bofarull's had been in the cellar of his own home. She stopped and steeled herself, forcing herself to continue. Inhaling deeply, she set off again to be swallowed by the lights and noise of the traders and re-enactors camping like excitable schoolchildren just metres from air-conditioned homes and restaurants.

It was a different park. The unusual sight of tents and torches and stands in readiness for the morning's festivities turned it into another beast, not one of painful memory, but a make-believe place where evil didn't enter. Savouring the scent of the trees and the sounds of low laughter and conversation, she found herself walking lightly through the groups of people getting ready for the night. The pressure of the two investigations seemed to float away from her, up into the leaves overhead.

She was surprised by a figure walking among the stands, talking to people as he went. She caught up with him by a group of re-enactors in French military costume.

'Sotsinspector Armengol?' she called him.

He turned to face her. In his hand, he held a sheaf of papers, the photos of Jaume Comas Miravent that they'd been distributing. He looked almost guilty.

'Elisenda.'

'Are you on your own?'

He shook his head. 'A few of my team are out, we're asking the newcomers who've come for the siege celebrations if they've seen Jaume.'

'Seguretat Ciutadana have already been here. You really don't have to.'

'There are more visitors here now. Most of them won't have been asked if they've seen him.' He paused for a moment, seemingly indecisive. 'I was talking to missing persons in Sabadell earlier. They were saying the flow of calls and messages has slowed down.'

Elisenda led him away from the group of re-enactors. 'Did they say why?'

'It coincides with every time Susanna Miravent makes a public appearance. When she's quiet, the public helps more. When she looks like she's using it for political gain, people switch off. It's upsetting. Naturally, the public wants to help when a child goes missing, but she puts so many backs up that everyone starts questioning the integrity of the whole thing. It's hampering the search.'

'And that's why you're out showing the photo?' She looked at the tents and stands fading under the line of trees. 'Here, give me some. I'll take the other end of the park.'

He handed her half his pile. 'One other thing,' he added. 'I've also been checking out the attack on Marc Comas. There's no record of anyone trying to use the stolen bank cards, which is unusual. Normally, I'd expect them to be used in the first hour at least. And my team's heard nothing about anyone trying to sell them on. The same with the mobile phone. It hasn't been used and no one's been caught trying to sell it. That's not normal for this type of robbery.'

'No word from any informants?'

Armengol gave a self-deprecating smile. 'My team have found nothing. And I'm new to the city, so I'm still building up my contacts. That's the problem of sending us all to different parts of Catalonia.'

'It'll come.'

Armengol smiled a second time as Elisenda turned to head off for the other end of the Devesa. 'I'm sure it will. I just need people to understand that we're all new at some point.'

Elisenda digested his last words as she made her way through the park, asking questions and handing out photos. She'd finished her stack of pictures towards the end of the Devesa furthest from the city centre when she found a figure standing in front of her. Staring into her eyes all the time, he bowed down low, the feathers in his cap brushing the ground at his feet. With another flourish, he stood up again and replaced his battered tricorne.

'Have you eaten?' he asked her. 'Food is on its way.'

'I want to talk to you,' she told the leader of the *cercavila*.

He turned and strode away, threatening to vanish into the shadows. 'Follow me.'

He led and she followed to the camp where she'd seen him the previous evening. He took out a lace handkerchief and slapped it across a stool before inviting her to sit. The other members of his troupe were a short distance away, engrossed in their own conversations. Despite herself, she accepted his offer.

'The story you were telling,' she asked him immediately. 'About a missing boy and a prisoner.'

He looked at her intently, his eyes glittering in the glow of the camping lamps. 'Just a story. I see what's happening around me and I turn it into a tale for people to feel self-righteous.'

'What do you know about a missing prisoner?'

'Ah, a police officer asking questions. That is always good to see. It makes me feel protected, wanted. Perhaps we should be more respectful in our depictions of you.'

'It's not so very long ago that you'd have been imprisoned for mocking a police officer,' she told him, instantly regretting the words, which sounded officious even to her.

He laughed, but not cruelly. 'Then we should all be grateful we live in a more enlightened age. One where we can tell our stories and not be worried about who's listening. I promise you, it's just a tale that I tell to entertain and send all good people to their homes certain of their own probity and morals. No one need take offence unless they have to. Why are you in the park at this time of night?'

Surprised at the change in direction, she didn't know what to say.

'Maybe you don't want to go home,' he continued.

Low in the darkness, his voice was more mesmerising still than it had been when it echoed in the narrow square of the old town. She felt herself being drawn in by its honeyed comfort.

He leaned back and studied her face, his gaze flickering from her one eye to the other and then back again. 'No, it's not that.' Suddenly he stopped. 'I'm sorry.'

'Why are you sorry?'

He looked down and seemed to pause for an age before replying. 'I had a wife and a son. I lost them.' He looked up at her again. 'I see it in you.'

A commotion nearby took away her need to answer. A sudden grin crossed his face.

'Food. I told you it was on its way.'

Elisenda turned around to see a motorcycle courier delivering a pile of pizzas to the nineteenth-century camp under the trees and the spell was broken.

'I can't stay,' she told him.

The wall behind him felt wetter.

He couldn't see it, so he had to feel as far as he could with his left hand. What had been damp before, then a film of water on the coarse stone, had become a slow but steady trickle. He felt it build up against his fingertips and flow around them like tree branches in a swollen river. He tried to reach further to see how far it went, but the pain of the metal band cutting into his right wrist pulled him back.

He sat forward from the wall to avoid the wet. Another wave of pain hit him. Hunger. And thirst. Cautiously, he took a drink from the plastic water bottle. It tasted all right, so he drank some more. Unwrapping the tin foil package with his left hand, he took out the baguette and bit into it. The bread was stale, the crust flaking, but the inside was soaked. The tomato and oil had seeped into the white of the bread and turned it to mush. He felt nauseous but he ate it. He didn't know when the next one would be coming.

Finishing the food, he instinctively turned to look at the plastic bucket standing within a short reach. His eyes prickled. He'd had to use it. The stench of his own faeces after the pulp of the sandwich almost made him retch the food back up. He'd put the bucket as far away from him as he could, but he still had to be able to reach it, so the smell was only ever an arm's length distant.

The door above him opened. It all but blinded him, used as he was now to the dark of the cellar. The figure standing in the frame looked down at him but said nothing. The light behind him was weak, and he couldn't see his face.

'You don't know what you're going to do with me, do you?' he called up to his captor.

Saturday

Chapter Forty-Eight

'You've done your homework.'

Elisenda stood on the landing. She hadn't even crossed the threshold into the counsellor's office. 'How can you know?'

'I told you I'd know.'

Puyals invited her in and tried to conceal a smile. The dark semi-circles that were a constant under Elisenda's eyes were in abeyance, her irises brighter than the counsellor had seen them all week.

'Do you want to tell me about it?' she asked once they'd both taken up their positions on chair and recliner.

Elisenda closed her eyes and tried to order in her mind what had happened after she'd got home last night. After the discovery of Bofarull's body, after breaking the news to his parents, after the disconcerting conversation with the leader of the *cercavila*, home was anything but a refuge. Giving up on bed, she'd wrapped herself in a sheet on the sofa and tried to blot out a lullaby curling misshapen through the corners of her flat. Shadows ghosted behind the paper screens and she'd felt for the first time that her redecoration had made the nights worse. She had nowhere to hide, nowhere to escape the darkness that ran through the open rooms of her apartment. In desperation, she'd tipped her bag out onto the coffee table to look for an aspirin when she found the piece of paper that Puyals had given her two days earlier. She'd read it and thrown it down in disgust.

'What a load of nonsense,' she muttered out loud.

'But you tried it?' Puyals asked her now.

'I tried it. I went and got paper and a pen and I wrote down a memory of Lina.'

What she'd written about was her daughter's fourth birthday, when it was just the two of them living in Barcelona. She'd taken her to the zoo, expecting Lina to be overwhelmed by the animals and the sights and sounds of the park. Instead, she'd barely noticed the big cats and the penguins and the snakes that had enthralled all the other children. Her boredom had quickly turned to fractiousness. For Elisenda, it had been turning into another day of disappointment until she'd suddenly noticed Lina wasn't next to her. She turned to see her on the path behind, calling Elisenda over urgently, her voice hoarse with excitement. She was looking down at the footpath.

'Look, mama,' she'd cried. 'Ants.'

'Ants?' Elisenda had wept with laughter and gathered her daughter up for a hug until she'd struggled and demanded to be let down again.

'I took her to a zoo,' Elisenda told Puyals, 'and all that interested her were the ants.'

'And?' Puyals prompted her.

'And I don't remember anything else until the sunlight coming in through the gaps in the shutters and waking me up. I'd slept through the night.'

She'd woken up to look at the notebook on the table. She was shocked to see she'd written pages and pages. She remembered nothing of the process.

'We'll be changing to weekly visits,' Puyals told her at the end of the session.

'Weekly?' Elisenda couldn't help feeling disappointed.

'You can call me if you need to. But if you keep doing your homework, that won't be necessary. We'll set our day for Saturday morning and leave it at that for a few weeks.'

'Saturday morning? What if I get lucky on Friday night?'

'Then we'll have something else to talk about on Saturday morning.'

–

Montse was waiting for Elisenda outside Susanna Miravent's house in Palau. The number of journalists in the huddle hadn't dwindled, despite the little news that the Mossos had been willing or able to release to them. The same reporter as before shouted out the same question about Jaume's disappearance being the work of a sex offender. Elisenda didn't bother replying this time.

'We have to expect this sort of interest to increase today,' she told Montse as they walked up the drive to the house. 'Since they can't report on the elections, the missing child of a controversial politician is the next best thing.'

It was Saturday, the day before the election, known as the day of reflection. Legally, parties weren't allowed to canvas and the press couldn't try to influence voters. Publishing the results of opinion polls had already been illegal for the last four days, although most of the papers got around it by reporting on polls shown in the foreign press.

'About time we got rid of it,' Montse commented. 'Everyone talks about the elections on Twitter anyway.'

'In theory, that's illegal too today. If they ever try and enforce it, we're going to need a lot more Mossos.'

Inside the house, Miravent was on her own in the living room. She was standing by the wall that stood at a right-angle to the glass doors leading out into the garden. It was covered in framed photos of the family and of her political career.

'You might want to sit down,' Elisenda told her.

'I'm perfectly fine where I am, thank you,' the politician replied.

Elisenda inhaled deeply without it showing, a trick she'd had to learn since joining the Mossos, and told Miravent that her campaign manager had been found dead the previous night. For once, there was a reaction of sorts, a muted shock that left her speechless and staring at Elisenda for a long moment.

'How?' was all she asked.

Elisenda explained the circumstances of Bofarull's death in as little detail as was necessary. 'It's important that you answer me,' she concluded. 'Is there anyone that you think might be responsible for this?'

'I presume you mean do I think that Pere Vergés would be capable?' Miravent replied. Her aloof coldness was back in place, although her eyes betrayed that she was fighting back tears. Elisenda wanted to tell her that it was all right to cry, but she knew the woman wouldn't appreciate it. 'I wouldn't have said so before his time in prison. Now, I really couldn't say.'

'And would he be capable of taking your son?' Elisenda asked.

Unusually, Miravent didn't reply immediately, looking instead at the wall of photos next to her. 'I suppose my answer would be the same. I doubt that the Pere Vergés I knew would be capable of it. But after all that's happened to him, I don't know.'

'I have to know if there is any reason he might blame you or your husband for what happened to him. If you haven't told me before, I need you to tell me now.'

'There really is nothing.' Her voice sounded strained, the first time Elisenda had heard that.

'We have to presume that he is involved,' Elisenda continued. 'Given what happened last night and that today is both the anniversary of the siege and the day of reflection, this might be the day that he makes his move. So I must insist that you accept protection from my team and from other Mossos. Are you or your husband planning on going out today? If you are, Montse here will be accompanying you. Is your husband here right now?'

'He's in his study. We will both be going into the city centre this morning to watch some of the re-enactments. As a candidate in the elections, I have to be there to show my face.'

She turned away to study the wall. Elisenda walked across to join her. She was gazing at pictures of Jaume at various sporting events and class graduations.

'I'm not as cold as you think I am, Elisenda,' she said in a low voice. 'My faith is what brings me through all this.'

On the wall directly in front of her, Elisenda saw a photo of a much younger Jaume holding a small trophy.

'What did he win the cup for?' she asked.

Miravent laughed, a faint trace of bitterness in it. 'Kayaking. It was one of the days I organise for members of our faith. We have a large picnic together and there are competitions for adults and children. Jaume won the kayaking competition. He was only ten at the time, the other children he raced against were a few years older.'

Elisenda peered at the photo, trying to place it. 'Is that near Susqueda?'

Miravent nodded. 'That is faith, Elisenda. I lost my older son to the water and I allowed my younger son to go back to the water.'

Chapter Forty-Nine

'I think the time's come to tell people what to look for.'

Àlex couldn't contain his frustration. 'We'll be showing our hand. It's the one thing we've got on this gang that they don't know we've got.'

Elisenda was adamant. 'We need to warn home-owners. We have to tell them about the symbols and get them to look around their own homes in case they've been targeted. If we don't, we're going to see more victims.'

Her unit were gathered in her office, except for Montse, who had stayed in Palau with Miravent. Between them, the day's copy of the local newspaper lay open on pages two and three. A double spread told of the religious pamphlets that had been found at the houses that had been attacked. Owners in isolated villages were being warned to report any religious callers to the police. It wasn't an initiative that the Mossos had put out.

'They'll just change their MO and we'll be back to square one,' Àlex insisted. 'We'd never be able to anticipate an attack.'

'We can't anticipate one now. You've seen that we couldn't ever hope to check out all the homes in the Baix Empordà, let alone the whole of the Girona region. We have to rely on people looking for themselves and warning us.'

'And warning the gang while they're at it.'

'It's a risk we have to take, Àlex. We have to hope they don't see the message, but we can't simply allow them to keep up their attacks and not warn owners. That has to come first.'

She could see that his frustration was because he knew she was right. She also knew that he had a point. Tipping the attackers off that the Mossos knew of the symbols could easily make them change their way of going about the robberies and set her team's investigation back.

Àlex pointed at the newspaper, his voice resigned. 'For all we know, this has already done it. If they see this, they'll change how they pick the houses. The paper probably found out about it because we've been asking owners if they've had a visit from these people. Any one of them could have told the press.'

Glancing for a moment at the paper, Elisenda called them back to Bofarull's murder. 'I think this means a convergence of the two investigations,' she told them. 'We can't be certain if he was killed by Vergés, or if it was part of these attacks, but his death inevitably means there's a connection, if only in terms of how we tackle it.'

'Isn't it too much of a coincidence?' Josep asked. 'Him being attacked by the gang when he's under suspicion for kidnapping the boy?'

'Or he was killed by Vergés but it's got nothing to do with the kid,' Manel interrupted.

Elisenda agreed. 'We won't know about Bofarull's bank accounts until later today, but the wine in that cellar was worth a fortune according to Riera. Científica will be taking an inventory, so we'll know exactly what it's worth, but the important point is how come he was able to amass that sort of collection? His only income is from his work and that wouldn't pay for it. That and his evident knowledge of computers points to him potentially being responsible for the fraud that Vergés was convicted for.'

'Vergés thought so too,' Àlex suggested, 'and went looking for payback.'

'You and Manel have been following up on the house attacks,' Elisenda asked him. 'Do you think Bofarull's murder is part of that or to do with the missing boy?'

Àlex let out a low whistle. 'Ordinarily, I'd say that with all the evidence we have, it was the gang that robbed the house and killed him. We don't know if he was forced to transfer his money, but the way he was tortured and killed suggests they were trying to force him to give up the codes. All the usual items were stolen and they took his car too. And we're certain that the next two attacks are going to be in the Baix Empordà, which this one was. That to me says it was the gang. The one thing I don't get is why the symbol wasn't crossed out. If it were the gang, they'd have done that.'

'They were interrupted?' Manel asked.

'Josep,' Elisenda said. 'Play devil's advocate. Tell me why it would be Vergés.'

Josep gathered his thoughts for a moment before speaking. 'Bofarull ran the fraud and framed Vergés for it. Vergés worked it out in prison and is looking for revenge. Not just on Bofarull but on Comas too, because he was involved in some way.'

'We have no evidence for that,' Elisenda interrupted.

'We don't. But Vergés might suspect it. He worked with Comas. And that's why Vergés has taken Jaume. Not for money, because he hasn't asked for anything, but for revenge. He lost his mother because he was wrongly convicted, so he's taken Comas's son. Vergés suffered, now he's making the people he blames for it suffer.'

'So why the symbol on the house?' Manel asked. 'That really would be some coincidence.'

'Vergés has been in prison for four years,' Josep argued. 'He got to know the gang members from his time there. He knows how they plan their attacks, so he's using it for his own ends. That would explain not crossing the triangle out.'

Elisenda shook her head. 'Do we think that Vergés has become that tough in prison that he's going to be accepted by this gang, which is pretty heavy duty, and be able to kidnap a fourteen-year-old boy and torture Bofarull? That's quite some change.'

'Four years in prison and you're innocent,' Josep countered. 'So's that.'

The four of them considered Josep's words.

'OK, Àlex and Manel,' Elisenda finally said. 'If we do think that Vergés knows how the gang works, it might be an idea to check up on whether any of the other home-owners had any links to him.'

Josep looked startled. 'I'm just playing devil's advocate. I don't know how far I go along with Vergés being responsible for Bofarull's death.'

'Neither do I,' Elisenda placated him. 'But it's all worth considering at this stage. Whatever happened to Bofarull, I think we still have to see Pere Vergés as a suspect for Jaume's disappearance and as a potential threat to Comas or Miravent. Those are the most likely avenues we have to pursue. For now, stick to the investigations you're working on, but be aware that we may be seeing a convergence between them. In what way, I don't know yet.'

'Do you really think Vergés has got Jaume?' Àlex asked as they made to leave her office.

'I hope so. Because that would mean he's still alive.'

-

Puigventós studied Elisenda and Àlex and considered their request. Armengol was also in the inspector's office, as was another figure.

'Sotsinspector Micaló is back from his course,' Puigventós explained.

'Surprised to see you here, Sotsinspectora Domènech,' Micaló said. 'I thought you were on sick leave.' As he said the last two words, he mimed speech marks with the first two fingers on each hand.

'No, I'm still here,' Elisenda told him affably. She'd caught a glance exchanged between Àlex and Armengol at the mime. 'I thought you weren't going to be back until Monday.'

Micaló sighed expansively. 'You don't seem to be able to do without me. Houses still being attacked, schoolboys still missing, what are we to do?'

'Quite,' she replied, turning to Puigventós. She'd heard Àlex's intake of breath, which helped divert her own irritation.

She quickly outlined her thoughts on telling the public to be aware of the symbols that the gang of house attackers was using to identify targets.

'We can use social media to spread the message. And get the newspapers to do the same. That way, we have a chance to get word out to home-owners to keep themselves safe.'

'It would also alert the attackers,' Puigventós argued.

'Yes, it possibly would. But there's also the possibility that with the public's help, we could identify the next target before the gang is aware that it's on social media. Apart from protecting the public, it could even work in our favour.'

Out of the corner of her eye, she could see Micaló gauging the inspector's reaction. Puigventós looked like he had his doubts.

'I don't know, Elisenda. We could find ourselves inundated with people calling about the most innocuous things on their houses, or even graffiti.'

'We'd tell people to look for a triangle, but we wouldn't give out any more details. That will weed out all the scrawls and squiggles. So if someone contacts us to say they've seen one with the lines coming out of the top, then we know it's genuine and we have to follow it up. Anything else, we just assure them that they're not at risk.'

'You might get pranksters drawing on other people's houses.'

'It's a chance we have to take. But we'll still be able to weed out the fakes the same way.'

Puigventós stared blankly at his desk for a moment and appeared to reach a decision. 'I think you're right. We have no other choice. Go ahead with it.'

'My thoughts precisely,' Micaló agreed. 'Go for it.'

'And now that Roger is back,' the inspector gestured to Micaló, 'you can count on the support of his unit in your investigations.'

'I'm more than happy with Esteve's help,' she said, nodding at Armengol.

Micaló held his hands up expansively. 'Of course you are. But any assistance I can give, I'd be only too happy.'

'You have no idea what that means to me,' Elisenda told him.

Turning to leave, she caught a gleam in Armengol's expression as he tried to suppress a laugh. Without meaning to, she smiled at him for the first time since he'd been working at Vista Alegre.

Outside the room, she was about to explode to Àlex about Micaló when a uniformed mosso came up to her with a message from the officer in charge of the cells.

'A prisoner wants to talk to you,' he told her.

Instantly calm, she told Àlex to get Manel and meet her in an interview room. Ten minutes later, the three of them were sitting there when Siset was shown in.

'I want to do a trade,' he told her the moment he sat down. His voice had lost none of its whine. 'If I tell you something, I want to go home.'

'Tell me what it is, and I'll decide whether you go home.'

Siset shook his head. 'I want a promise, Elisenda. I'm not telling you unless you promise.'

'OK, Siset, tell me something useful and you will go home.'

He bit at the fingertips on his right hand for a few moments. 'These people I trade with. There's going to be a job tonight.'

'You told me there was going to be one last week and you were wrong.'

'No, I wasn't. There was an attack, I just got the wrong place.'

Elisenda sighed. 'You really are hopeless, Siset, do you know that. So there's going to be an attack tonight? Where?'

He looked uncertain for the first time. 'I don't know. They just told me to be at home tomorrow because they're going to bring me some stuff.'

'How long have you known this, Siset?'

He shrugged his skinny shoulders. 'A few days.'

'And you're telling me about it now? And you don't know where it's going to be? What am I supposed to do with that? I said "useful".'

'That's your job, Elisenda. You're the cop.'

She stood up. 'OK, Siset, you can go home.'

'I can?'

'Sure you can. Tomorrow, when the seventy-two hours are up.'

Chapter Fifty

In a clearing, two soldiers faced each other across a divide under the trees yearning for light. Slowly, they approached, each one mirroring the tentative step of the other. When some ten metres still separated them, they stopped. In the hush that fell, a baby cried, its mother hurriedly calming it. The rest of the onlookers remained silent, held in thrall by the events happening in front of them.

'Will you surrender?' the Irishman in the uniform of Napoleon's army called.

'No. We will defend our city,' the Irishman in the uniform of the Ultonia regiment, a force in the Spanish army made up of troops of Irish ancestry, replied.

The two men faced each other as a drum in the Spanish army ranks began to mark a slow and insistent beat. Nodding at each other, the two soldiers turned their backs and joined their armies. The Irishman in the French uniform, a baker from Barcelona and Catalan, reported back to his commanding officer. The other Irishman, in the Spanish uniform, an office manager from Girona and also Catalan, rejoined his troops, other re-enactors in Spanish uniform and a ragtag force of *miquelets*, Catalan militia.

The drum beat stopped and the two armies marched slowly towards each other. They stopped and fired their weapons once above the heads of the opposing force before moving forwards again, steadily quickening their pace. They met in the middle and skirmished with studied sword blows and clashing pikes. Finally, the French troops were pushed back and they withdrew to their tents, set up in the shade near the traffic lights. The defenders moved back to the cheers of the people under the trees, filming it all on mobile phones and explaining what had just happened to their children.

'That was the first siege,' a mother told her wide-eyed young son. 'The French sent an Irish soldier serving with them to demand surrender and he met another Irishman in the Spanish army defending the city. The French will attack two more times in this siege, but we'll push them back every time. Then there'll be two more sieges after that.'

'Do we win every time?' the little boy asked.

The mother laughed. 'No, not every time. We lose the third siege.'

The boy looked crestfallen to hear that, but he suddenly perked up. 'So we won two-one?'

Under the trees in the Devesa, Elisenda listened to them and smiled. These re-enactments of the Napoleonic siege of Girona during the Peninsular War had only been celebrated for the last few years. It wasn't something she'd grown up with or been able to bring her daughter to see. Now it was a big celebration with mock battles all over the city and story-telling and stands selling all sorts of food and trinkets and stuffed or wooden toys for a new generation captivated by their own history.

Her eyes roamed the park again. All through the staged fight, she'd scanned the people in the crowd. In front of her, Montse was standing near Susanna Miravent and Marc Comas, the couple subdued in their viewing of the events. She watched as another couple came up to them and spoke to them, the wife holding on to Miravent's hand all the while. All around, there were increased numbers of Mossos, not all in uniform. Because of the siege celebrations and the missing boy, all weekend leave had been cancelled. Other Mossos were touring the park and the rest of the city, all briefed, all with photos of Jaume and of Pere Vergés. All watchful, Elisenda hoped. One of the few exceptions was Josep, back in the gloom of Vista Alegre, scouring through the leads and reviewing all the information they had. Àlex and Manel, too, were on other duties, following up Bofarull's murder and looking for a way to stop the next attack. She sighed. It was like looking for a single face in the forest of people under the trees.

With a lull in the re-enactments, Miravent and Comas followed the lead of many of the other visitors to the park and drifted back into the city centre. Montse followed closely, Elisenda at a short distance, looking for anyone tracking the couple. In the odd moments that she caught sight of their faces, she saw the strain the politician and her husband were under. Miravent was turning on the charm when they ran into friends or when would-be voters recognised her, but Comas could barely contain his evident wish to get away. Although she couldn't share Miravent's hard-core beliefs and she knew in her gut that there was something not right about Comas, she felt sorry for them both in different ways because of the pain they were going through.

On Carrer Santa Clara, the crowd seemed to gather focus, and she saw that they were falling in behind a small troupe up ahead. Craning her neck, she was surprised to see that it was the *cercavila*, dancing in their faded costumes along the narrow shopping street to the strident screeching of the bombards and shawms they were playing. The leader weaved in and out of the people in front of him, waving his sword at the children, who ran screaming in joy from him.

They stopped on the Pont de Pedra, the stone bridge connecting the old town with the new, and took up formation. The leader now faced the crowd that had been following him. Behind him, two of the troupe fired their blunderbusses, making everyone flinch with the noise. One of the bombards tweeted and the crowd laughed. The leader put down a low stool on the cobbles and flapped at it with his frilly handkerchief before stepping up onto it. From his position, he caught sight of Elisenda and bowed low, almost wobbling as he did so. The crowd laughed and he held his hand up to them, showing that everything was under control. Elisenda dragged her eyes away from him to look around the people gathered on the bridge and by the parapet on Carrer Santa Clara.

'A story,' the leader pronounced. The crowd fell silent.

'A story of lies, deceit and a loud gun.' Behind him, one of the team fired their blunderbuss, which echoed with a huge retort. He ducked. 'That was the gun.'

As the audience hushed again, four of the troupe came and stood in front of him and he held one hand up like an ancient Roman making a proclamation.

'Bla bla bla bla bla.' He paused and began again. 'Bla bla rubbish, nonsense, crap, bla.'

His fake audience of four ignored him as he spoke, talking instead to each other and pointing at the buildings around them and the river to either side of them.

'Bla bla bla, better with Spain, bla bla, take back control from the nationalists, bla bla bla, and give it to other nationalists.'

Seeing that his audience wasn't listening, he turned and called over one of the two standing behind him and whispered in her ear. She nodded and gave a giant comical wink and went back to the other member. Taking something out of a sack, she walked up to the leader and proffered it to him. It was a doll. He pretended to sing a lullaby to it and jiggled it up and down to soothe it. Suddenly, the remaining member of the band walked up and took the doll from him. Stuffing it under his jacket, he sauntered off, whistling.

The fake audience in front of him suddenly took notice of him and he began to speak again, this time in Spanish instead of Catalan but with a strong Catalan accent. His words held them in thrall and they danced extravagantly, pretending to rejoice in his message.

'We are nationalists. We love our country, we love our capital and our capital is Madrid. Vote for me and you'll never have to worry about voting for the Catalan government ever again. You can do better things with your time. Better still, we'll go back to how it was before and you won't have to bother voting in any elections. That's how we see democracy. At least, that's how we see it for you dirty separatist Catalans.'

Stunned at first, the crowd got the joke and began to clap and laugh. Some of them were carrying the *estelada*, the unofficial flag with a star in a triangle at one end of the red and yellow stripes, the symbol of the call for Catalan independence, and began to wave it in joyous arcs. From where she was standing, Elisenda saw Miravent look on impassively, the *cercavila*'s message mocking her and every policy she stood for.

The troupe was about to fade away when a figure strode out to them. It was Micaló. Elisenda hung her head and began to move forward. She approached the two men, now joined by the rest of the *cercavila* and the curious crowd, and heard Micaló's opening words.

'I could charge you for failing to respect the day of reflection before an election. What you are doing is tantamount to electioneering.'

The leader climbed down off his low stool and smiled disarmingly. 'Tantamount? That is a fine word. I applaud you.'

Elisenda saw Micaló bristle and knew he was seconds away from arresting the lot of them and potentially causing a riot with the crowd, most of whom had enjoyed the story the troupe had told.

'I am charging you…' Micaló began, but she cut him short.

'You're charging no one. Look around you; any high-handedness from us will turn this sour in seconds.'

Micaló looked at her in shocked anger and then at the crowd. His face quickly registered recognition that she was right. She turned to the leader of the *cercavila*. He looked at her full-on, a smile at the corners of his mouth.

'You are electioneering,' she told him. 'It will stop. Entertain the crowd, don't incite them.'

He bowed his head. 'I will do as you ask.'

She turned to Micaló. 'I can manage this.'

Realising that he was on the back foot among so many people, the other sotsinspector nodded curtly. 'I'm sure we've made ourselves clear,' he said to the leader and left, hoping his pride was intact.

'A poltroon,' the leader whispered to Elisenda.

'You went too far invoking her son. I won't be able to protect you again.'

'I am in your debt.'

He bowed down low, doffing his hat extravagantly, and rejoined his companions.

Elisenda watched them go and turned to see that a man had joined Miravent and Comas and was talking to them. Walking towards the group, she couldn't place him for a moment, but then recalled his face. Salvador Canet, a local builder, one of the men that David Costa had included in his list of Marc Comas's possible partners in corruption. She certainly knew him as another figure that appeared to have more to hide than he should, but there was never any evidence or word anywhere that he was up to anything illegal.

'You probably are, though,' she muttered.

As she drew near, she heard Canet talking to Miravent. 'Perhaps your husband has spoken of me, Susanna. May I call you Susanna? We've been discussing me joining you one day on one of your famous outings.'

'Have you really?' Miravent asked him, flashing a look at her husband.

'Yes. I'm very fond of Marc here. We speak the same language. As I'm sure you and I do. We have our faith to bring us together. I'm sure you understand. But where is my compassion? Of course, all this must wait until young Jaume is safely returned to the bosom of his family, and then we can discuss it more at our leisure.'

Before he could say any more, Comas introduced Elisenda and Montse. 'They're in the Mossos, helping us look for our son.' As he spoke, he nursed his right hand.

Canet smiled wolfishly at them both, looking them up and down. 'I am impressed. Well, I mustn't keep you.'

He smiled once more at all four of them and walked away, lost in the throng packing Carrer Santa Clara.

'How do you know Salvador Canet?' Elisenda asked Comas.

'Through work. It's my job to know all the people involved in construction in Girona.'

She gestured at his hand. 'Is it hurting?'

'I fell and knocked it again trying to break my fall. It needed resetting.'

Elisenda studied his face. 'Well, once we find Jaume, I promise you that I'll be taking a close look at the attack on you. I'll make sure I get to the bottom of whoever it was that mugged you.'

He smiled faintly and turned away. Elisenda watched the couple walk off, across the bridge, with Montse in tow. She took out her mobile.

'Josep? Take a look at everything we've got on Salvador Canet. What his connection with Marc Comas is. Any property he owns.'

She hung up and looked thoughtfully at the three figures crossing the stone bridge over the river, the rush of water louder than usual, a growl underlying the chattering lies of politicians and people.

Chapter Fifty-One

Elisenda turned away and walked back the way she'd come along Carrer Santa Clara. Crowds were coming and going along the shopping street and she found herself swept naturally along in a flow of bodies heading away from the stone bridge like a river in noisy torrent. Past the post office, she went into the Institut de Medicina Legal.

'Good of you to do this on a Saturday,' she told Riera once she'd gone into the cutting room. She stood just inside the door as he appeared to be finishing.

He glanced over to her as an assistant began to clear up. 'Beats having to waste my morning listening to those bloody fools outside with their antique guns and silly costumes.'

'Not a fan of history, Albert?'

'I'm quite happy with it as long as it stays in the past.'

'Your argument is faultless.' She gestured to the body on the table in front of the pathologist. 'Any news for me? I thought you weren't going to be starting until now.'

He walked over to her, taking off his cap and revealing his shock of white hair, which he smoothed back over his head. 'Couldn't be arsed to wait. I know you'll trust my findings. Not my problem if you don't.'

He led her out of the room into an anteroom, where he washed his hands at length. Not for the first time, Elisenda watched his delicate, deliberate movements with rapt attention. He had a gentleness of movements that was at odds with his abrasive tongue.

'It's Saturday and I'm tired,' he finally announced. 'I refuse to waste my time with the technical stuff even though I know you're one of the few with enough brain cells to understand it. You can see all that in my report on Monday. Suffice it to say he drowned. Aspiration of liquid in the lungs. Red wine. Good stuff too. That and vomit.'

Elisenda had more or less presumed that that had been the cause of death. For the time being, other aspects interested her more. 'How many people do you think were involved?'

'Extensive bruising to the chest. He appears to have been held down by a hand, sometimes flat, other times in a fist.'

'Two different hands?'

He shook his head. 'Impossible to say. He would have been thrashing around a lot, so it could be one hand changing position and stance. I would say, though, that the perpetrator or perpetrators would have had to hold his head still for the pouring of the wine on the material to be effective.'

'Which would indicate more than one person.'

'I would say so, but that's for you to determine.'

She took in his words, trying to imagine the scene in Bofarull's cellar. First with one attacker, then with two. Of course, even if it were two or more, that still wouldn't rule out Vergés. He could conceivably have met anyone in prison willing to help him. She recalled Josep's devil's advocate theory that Vergés got to know someone in the gang of house robbers while he was inside.

'Could it have been accidental? He died while someone tried to get information out of him. Or deliberate? He was tortured to the point of death?'

Riera stopped what he was doing and looked at her. 'Ditto, Elisenda. That's for you to determine. I've given you the historical facts, you can do the re-enactment.'

She turned to leave. 'Very apposite, Albert.'

Outside, she made a phone call. As it turned out, the person she was speaking to was a short distance away on Plaça Independència.

'Stay there,' she told him. 'I'll come and find you.'

David Costa was standing on the opposite edge of the square by the Pont de Sant Agustí footbridge that crossed over to the old town. Almost hemmed in by the people thronging past them, they found a quiet spot halfway across the river and leaned against the railings. Below them, the river tumbled through the city, the water higher than normal. In front of them, the cathedral rose up above the houses and the old apartment block where Elisenda lived. She could see people sitting in the window of La Terra, taking in a vermouth and a view. For a brief moment, she envied them.

'What can I do for you, Elisenda?' Costa asked. 'I can't give you long. This is a busy weekend.'

Elisenda turned to see the crowds wending back and forth behind them. 'You're telling me. Your newspaper published reports of the fake religious callers. How did you find out about that?'

The journalist was taken aback. 'You always were direct. We had phone calls from people the Mossos had asked about a religious pamphlet and about people going round door to door. It sounded like something we should be telling our readers about.'

'You're probably right.' She could see from his expression that her comment had surprised him. 'Have you had any follow-up? Anyone reporting on it today?'

Before replying, he checked the paper's social media account. 'I've had nothing, and I don't see anything here.'

'You will tell me if you do.'

'If you tell me of any developments before you tell anyone else.'

She gazed up at the cathedral, the stone tower proud against the blue sky.

'All right, I will. But I want you to do something.' She told him about the symbols found at the houses, leaving out the detail of the lines emerging from the top of the triangle. 'We're warning people on our social media to look for the symbol. I want your paper to do the same.'

He looked doubtful. 'Why are you sharing this with us?'

'We have to stop more attacks. We can't search every house in the region, so we need owners to check their own homes and tell us if they find a triangle. The more we get the message out, the more of a chance we have of catching this gang.'

He considered for a moment and then composed a message on his phone. He showed it to her. 'Something like that?'

She read it. 'Perfect.'

After he'd pressed the button to post the message, he stood up straight. 'I have to go.'

'One other thing,' she said, also straightening up. 'Salvador Canet. You mentioned him the other day. What have you got on him?'

The question took the journalist by surprise. 'Is this to do with Marc Comas?'

'Why do you ask?'

He waited until a noisy group went past. 'Canet is a builder. He's someone I would say would benefit from having a tame councillor like Comas on the planning committee, and there are always rumours about someone who's built up such a successful business and kept it afloat in the middle of a recession. The trouble is I've never found anything on him. Any dealings of his that I've ever looked at have turned out to be above board. He looks clean.'

'But you don't think he is?'

Costa stared at the river rushing below. 'The truth, Elisenda? I really don't know. If he isn't, he's damned good at covering it up.'

'That's why you have people like Marc Comas,' she muttered. 'To take the fall.'

Or Pere Vergés, she thought, keeping that to herself.

'Are you investigating Canet?' Costa asked her.

'Not yet. Not for corruption, anyway.' She started to accompany him to the other side of the river through the crowd. 'That's going to have to go on hold for another day.'

-

'Nothing,' Josep told her. 'There's nothing I can see that links Salvador Canet's businesses to Marc Comas or Susanna Miravent.'

She pulled out a chair at the desk he was sitting at in the outer office and sat down. 'There's got to be something. Maybe it's not business-related. I just heard Canet talking to the two of them, angling to get Miravent to get him into Opus Dei.'

Josep turned away from the screen to look at her. 'In which case, it will be business-related. He'll be wanting all the contacts and opened doors that being in Opus will get him.'

She nodded. 'And that still wouldn't rule out some sort of collusion between him and Comas. They're both in a position to help each other.'

'Do you want me to go digging?'

'I think that's going to have wait for a later date. Our concern at the moment is finding Jaume. I want you to look at Canet from the point of view of his possible involvement in kidnapping the boy. If he wants an in with Opus Dei, he could be using Jaume as a bargaining chip.'

Josep looked surprised. 'You really think he'd take the boy for that?'

'Between Comas at the council and the contacts through Opus, the benefits for his business would be worth it, I reckon. If Miravent is reluctant to let him join her club, he might resort to that. I think Comas's mugging is possibly down to him. Did you find a list of Canet's property?'

'He's a builder,' Josep replied, frustration in his voice. He turned back to the computer and called up a file. 'He has dozens of pieces of land and property registered in his company's name.'

A list appeared and he began scrolling down through it.

'OK, I get the picture.' She stared at the names. 'Go through it and look for anywhere he could possibly be keeping Jaume. Get Seguretat Ciutadana to check them out.'

'What about warrants?'

She looked at him askance. 'Wash your mouth out. We're looking for a missing boy, we don't need warrants if we're simply searching.'

Josep grinned, his shoulders straightening as he began to tower over Elisenda in his chair. 'One other thing. The phone call that Francesc Bofarull got, supposedly from the water company. Científica have told me that it came from a call box in La Bisbal. That's all they've got. So it could still be anybody.'

Elisenda stared at the lists on the computer screen and the folders strewn across Josep's desk.

'Couldn't it just.'

Chapter Fifty-Two

'Girona drivers,' Manel cursed.

Àlex looked up as the caporal overtook an olive-green cinquecento on the road to La Bisbal, veering back into lane as a silver BMW approached them from the other direction at speed, flashing its lights angrily. Manel turned the blue light on for a moment and gave a warning beep on the siren. The BMW slowed down immediately, the driver staring fixedly ahead as the two cars passed. 'Arsehole. Wouldn't be given a licence in Lleida if he drove like that.'

Àlex was surprised to find himself for the first time not irritated by Manel's monologue. Instead, he went back to checking his phone. None of the replies to the Mossos' or the newspaper's social media messages about triangles drawn on houses looked promising. He'd just spoken to Josep, who told him that nothing of interest had come in so far. Sighing, he darkened the screen and put the phone back in his pocket. He seriously hoped Elisenda's idea of releasing the information about the symbols wouldn't hamper their investigation. They had precious little to go on as it was. The breaks they'd had in working out the different teams, the symbols and the broad geographical pattern of the attacks were a good start, but he still felt as far away as ever from actually catching the perpetrators.

'It's odd,' he said, 'how when you ask the public to tell you if they see a triangle, they post photos of every vaguely geometric shape that isn't a triangle.'

Hunched over the wheel, Manel shrugged. 'That's Girona for you.'

In Vulpellac, Manel parked two doors away from Bofarull's house as the area directly in front was cordoned off with tape. A Seguretat Ciutadana mosso from La Bisbal was standing outside.

'Anything of interest?' Àlex asked him once he and Manel had got out of the car and shown their ID.

'Not a thing,' the mosso said, stifling a yawn. The sun was shining directly overhead into the narrow road and he had nowhere to shelter from its warmth. Tears of sweat ran down his forehead from under his peaked cap. The air was humid, a storm threatening for later. 'Some of the neighbours have walked by about half a dozen times each, but that's all.'

Àlex grinned. 'They'll be nosing about more as the day goes on.'

The mosso shrugged. 'That's the next guy's problem. I'm off in an hour.'

Àlex studied the symbol painted on the meter box again. It had been photographed last night, under the unforgiving light of arc lamps, but it looked horribly innocuous in the bright sunshine. A small, childlike scrawl in black felt-tip on the light grey cover of the inset cabinet.

'Any activity inside?' he asked the mosso.

'Científica left a short while ago. That's all.'

Before questioning the neighbours, Àlex and Manel went inside, keeping to the designated areas, for another look. The kitchen with its dusting of fingerprint powder, white pyramid evidence markers and plastic tape reminded Àlex of the drawing outside, mundane souvenirs of a horror now past. He knew he wasn't going to get any more of an image of the scene than he'd taken away last night, so he signalled to Manel that they should leave. The neighbours either side had already given statements the previous night, but Àlex and Manel knocked on both doors to see if they could remember anything more.

'We didn't hear a thing,' the elderly couple to the right told them.

That was hardly surprising, Àlex thought. The volume of their TV was deafening in the narrow living room at the back of the house, the sound reverberating between the walls and occasionally rattling a ceramic plate on an antique dresser. They got the same story the other side, and the further away along the street from Bofarull's house, the less the owners had to say about last night's events.

'Old stone houses,' he told Manel as they approached the last in the short row. 'They built them solid in those days. You wouldn't hear a thing.'

Manel shook his head from side to side after yet another loud TV. 'I still can't,' he complained.

The last neighbour they called on lived at the end of the street. She opened the door and insisted on coming outside rather than letting them in. She wore a cotton housecoat that she held together at the front in her tight, little fist. She had a voice that reminded Àlex of a primary school teacher he once had, a small and birdlike figure with lungs that could overcome a class of fractious seven-year-olds with a single word.

'Scandalous,' the woman repeated for the third time. 'The noise you lot made with your cars and your electric lights. I didn't get a wink of sleep all night.'

Yet a horrific murder four doors away didn't worry you, Àlex was tempted to say. Instead he asked her if she saw anything, holding out little hope for a helpful answer.

'Four men,' she told him. 'Don't know who they were or what they thought they were doing, but there were four of them. Outside that Bofarull's house. Stuck-up little tyke he was, God rest his soul, never spoke to anyone, even though we all knew him when he was a snot-nosed little kid, God rest his soul.'

'Four men?' Àlex tried to bring her back to the point. 'Did you tell the Mossos this last night?'

'You didn't ask me last night. Too busy making enough noise to wake the dead, you were. Four of them, there were. Talking Spanish, even though they were foreign.'

'Foreign?'

'Accents. All of them. Two of them, anyway. A couple of them sounded Spanish, the others were foreign. South American or something. They didn't talk much and they shut up when I went past.'

'Where exactly did you see them?' Àlex was struggling to remain patient.

'I told you. Outside Bofarull's house. They were putting stuff into a car and talking. Shut up when I walked past. Right outside his front door, they were, don't know what they were doing, but they stopped doing that too. Just got in the car and drove off.'

'Did you see what sort of car?'

She shrugged and pulled the housecoat tighter around herself. 'A car.'

Àlex pushed her for more information, but she couldn't say the type of car or even the colour because of the distorted light from the street lamps.

'Could you describe any of the men?' he tried once more.

'Foreign.'

Realising they weren't going to get much more out of her, Àlex thanked her and he and Manel walked back to Bofarull's house. Outside, they studied the symbol of the triangle with the three lines emerging from the point at the top.

'They didn't draw the line through it,' Àlex commented, 'because they were disturbed by the woman.'

'But it is the lot we're after,' Manel agreed. 'Nothing to do with this missing kid or the elections. Just another gang robbery. Bofarull's house just fit the bill.'

Àlex continued to stare at the crude lines of the drawing. 'So, he was just another victim of the robbers. It had nothing to do with Pere Vergés.'

He stared at the symbol, its outline blurring the harder he looked. Just as one piece of the investigations came into focus, others faded into the mist.

'Where does that leave Vergés?' Manel asked.

Àlex shook his head to clear it. 'It doesn't rule him out of the picture for Jaume's disappearance. He might still be wanting retribution from Miravent or Comas. Even if he wasn't behind the attack on Bofarull.'

Manel nodded at the symbol. 'Vergés could even have tipped the gang off about this guy. Part of his revenge.'

Àlex considered that as he took his mobile out. 'Possibly. Or his gripe is solely with Jaume's parents.'

He was about to call Elisenda to let her know of their findings when his phone rang. It was the Mossos station in Palamós. Tempted to ignore it so he could call Elisenda, he answered it nonetheless and listened in increasing interest. At the end of the call, he hung up and stared at Manel.

'Someone from a house in La Fosca has called Palamós. They've found a symbol on their house that wasn't there yesterday. A triangle.'

Chapter Fifty-Three

A soldier in the uniform of the Terç de Miquelets, a regiment made up of local Girona volunteers in 1808 to defend the city from Napoleon's troops, snapped to attention and watched his companions form a double column. Dressed like him in dark blue breeches and jacket with a crimson facing and two rows of brass buttons over leather gaiters and red and white laced espadrilles, they were slowly coming together in two rows, their muskets jostling for space over their shoulders. He placed his headgear on, a curious black brimmed affair like a truncated top hat with a bright red plume and left his wife and son to join their ranks. As he took his leave and walked across the cobbles on the square in front of the university, his mobile phone rang in his trouser pocket. Sheepishly, he grabbed at it to turn it off. The officer at the head of the column raised his eyebrows at him and he gave an apologetic look back.

Elisenda watched them march away from the square, heading for the cathedral and the climb down the rococo steps to the little square at the bottom. She'd rejoined Montse and her two charges in the middle of the second siege of the city. The French had breached the walls with cannon-fire but had been held back by the defenders. Now the *miquelets* inside Girona and the Spanish army outside were launching a raid on the French artillery to capture the siege guns. That would be the end of the second siege and of the re-enactments for the day. Sunday would see the third siege, which took place some months later in 1809.

As part of the crowd trailed in the soldiers' wake to watch them steal out through the city walls, others waited expectantly in the university square. More joined them, huffing and puffing after the ascent of the steep stone steps that emerged opposite the main faculty or streaming down from the other two sides of the square, quickly filling the spaces left vacant by the retreating sound of the soldiers and their followers. They didn't have to wait long. A blunderbuss sounded to the right, and a wail of bombards and shawms heralded the arrival of the *cercavila*. At its head, the leader appeared to be searching the audience. His gaze alighted on Elisenda and the people around her and he called a temporary halt to his band and bowed down low, doffing his hat with a flourish and half-smiling at her. The rest of the troupe made the most of the unplanned stop and bumped into each other. Sorting themselves out to the crowd's amusement, they continued to the middle of the square and took up positions. A second blunderbuss sounded, flame flashing from its flintlock and the noise reporting back and forth amid the stone walls of the square and ringing in the audience's ears.

The leader held his hand up. In the expectant hush, he waited, a smile slowly crossing his face. He spoke, his voice once again beguiling and authoritative.

'There are three types of people. Those who have an education. And those who don't.'

He waited until the penny dropped before continuing.

'We are creating the third sort.'

Some of his troupe ran out in front of him and set up a makeshift classroom, the teacher at the front moving dynamically about, explaining some strange and fascinating concept. The children, a boy and a girl, looked on enthralled. On the blackboard, there were diagrams and pictures, equations and quotations vying for space.

The leader spoke now in a stage whisper. 'I would say it's the politicians who are doing that for us, but we're all reflecting today so I'm not allowed to say things we already know.'

The crowd responded with nervous laughter, unsure where it was going. He returned to his normal speaking voice.

'This is the picture they all have for us now,' he said, sweeping his hat at the classroom tableau.

The teacher picked up a cane and strode forward to bring his cane crashing down on the desk. It split in two. More members of the troupe dressed as functionaries came out and separated the boy and the girl, forcing them to sit apart at their own half of the table.

'Education. Back to the old days, back to the old values. Back to a time where you got what you paid for. And if you couldn't pay for it, you didn't get it.'

The tableau transformed. Now the teacher stood at the front, pretending to spout knowledge. The boy and the girl had moved further apart and were staring ahead fearfully. The blackboard showed a list of Spanish prepositions, something generations of children had had to learn parrot-fashion, but with some of the words misspelt.

'We're being sent back to a time when children were educated separately. Boys from girls, rich from poor.' He looked pointedly at Susanna Miravent in the crowd. 'The sacred from the profane. And when they take education back, you know what they're doing, don't you?'

The crowd giggled nervously, each individual afraid to reply.

'They're taking society back.'

The three figures in the tableau now stood up and began to sing *Cara al Sol*, the Fascist hymn that children were forced to sing at the start of the school day during the years of the Franco regime. Slowly, they raised their right arms in a salute. The crowd gasped. At the height of the salute, the three players suddenly burst into a smile and waved their hands, dancing off to the rear like bad music-hall stars. With an audible exhalation of relief and a release of tension, the crowd burst into laughter and applause.

The leader bowed down low and turned. He caught up with his troupe and joined them as they danced out of the square, slapping hands with the crowd as it parted, the bombards and shawms regaling their passage.

Miravent turned to Elisenda. 'Are you really going to allow him to get away with that? It's outrageous.'

Before she could reply, Elisenda saw a figure approaching them. It took her a moment to place him. It was Joaquim Benach, Jaume's tutor at his school. He walked up to Miravent.

'I just wanted to say how much I feel for you,' he told the politician. 'Jaume is such a nice boy.'

Miravent was momentarily nonplussed. Benach had to remind her who he was.

'Of course,' she said, her calm restored. 'Thank you.'

'If there's anything I can do,' he replied, 'please, you only have to ask. I'm sure Jaume's all right. I'm certain he'll return safe and sound and that there's really nothing to worry about.'

With those words, he turned and walked away as quickly as he'd arrived, to be quickly swallowed up by the people milling about the square. Elisenda lost sight of him almost immediately, but she had other plans. Making her excuses, she hurried off after the *cercavila*. She caught them as they were pausing between the university and the cathedral, under the trees on the tiny Plaça dels Lledoners. Some of them were drinking from plastic bottles of water, but the leader stood apart from the rest, breathing heavily. He looked more like he was trying to calm down rather than getting his breath back.

'You push it a bit too far,' Elisenda told him.

'You really think so?' He gazed at her, his eyes tired. Blinking a few times, he seemed to regain strength. Suddenly, the smile and the persona were back in place. She felt she'd seen the stage curtain reveal a momentary secret. 'I'd say it's the people I'm railing against who are the ones pushing it too far.'

'Why education? Because Miravent sends her sons to private schools?'

'Because I was a teacher. Because I hate the way central government is mangling and demolishing the education of our children to suit their own ideologies and to punish any part of the country that disagrees with them. They're taking education back to the days when it served a wealthy, elite few and brainwashed generations into submission. They're cutting the amount of time we're allowed to spend learning in our own language and they're forcing a time-warp religious indoctrination on us that we haven't seen since Franco's day. I'm not the one that's pushing it too far.'

'How do you know Susanna Miravent?

He looked surprised. 'I don't. Not personally. But we all know a Susanna Miravent. Sadly.'

Elisenda studied him intently. 'Do you know her son?'

He laughed wryly. 'No, I don't know her son. I've never known her son. Just as I no longer know my own son.'

'Can you tell me your name?'

Seeing the other members of the *cercavila* move off into the flow of people streaming past, he quickly followed them, being instantly engulfed in the torrent of bodies.

'My name?' he called back to her. 'My name is...'

He said something, but his voice was swept away with the sound of a shawm and the babble of humanity tumbling through the narrow streets.

Chapter Fifty-Four

'That is a triangle.'

Àlex listened to Manel's words and continued to look at the marking scrawled on the gateway leading to a house in La Fosca. Just like Bofarull's house, it had been marked in black felt-tip on the cabinet housing the meters, this time set into the wide stone gatepost at the entrance to the drive. Two lines emerged from the top of the drawing.

'Is it what you've been looking for?' the uniformed caporal from the Palamós station asked him. He'd met them at the road into the development of second homes and led them to the house, a modern building set back from the narrow road.

'And it wasn't here yesterday?' Àlex asked him.

'Apparently not. The owners are elderly and don't go out much, but their daughter visited them yesterday and again today. She's the one who contacted us as she'd seen it on social media.'

'How did she tell you?' Manel grunted, holding his phone up, looking for a signal.

'Once she saw it, she drove to near the main road. You can get a signal there.'

'Do her parents live here all the time?' Àlex asked.

The caporal nodded. 'All year round. They used to have an apartment in Girona, but they came out here when the husband retired and fell ill because the house is on one floor. He can't climb stairs.'

They opened the gate and walked up to the house. Waiting on the porch, the daughter let them into the house. Her mother was sitting in the living room, looking small but defiant among a lifetime of bric-a-brac. On the coffee table in front of her was the same religious pamphlet they'd found at other houses. Àlex introduced himself and gave the two women some idea of the attacks that homeowners had been subjected to.

'You really need to leave your home,' he told the mother. 'Can you stay with your daughter at least for tonight?'

The daughter replied first. 'The problem's my father. He's bedridden and can't be moved. Not without an ambulance, and even then it's problematic.'

'We can arrange transport for him,' Àlex told her.

'I'm not going anywhere,' the older woman suddenly said. Her voice had the brittleness of age but there was an underlying strength to it. 'This is my home. I'm not being driven out.'

'You aren't being driven out, senyora,' Àlex assured her. 'It would just be while we sort out this problem.'

The woman shook her head vigorously, the veins on her neck taut under the loose skin. She turned to her daughter. 'I'm not going. You know your father wouldn't be able to take it.'

Àlex turned to the younger woman. 'Does your father know about the symbol on the house?'

'We haven't told him yet. We don't want to worry him.'

'I've told him,' the mother interrupted. 'He has a right to know. And he feels the same. We're not going anywhere. Let these people come, we'll see them off.'

Àlex stifled a sigh and asked if he could see the bedroom where the husband was.

'He's asleep,' the mother said. 'I'm not disturbing him.'

Instead, Àlex walked to the window overlooking the front garden and asked the daughter to join him. 'Is there any way you can convince her to stay with you for a few nights?'

The woman laughed almost bitterly. 'If I do, it'll be the first time in living memory.' They both turned to look at the mother, scowling at Manel. 'You've seen how stubborn she is.'

The two of them went back to the sofa where the mother was sitting and the daughter sat down next to her. The younger woman spoke to Àlex. 'I have to say, if my parents won't go, I'm staying here with them.'

Àlex looked directly at her. 'You will all be at risk. These people are very violent.'

'I don't care,' the mother said.

Àlex looked at them both. 'If you'll just excuse us for a moment.'

He beckoned Manel and the caporal from Palamós over and the three of them went outside.

'Mad old biddy,' Manel commented. 'Does she want to die?'

'She wants to stay in her own home,' Àlex told him.

Together, they walked around the house. The garden covered two sides of the property, the front as far as the gate out into the road, and the side, which Àlex saw was where the kitchen was. Beyond the gate, there was just a small gap separating it from the little street, without even a pavement. The other side of the road was a copse of tall stone pines, offering no place for anyone to hide. He went out into the road and looked up and down. It was narrow and straight for some metres either way. Any van or cars parked there, staking the place out, would be noticeable. He walked back into the garden and looked back to the house. The property was small, with no place to keep any appreciable amount of Mossos hidden while they waited for the gang to attack. He rejoined Manel and the caporal.

'There's no way we're going to be able to get enough people into here unnoticed to trap this gang. And we can't allow the owners to stay.'

'That lady's not going anywhere,' Manel muttered.

'We can't allow this to happen,' Àlex said absently. 'But I can think of one way around it.'

He asked Manel and the caporal to stay with the family while he drove to the main road to find a signal to call Elisenda.

Chapter Fifty-Five

The heels of her short lace-up boots thumped dully on the expensively-tiled floor as she walked across the living room. A stone in the tread of the right one scraped across the light brown surface of the floor like fingernails down a blackboard. The sound grated through the house.

'Sorry, Catalina,' Elisenda whispered to herself. Bending her leg at the knee, she picked the tiny stone out and looked for somewhere to put it. Shrugging, she threw it in the open fireplace and apologised to her sister again.

She was on her own in the room, pacing edgily in the spaces between and around the three large sofas. She stopped now and stood by the fireplace, her right foot raised on the cold grate. Sturdy chunks of wood and fine kindling were stacked in a neat pyramid in the centre, more a design statement at this time of year than in readiness to be lit. She turned around to face the room, the front door just out of sight at the top of three steps leading to the little hall. To her right, the darkness outside pressed against the window that gave onto the front garden and the coastal footpath. She was on display and had to fight an urge to turn the bright ceiling lights and floor lamps off so she could see out into the night. In front of her too were the two giant ceramic pots, stylishly distressed and supposedly held intact with giant staples, that Sergi her brother-in-law loved. So did she, but not in a minimalist, modern living room and most certainly not now. She had to suppress a whim to check there was no one hiding inside them.

The music was turned up loud, the speakers in every room blasting out Sopa de Cabra's *L'Estació de França*. She'd brought her own iPod to insert in the dock. She didn't mind facing danger, but she refused to put up with Sergi's taste in music. The song's lyrics about the human fauna found at one of Barcelona's oldest stations and the energy of the two guitars were pumping her up for what she hoped lay ahead. It was also a beacon in the night, the house on the low cliffs a haven of light and noise to attract moths to their fate.

She wasn't alone in the house.

She knew that, but she still felt nervous. She was on her own downstairs, but the upstairs rooms and the garage at the foot of the narrow flight of stairs down from the kitchen were occupied. Àlex and Puigventós were at the top of the landing, Manel in the garage. All four were accompanied by small deployments of ARRO teams, the anti-riot force, armed and armoured in readiness. Outside, vans hidden behind other houses and in the dense pines along the road concealed back-up teams from Armengol and Micaló's teams. Nevertheless, Elisenda had to admit to herself that she was scared.

When Àlex had rung her from La Fosca a little over two hours ago with a proposal, she'd only taken a moment to agree to it. Once he'd described the symbol on the elderly couple's house, their refusal to leave and the layout, she'd known he was right. All she had to do was convince her sister. That, in turn, had been easy.

'How will Sergi see it?' she'd asked Catalina.

'I won't tell him until tomorrow,' her sister had replied.

Leaving the living room, Elisenda walked into the kitchen. Standing by the sink, she looked out of the window into the night. The layout of the land meant that the kitchen was on the ground floor in terms of the front entrance and on the first floor at the rear, above the garage. Staring out, she could see more than she could at the front of the house. The pine-lined road snaked off towards the rest of the development, the sparse street lamps lighting little of the area but showing enough for her to see out. There was no movement. She took a deep breath and carried on what she was doing as naturally as she could. Anyone watching the house for the last hour would only have seen a woman alone inside.

Àlex's idea had been simple. The elderly couple's home was just two streets away from Catalina's beach house. If they were right about satnav coordinates and the symbols, that should be enough to fool the gang. He'd taken a pot of paint to the meter box and covered over the symbol. Then he'd hurried to Catalina's house. The cabinet there was on the side of the house, by the steps leading up from the road to the footpath at the top of the cliff. It was ideal. He'd scrawled the same triangle with two lines on it. Fortunately, the other three houses in the row were empty. In the meantime, Elisenda had gone back to Vista Alegre to organise the setup with Puigventós, who had in turn arranged the ARRO support. Armengol had immediately offered his help, followed a little reluctantly by Micaló.

The one problem was the phone signal, which meant that they couldn't rely on a call from Elisenda, who would be acting as the tethered goat, getting to teams waiting outside. Instead, the back-up had to be inside, so the challenge had been to get all the support in place as quickly and surreptitiously as possible before any attack was likely to happen. Part of her nervousness was due to the possibility that the operation was already compromised and all of her waiting was in vain. The lack of a phone signal also meant that for help from the outside teams, they had to rely on their radio network, which they shared with the other emergency services in Catalonia. It was proving to be only marginally more reliable right now, the signal coming in and out of range constantly. She hoped that with the numbers of Mossos inside the house, that wouldn't matter.

Walking back into the living room, a sound startled her, until she realised it was someone moving about upstairs, the noise amplified by the ceramic tile floors. The music on the player shuffled through the playlist, one she always used when she wanted to raise her energy.

'Music to act as decoy for a violent gang by,' she muttered out loud, chuckling nervously. 'Might have to tweak the marketing, but it could work.'

The doorbell rang and she froze.

Glancing over, she thought she saw a shadow move at the window. She had to resist looking back to make sure. Where she was standing by the fireplace, the front door was just out of sight. Suddenly leaden, she had to will herself to walk towards it. The three steps leading up to the hallway were the steepest she'd ever climbed. She slowed down, controlling her breathing, making the adrenaline work for her.

As she approached, it rang again.

That was the push she needed. The insistence of the caller had fired up her anger, their eagerness to make someone else a victim the best motivation she needed in that final moment when her hand hovered over the door handle. Even so, she was surprised by the violence of the shove against the door once she released the catch. It caught her a blow to her right shoulder and cheek and forced her to stagger backwards. It swung open as she stumbled and she knew that she daren't fall to the ground. Two figures came in quickly, both wearing balaclavas. The first one pushed her, but she managed to keep to her feet. Sensing the steps behind her, she had to turn her back on them to make sure she didn't trip. She jumped down all three and turned quickly to face them, but the first attacker was on her immediately and punched her in the jaw. She ducked enough to lessen the blow but the pain still burst across the side of her face. Behind her assailant, she could see that there was still one figure outside the house. She knew they all had to be inside for the Mossos to catch the lot of them. Hurriedly backing away, she kept one eye on the figure directly in front of her and the other on the door and the person still outside. The first one threw another punch at her, but she danced back to avoid it. She was getting near the door to the kitchen. She wanted to stay in the living room so that the team upstairs could get to her more quickly, so she sidestepped another punch and went to her right, towards the sofas.

She was just losing sight of the front door when she saw the third figure come in. The one immediately behind her assailant was about to join in the attack on her, so she shouted out, her voice louder than the guitar riff thumping out through the sound system. Taken by surprise, the first attacker stopped, so Elisenda lunged forward and caught him a blow straight to the stomach. Winded, he doubled up, blocking the second attacker's path to Elisenda, but not hers to him. She quickly rammed the heel of her right hand under his nose, the sound of his yelp of pain instantly satisfying.

Her blow had barely landed when she heard the sound of shouting and the thundering of footfall down the stairs. The ARRO team quickly overcame the two figures in front of her. Manel came through the kitchen door at the same time and picked the two bodies up by the neck, his huge hands engulfing them. Elisenda looked up to see Àlex hurdle the sofas and race to the door to catch up with the third figure, already retreating across the hall. He was almost on him when the would-be burglar suddenly slumped and fell. Behind him, Armengol was coming through the door, ready to deliver another punch.

The uproar settled and Puigventós turned the music off, the silence that ensued more forceful than the tumult of a moment ago. Elisenda looked around. All three attackers had been subdued. Manel had pulled the balaclavas off the first two. She was surprised to see how ordinary they looked. They would have passed unseen and unassuming in any other circumstance. Missing the beat of the music, she exhaled slowly, on a high after the success of the setup.

Armengol came further into the room, followed by two more of his team. Between them, they were holding a fourth figure.

'This one was at the top of the stone steps,' he explained. 'We saw them and thought we'd better take up position nearer. The radio link wasn't working at all, so we had to take the risk.'

Catching her breath, Elisenda laughed and mouthed a breathless thank you at him.

Through the open door behind Armengol, Micaló walked in, followed by one of his team. He surveyed the scene and gravitated to where Puigventós was standing, near the fireplace.

'We did it,' he pronounced.

Armengol looked across at him. 'I'm sure we'd all like to congratulate you, Sotsinspector Micaló. That course of yours really did its stuff.'

Elisenda caught Armengol's eye and gave him the broadest grin she could ever remember giving. 'That's all you had to do,' she told him.

The water had reached his knees.

He was half-standing in the flow, his right hand still manacled to the wall, and he felt the level rise as high as his thighs.

He screamed to the person above.

The river roared. The slabs beneath his feet buckled in its anger and rough stones in the wall crumbled under the force. More water surged through. He pulled on the iron ring, not caring about the pain searing his wrists, but it wouldn't move, the wall where it was embedded standing firm against the flood.

He screamed again.

The door opened and he looked up.

'You have to do something.'

Without a word, his captor lowered the ladder into place and began to climb down. In the cellar, he almost cried in gratitude. The figure thrust something into his hand. Opening his fist, he looked at it. It was a pair of pliers.

Fumbling against the cold of the water and his own panic, he forced the edge of the pliers between the metal band and the raw skin of his wrist. The pain shot up his arm. Finding a purchase, he squeezed as hard as he could, but couldn't get enough of a grip. Crying in rage and pain, he twisted the tool into his flesh and tried again. This time it bit. He felt the thin metal cut in two, releasing him.

Looking up, he saw his captor struggling to get back to the ladder. He stood up and was horrified to find the water up to his waist and rising. The bucket he'd been using for a toilet tumbled past him, its contents swirling with the water, bringing up bile in his throat. The roiling brown flood clung to him as he waded past the plinth of crumbled steps towards the other figure.

He made it past the plinth to the foot of the ladder, the water up to his chest, when another surge as more stones crumbled sent a wave rolling towards him. He kept his feet, but turned to see the ladder swept away and sent tumbling in the relentless flood. His captor frantically lunged after it, but it barrelled out of his grasp.

Crying, he forced his body through the water, wading after it.

Between them, he and the other figure caught hold of the ladder and managed to fix it in place. Each one trying to gain a foothold on the bottom rung, they turned at the sound of another roar of tumbling stones sending a wave cresting towards them.

They looked at each other, panic reflected in each other's eyes.

Sunday

Chapter Fifty-Six

Salvador Canet sat in the small office at the rear of the warehouse. With his left hand, he was turning a gold lighter over and over on the desk. It made a sharp click every time he upended it. His right hand held a bling-encrusted mobile to his ear. He told whoever was at the other end to meet him at his office in Girona and hung up.

Opposite him, Àlex reached across the desk and made to take the lighter out of his hand. Canet held on, staring Àlex in the eyes. Àlex grinned and tightened his grip. Canet had spent too long away from actually working on building sites and his clasp wasn't as strong as it once was, so he released it as the pain grew stronger. Deliberately, Àlex placed the lighter gently down on the dusty metal table, not once removing his gaze from Canet's face.

'Now isn't that better,' he told him. 'Because it was irritating the shit out of me.'

It was Canet's turn to grin, a wolfish leer that had intimidated many a business partner. 'So sorry, sergent. I forgot, you no doubt can't afford an object like this.'

Àlex looked down at the gaudy lighter and back at Canet. He laughed. 'You've got me there. There's no way I'd own such an item as that.'

He could see in the other man's eyes that the barb had hit home. Social climbers, no matter how menacing their background, were always prey to self-doubt.

Canet leaned back and yawned. 'Will this take long? I have to go to church.'

'Of course you do.'

Outside the office, a team of Seguretat Ciutadana and four Científica officers were combing through the warehouse. Manel was with them, searching through the small rooms that led off the main storage area. It was one of two properties belonging to Canet that Josep had found in his search that could fit the bill for keeping Jaume hostage. This was a huge and empty complex of one large room and various side rooms and outbuildings. Currently unoccupied, it stood in an industrial estate on the road north from Girona. So far, they'd found nothing.

Àlex and Elisenda had gone to Canet's home in Montjuïc early that morning, dragging him away from his lavish breakfast. Without a word, his wife, younger than Canet and dressed in a short silk kimono, had got up and closed herself in their bedroom, not appearing the rest of the time they were there.

'We have a warrant to search two of your properties,' Elisenda had told him, showing him the paper.

On the way to Canet's house, she'd told Àlex that from now on she was always going to apply for warrants at the weekend. The duty judge, a woman Elisenda's age with almond eyes and a Sunday-morning air, had issued the orders without a moment's hesitation.

'I shall reserve all crime-fighting for when Jutgessa Roca is safely tucked up in bed,' she'd told him.

Her voice was slightly muffled, her jaw stiffening up and bruising after the glancing punch she'd received the night before.

'Matches the other cheek,' Àlex had told her. 'Suits you.'

Àlex had then met Manel and the uniformed and Científica teams at this warehouse, while Elisenda had hooked up with Josep and more Mossos at the other property, an empty suite of offices set among a park of beech trees away from the road to the west of the city.

Canet had decided to go to the one that Àlex was searching, having told someone else on the phone to get to the second one. Àlex had wondered at first if it was significant, but it was becoming evident that the boy wasn't being kept at the site. Manel came in ten minutes later to confirm it and Àlex stood the teams down.

'So sorry not to be of more help,' Canet told him. He picked up the lighter and turned it over once on the table, the sound reverberating on the metal.

Àlex stared back at him as he made to go. 'Don't worry, I'm sure you will be one day.'

For her part, Elisenda was getting the same result. The person Canet had told to get to the site was a large and taciturn bruiser of a man who sat at the dusty reception console and smouldered as teams of Mossos went systematically through the empty offices. His face impassive, his eyes constantly roamed the corridors emanating from the lobby to keep close watch on what the police were doing. A uniformed sergent came in through the glass front doors, opaque with disuse, and approached Elisenda.

'There's an outbuilding,' he told her, 'and none of the keys we've been given fits.'

Elisenda looked at Canet's employee and raised her eyebrows in question.

'They should all be there,' he said, the first words he'd uttered in the last hour.

'If you wouldn't mind coming with me,' she invited him, getting up.

Reluctant at first, he evidently quickly realised that he couldn't allow the Mossos access to the building without his presence, so he stood up and followed Elisenda and the sergent out of the doors. The sergent led them to a modern single-storey block fifty metres from the main offices. There were no windows, just a couple of grilles set high into the walls.

'We think it must be a generator,' the Mosso told her.

Elisenda turned to the other man. 'Do you have a key?'

He simply looked at the small building and shrugged.

'Break the lock,' Elisenda ordered the sergent.

The burly man lunged forward and stood in front of the door. 'Senyor Canet won't like it.'

Elisenda smiled disarmingly up at the man's craggy face. Her jaw was hurting and she needed a painkiller to stem an incipient headache nagging away behind her forehead. 'I don't give a shit what Senyor Canet will or will not like. If you haven't got a key for this door, we're breaking it down. I haven't got time to waste.'

He took the keys from the sergent and looked through them, trying all the ones that would fit the type of lock on the door. None of them worked.

'Break the door down,' Elisenda repeated to the sergent.

The other man looked for a moment like he was going to refuse to move.

'I will arrest you if I have to,' Elisenda told him, her voice strained. 'Get out of the way.'

Two other Mossos came up at the sergent's orders with a ram and knocked the door off the lock with their second blow, pushing it inwards with a sharp judder. A stale smell of diesel and dust greeted them. The sergent went inside with his torch sweeping around the one room, which was dominated in the middle by a huge generator, a back-up power supply to the main offices. It was caked in dust. Elisenda looked down at the floor. From the undisturbed weft of grime, it was obvious that no one had been in here for ages. Nevertheless, the sergent and the other two Mossos searched the room, their torches picking out giant brown moths asleep on the walls and a lattice of grey and grisly cobwebs in the corners and at the angles of the ceiling.

'Nothing,' the sergent confirmed.

'That lock'll need repairing,' Canet's man told Elisenda.

'Won't it just.'

She and the man returned to the reception area and sat down. He tried making a phone call, no doubt to Canet, but there was no reply. In the end, as officer after officer came in and shook their heads, she had to admit that they weren't going to find anything there. She stood her team down and thanked the man for his cooperation. Without a word, he stood up and waited for her to leave, his face restored to its impassive stare.

Outside, the air was damp with moisture. Over to the west, she could see vertical wavering streams of lighter colour amid the black clouds, telling her that the mountains that way were getting a soaking. The rivers in Girona would be higher still when she got back.

'I'll see if there are any others where he could be kept,' Josep told her in the car on the way to Vista Alegre. There was anger and frustration in his voice. 'But of them all, these were the only really likely ones.'

'Do what you can. We might be barking up the wrong tree with Canet, but he's got some hold on Comas, so we need to be sure.'

'I'll keep digging. With Vergés too.' He paused for a moment. 'Have you seen this morning's newspaper? It's on the back seat.'

She turned and reached for it, scanning the front page and opening it to read inside. After just a few moments, she crushed it in her lap. 'Bastard.'

Àlex and Manel were waiting for them at the station. Montse was with Miravent and Comas in the house in Palau. They'd be going out to vote in the elections, and Elisenda wanted someone from her team to be with them, both for their safety but also to keep a close watch on the couple.

'Josep needs to be checking up on some things,' she told Àlex. 'We'll have to interview our burglars between you, me and Manel. Apart from bringing down the rest of the gang, I want to make sure it was them who were involved in Bofarull's murder so we can rule out any link to Jaume's disappearance.'

She got a call on her internal phone. It was the officer in charge of the cells. Sighing, she hung up.

'It's Siset,' she told Àlex. 'Apparently he's revolting. Give me five minutes and then we'll start on the interviews.'

She collected her informant from the cells and took him to an interview room.

'You've got to let me go, Elisenda,' he complained.

'Few more hours of your company yet, Siset. I wouldn't want to miss you. You can go soon, but first, tell me what you know about Salvador Canet.'

His eyes flickered. 'I don't know him.'

'Yes, you do. What do you know about him? And don't piss me around anymore because my jaw is aching and I'm in a foul mood and you're about to be on the receiving end of it.'

He looked at her to make sure she was being serious. 'I know who he is, Elisenda, but I don't know anything about him. I don't do white-collar crime.'

Elisenda considered the glowering menace of the builder. 'He's hardly white-collar, Siset.'

'He is compared to me.' There was no irony in his voice. He looked doubtful about saying any more. 'People talk about him like he's part of the world, but I've never had anything to do with him. I know people who've worked for him, but they won't say a thing about him or what they do for him. He's mean.'

'Mean,' Elisenda repeated. That was about the most damning thing Siset could say about anyone as it meant he was scared of them. It also meant that he was unlikely to give anything away about Canet at this stage. 'If you hear anything, you make sure you let me know.'

He pulled his face into a grimace, which she recognised as Siset's attempt at a smile. 'I can't find anything out when I'm in here.'

She sighed and stood up. 'All right, you can go.'

He almost whooped in joy and made to get up. She put her hand on his shoulder forcing him back down.

'There's just one more thing I need you to do.'

Chapter Fifty-Seven

'Do you know any of them?'

Siset stood next to Elisenda peering through a grille near the cells. Four men were being taken out of a cell one at a time and made to stand in view of Siset for a moment. They couldn't see him.

'I don't know any of them,' he whispered to her.

'Are you telling me the truth, Siset? Because I can hold you for a few more hours.'

Siset looked panicked. 'I swear it, Elisenda. I don't know any of them.'

'These aren't the ones who sold you the goods from the robberies? Or who told you when to expect them?'

He shrank back into the small room and whispered even lower. 'Is that them?' He stared at the last one in awe. 'No, it was only ever two who came to see me. An older one and a younger one. But their faces were always hidden.'

She believed him. He was too scared to be lying. 'The two you met? Where were they from?'

He looked at her in surprise. 'Here. Well, Spain anyway. They spoke Spanish. Why?'

She considered that for a moment. 'No reason. Come on, you can go now.'

They waited until two of the men had been led upstairs to the interview rooms and the other two put back in separate cells. Siset walked with Elisenda nervously to the sergent in charge of the cells to be discharged.

'They can't see me, can they?' he asked her.

'Not at all.'

He only began to cheer up when the sergent handed his leather satchel back to him, and he started rummaging through it.

'It's a bit lighter,' Elisenda told him. 'We've taken out anything we think was stolen, which was pretty much everything. You'll be hearing about that when I can be bothered with you. Now go and vote. There's an election today.'

'Is there?' He shook his head. 'I never vote. Politicians, load of crooks if you ask me.'

She rolled her eyes at the sergent behind the desk and accompanied Siset to the door leading out of the police station. He'd no doubt be back before long, she thought.

–

'Venezuelan.'

The man in the first interview room patted himself on the chest and repeated the word for the seventh time.

'No, you're not,' Elisenda told him, her voice tired.

'Venezuelan.'

'So how come you claim you don't speak Spanish?'

'Don't speak Spanish. Speak Venezuelan.'

Elisenda looked at Manel and shook her head in disbelief.

'Say something in Venezuelan then,' Manel told him.

Muscular and tanned and wearing a white T-shirt and jeans, the man looked insolently at Manel and began to speak in a language that most certainly wasn't Spanish. The first time he'd tried speaking it half an hour ago, Elisenda had thought she'd recognised it, so she'd called for an interpreter from the pool that the Mossos had in Girona. The woman was sitting in a corner of the room now, having entered a short while ago without saying a word. After the man had been speaking for a few moments, she replied to him, her voice calm. He blanched and stared at her.

'Thank you,' Elisenda told the woman. She turned back to the man. 'So you speak Romanian in Venezuela, I take it.' She paused the interview for a moment and left the room with Manel and the interpreter.

Two of the other three would-be robbers that the Mossos had caught the previous night were also claiming to be Venezuelan.

'They at least speak Spanish,' Elisenda told Àlex outside in the corridor. 'Although their accent doesn't sound Venezuelan to me.'

'I'd say Peruvian,' Àlex agreed.

'Why are they claiming to be Venezuelan?' Manel asked, puzzled.

Àlex grinned at him. 'Country boy.'

'Because Venezuela and Spain don't have an extradition treaty,' Elisenda explained to him. 'A lot of crooks from Latin America buy fake Venezuelan IDs, so that if they're caught, they can't be sent back to their own countries after serving their sentences here.' She grinned too. 'But this is the first time I've ever seen a European trying that one on.'

Elisenda went into the other interview room, where the fourth suspect was slumped on an upright chair. Thin and with vulpine eyes that glowed with malice, he folded his arms and sat up straight when she walked in. His nose was heavily plastered from where Elisenda had hit him during the attack on the house. She felt a pulse of pain in her own jaw and couldn't help feeling satisfied at the bruising around the man's nose and cheeks. His lip was swollen, but that hadn't stopped him from snarling threats at her and Àlex on and off for the last hour. He was the one Spaniard among the gang.

'I'm not saying a fucking word,' he repeated to Elisenda now.

'No need,' she told him. 'You see, I know how your operation works. You have three teams, each one allocated a house to rob. Yours is team number two, so it's obviously not the best.'

He leered at her. 'That won't work on me, girlie.'

'And you have a couple of people who check out the houses and tell you which ones to rob,' she carried on regardless. 'Now, what I reckon is that each team has a leader who's more senior in the setup. You're the leader of your merry little bunch. And you will be the ones to get the longer sentences when we put you all away. Unless you decide to be a little more helpful than you have been and give me some names.'

He leaned forward and peered at her. 'You are fucking joking, aren't you?'

'Of course I am. One of your friends has already told us.'

He smirked and sat back. 'You really think so? They couldn't even if they wanted to.'

'And why's that?'

Leering at her, he shook his head and kept quiet.

Telling Manel to come in and sit with the man, Elisenda joined Àlex in the first interview room. She shook her head at his silent question about how things had gone with the other suspect. Àlex had sent the Romanian back to the cells and was questioning one of the two non-Venezuelan Latin Americans. Elisenda recognised him as the one she'd punched in the stomach. She was struck again by how ordinary he looked without the balaclava. A short, wiry man in his thirties, he was all fibre, the veins standing out like thin rope on his tanned forearms, his dark hair thinning on top. He appeared to be more forthcoming than his friends.

'We don't know who the others are,' he was telling Àlex in Spanish. 'We're told where to go. We just do as we're told to do.'

'You must meet the others when you pass on the goods you steal,' Àlex demanded.

He shook his head. 'Only Esteban does that.' Esteban was the Spanish gang member. 'And he only knows two others. He used to take the stuff to them. But he doesn't know who's in the other gangs. None of us do. They're nothing to do with us.'

'One of your gangs murdered someone on Friday night,' Elisenda interrupted. 'You will all be charged as accessories.'

The man looked shocked. 'We never killed anyone. That's nothing to do with us.'

'It will go easier on you if you give us some names,' Àlex told him. 'You must have heard names at least.'

He was frightened but insistent. 'I don't know anyone. They did that deliberately so we wouldn't all go down if one of us got caught.'

Elisenda called a pause and she and Àlex went outside.

'I don't see how we're going to get to the other parts of this gang,' Àlex muttered. 'They've done a good job in keeping them all separate.'

Elisenda swore under her breath. 'We can get these four put away without any problem, but I don't see how we're going to get to the others. I've got to see how Josep is doing with Jaume, but you keep at it with these. See if you can find any way in.'

-

'I was just about to come and get you,' Josep told Elisenda, opening the door to her office.

He stopped talking when he saw she was on the phone. In front of her was the newspaper he'd shown her, open on the article that David Costa had written, questioning Susanna Miravent's attitude to her two missing children.

'I trusted you, David,' she was saying into her mobile. She slapped her hand on the page open on her desk. 'This is every bit as bad as Miravent's electioneering. I dislike her politics as much as you do, but that's no excuse to come down to her level and use it for the same purposes. You've used her missing child to rubbish her election chances.'

'*It's in the public interest, Elisenda. How can the electorate trust a woman like that?*'

'That's bullshit and you know it. You're pandering to your readers.' She looked at a line that mentioned how the politician's attitude was hampering the police investigation, and her anger peaked. 'You've surpassed yourself this time, David. I didn't think even you would be so underhand. I trusted you.'

She stabbed at the off button on the screen before he had a chance to reply. Putting the phone down on the desk, she took a few deep breaths before looking up at Josep. 'Bring me good news, Josep, I'm warning you.'

He looked uncertainly at the bundle he was holding. In one hand was a printed report while the other held his laptop. He placed the computer on Elisenda's desk. 'Científica have given us Pere Vergés's desktop computer back. They found nothing on it to suggest any wrongdoing. Crucially, there's nothing on it that would suggest any involvement in the fraud he was convicted of either.'

'I said good news.' She looked at the laptop. 'I'm convinced that Francesc Bofarull was behind that, but we've no way of knowing for certain as we can't check his computers. This is turning out to be one hell of a shitty Sunday.'

'There is one thing. Científica retrieved all the files that Vergés deleted. There was nothing too sinister about them, otherwise he'd have known enough to wipe them completely. But there are a number of emails that he sent to Susanna Miravent.'

He gestured at the laptop, and Elisenda turned it to face her. 'Miravent?'

Josep leaned down next to her and opened a file with a string of emails. 'He sent them between the time that he was being investigated for fraud and when he was arrested and held in custody until his trial and conviction.'

Elisenda quickly scanned them. 'That is one angry man.'

'All his Opus Dei friends were shutting him out. He complains here how no one would help him and how he felt he'd become an outcast.'

'And he blames Susanna Miravent for it,' she commented, looking through the mails he'd sent her. 'She doesn't reply to any of these?'

'Just two, one telling him that she'll get an injunction if he continues to harass her. And the other one to tell him that he is now dead to her and to their faith.'

'Very Christian.'

'If you look, his mails get increasingly more threatening. He tells her he'll haunt them if he's convicted. He also talks about a get-together that she was organising. He was told he wasn't welcome.'

Elisenda found the email Josep was referring to. She let out a low whistle. 'And he wasn't happy about it, was he?'

The final email told Miravent that he would find a way to make her pay for her treatment of him. Elisenda sat back thoughtfully.

'So why hasn't Susanna Miravent mentioned this?'

-

The politician looked at the printout that Elisenda had given to her.

'Why haven't I mentioned it?' She riffled through the papers. 'Look at it. They're the outpourings of a bitter man. I didn't take them seriously at the time. I haven't mentioned it simply because I'd forgotten about them. I deleted them straight after he sent them.'

Elisenda glanced at Montse, who was standing by the window in Miravent's house in Palau. The three of them were by the table overlooking the garden, in front of the wall of family photos. When she'd arrived, the politician and her husband had just been getting ready to go and place their vote and then they were going on into the city centre to see more of the siege re-enactments.

'I don't want to go,' Miravent had said, 'but in my position as a political candidate, I have to.'

Her face was looking drawn for the first time. Montse had told Elisenda that she'd been staring at the pictures on the wall. It was the only semblance of an emotion she'd shown about her missing son.

'I just don't get her,' Montse had muttered.

Elisenda joined the politician at the wall and looked at the pictures. She found again the one of Jaume with his kayaking trophy.

'That was four years ago today,' Miravent told her. 'Near the reservoir in Susqueda.'

'Today?'

She nodded. 'I always used to organise one this weekend. That's why we've never seen the re-enactments in the past. It always clashed with our autumn outing.'

'And you did this every year?'

'Every year. For the association. Jaume used to love it.' For a moment, Elisenda thought that some facade was about to come down, the faith failing to keep emotion back, but Miravent held herself in check. She corrected herself. 'Jaume loves it. I only didn't organise one for this year because of the elections. With what's happened, that's been a blessing.'

Elisenda turned to face her. 'Is this the get-together that Pere Vergés talks about in his emails?'

'I have no idea.'

Elisenda grabbed the printouts back and looked at the dates. 'It was this outing four years ago that you banned him from going to. It would have been this weekend. Today.'

Miravent tore her eyes away from the wall and glanced at the sheets of paper. 'If you say so.'

'I do say so.' She pulled her mobile out and dialled while still speaking to Miravent. 'Where exactly was that picture taken?'

Chapter Fifty-Eight

They were thirty minutes out of the city when they hit a wall of rain. Thunderous black clouds writhed and twisted above them and a roar of water pummelled the roof of the car, beating a clamorous counterpoint to their urgency. Instinctively, the driver of the four-by-four quickened her pace in time with the anger of the skies. Taking a sweeping corner to the left, the patrol car aquaplaned, gliding ominously towards the middle of the road and an oncoming lorry. Calmly, she pulled it back under control without skipping a beat and accelerated after the curve along one of the few straight stretches. In the passenger seat, Elisenda closed her eyes for a moment, but quickly opened them again when she realised that that was worse.

The road followed the valley carved out of the mountains by the Ter to the east of Girona where it flowed westwards from the mountains and the reservoir at Susqueda. The river was over their right shoulder all the way, a boiling mass of brown and white rising up to meet the rain falling down it, swelling it as it ran. As they drove, they crossed several small tributaries in turmoil, each one tumbling eagerly to the chaos of their wayward offspring.

'Both the places we want are before we get to the reservoir,' Josep said from the rear seats. He had to shout over the uproar of the rain and the keening of the sirens.

Sitting next to him were Susanna Miravent and Marc Comas. They'd insisted on coming with the Mossos after Elisenda had thought there was a possibility that Vergés was holding Jaume somewhere near the site of the autumn outing he'd been banned from going to.

'I know the way better than you do,' Miravent had argued.

Elisenda had had to admit that she was right, but it also meant that she couldn't voice her concerns to Josep as they drove. She knew there was a good chance that Vergés had taken Jaume, and that if he had, it was a likely place to exact any revenge that he sought, but she had to accept that it was still a long shot.

'One of the houses is occupied,' Josep continued, 'but the other one's abandoned. I think that has to be the better bet.'

'We always have the picnic near the abandoned house,' Miravent added. 'It's a short drive from the river where we do the kayaking. The one by the house is too small but it's good for the children to splash about in.'

Elisenda turned around in her seat. 'There's a river by the house?'

Josep checked his maps. 'A tributary of the Ter.'

Elisenda faced forward again to hide her concerns from the couple in the back seat. They were in the lead car. Behind them, Àlex, Montse and Manel were in the first of three more four-by-fours speeding along the fast new road as it temporarily left the river before crossing over the Ter and taking the tortuous route that clung to the side of the valley. Normally used to seeing it tranquil, she was shocked at the violence of the river beneath them, now over to her left. She hoped the level wouldn't rise as high as the road they were on. Turning off onto a smaller track still, they climbed steadily.

'That's the way to the occupied house,' Josep suddenly called. He was pointing to a muddy path to the left. 'The one we want is another kilometre on the right.'

Elisenda turned again to see Miravent nodding at Josep's directions. Comas sat in silence, his head staring down at his lap. The kilometre seemed to take forever, progress slow and uncomfortable across the bumps and potholes of the track.

'Over there,' Josep called.

They turned off the track onto a smaller one still. She peered through the water washing down the windscreen, the wipers barely forging a path through the torrents before thick new raindrops instantly merged to form a new prism of blurred colours. She could just make out a small patch of grey ahead of them, an artificial geometric shape against the swirling ground of green, melting from view in time with the swish of the blades. The car slowed almost to walking pace and finally stopped.

'This is as far as we can go,' the driver told them.

Elisenda could see the house in front of them, drifting in and out of vision through the rolling curtain of rain. Two empty windows and a doorless frame downstairs looked like an uneven row of cracked teeth, the apertures upstairs like empty eye sockets. A sightless home crumbling and decaying under the relentless oblivion of sun, wind and rain.

The car door was almost blown out of her hand when she opened it. Telling Miravent and Comas to stay inside, she struggled out. Josep joined her, but Elisenda turned to see Miravent following him.

'I'm coming,' the politician shouted above the roar.

It was when they got out of the car that another sound had risen up. The thundering of water, not from above, but from somewhere beyond the house. A mountain stream swollen with weeks of rain and released bucking from its gentle servitude.

Elisenda decided not to waste time arguing with Miravent. They were joined by the rest of her unit and the teams from the other cars. Shouting instructions, she headed the trudge along the treacherous path. The mud was superficial, a thin layer crusting decades of compacted earth. It didn't suck them down into the ground and hamper their progress, instead, it sent their boots slithering across a thin icing of rust-coloured slush. They soon found that the edge between the worn track now in disuse and the natural tangle of stubby grasses encroaching on it was an easier line to follow.

Concentrating on keeping her feet, Elisenda nearly missed the figure emerging from the house, but a colourful blur of movement in the misting grey air caught her eye and she looked up in time.

Someone was running out of the front door. Not along the path towards them, but away from the house at an angle.

'Àlex and Josep,' she shouted, turning and pointing at the figure.

They immediately set off across the grass and low brush in slow pursuit, all three figures in exaggerated motion. Two other Mossos went with them. Elisenda and the rest continued towards the house, picking up speed as best they could. They were drawing near. The sound of the wind and the water diminished slightly in the lee of the old building. To the right of the house, a blue Renault was parked under a tree, facing away from them.

Elisenda told Montse to make sure that Miravent stayed outside. She noticed that Comas hadn't followed them out of the car. Inside the house, a tiny room with bare earth and rain blowing in through the glassless windows revealed nothing more than an interior door. Once painted brown and now flaked and warped, it stood open, held in place on the ground. A swathe of flat earth showed where it had been opened and closed recently.

She went through it into a second room, her caution mixed with an impatient urgency. The one window, on a wall giving onto the side of the house, was still glazed. The temperature was instantly a little higher, the damp not so cloying. In a corner was a sleeping bag, spread over a second one acting as a mattress. A battery lantern stood on a little camping table and plastic supermarket bags looked to be stuffed with food. Empty ones lay strewn on the floor.

Another door gave off this, also open, and she went through. An old stone sink and ancient cupboards told her it was once the kitchen. Parts of the rear wall around the windows were gone and the view gave onto the river. The sound of it returned, a roar bellowing along its course, just metres beyond the house. As she watched, an uprooted tree was borne past, rotating helplessly in the river. She could see how the level had risen, the water just a couple of metres below the room where she stood, bursting its banks on both sides.

She turned to see another door and her heart missed a beat.

It was a cellar door. Closed.

Rushing over, she tugged to open it and looked in.

It was dark, and she called for a torch. Shining it in, she saw a room, its bottom couple of metres filled with water tumbling over and over itself. The sound of its rushing was deafening. Most of the original old steps had evidently crumbled away years ago, leaving just a few at the bottom, rising out of the muddy flood that had invaded the cellar. A gap too large to climb down remained between the top step and the door where she was kneeling. She leaned down to see if she could reach, but it was impossible. In the murk, she spotted a ladder being turned over in the water, dragged under to be released again moments later.

She saw something else given up by the flood.

Turning, she saw Miravent at the door into the kitchen. Montse was barring her way.

Elisenda turned back to peer into the cellar.

She saw it again and closed her eyes.

'Please, not that,' she whispered.

Chapter Fifty-Nine

Elisenda watched Albert Riera working.

She had asked if she could be present and Jaume's parents had had no objection.

For once Riera was silent. His hands moved gently over the boy's body. Systematically, he checked his face and head, his hands and arms. Centimetre by centimetre, he looked at the boy's torso, looking for abrasions or contusions. He opened his mouth and checked inside, peering at his teeth and gums. He shone a torch into his eyes to examine them closely. He examined his lower limbs and feet, looking for bruising or injuries, any marks that had been inflicted deliberately or by accident. Elisenda had had to turn away at some points. Riera checked the boy's genitals.

Elisenda turned back and looked again at Riera's smooth, economic movements. He wasn't just a pathologist. His proper title was forensic doctor. As such, his task was not only to conduct post-mortems on the bodies of suspicious deaths, but to examine the living victims of crimes.

He stepped back and took another look at Jaume.

'You're perfectly all right, young man,' Riera told him. 'You can put your things back on now.'

Next to her, Elisenda heard Miravent let out a long, low sigh. She rushed forward and embraced her son. Embarrassed, the boy brushed her away and began to put on the spare clothes that his father had brought from home on the way to the Institut de Medicina Legal.

'Is he really all right?' Miravent asked Riera.

The pathologist frowned at her. 'You heard my opinion. There's nothing wrong with him that a hot meal and night in a warm bed won't cure.'

Like Elisenda, his mother hadn't left his side from the moment Àlex and Josep had wrestled him to the ground as he'd fled the abandoned house. She'd returned to Girona with the mother, father and son and left Àlex in charge at the house by the river.

'Why were you running away from the house?' Elisenda asked Jaume once they'd all moved into a more comfortable room with sofas in the forensic institute.

Someone had brought him a hot cup of chocolate milk at his mother's request. He held it in his hands, warming up in the cool of the air-conditioned office, and took small sips.

'I thought he was behind me,' the boy said. 'I just saw people running towards the house and I didn't know who you were. I wanted to get away.'

Elisenda asked Miravent if she could continue to question the boy, and the politician agreed. Marc Comas was sitting on another sofa and had barely said a word since coming with the clothes. All the way back from the house, he'd wept openly and tried to hug his son, but now he was more reserved. He looked across at Jaume every so often and smiled encouragement at him, but the boy scarcely reacted.

'Tell me what happened, Jaume,' Elisenda told the boy. 'In your own time. There's no hurry.'

Without looking at either of his parents, the boy began to speak.

'I was in the cellar. I couldn't get out because the steps didn't go all the way. Every time he came to bring me food, he put a ladder down so he could get in.'

'Did he say why he was keeping you there?'

He shook his head and took a sip of chocolate. 'He didn't talk much.'

'How did you get to the house, Jaume?' Elisenda asked him.

'He drove us there.'

'You got into his car. Why was that?'

'He offered me a lift. When I got off the bus in the centre. He was driving past and I knew who he was. He said he was going to see my parents to talk to them about something. And then he just kept driving and he took us out to the Susqueda reservoir, where we always went on picnics. He told me not to worry as he just had to pick some things up and then we'd be going home.'

'Why didn't you try ringing us?' Miravent asked. Elisenda looked at her and signalled that she should be quiet for a moment.

'I tried. But he told me there was no signal. He took my phone from me in the car and wouldn't give it back. That's when I got frightened, but I couldn't get out, because he was going too fast.'

'Why did you tell Carles Pascual that you were going out for dinner with your parents?' Elisenda asked him.

The boy shrugged. 'Pascual's such a dweeb. I didn't want to go around to his house anymore.'

A budding friendship dismissed in a thoughtless second, Elisenda thought. It occurred to her that Jaume was more like his mother than his father and she glanced over at Comas, sitting apart from his wife and son, largely ignored by them both.

'How did he treat you, Jaume?' she continued.

'He was nice. He gave me food and made sure I was all right at night. It was a bit scary down there in the dark, and he brought me a lamp.'

His answer surprised Elisenda. 'So what happened today, when it was raining?'

'The water started coming in through the floor and the walls. I shouted to him. But he didn't come for ages. I don't know where he was. Then he saw the water coming in and it was up to my chest, so he put the ladder down and came down to let me out. He used to tie my hands to the wall, so he cut the bits of metal and helped me up the ladder.' The boy started to cry. Tears ran down his downy cheeks and he suddenly seemed the young boy that he was, despite his height. 'When I got up to the top, I just wanted to run away. I heard him shout, and I turned. He was climbing up the ladder behind me and he fell off into the water. And the ladder slipped and fell back into the cellar. I didn't do anything. I ran away.'

He was crying more forcefully now, racking sobs that shook his body.

'You've done nothing wrong, Jaume,' his mother told him.

For the first time, the boy allowed her to comfort him. Comas remained where he was and made no attempt to sit with his wife and son.

'I'll have to ask you some more questions another time, Jaume,' Elisenda told him.

She went outside, where Riera was waiting.

'I've got a body on the way, I take it,' he told her.

'I'm afraid you have, Albert,' she replied. 'Pere Vergés.'

She described a little of the scene at the abandoned house.

'He was trapped in the cellar,' she told him. 'The flood water was coming in too quickly and he couldn't get out. When I left, a couple of Científica were going down to try and retrieve the body. Àlex has told me that they found metal ties down there, cut with a pair of pliers, and that there are old metal rings set into the wall. They also found some pliers and empty food containers and water bottles.'

Riera shook his head. 'Poor kid. What makes a man do that?'

The door opened and the small family came out.

'We're going to go home,' Miravent told them.

'I'll come by later, Jaume,' Elisenda said, 'to make sure you're all right and to ask you a few more questions.'

The boy nodded and gave her a small smile.

'But first,' his mother said, 'we've got to go and vote. We can all go together and the city can see that I've got my son back.'

They walked off down the corridor. Elisenda watched them go.

'Another one prepared to use a child for their own ends,' Riera muttered bitterly. 'Even her own child.'

Elisenda took her leave and walked out into the surprisingly mild weather of the city. There was a scent of moisture in the air, the only hint to the rain pounding down on the reservoir just an hour away. A breeze blew through the trees and she held her head back to breathe in deeply. Opening her eyes, she saw a figure walking away from her, heading for the shelter of the towering trees in the Devesa.

Watching him, she made up her mind and set off after him.

Chapter Sixty

'We should go and question these house attackers some more,' Àlex told Manel. 'The clock's ticking.'

Manel nodded his head and sighed deeply. The two of them were sitting with Josep and Montse in the unit's outer office. All four had showered and were dry and in clean clothes, but they were exhausted, their energy sapped after the events at the abandoned house in the country. None of them was talking.

'I really didn't think it was going to be Vergés,' Josep suddenly said.

'Doesn't always go the way you think,' Manel replied.

'You don't have to have an answer for everything, for Christ's sake,' Josep snapped.

Àlex stood up and signalled to Manel before he had the chance to say anything in reply. 'With me. We've got interviews.' He turned to Josep. 'Can you check the social media? See if there's anything new about the attacks. We'll be winding down the missing persons investigation, but we need to keep on top of everything else.'

He knew how the anti-climax of an unexpected result could drain the energy from a team, so it was important that they should have something to focus on. Josep nodded and turned straight to his computer. He looked up almost immediately but Àlex and Manel were gone. Seeing the expression on his face, Montse got up and went out into the corridor to call them back.

'What is it?' Àlex asked when they came back in.

Josep pointed to the screen. He had a map of the Gironès region showing.

'The couple calling with the religious pamphlets. We've got messages coming in right now that they're knocking on doors.' He pointed at the map. 'Forty-five minutes ago here, twenty minutes ago here. And just over five minutes ago here. They're following the Sant Adri road.'

Manel peered at it. 'It's a route. We can see the trace of where they've been.'

'Better than that,' Àlex told them. 'We can see where they're going.'

-

Elisenda walked through the crowds in the park, shadowing the figure that bobbed in and out of view ahead of her. Judging by the numbers of people, she realised that the city had just fallen in the third and final siege. After seven months of bombardment and starvation by Napoleon's troops, the defenders besieged inside the city had capitulated. The food had gone and they'd eaten all the rats and mice, dogs and cats, living among the decomposing bodies of their fellow citizens and dying in their droves from disease and it was time to give up. The Spanish soldiers had been led out of the Portal de Sant Pere to captivity and the half of the city's population that had survived was preparing itself for occupation by the French.

And now groups of *miquelets* chatted with Napoleonic troops while children skittered in and out of them and laughed. Soon they'd be going home or taking a stroll through the old town or through the park before a drink and a bite to eat. And she was following a lone figure while Pere Vergés was being driven to the mortuary and Susanna Miravent was taking her son with her while she cast her vote in front of the cameras. The thoughts nagged at her.

The figure stopped at his tent and she caught him up.

'Are you following me?' he asked her, but the spark was gone from his eyes.

'Yes. I want to know how you know Susanna Miravent.'

He sat down on the log stool and took his hat off. This time there was no flourish.

'I told you. I don't know Susanna Miravent. We have a common history but I don't know her. It's Pere Vergés that I knew.'

'Vergés?'

'Yes. I was going to kill him.'

-

The man in the house tucked away at the end of a winding drive off the Sant Adri road glanced out of the window at the front of the house, but it was all quiet out there. The rain that had fallen over by Susqueda earlier in the day had clipped the house in passing and the ground outside was wet. He could see coils of steam rising as the sun dried it out.

Moving easily through the downstairs rooms, he looked out of the rear window. A car was parked there, but there was no one sitting in it. He knew there was another car out on the main road, past the entrance to the house. He tried sitting down on the faded sofa in the living room, but he couldn't settle, so he wandered through the rooms again and examined the photographs on the wall in the dining room. It was the story of a mother and father turning grey and becoming grandparents to children that grew up to go to university, the colours less faded as the tale came into the present day. He smiled at the pride in their eyes at graduations and christenings and first communions.

The dining table was still cluttered after Sunday lunch, the plates and glasses in convivial disarray. The family here for a family meal, young and old, the traditionally confused and the social media savvy.

The doorbell rang.

Taking a deep breath, he looked out of the living room window. A car was parked at the front of the house. Beyond it, a second car was driving slowly along the drive, half-hidden by the trees.

The man went to the door and paused a brief moment before opening it. In front of him were two men in their thirties, dressed in short-sleeved shirts and trousers. Neither of them would have stood out in a crowd, both wore ingratiating smiles. In his hand, one of them was holding a small pile of pamphlets.

Holding onto the door he'd just opened and watching the unmarked car slowly come to a halt behind the two men, Àlex smiled back at them.

'I've been expecting you,' he told them.

-

'You were going to kill Pere Vergés?'

'Yes, but it's too late now. He's dead.'

Elisenda was stunned. 'How do you know that?'

'Susanna Miravent. She's posted it on social media. Apparently, her god has given her back her son and he's punished the man responsible. So all is right with the world.'

Elisenda looked up at the trees reaching above her and swore. Bringing her gaze back, she looked at the man sitting opposite her. 'Why were you going to kill Pere Vergés?'

He laughed gently and replaced his tricorne on his head. Some scintilla of the normal gleam returned to his eyes. 'I am a storyteller. Let me hide behind that one more time. But first, don't you want to know why I have a shared history with Susanna Miravent?'

'I want to know everything.'

Seamlessly, he adopted his persona, the iconoclastic teller of tales, always on the brink of chaos.

'Two children. One rich, one poor. Well, not poor perhaps, but certainly not as rich as the first one.'

'You've already told this story.'

'I know I have, but you didn't get it the first time.' He gazed frankly at her and she nodded that he should continue. 'Two children. I have painted the picture for you already. So one day, the first child goes missing and is then believed to have died. And all the finest people in the land got all the finest searchers in the land to upturn every stone and to pin every known miscreant to the wall, and all the modern-day storytellers, or the media as we call them, gave us hour-by-hour tales of everything that was happening. And the child's mother, an infamous comedy villain who the modern-day storytellers had allowed to infest our every waking hour, appeared every day asking us all for our support as the help she was already getting from all the institutions in the land apparently wasn't enough.'

'Jaume Comas Miravent,' Elisenda interrupted.

He gave a small shake of his head. 'Albert Comas Miravent. This story took place once upon a time four years ago.'

'His brother?'

'I told you there were two children. But Jaume isn't one of them. Our two children are Albert Comas Miravent and another child called Jordi Sobrerroca Punyent.'

'I don't know who that is.'

The sparkle in his eyes flashed the colour of steel for a moment and was quenched.

'No one does. Not then. Not now. But he also died on the same day as Albert Comas Miravent. And he died just a short distance away from where Albert died. The problem is no one got all the finest searchers in the land to find who was responsible for it and none of the modern-day storytellers had any room for his story as they were too taken up with the story of the rich child. So he died unnoticed and his death went unresolved and now the searchers don't even know his name.'

Elisenda gasped. 'The hit-and-run. The same day Albert went missing, a mother and child were killed on the road.'

'My son,' he told her. 'And my wife. They died on the same day a wealthy politician's child went missing and no one gave a moment's care to their deaths.'

'I'm so sorry.'

He took several deep breaths before answering. 'You of all people should know what it feels like.'

She had to search for her own calm before she could continue. 'Why Pere Vergés?'

'He was driving the car that killed my wife and my son.'

She gasped for a second time. 'How can you know?'

'I investigated. The Mossos d'Esquadra weren't doing it and the media weren't doing it, so I had to. I was a maths teacher, I was used to logic and supposition, probabilities and outcomes, and I looked for the last four years and I discovered who it was who had killed my family. And it was Pere Vergés. And I discovered that he had been released from prison for a crime that he didn't commit, and I was going to punish him for a crime that he did.'

'While he was after revenge of his own for the injustice against him.'

The man was lost in thought for a moment. 'Are you so sure of that? I don't see why he would be. He'd stand to lose so much more if he started digging up what really happened that day. His actions were far worse than any fraud. His own punishment would have been worse than anything he'd already experienced.'

Elisenda digested his words. They added to the questions she was already asking herself.

'Would you really have killed him?'

He shrugged. 'I'll never know.'

The quiet under the trees amid the hubbub of the people in the park was shattered by Elisenda's mobile. She was about to cancel the call but then she saw who the caller was.

'I have to answer this, I'm sorry.'

It was Albert Riera.

'*Elisenda? There's something here you need to see.*'

She hung up and sighed and walked away from the leader of the *cercavila*.

Chapter Sixty-One

'Is your husband in?' Elisenda asked Susanna Miravent. 'I think he should be present.'

Miravent stared up at Elisenda and Montse from her sofa. Jaume was sitting next to her, a second hot chocolate on the coffee table in front of him. 'I really don't see that that's necessary. I'm present, that should be sufficient.'

'Please, Senyora Miravent.'

Elisenda waited while the politician ill-naturedly called for Encarna and told her to fetch her husband.

On the way from seeing the pathologist, Elisenda had stopped at Vista Alegre to pick up Montse to go with her to see the family in Palau. While she was there, Àlex had told her about the pamphleteers.

'They're in the other cells now,' he added. 'We're about to question them.'

Elisenda had to focus on what he was saying. It really was a breakthrough. 'That's excellent news. Well done.'

'This could be the key to getting into the whole of the gang. These two are going to have to know at least each of the team leaders. We haven't got the other two teams, but we've got one of them and the two people who organise the attacks. That's got to mean we've pulled the teeth of the operation.'

She considered his words. 'Yes, I think you're right. Without the two organisers, the other teams are in disarray at least.'

'And I think we'll be able to get to them through the ones we've already got. Even if we can't, with the people we've arrested, we've brought the operation down. They can all be as Venezuelan as they want, we've got them.'

She also spoke to Josep while she waited for Montse to check out a pool car.

'The hit-and-run accident on the same day Albert Comas Miravent went missing. Find out everything we have on it, and check Pere Vergés's movements that day if we still have any record of them.'

Josep looked surprised at the request. 'I don't know how much I'll be able to find.'

'Do what you can.'

In the house in Palau, Marc Comas walked into the living room, surprised to have been summoned.

'I just have a few more questions for Jaume,' Elisenda explained. 'I think you should both be here.'

She was sitting at the end of one of the sofas where it met the other one at a right-angle. Jaume was sitting on the second one, in the corner nearest to her. She spoke directly to him.

'You've been through a terrible experience, Jaume, and I understand you're very upset, but there are some things that I have to ask you. Take your time with your answers.'

He looked directly back at her. He still looked the child on the cusp of adulthood he had earlier, but some of the self-assuredness with which people had described him appeared to be returning. His gaze had the same lazy confidence that his mother's had. Elisenda reached forward and took hold of both his hands. Surprised by the gesture, he made no attempt to withdraw them.

'When Pere Vergés held you in the house, did he hurt you in any way, Jaume?'

'No, I told you. He was always nice to me.'

'But he tied you up, didn't he? We found the metal ties in the water in the cellar.'

The boy gulped. 'Yes, he did.'

'Why was that?'

'I don't know.'

'You see, you were unlikely to be able to get out of the cellar without the ladder there. Did he leave it in place while you were on your own?'

Jaume looked uncertain. 'No, he always lifted it out.'

She nodded and rubbed his hands, pushing his sweatshirt sleeves up. 'You see, the thing is, Jaume, you don't have any marks on your wrists where the metal ties would have dug in.'

They both looked down at the unblemished skin on his wrists.

'What is this all about, Sotsinspectora?' Miravent complained but Elisenda ignored her.

'I've just been to see Doctor Riera,' Elisenda continued talking to the boy. 'The doctor who examined you. He had something he wanted to show me. You see, Jaume, Pere Vergés did have wounds on one of his wrists where the metal ties would have been. That's because he was the one who was tied up, isn't it, Jaume?'

The boy opened and closed his mouth but no sound came out. Miravent moved forward nearer to her son.

'What is this?' she demanded.

'I've been talking to someone else, Jaume,' Elisenda persisted, her voice gentle. 'Someone who knows what happened on the day that Albert died.'

For a moment, she thought he was going to be able to brazen it out, but his face suddenly crumpled and he began to cry. She held on to his hands, squeezing them to calm him.

'It wasn't my fault,' he said between sobs. 'Not really. I was just making fun of Albert because he wouldn't go swimming, and he jumped in the water before I knew it.'

Miravent gasped and shrank back. 'You did what? But you knew he wasn't a good swimmer.'

Her son rounded on her. 'He was always your favourite because he was the bright one. You were always telling him how clever he was. Never me. But I was stronger. It was the one way I could beat him.'

'What did you do, Jaume?' she whispered.

'I made him go in the water. I made fun of him until he did it. It was my fault. I didn't think he would.'

Elisenda couldn't help feeling sorry for the boy at the maternal support that was so easily taken back when it suited his mother and the coldness of faith that he must have experienced his entire life.

'But what did you think we'd do?' his mother asked him.

'You'd have said it was my fault. You always made me look after him, but he was older than me. I shouldn't have had to look out for him. I'd have got the blame. I always got the blame.'

'What happened next, Jaume?' Elisenda encouraged him.

The boy calmed down a little. 'He got out of his depth and he just disappeared. I didn't see where he went but he was just gone. I couldn't do anything about it. It was too late.'

'Did you bother to go into the water after him?' Miravent demanded.

'Please, Senyora Miravent,' Elisenda silenced her. She continued to look at Jaume. 'And then you saw someone, didn't you?'

Jaume looked up at her and nodded. 'Senyor Vergés. He was on the other bank, watching. He didn't say anything, he just watched what happened. He saw what I'd done.' His sobbing renewed at the last utterance.

'What was he doing, Jaume?'

'He was cleaning his car. He was getting water from the riverbank and cleaning the front of his car. And then he drove off. He just looked at me and he didn't say anything, he just drove off. And I thought he'd tell on me, and when he went to prison, I was so happy because I thought no one would believe him if he said anything.'

'And then he came out of prison,' Elisenda prompted.

'He came out of prison and I thought he'd tell on me now and I didn't know what to do. I couldn't let him tell my parents what I'd done. So I telephoned him and asked him to come and pick me up in the city centre. I had it all planned.' Strangely, there was a slight note of pride in his last words. 'I asked him to drive us out to the house by Susqueda because I had something to show him.'

'And he willingly went,' Elisenda surmised. She stifled a sigh. Vergés would have gone with the boy because he thought that

Jaume was going to blackmail him about having seen him in the area where the mother and child were killed that day. And Jaume thought Vergés was going to spill the beans about what happened to his brother.

'I asked him to go down into the cellar,' the boy continued. 'And when he was down there, I pulled up the ladder. He started shouting at me to let him up, but I couldn't. He started getting angry and I was afraid what he'd do.'

'Is that why you tied him to the rings in the wall?'

He nodded. 'I had some sleeping pills my father kept in his drawer, and I put them in a bottle of water and threw it down to him. When he was asleep, I went down and tied one of his hands to the rings.'

'Sleeping pills,' Miravent shouted. 'Marc, how could you?'

Elisenda ignored her and carried on talking to Jaume. 'What happened on the day it rained?'

'I could see the water rising, but I didn't know what to do. I thought if I went down, he'd be angry and leave me down there while he got out. He was shouting at me, begging me to let him out, and I didn't know what to do. And then the water was up to his middle and I had to go down and cut him loose. But the water kept coming in and I made it up the ladder, but when he tried, it slipped into the water again. I didn't know what to do, so I ran. I was going to go for help and then you were all there and I panicked. I didn't know who you were.'

He ran out of words to say and the room was suddenly silent, the four adults shocked.

'What did you think you were going to do?' his mother asked him.

'I don't know. I just knew I couldn't let him tell you what I'd done. I didn't know what I was going to do.'

'Jaume,' Elisenda told him. It was one of the hardest things she could ever remember having to say. 'You weren't to blame for Albert's death. It was an accident. Brothers and sisters are always goading each other, it doesn't mean they're to blame for anything. The day he died, Pere Vergés killed two people in another accident. But this time, he was to blame. You hadn't done anything wrong, he had.' She watched his face crumble into tears again. 'He would never have told on you, Jaume, he had more to hide than you did.'

'So where does that leave us?' Miravent demanded.

Elisenda ignored her and continued to hold on to Jaume's hands as he cried.

Chapter Sixty-Two

The evening was drawing in as Elisenda walked through the Devesa. The tents where the *cercavila* troupe had been sleeping were packed and gone. The stands selling toys and crafts were still going strong for another hour or so, a huge and shining copper still bubbling aromatically away at one of them. The last of the re-enactors were getting on a coach, their muskets and uniforms stowed in the hold until their next weekend battle. Lights were strung between the trees and glowing from the bars and restaurants on the edge of town. Another Sunday evening.

She'd given the unit the rest of the afternoon off. They were drained and the house robbers could wait until Monday. Her team had more of a chance of breaking the gang now and she'd decided that their need for some time to themselves was more pressing right now than any urgency in questioning the gang members.

She'd taken the chance to go and vote and had then called her sister and suggested a walk through the park to catch the last of the weekend's festivities. Catalina was talking now to someone she knew at a stand selling decorated ceramic tiles and Elisenda was under the trees, holding her niece. She looked at her reacting to the lights and sounds in the park. A modern lullaby came on over the loudspeakers, *Bona Nit* by Els Pets, a rock band. Elisenda started dancing gently to it, bouncing Enriqueta lightly up and down and watching her gurgle in enjoyment.

'You hear this, kid,' she told her niece. 'This is proper music. You stick with this and you can't go wrong. Forget that twinkly crap your parents like.'

She laughed back at her and danced some more to the rich acoustic guitar sound. In her mouth, Enriqueta was chewing on the end of a stuffed toy that Elisenda had just bought for her at another stand. It was an El Tarlà doll, the medieval clown in the city's legends who'd entertained the people when they were quarantined during the plague. Enriqueta just knew it felt comfortable in her mouth and she liked the sound of the rattle in the doll's cap.

'That's the way to go,' Elisenda encouraged her. She wandered along the path through the stalls, breathing in the cool evening air. 'You know what, kid? Adults are funny creatures. We always want there to be a connection between everything. But sometimes the connections just aren't there, and that's what makes you go chasing after the wrong things. We had a kid who went missing, a man who got out of prison for a crime he didn't commit, a politician no one likes, a supposedly corrupt councillor, a murdered campaign manager, a social-climbing businessman and a load of houses getting robbed. And you know what? They weren't at all connected in the way we thought they were.

'The kid did a wrong thing because he thought he'd done something else wrong when he hadn't really. And that's the thing with kids. They don't see connections. They just see themselves, and they think everyone thinks they've done something wrong when the adults are really just thinking about themselves as well anyway. So the kid tried to hide something he'd done in the past that made him feel guilty and unloved by doing something even worse.

'And the man who got out of prison, the one the kid thought was going to tell on him. He never would have. He'd done something far worse and got away with it but then got punished for something he didn't do. And we saw the wrong connection. We thought he was after Jaume because of something Jaume's mother or father might have done, or that the businessman was involved, or there was some strange Opus Dei conspiracy. And we thought he'd got to know the robbers in prison and got them to get revenge for him on Bofarull when in fact nothing of the sort had happened.'

Enriqueta tried to force the stuffed toy into Elisenda's mouth.

'Not now, kid, I'm in full flow. There were no connections. Not in the way we'd seen them. There were people who were connected to each other who'd committed isolated acts and we'd kidded ourselves into thinking they had to be part of some bigger picture. Miravent wasn't targeted because of her politics, Comas wasn't being punished for his part in a fraud. There was no shadowy Opus Dei shenanigans going on, no revenge for past slights or extortion. Just random acts by individuals who knew each other.'

She stopped walking for a moment and pulled her niece closer. 'Do you know what, though, kid?' she whispered. 'Sometimes there still are connections. Bofarull. His part in the fraud that got Vergés put away, that became obvious. We couldn't punish him for it, but we now know what happened. The robbers. They're all connected to each other, the various teams and leaders. And that connection's what's going to help us bring them down. And Marc Comas and Salvador Canet. Thanks to all of this, we've got a good idea that there is something going on, so that's what your dear old aunt is going to be looking at first thing tomorrow morning.'

She looked down. Enriqueta was asleep.

'You sleep, kid. The bad guys don't get away with it.'

Elisenda danced slowly back to where she'd been as the music was fading out of earshot. In her arms, her niece had woken up again and felt Elisenda's face where one of the bad guys had hit her. Elisenda winced and smiled. She found herself by a tree and she looked at the little row of tiny black figures tracing a path up and down the two-tone bark, carrying on with what they had to do no matter what. She pointed at them and moved Enriqueta closer to them.

'Look, kid. Ants.'

Elisenda watched the industry on the tree and smiled at her memory.

After an early dinner, she left Catalina and Enriqueta and went home to her empty flat. She checked the television news for any election results. Susanna Miravent had stepped down from her party list, not that it appeared she would have won a seat anyway. Elisenda turned it off and took out a notepad and pen. She sat down on the sofa and wrote some more about her daughter, filling page after page of the squared paper as the lights across the river slowly went out.

Closing the book, she placed it on the coffee table and listened. She heard no lullabies, no singing floating through the paper screens. No shadows flitted across the walls.

'Good night, Lina,' she whispered.

She turned the lamp off in the living room and went to her bedroom, where she slept a night filled with joyful dreams of her daughter.

'Your dad's accent is just so cool.'

'No way.'

'It so is,' the third young teenaged girl said.

The three of them were walking the short distance home from school. They turned off the wide avenue into a leafy side street, chatting as they crossed the affluent Altamira neighbourhood of Caracas.

'I'll tell you what isn't cool,' the second girl said. 'History. I hate it.'

The first girl laughed. 'You hate La Vieja.' La Vieja. The Old Fogey. Their name for their history teacher.

'That's because she always marks you down,' the third girl said.

The second girl sucked her lips in and impersonated their teacher. 'That's because you don't know anything about the history of Venezuela, girl. You're not a part of it.'

Her two friends laughed. She let her mouth fall back to its normal shape, the slight overbite that she hated showing again.

'Too right I'm not,' she carried on. 'It's my history I want to know about.'

Her friends laughed again. Suddenly they stopped.

'It's your dad,' the first girl said. 'He's so cute.'

'Ew, he's my dad,' the second girl said.

Her father approached them and said hello to her two friends before kissing his daughter on the cheek.

He spoke to her in his accent that sounded so strange to her Venezuelan friends.

'Hi, Lina. Did you have a good day?'

Acknowledgements

As always, there are so many people to thank for their help and support with this book. I've been bowled over by the generous response to the Elisenda Domènech series, and I'd like to thank all the wonderful readers and reviewers who have left such kind reviews and sent me such positive messages. The books have also been well received by readers from Girona, which is particularly gratifying. Special thanks here go to Jordi Serra-Mestres and Jordi Camps.

I'd like to thank the lovely people at Canelo for their vision and for their faith in Elisenda and in me: Michael Bhaskar, Iain Millar, Nick Barreto, Simon Collinson and Louise Cullen. Thank you also to Elodie Olson-Coons for her insightful copy-editing and to Chris Shamwana for the haunting cover designs for my books. Thank you as well to Faye Rogers for all her hard work in organising a great blog tour and her help in promoting the series.

I know I keep harping on about my agent, the brilliant Ella Kahn, but she really is the best you could ever wish for. Thanks as always to her for all her hard work, support, encouragement and belief in me.

And finally, and as always, I want to thank my wonderful wife Liz for everything. She's kept the wine flowing.